CITY OF GOLD

CAROLYN ARNOLD

PROLOGUE

THE SOUND OF HIS THUMPING heartbeat was only dulled by the screeching monkeys that were performing aerial acrobatics in the tree canopy overhead. Their rhythmic swinging from one vine to the next urged his steps forward but not with the same convincing nature as did the bullets whizzing by his head.

Matthew glanced behind at his friends and was nearly met with a bullet between the eyes. He crouched low, an arm instinctively shooting up as if he'd drop faster with it atop his head. The round of shots hit a nearby tree, and splintering bark rained down on him.

"Hurry!" he called out, as he peered at his companions.

"What do you think we're—" Cal lost his footing, tripping over an extended root, his arms flailing as he tried to regain his balance.

Robyn, who was a few steps ahead of Cal, held out a hand, her pace slowing as she helped steady him.

"Pick it up, Garcia!" Matthew didn't miss her glare before he turned back around. He hurdled through the rainforest, leaping over some branches while dipping under others, parting dangling vines as he went, as if they were beaded curtains.

His lungs burned, and his muscles were on fire. One quick glance up, and the monkeys spurred him on again. Not that he needed more than the cries of the men who were chasing him. The voices were getting louder, too—growing closer.

Robyn caught up to Matthew. "What happened to natives

with poison darts?"

"The modern-day savage packs an AK-47 and body armor."

Several reports sounded. Another burst of ammunition splayed around them.

"If we get out of this alive, you owe me a drink." Her smile oddly contrasted their situation.

"I'll buy you each two," Matthew promised.

Cal ran, holding the GPS out in front of him, his arm swaying up and down, and Matthew wasn't sure how he read it with the motion.

"Where do you expect to take us, Cal? We're in the middle of a damn jungle," Robyn said.

"Round here. Go right," Cal shouted.

Another deafening shot rang out and came close to hitting Matthew.

"You don't have to tell me twice." Matthew ramped up his speed, self-preservation at the top of his list while the idol secured in his backpack slipped down in priority.

Most of their pursuers were yelling in Hindi, but one voice came through in English. He was clearly the one giving directions, and from his accent, Matthew guessed he was American, possibly from one of the northern states.

"I have to stop…and…breathe." Robyn held a hand to her chest.

"We stop and we're dead. Keep moving." Cal reached for her arm and yanked.

Matthew slowed his pace slightly. "Robyn, you could always get on Cal's back."

"What?" Cal lowered the arm that was holding the GPS.

She angled her head toward Matthew. "If you think I'm going to get up there like some child, you are sorely mistaken."

Matthew laughed but stopped abruptly, his body following suit and coming to a quick halt. He was teetering on the edge of a cliff that was several stories high, looking straight down into a violent pool of rushing water. He lifted his gaze to an upstream waterfall that fed into the basin.

Cal caught Matthew's backpack just in time and pulled him back to solid ground.

The rush of adrenaline made Matthew dizzy. He bent over, braced his hands on his knees, and tucked his head between his legs. He'd just come way too close to never reaching his twenty-ninth birthday.

Robyn punched Cal in the shoulder. "Go right, eh? Good directions, wiseass. Maybe next time we'll just keep going straight."

"Sure, blame the black guy," Cal said.

More bullets fired over the empty space of the gorge.

"What do we do now?" Cal asked.

Matthew forced himself to straighten to a stand. He hadn't brought them all the way here to die. He'd come to retrieve a priceless artifact, and by all means, it was going to get back to Canada. He pulled off his sack, quickly assessed the condition of the zippers, and shrugged it back on. He tightened the straps, looking quickly at Cal and then at Robyn. One stood to each side of him. He had to act before he lost the courage. He put his arms out behind them.

Robyn's eyes widened. "What are you doing, Matt? You can't honestly be thinking of—"

Matthew wasn't a religious man, but he was praying for them on the way down.

CHAPTER 1

DRENCHED IN SWEAT, CAL MYERS gripped the sheets and bolted upright, his body heaving, his lungs hungry for oxygen. The scream that had woken him was his own.

"Cal?" Sophie's hand touched his shoulder, and he sprang out of the bed. She rolled over to face him. "Another nightmare?"

That was one way of putting it. He'd been running and dodging bullets one minute, and the next thing he knew, the ground had disappeared from under him and he was falling, falling, falling. Just when it had seemed bottomless, there was the raging river with its white caps and jagged rocks dotting its surface.

"Maybe you should take a break from all these adventures." Her words were soft, thoughtful.

His gaze met hers. Sophie Jones was his girlfriend of five years. Given their similar personalities and restless natures, it was hard to believe they'd managed to stay monogamous for that long. They had yet to commit to living together or the big M-word, but she grounded him—her words, not his—and she was the one who gave his life any semblance of normalcy. Besides their long-term relationship, nothing else fit within the confines of an ordinary existence. He blamed—and thanked—Matthew Connor for that.

Sophie patted the mattress. "Come back to bed, baby."

The alarm clock on the dresser read 5:15. He had no reason to be up this early, but getting back to sleep was going to be impossible. His imagination would only continue to replay the dream.

"You went through a lot in India," she said. "I'm sure that Matthew would understand if you took some time off."

He refused to acknowledge her line of reasoning. Before Matthew, his life had been anything but exciting. While it was true that Cal had explored the world, writing travel pieces and photographing some of the most popular landmarks didn't hold a flame to treasure hunting and being shot at and— What was wrong with him? Why did he crave the element of danger? It wasn't healthy. If anything, his recurring nightmare confirmed that. Some time off might do him good.

He slipped back into bed, and Sophie snuggled against him. She traced her fingertips over his chest, her touch working to dull the flashbacks.

"Was it the same dream you've been having lately?"

He swallowed, trying to keep the calm she was compelling him toward. "Yeah, the one where the ground just disappears."

"I didn't think the ground disappeared from under you in India," she teased gently.

She was trying to make him smile, even for a second, and he loved her for that, but he didn't want to remember what had truly happened. Was it possible he had a touch of PTSD?

"Close enough," he said. "I still can't believe he pushed us over the edge like that."

She reached for his hand and gave it a small squeeze. "But all of you survived and you're fine."

"If you consider constantly having vivid flashbacks and nightmares *fine*."

"They will pass in time."

He exhaled loudly. "It's almost been a month."

"Hardly enough time to recoup from an experience like that."

"You make it all sound so positive."

Sophie laughed and flicked his nipple.

"Hey!" He squeezed her hand and then rubbed where her nimble fingertip had grazed.

"It's your life, you know," she said, becoming serious again. "It's up to you what you do with it."

Cal thought back on his life before Matthew. He had survived on a paycheck-to-paycheck basis and was deep in debt with student loans. He couldn't afford a car and he'd lived in a low-rent building where the landlord tracked the comings and goings of any visitors he had.

In addition to material freedom, Matthew provided Cal with adventure and satisfied his lust for action. It was more stimulating not knowing what each day had in store. If given the option between a calm and peaceful existence and a fight for survival laced with adrenaline, his choice would easily be the latter.

He glanced at the clock again: 5:20.

"I'm getting up, babe." He kissed her forehead and maneuvered his arm out from under her.

Sophie let out a moan. "It's so early."

"Yes, but *you* can go back to sleep."

"What are you going to do?"

"Don't worry about me."

Sophie sat up, putting her back against the headboard. "That's the problem. I do." Her face contorted in a way he was very familiar with. Her left eyebrow was jacked up, and her eyes held a deep intensity. If that wasn't enough to give away her agitation, she tousled her short, dark dreads before crossing her arms.

"There's nothing to worry about. You just said I'm fine."

"I was trying to make you feel better, but people were shooting at you and you jumped off a cliff—"

"I was actually push—"

"There you go," she interrupted as she unfolded her arms and kneaded the comforter. "Either way, things are out of your control when you…" She rolled her hand, searching for the right words.

He knew what she was doing because she didn't like the term *treasure hunting* and did her best to avoid it. Even the Indiana Jones movies were not her thing, and while she supported Cal in his "outings" or "adventures," she far from encouraged them.

"Gather historic objects," she finally said. "I know it makes you happy, for the most part anyway. I just don't like seeing you having nightmares and waking up in the wee hours."

It was his turn to laugh. "Wee hours? I would think that applies to two or three or—"

"You're missing the point." She threw the comforter off her and got out of bed, then gathered her clothes from the floor and tossed them onto the mattress.

"And what point is that?" They rarely fought, but when they did, they tended to revolve around his expeditions and treasure hunting.

She pulled her sweater over her head. "You might be in danger, you know. What if the men from India tracked you back to Toronto? They could know where you live."

He raised an eyebrow at her. "Now you sound like you've been watching too many movies."

"Do I?" She plucked her skirt from the bed and pulled it on.

Faced with the direct, two-worded question, his inclination was to back down. It was packed with fervor, and paired with her tone, it had the potential to set the room ablaze.

"Even Matthew operates under an alias," she continued. "If it's not because of risk, then why would he do that?"

"You know why."

"Uh-huh. His father, the mayor? You're still buying that? He's a twenty-eight-year-old man who can't be straightforward enough with his own father to let him know what he does for a living. Although I'm not sure how much of a living it provides when you put your lives at stake to do it."

"Why are you being like this?" It wasn't like they were married, or even living together for that matter. She had no right to tell him how to live his life. No one had permission to do that.

"Are you sure you want to know?" she snapped.

"I asked, didn't I?" He put his hands on his hips and realized he was standing there in his boxers. The lack of clothing somehow seemed to take away his power. He put on the pair of jeans that had been lying at his feet.

"All right, well, here it is. And so help me God, if you snicker or make fun of what I'm about to say, it's over, Cal. Do you hear me?"

And they were back to this. While he liked to believe that what they had was the real deal, whenever it came to verbal blows, her strike was always an uppercut to the jaw. She always pulled out the "I guess we're over" and "We had a good run" crap. At least they didn't fight often.

"Do you promise?" Her question was accompanied by a glare.

"I promise."

"I feel like someone's watching us."

He had made a promise not to jest about what she had to say. Hearing her voice her fear made him want to scoff, though. Was she serious?

He cleared his throat. "Why do you think that?"

"Don't patronize me, Cal Myers." She pointed a finger at him. "I see it written all over your face."

"Come on, baby. I just didn't expect you to say that, that's all." He found his legs taking him to her now. He reached for her arm, but she pulled it out of reach.

"Have you been listening to me at all? And you promised not to make fun of what I was going to say."

He held up his hands. "I'm not making fun. I swear."

She tilted her head to the left and studied his face. "Fine. You gonna listen?"

He nodded. The option was either that or hitting up a florist at some point during the day. Hell, he might end up doing that anyway.

"When we were out last night, I kept seeing this one guy. Whenever I'd look in his direction, he'd turn away really quickly."

Cal sensed her energy and saw it in the softness her features took on and in the way her eyes changed. She was afraid.

"You have nothing to worry about." He attempted to touch her again. This time she allowed it.

"Can you promise that? Because I don't think you can. I didn't like the way this guy looked."

"And how was that?"

She gazed into his eyes. "Like Liam Neeson."

"Liam Neeson?"

"Yeah, you know, the actor? *Taken, Clash of the Titans, The A-Team*?"

He dismissed her with a wave. "I know who he is. I would like to know what you have against him." Her face fell, and he felt like a heel for causing that reaction. "I'm sorry. It's just I've been hunting treasure for two years now. I'm still alive. I'm not going to lie and say that it's the safest profession."

"If you did, I wouldn't buy it anyway."

"So? Liam? What made you suspicious of him?"

"You said that when you were in India, the person commanding all those men who were chasing you spoke English and was likely from North America."

Now he regretted having said anything to her about the trip. "Yeah, but that could describe a lot of people, Sophie."

"I'll give you that. It's just… What if he tracked you down? I don't want you to go tonight."

Tonight was the exhibit opening and gala to celebrate the Pandu statue they had recovered in India. He wanted to be there. He couldn't believe she was asking him to sit it out. "You what?"

"It's just that… I don't think you should go. Something's going to happen."

"And you're psychic now?" He put up with her feelings, her hunches, her suspicions, but if she was starting to foresee the future, it might be time to give her the "We had a good run" speech himself. And mean it.

She shook her head. "Of course not."

He let out the breath he had been holding. He'd grown accustomed to having her around.

"I just *know* that he was watching us and trying to act as if he wasn't," she went on. "I can feel it. He left the restaurant at the same time we did. When we were waiting at the curb for the valet to bring your car around, he was standing there and he lit up a cigarette." She stopped talking, but he sensed there was more.

"And?" he prodded.

"When we were pulling away, I saw him get into a black SUV."

The laugh erupted on its own.

She narrowed her eyes at him, and he could almost feel the daggers landing in his skin. "That's it, I'm outta here," she clipped. "I have a busy day ahead of me. Houses don't sell themselves."

He reached for her hand, but she swatted him away and kept moving.

"Babe, are you sure you haven't watched too many movies?" he called after her.

"Shove it, Cal."

The door slammed behind her.

Cal wanted to punch a wall. His fist was balled and ready, but somehow, he had mustered the control not to go through with it. Self-preservation, maybe. Instead, he drew back the blind and watched her drive off. He was about to retreat from the window when he saw a dark-colored Escalade parked on the other side of the street. And a man was silhouetted behind the wheel.

CHAPTER 2

THE GALA WAS A BLACK-TIE affair, and according to his father, *anybody who's anybody* was going to be there. Matthew recognized it for what it was: an opportunity for the prestigious to measure and compare their financial portfolios and charitable donations. Growing up with his father, he was well acquainted with the subject matter, but he refused to let that sort of thing define him.

The event tonight was, in actuality, meant to celebrate a relic acquired by the Royal Ontario Museum—a certain artifact that Matthew had taken part in obtaining. While the statue would remain in the museum, encased behind bulletproof glass and security systems, his father, William Connor, had insisted that the banquet take place in the family home. Not that the house fell within the regular classification of a "family home." It was a 26,000-square-foot castle located in Toronto's affluent Bridle Path neighborhood and was capable of accommodating a few hundred people.

Matthew often thought that his grandparents would roll in their graves if they knew what their son had done with his inheritance. They had been salt-of-the-earth people who put more stake in humanity than the almighty dollar. His grandmother's mentality was that she had grown up with little and it hadn't hurt her. As a result, instilling culture in her children trumped materialism. Matthew's father had failed to grasp the lesson, though. He flaunted the palace any time he had the opportunity. When he didn't have a reason, he invented one.

While Matthew may have hunted treasure, it wasn't to line his own pockets; it was to give back to humanity. He subscribed to a utilitarian mindset, so whatever he found was donated to museums for the world to enjoy. His finder's fees were sufficient to cover any expenses involved, but not much more. He assigned a larger portion to Cal and Robyn than he did to himself. It was Daddy's money that funded his expeditions, but it wasn't as if the family accounts were going to dry up anytime soon. Interest on his investments alone could fund many families.

Matthew believed his mother would be proud of his dignity and worldview, but he'd have to take that on faith. She'd lost the battle to breast cancer ten years ago. Where was Daddy's precious money then? It had been powerless against the malignant growth. In fact, that was probably why Matthew recognized the limitations of wealth. It didn't have the ability to breathe life into a soul. Cash was a tool—nothing more, nothing less.

Matthew finished tying his Windsor knot and gave himself one last look in the mirror. A strand of dark hair shifted, revealing the scar on his forehead, a souvenir from his most recent expedition dodging bullets through the jungle of India. He brushed his hair back to inspect the wound more closely. It was barely noticeable.

Dressed in a fitted Ralph Lauren tuxedo and black Hugo Boss high-polished shoes, he'd still fall short of his father's expectations. His face was cloaked in a five-o'clock shadow, which suited him more than a clean shave. If that wasn't enough to wind up his old man, the necktie would finish the job.

Matthew caught his own arctic-blue eyes reflecting back at him. "Well, Gideon, you're looking pretty dapper."

Gideon Barnes was the fake name he used to give credit to his finds. It was a secret among less than a handful of people—people he trusted with his life. If his father found out what he really did to keep busy, he'd likely be cut out of the will. If that happened, he'd lose the necessary backing to support his passion. No, it was best that his father believe that he was an archaeologist, not a treasure hunter. And he had the necessary schooling to back that story.

He had majored in archeology and had even obtained his doctorate. His knowledge of history had proved useful out in the field on many occasions. Even with his esteemed education, his father had preferred that he become a doctor or a corporate manager of some sort. It would've been ideal for William if Matthew followed in his father's footsteps and entered the political arena one day, but witnessing William's stressful climb up the proverbial ladder was enough to squash any drive for power and dominance. William had barely survived two heart attacks and he was turning fifty-three this November.

Yet, his father's Achilles' heel was his unquenchable lust for wealth, so he kept pushing. There would never be enough. It didn't matter that the family home had been paid for in cash at the sum of thirty million dollars and that their worth was well into the billions.

Matthew sighed, straightened his spine, and sprang down the winding staircase, his steps light. When he was a child, he used to slide down the walnut banister whenever his father wasn't around. Lucky for his younger self, that was often. A mischievous part of him wondered how people would react if he did so tonight. It was tempting to see how worked up William would get over it, but he resisted.

The main level was filled with the droning hum of multiple conversations converging. His father's associates, who were mostly strangers to Matthew, flitted about in their designer suits and gowns. The women were all a little too perfect to be natural. Their foreheads had clearly been peeled back and tightened, and their skin stretched, appearing almost painful when they smiled. Their lips were full and their breasts plump and too large for their slender frames. The majority were blondes. The lot of them could have come off an assembly line.

Most were trophy wives who entered on the arms of men old enough to be their fathers, and in some cases, grandfathers. Most of the men in his father's circles were on their second, third, or fourth marriages. To them, nuptials were an arrangement of convenience and manipulation, to provide the appearance of stability.

As Matthew wove through the crowd, the guests' myriad colognes tickled his nose, creating a heady elixir. He put on a pleasant front, offering gentle nods of greeting and subtle smiles to anyone who caught his eye.

"Matthew, sir?" Lauren Hale, his father's head housekeeper, held out a tray of champagne. She served along with a hired wait staff.

"I think I'm going to need one." He took a flute. "Thank you."

"You always talk like that, but you still have a good time." She gave a small curtsy before leaving to serve the guests.

Matthew watched her move through the crowd. Maybe one day, his father would get over himself enough to acknowledge the feelings that existed between them. But even if his father did come around, Lauren was too nice a person for his father anyway.

Speaking of the old man…

Matthew let instinct guide him into the grand room. With its coffered ceilings, glass chandeliers, marble floors, and tall pillars, it resembled the lobby of a ritzy hotel more than a place of residence.

He heard his father before he saw him. His timbre always boomed over the crowd. William was conversing with a couple that passed Matthew polite smiles as he approached. His father was what most would consider handsome. He had a head of silver hair and electric blue eyes, and he kept himself in shape with regular exercise and a proper diet. Despite living most of his life in a suit, he never quite filled them out, even though they were always designer and specifically tailored for his body.

"Son, how nice of you to finally join us."

His father said *finally* as if forever had come and gone. It was a jab at the fact that Matthew had bowed out of attending the official event at the museum. The surrounding guests carried on with their conversations as if they hadn't heard him, but Matthew knew they had. No one could *not hear* that bellow.

"There's nowhere else I'd rather—"

His father gripped Matthew's shoulder tight, cutting off his words, and leaned in, bringing with him the smell of whiskey and cigar smoke, the latter being strictly a social vice. "It would have been nice if you cleaned yourself up a little. And no bowtie?"

If William wanted to embarrass him, he'd have to try harder. Matthew cut a glance to the couple, and they excused themselves.

"Why did you have to do that?" William's voice was only slightly lower than before.

"You know I don't like bowties." And so began another painful attempt at conversation with his father. Why he even tried was beyond him. Except for their genetic similarities and the fact they had both loved Matthew's mother, the two of them had nothing in common. It was what made it easier to think of his father as *William* as opposed to *Dad*.

"It's not about what you like, or don't like, it's about—"

"Yes, I know. Appearance." Matthew drained the rest of his champagne. "But like you said, at least I showed up."

William's jaw tightened, and his lips pressed into a straight line. "As long as you—"

"Yes, Father, as long as I live under your roof."

"Are you mocking me?"

"I don't know, William, what do you think?"

"I've told you to call me Dad," he ground out.

The ensuing eye contact simmered. It wasn't as though Matthew needed to live in this place. So why did he still bother? Did he actually believe he might develop a bond with the man? It hadn't happened in twenty-eight years, so why would one form now?

Lauren came by then, and without taking his gaze off his old man, Matthew exchanged his empty flute for a fresh one. He took a swallow of the bubbly liquid, and his mind cautioned his ego to slow down and not allow his father to have such control over him.

William waved Lauren away and gestured to Matthew's temple. "What happened to your face? How do you manage to always cut yourself up? You're an archaeologist for crying out loud."

"For your information, that happened a month ago. It's great to know that you are paying attention, *Dad*."

"I've always taken care of you."

Matthew glanced around. This wasn't the time or the place. While it was true that William had taken care of him materially, Matthew would have preferred his company to a guilt offering. It was just one reason why their relationship had always been strained.

"You really want to get into this right—" He turned back to his father only to realize the man had left and was now positioned behind a microphone.

This night couldn't end fast enough. He downed the champagne, his mind on the next adventure, knowing that whatever and wherever it would be, it would take him away from *William*.

"Good evening, ladies and gentlemen. I want to thank you all for coming to celebrate this monumental find." William paused to soak in the enviable applause. He definitely had a way of extorting the response he wanted.

After the clapping died down, he continued. "The Pandu statue is unquestionably one of the greatest discoveries of the twenty-first century. We are indebted to those who brought the Pandu here for us to appreciate."

The statue was suddenly projected behind him on a large screen, the introduction to a slideshow presentation.

Matthew ran his hand along his jawline as he scanned the room. For the most part, everyone's eyes were on William. All except for a few wandering and lustful gazes that traveled over him. A brunette, who appeared to have reached drinking age last week, sucked on her finger, the implication obvious.

Matthew returned his attention to the podium, even though it made him nauseated to listen to William speak about his discovery. If the man had any idea that it was because of his son—and his son's two best friends—that this celebration was even possible, it might give him his third heart attack.

"If you have any questions about the Pandu, I am certain that the museum curator, Miss Robyn Garcia, would be happy to answer them. You can also ask my son, Matthew Connor"—he extended his hand toward Matthew—"who is an archaeologist."

Despite the twist in his gut, Matthew lifted his glass in response, purely out of etiquette.

"Yes, well, without further pomp and circumstance, Miss Robyn Garcia." William stepped to the side, clapping, and Robyn joined him on the podium.

It was the first time this evening that Matthew saw her. How he had missed her, even in a crowd, was remarkable. Matthew let out a deep breath at the sight of her.

She wore a black evening gown that complemented her tanned complexion. Her long, dark hair was straightened and slicked behind her shoulders and left to drape over her bare upper back. The dress was floor length with a slit on the left side that reached midthigh. Beads that sparkled like diamonds covered the bodice, and the fabric was attractively gathered where it cupped her breasts. She'd paired the gown with diamond earrings and bangles.

Robyn positioned herself behind the microphone and let her eyes trace over the crowd. If she was nervous about public speaking, it wasn't evident. They met each other's eyes, and her lips curved upward slightly. He was certain his mouth was gaping open and his expression resembled that of a goofy teenaged boy with a crush. It was a lot easier to see her as an equal when she was wearing khakis and boots, her shirt stained with sweat and her hair pulled back into a loose ponytail.

Robyn gestured to the screen behind her. "It truly is a remarkable gift we've been given. Thank you to William Connor for extending this celebration to his home." She clapped, encouraging everyone to follow suit. Even Matthew found himself putting his hands together.

William dipped his head in silent acknowledgment and then waved, implying that it was no big deal.

And really, it wasn't. Lauren and Daniel did all the hard work.

Lauren's primary charge was keeping the house tidy, and Daniel was the butler and property manager. At the end of the day, everything was their responsibility.

Speaking of Daniel, there was no sign of him. That was strange because he was the one who had led them to India in the first place. He was Matthew's aid when it came to researching and picking expeditions. Maybe Daniel working for both father and son wasn't the ideal situation, but it was what it was.

Robyn continued. "The Pandu is believed to date back to the third century. If you joined us at the museum earlier, this isn't news to you, but the sacrifices that Gideon Barnes made to bring this to us are significant."

"Is that why he's not here tonight?" a man in the crowd called out. If Matthew remembered right, his name was Jacob.

No one was looking at him, yet Matthew felt under a microscope. Where was Lauren with more champagne? He always felt uncomfortable in these situations and was impressed by Robyn's restraint in not letting her eyes drift back to him. She was a pro.

"Mr. Barnes regrets that he was unable to be here tonight, but he sends his love and appreciation."

A man standing next to Matthew bumped his elbow. "The guy never shows up for his own contributions. If it weren't for the artifacts and some pictures, I'd doubt his existence."

"He might value his privacy," Matthew said. And that statement wasn't far from the truth. As for the pictures, Matthew had hired a man to be the face of Gideon Barnes, but it was to get his father's backing, nothing more.

Robyn went on, providing more background on the Pandu. His mind wandered as she spoke. He was ready for the next mission. Time was too precious to sit around basking in past accomplishments. Life was about seizing the moment.

Matthew looked to the doorway and noticed Daniel standing off to the right. Daniel's Norwegian gray eyes were locked on him.

"Excuse me," Matthew whispered as he weaved through the

mass of people to Daniel. Matthew handed his empty glass to the man.

"Refill, sir?"

Matthew directed Daniel to move down the hall and out of sight of their guests. "That's not why I'm here, and you know it. You have something. What is it?"

Daniel considered their surroundings before responding. "One of the greatest legends, sir."

Matthew's heart palpitated, a natural and habitual occurrence when the prospect of a new adventure came calling.

The two men shuffled farther from the entrance to the grand room.

"And you think it's worth checking out?" Matthew asked, his voice low.

Daniel nodded. "Absolutely. You will change the world with a find like this one."

The guests in the other room laughed and clapped. He then heard his father's closing words encouraging everyone to drink and have fun. After a final round of applause, the music began, meant to inspire the guests to dance.

"In five minutes, make your way upstairs," Matthew whispered to Daniel. "I'd like that refill after all." Matthew rushed up the stairs, taking two steps at a time. It sounded like this quest had his name all over it. Daniel had said it was one of the greatest legends and capable of changing the world. What could it be? A precious object that would alter the way people viewed the world? Change what society knew about the beginning of time, maybe? Rock the foundation of established religion?

He entered through the double doors to his room. The space itself was large enough to be considered a luxurious apartment in Manhattan or even downtown Toronto for that matter. It was two levels, and a loft overlooked the sleeping and living areas. A studio apartment could fit inside his en suite alone, and his balcony had a view of the tennis court. A wall of windows extended along both levels on one side, and natural light streamed in during the day. With it being night now, the drapes had been drawn shut.

He looked around his room. The palette for his bedroom was geared toward neutrals, all shades of whites and brown. His bed was king-size, and he'd had one that large since he was ten. He had adjusted to the dimensions, and because of that, it was hard to share with someone else. He'd been accused of being a bed hog more than once.

He closed the doors behind him and jumped a foot. "What the—" Matthew flicked on the lights to find Cal sitting in the living area. Cal's black skin had been almost completely camouflaged him in the darkened room.

"Sorry, Matt," Cal said. "I didn't mean to scare you."

"What were you thinking?" Matthew loosened his tie, wondering why Daniel hadn't mentioned Cal was up here. "What are you doing here?" Cal wasn't dressed for the gala by any stretch of the imagination in his faded T-shirt and tattered blue jeans.

"You know how Sophie gets feelings about things, right? Like her premonitions or whatever? Well, she's freaking me out a bit."

"Is that why you didn't come to the banquet tonight? You know, just because she has a feeling doesn't make it fact."

"This time, though… I don't know. Something is off."

"Are you still having nightmares?"

Cal met his eyes. "Like you wouldn't believe."

"It's not the first time we've been shot at—"

"It's not the bullets that have me drenched in sweat at night. It's going over that…that…cliff. Thanks to you." Cal pointed a finger at Matthew.

"What are you complaining about? You're still alive." It was a play on a line from *Robin Hood: Prince of Thieves*, which was one of Cal's favorite movies.

"That's easy for you to say."

Matthew laughed and joined Cal on the sofa. "Tell me what happened."

"It's not so much as what has happened, but Sophie feels like we're being watched."

"She thinks you're being watched?" He raised an eyebrow at his friend.

Cal narrowed his eyes. "Don't look at me like that. Sophie does have a way with these things."

"I'm going to need more than that."

"Fine, you want more?"

Matthew splayed his hands and gave Cal an exasperated look. "Sophie and I went out for dinner last night."

"This story is starting off exciting already."

"Would you cut it out? This is serious."

Matthew forced his face to a blank expression. "Continue."

"She says there was someone watching us. I never saw him."

"You never saw him?" A smirk lightened his expression.

"Shut up, wiseass. Sophie did see him. She said he looked like—" Cal hesitated.

"Like?"

"Oh no. If I say it, you're going to laugh. I know that much."

"Try me."

"Fine. She said the guy looked like Liam Neeson."

Matthew snickered.

Cal shook his head. "See? I knew you would laugh."

"Are you sure Sophie hasn't been watching too many movies?"

"That's what I said. I wanted to believe that's all it was, but… What if those people from India followed us home or somehow found us?"

"Unlikely," Matthew said, brushing it off.

"Yeah, unlikely but not impossible."

"Nothing is impossible."

"That's reassuring."

Matthew shrugged. "What do you want me to say?"

"Never mind. Anyway, Sophie and I had a huge fight. I watched her leave and—"

"Ah, how sweet."

"Can you keep quiet long enough to let me tell my story?"

"Okay, okay." Matthew loved how easy it was to tease his friend.

"The same vehicle she saw him getting into the night before… well, it was parked in front of my building."

"Let me guess. A black SUV?"

"I'd say more of a charcoal gray. Wait. How did you know? Have you seen one lurking around?"

Did his friend really want his answer? He'd give it anyhow. "You say there's a guy following you who looks menacing. A dark SUV completes the picture."

"Ah, so we're back to the too-many-movies theory."

"I'm starting to wonder if you both have watched too many."

"Sure, fine, laugh it up, funny boy, but when something happens…"

"Nothing's going to happen."

"You can't promise that, man."

They both fell silent for a moment, and then there was a soft rap on the door.

CHAPTER 3

ROBYN WAS HAPPY TO HAVE the speech behind her. Contrary to the praise she received for public speaking, it wasn't something she enjoyed. Her insides always jumbled into a mangle of nerves and she had to clasp her hands to calm herself. To others, she must appear as if she were cold in those situations, but in actuality, her palms were sweaty and all she could think about was stepping out of the limelight. Tonight, she'd had to address a crowd twice—one at the museum and now another one here. And she'd do this for William, or Bill, as he preferred she call him.

She had known him since she was a teenager and he'd always accepted her as if she were his daughter. For her, this was with reservations. There was a self-serving quality about him, but she wasn't sure if it was prejudice from all Matthew had told her over the years or her personal opinion. She never had much luck with her own parents. Her father had left before she was born and her mother had worked fifteen hours a day to keep food on the table, making Robyn a latchkey kid. As an adult, Robyn didn't speak to her mother.

Stepping back from the microphone, she let out a deep breath, the tension in her neck releasing with her exhale. Her body remained tender from the fall in India, even though it had happened about a month ago. She was thankful that was the worst of her symptoms. She'd pay Matthew back for pushing her over that cliff when he least expected it.

She stopped shy of rubbing her neck. With a level of professionalism to be maintained, she didn't need to look as if she had a headache, even if one was already blooming behind her eyes.

The men in the room followed her every move with lascivious gazes. She smiled politely at a few with no intention or underlying implication. She was fantasizing about popping an Advil, truth be told. Her fingertips brushed the points of her earrings, and she let her arm fall to her side.

"Bravo." William Connor clapped. "You were absolutely spectacular, my dear. You should be very proud of yourself."

"Thank you. But really, it's Mr. Barnes who made tonight possible."

"Yes, and speaking of Mr. Barnes…" The flicker in his eyes revealed his ego was taking the hit for the archaeologist's apparent no-show. If only he knew that the man behind the name lived under his own roof. Sometimes carrying the secret between father and son seemed too heavy a burden.

"He really is sorry he couldn't make it tonight."

"Yes, I am sure he is," William said coolly.

The band played a classical waltz number, a piece of sheet music she ought to recognize by name as she'd heard it many times before. Fancy balls were a part of her chosen lifestyle. But her love, her passion, wasn't for musical composition; it was for studying ancient civilizations and the relics they left behind.

"Miss Garcia?" A portly older gentleman extended his hand. "I would be honored if you would grant me this dance."

His blue eyes no longer carried the spark and vitality of a man half his age, but they were soft and sincere. If she based her assessment of him on his greeting and appearance, she'd accept that his intentions were pure, but she knew better. It didn't matter that he neglected taking care of his physical body, the man was worth billions and had his pick from any money-hungry bimbo from Toronto to Tokyo.

His name was Nicholas Hartman, and he came from old money. His large contributions to the museum made her somewhat obligated to grant him at least one dance. If his hand slid too low down her back, however, it would be over. She slipped her hand into his, and he smiled. He guided her to the floor with a cultured grace and took the lead.

The song ended, and everyone applauded before the band carried on with the next melody.

"Thank you for the dance, Mr. Hartman," she said with a slight bow of her head.

"Thank you, darling." He kissed the back of her hand.

She sensed his hesitancy to let go but was pleased when he did. He might be used to getting his way in a courtroom—and with insecure women—but Robyn didn't fit into either category. She wouldn't be submitting to him anytime soon.

Now, where was Matthew? They had made eye contact during her speech, but she'd noticed him leaving part way through.

She scanned the room. It was bad enough he didn't attend the exhibit opening, but for him to pull a disappearing act at this point was unacceptable. As it was, she never understood how he could risk his life to make such historic discoveries and then stand quietly at the back of the room. When Matthew had decided it best to hide this side of his life from his father, though, it affected more than just him. Robyn herself found it hard to keep quiet about her own role in the acquisition.

"Such a beautiful dedication speech." Another man put his hand on her forearm as she worked her way through the crowd.

"Thank you." She smiled pleasantly, but the second her back was to him the expression faded. She'd had enough of human interaction for one evening—at least with these types of people. She did have some choice words reserved for Matthew, however.

She headed for the staircase, certain he must be with Daniel and on the verge of another adventure. When she'd met Matthew's eyes earlier, she'd seen that familiar spark. He could never stay put for long. His energy was only this electric when…

Her cheeks flamed with the acknowledgment that more than one thing had this effect on him. It was best she disregard the second and more personal reason.

Her fingertips brushed across her neckline, the light touch transporting her to a time when they were more than friends.

She shook herself out of it. This was ridiculous. Their romantic relationship hadn't worked for many reasons.

As she reached the base of the stairs, Daniel rounded the corner with a tray of champagne in hand, clearly intending to take it upstairs with him.

Something was definitely going on. He had two flutes and a bottle. Maybe she had jumped to conclusions about the purpose of Matthew's determined stride. It could be in regard to the more intimate reason and not work-related at all.

Daniel dipped his head toward her. "Miss Garcia."

"Good evening, Daniel. Do you know where I could find Matthew?"

"Certainly."

Awkwardness sparked in the air between them. No elaboration most likely meant Matthew really did have a woman in his room. She was probably the reason he had missed the dedication, too. It should have made her want to retreat and afford him his privacy, but a rush of anger surged through her. Of all the times for him to be distracted! It wasn't solely his hard work he was disrespecting; it was hers and Cal's, as well. With all they'd been through to retrieve the Pandu statue, she couldn't believe he was willing to sacrifice its celebration to an evening of cheap sex.

She planted her fisted hands on her hips. "Where is he?"

Daniel propped the tray in one hand and bobbed his head toward the second landing.

"He's in his bedroom?" she asked for confirmation.

"Yes, Miss Garcia."

It was in his tone. This wasn't about a woman. This was about Matthew trying to "protect" her from another adventure. Her heart fluttered in her chest, and she released a deep breath. "You have another mission for us? For him?" she whispered.

He remained silent and expressionless. He could've rivaled the Queen's Guard at Buckingham Palace. She studied him more closely as he stood there. To others, he was a manservant simply taking drinks to his master's suite. No one would think anything more of it, especially not William Connor. But Daniel was the hinge point from which all their excursions began. His unofficial responsibilities included researching lost treasures and legends.

"I'm in." She brushed past him, charging up the stairs. It would take more than a few body aches to keep her from another quest.

Chapter 4

Ian Bridges usually took pleasure in knowing what most others did not. In this case, he knew that the famous treasure hunter, Gideon Barnes, was none other than the mayor's son. And it wasn't welcome news. An interested third-party had hired Ian to get the Pandu statue back at any cost, but with it now secured behind bulletproof glass and the high-profile identity of its discoverer, the situation had escalated, leaving him with limited options for the object's retrieval. Sadly, murder, although it was his gifted skillset, wasn't a service required by this employer. And bribery presented too much risk and was certain to attract undesired media attention.

The crowd at the exhibit had thinned, leaving behind those who didn't rank high enough in society to secure an invitation to the Connor mansion. Ian made his way toward the statue, his confidence building with each step. Yes, the situation certainly posed a challenge, but he had faith in his abilities. He wasn't familiar with failing, and he wasn't about to learn the lesson now.

The statue was enclosed in a glass cube atop a four-foot-tall pedestal. A red rope with brass hardware surrounded it, encouraging people to stand a couple feet out of its reach. The area was obviously off-limits. But he still considered stretching out to touch the glass. He'd love to smear his fingerprints all over it simply because its contents were so highly esteemed. It was treated more regally than some people were, and yet when he looked at it, he saw nothing more than an ugly man in a dress. Clearly burying an item in the sand for thousands of years transformed even worthless idols into sought-after treasures. What his employer saw in it or why it was sought after in the first place wasn't information Ian required to do his job. Whether it was to provide bragging rights to its owner or to sell it or something else, he didn't care.

"It's beautiful," a woman said. He turned in the direction of the sound and a woman in a black evening dress sidled up next to him. Her hair was a rich red and fell over her shoulders in flowing curls. Her fingers were long and adorned with rings, her wrists were slender and wrapped in silver bracelets. She also wore a silver cuff on her upper arm. Now *this* woman had a brand of beauty he could appreciate.

She seemed to assess him as he did her. "Where are my manners?" She positioned her purse under an arm and extended her hand. "My name is Veronica Vincent."

"Ian." He took her hand and was certain to make eye contact as he shook it. While some women might find the move too familiar and bold, this was the territory upon which he loved to tread. Eyes truly were the windows to the soul.

"Just Ian? Or do you have a last name, too?" Her seductive smile curved one side of her mouth slightly higher than the other. With it, her eyes narrowed marginally. Oh yes. This woman welcomed the attention and reciprocated his attraction.

"My friends just call me Ian." He had to keep some anonymity. His line of work didn't afford him the luxury of screwing up because he wanted to get laid.

"All right. Mysterious. I like it." She slipped her arm through his.

They stood like that for a while, him watching her, her watching the statue.

"You think that thing is beautiful?" He'd come to learn that women found a controversial subject more entertaining than one that had him acting the yes-man.

"Absolutely." She pried her eyes from the robed sculpture, letting them drift to meet his. "I take it you do not?" There was a small hitch in her eyebrows, and he knew he was in.

He shook his head. "Not in the least. They do say that beauty is in the eye of the beholder, of course, but I am starting to wonder if we're looking at the same thing."

She pouted. He was scoring gold here.

"And while this statue is the most hideous thing I've ever seen, you, on the other hand, are very stunning." He threw her an arrogant smile. He was due for a night of blowing off steam, and there was no better place to clear the mind than between the legs of a beautiful woman.

CHAPTER 5

MATTHEW OPENED THE DOOR AND ROBYN burst into the room, Daniel trailing her as he tried to keep up.

"What are you do—"

"Matthew, don't you dare ask me what I'm doing here. If anyone should be asking questions, it's me. Why didn't you go the exhibit opening? And why did you leave during the middle of my speech?" Her eyes were ablaze, and her cheeks were flushed.

She was so gorgeous when she was worked up. "You know, you're so—"

"I swear to God, Matthew, if you say that I'm pretty when I'm angry one more time…"

He held his hands up in surrender. "Fine."

"Fine *what*?"

He smiled at her. "Fine, I won't say it one more time."

"You're such a damn brat." She playfully shoved him.

He kept his balance. There was no sense in defending himself. He couldn't help it. Frustration gave birth to anger, and anger ignited her fiery nature. And that turned him on. It was a game he was rigged to lose. She had made it clear that they fared better as friends. He just wished that she dated more often, as he did—if you could call bedding women around the world *dating*—but then he realized that every time she did date, he became jealous as hell.

Daniel closed the door behind the two of them.

Robyn seemed to catch her first glimpse of Cal at that moment, and her eyes traveled over his outfit. She laughed. "You really don't get the concept of dressing up, do you?"

"I don't see what's wrong with an old-fashioned pair of jeans."

"I'm not sure *old-fashioned* is the right term for *those*. Look at all those tatters! How old are they?" She shook her head. They all knew it wasn't a question that needed an answer. When her gaze turned back to Matthew, her expression had softened. "Why can't you come to a single exhibit dedication?"

He wasn't going to bring up the fact that Cal had missed this one, too, even though the temptation was strong. "You know why."

"I do? If you're referring to your father, he remains in the dark as far as Gideon goes, but he believes you are an archaeologist. Your interest in new findings is to be expected."

It wasn't like he never visited the artifacts he'd tracked down. He just preferred not to see them on their opening nights.

Despite his strained relationship with his father, he loved it when she brought him up and showed concern for the man. William Connor had initiated the role of a surrogate parent to her. It was ironic that Matthew was the man's flesh and blood—and at times he wished he weren't—while Robyn had eagerly accepted an unofficial invitation into the family. At one point, Matthew had wanted to make it official. But that was many years ago. Before treasure hunting and life became so complicated. While one of their reasons for separating had been the dangerous lifestyle he had chosen, she had come to adopt that way of living, too, and it now bonded them. Another of life's ironies.

"Would you stop looking at me like that? It's like you're not even listening." Robyn filled a glass with champagne and fell into a chair. She put her feet up on the table in front of her and crossed her ankles.

"I was listening to you. It's just…" Matthew shook his head. "Never mind." This particular conversation wasn't one worth finishing. He entertained telling Robyn about this Liam Neeson character following Cal and Sophie but decided against it. Until confirmed as a threat, he didn't need to frighten anyone else.

Matthew took another flute out of a corner hutch, set it next to the bottle, and took a seat on the sofa beside Cal. There was no way Matthew would be having another glass. His head was already spinning from the two he'd drunk in quick succession downstairs.

"Go ahead if you'd like, Daniel," Matthew offered. "Have some bubbly, take a load off."

Daniel didn't accept Matthew's suggestion and remained standing.

"So what do you have for us, Danny?" Robyn winked at him before taking another sip of her drink. She was the only person who got away with calling him Danny.

"I have come across something of immense value. People might start believing in their dreams again, that anything they can imagine is possible. This discovery, if successful, will change the world." Daniel slid his gaze to Matthew.

For such claims, the implication of danger was inherent. But where there was great risk, there was great reward.

"What if I told you that the City of Gold may exist?" he asked.

"The City of Gold?" Cal guffawed. "You mean like El Dorado? Isn't that purely folklore? I find it hard to believe it's anything but fictional. Streets paved with gold? Nope, I'm not buying it."

Daniel's pulse tapped visibly in his jaw as he continued. "There is reason to believe that it may be more fact than fiction."

"Did you hear this from the leprechaun at the end of the rainbow?" Cal's laughter shook the couch.

Daniel pointed a finger at Cal and dragged it toward Matthew. "If you don't tell your boy here to back off, I'm not going to say another thing until he's gone."

Cal held his hands up, continuing to fight off his chuckles.

"Continue, Daniel," Matthew said with a nod.

"People have been searching for the lost City of Gold for centuries without any luck. It's been relegated to the status of legend, but I believe it does exist. And I believe that it hasn't been found because everyone has been searching in the wrong place. People have scoured northern Peru, near Machu Picchu and Cusco to no avail, but I think it's in the northeastern Bolivian jungle."

Matthew found his heart racing again. Discovering the city really would change the world, just as surely as Daniel had surmised. And Matthew and his friends could have a part in making that happen. "What makes you think it's located in Bolivia?"

"This." Daniel slipped a folder out from beneath the drink tray he had set down. He removed and distributed photographs to each of them, and by the looks of it, there were more in the folder.

"What are we looking at?" Matthew asked. The picture he had was an aerial image. Based on the coloring, he'd guess it was taken using some technology that penetrated the ground.

"These photographs were taken with special cameras that detect heat and depth. You are looking at what I believe to be the *real* City of Gold—Paititi."

"You mean El Dorado." Cal had composed himself by then and was sitting with one leg crossed over the other, his fingers drumming on his shin.

Daniel passed looks to all of them and stopped on Cal.

"What?" Cal ceased tapping.

Daniel let his gaze linger on Cal, and Matthew fought to keep his smile from showing.

Of the three of them, Cal was the least educated when it came to history. He was a man who hungered for travel and adventure, not for a classroom. Matthew often wondered how Cal had made it through college with his seeming aversion to textbooks.

Cal repeated himself. "El Dorado, right? That's the City of Gold?"

Daniel let out a rush of air. "That city is mythical. El Dorado is actually a ritual, not a place. It was a ceremony performed by a Muisca chieftain called the Golden One. He was said to be sprinkled with gold dust. He'd set out across the lake on a raft and submerge himself into the water with precious metal and jewels. A small gold replica of his raft was found in 1969. It's all quite fascinating actually."

"Yes, fascinating." Sarcasm soaked Cal's words. "But I've never heard of Paititi."

Another warning look from Daniel to Matthew. Cal picked up on it and twisted his fingers in front of his lips as if locking them with an imaginary key.

Daniel sighed. "The brief history lesson is this," he began. "The Spanish and the Incas of Peru had been at war for nearly forty years. It led to the Incas retreating to the Vilcabamba mountains where they were safe until 1572."

Robyn put her feet down and picked up the story. "And by the time the Spaniards found and conquered what remained of the Incas, most of the treasure was gone."

"Correct, Robyn," Daniel said.

"It's believed the Incas hid the bulk of their treasure in Paititi, a city speculated to be somewhere in the remote rainforests of Bolivia, Brazil, or Peru," Matthew added.

Daniel nodded, and Robyn carried on. "Some say that the Spaniards created the legend of a golden city to provoke excitement back in Spain. They wanted more people to accompany them on return trips. Though they had already found great riches, they were greedy for more gold."

"See, there is too much talk about Paititi for it to not be real. Think of it this way…" Daniel said. "There are always three sides to things—two opinions and the truth, which usually lies in the middle. Even with gossip magazines, for example, we know their claims are likely false overall but that they are also built upon a snippet of fact."

Cal uncrossed his legs. "So, by extension, you believe there's some city hidden in the jungle full of gold? It sounds kind of crazy to me. How much would a place like that be worth, assuming it does exist?"

"Are you sure this man is a friend of yours?" Daniel asked Matthew.

"Hey," Cal said, "you're just a maid, remember?"

Daniel took a few steps, his strides large enough that just those few took him across the room. He stopped in front of Cal.

Matthew jumped up between the two men. Cal was smirking, and Daniel was fuming. His energy was pulsing beneath Matthew's hand. All Daniel did was stare in Matthew's eyes. No words were said. Nothing needed to be.

"Daniel, please, pour yourself a drink and take a seat," Matthew said.

"He's so skeptical," Daniel said, shaking his head. "And how can one even put a price tag on history? He's ignorant."

"Sit." Matthew stared at Daniel until he backed off and pulled down on his suit jacket. "Are you okay?"

"I will be fine, but I swear to you, that boy bugs the living hell out of me."

"Well, he's part of the team, and he's not going anywhere. Can you accept that?" Matthew hated being placed in the position of referee and wasn't about to pick favorites.

"Yes, fine."

"All right, then. Answer his question."

A bolt fired through Daniel's eyes. "How is it even possible to place a monetary value on a find like this? It really is beyond me."

Matthew ignored his rant and raised a commanding eyebrow.

Daniel grumbled unintelligibly for a moment, then said, "Ten billion."

"Is the find explicitly gold?" Matthew asked, trying to appear calm and not like his blood was pounding in his ears the way it actually was.

Robyn answered the question this time. "I studied the Incas and the City of Gold, but it was years ago. While its name was obviously derived from the presence of gold, it is known—or at least was rumored—to include jewelry and other valuable trinkets." She worded the part about it being a rumor as if she questioned that viewpoint. "But even though the ancient Incas had all this wealth, they never looked at it from a materialistic perspective. Gold was sacred to them and used in their worship. They believed it brought them closer to their sun god, Inti."

"Impressive," Daniel said. "You know your Incan history well."

Cal flicked the photograph he held. "So all we have to do

is drop into the middle of a jungle, face the dangers inherent in said jungle, and find a city that may or may not exist. Am I understanding this correctly?"

Daniel finally poured himself a glass of champagne and took a sip.

"What made you look in Bolivia?" Robyn asked, ignoring Cal. Her gaze was on the photograph in her hand, and Matthew looked at his again, too. He wasn't an expert in this field, but it looked like there was something beneath the surface.

"I compared several accounts before arranging for an expedition team to fly overhead." Daniel sat on a chair. "I'll try to give you the simplified version. The details are compiled, of course, and I have them for you, Matthew. I'll deliver them tomorrow."

Matthew nodded. Normally, Daniel would whet his appetite by pitching the mission on a broader scale, then provide the finer details.

"The Incas did allow some people to see the city," Daniel continued. "It's rumored that they were blindfolded and led there so they couldn't return. A Spaniard lived with the Incas for a time. He even wrote a book about his experience. Then in 2001, an Italian archaeologist, Mario Polia, studied a Jesuit document, thought to date back to the sixteenth century, that described the city of Paititi. Records point this way and that, even contradicting one another, but I zeroed in on the northeastern jungles of Bolivia. As a side note, Paititi translates to 'city of the jaguar' and 'all white and shiny' or 'white gold.'"

"They can't even get their facts straight." Cal apparently didn't mind tempting fate again.

"I'm not understanding what led you to Bolivia," Robyn said.

"There is one account of Paititi which describes the city as an immense kingdom located 'approximately close' to the Bolivia–Brazil border. But it was a number of things that brought my attention there. Do you know who Manco Cápac is?"

"The name sounds familiar but refresh my memory," Robyn said.

"Cápac was worshiped and viewed to be the son of Inti. While the legends vary, they both center on Lake Titicaca. In one version, Cápac emerges from the lake and, in another, from a cave near the lake. Both have him carrying a *tapac-yauri*."

"A golden staff," Robyn added.

"Correct. Now, Cápac was directed to build a temple in honor of his father and it was to be where the staff sank into the earth." Daniel paused and looked at Cal. "Please don't say that could be anywhere."

Cal shrugged and smirked. "I don't have to. You just did."

Daniel rolled his eyes.

"I remember now," Robyn said. "Many Incan myths hinge on Lake Titicaca. Are these pictures from a mountain range near the lake?"

"Not exactly. Legends describe the trek to Paititi as taking days. As a point of reference, the journey started at Cusco."

"Paititi has been described as being in southeastern Peru. Among other places." Matthew added the last part as an afterthought. The truth was, people had searched for Paititi throughout South America.

"Lake Titicaca is shared by both Peru and Bolivia," Cal said with a shrug. They all looked at him at once. "What? I know geography."

Daniel shook his head, then continued. "There have been discoveries of Inca tunnels under Cusco. It's believed that the Incas traveled underground."

"I remember hearing that, too, and it makes sense. They lived in some rough terrain—jungles, mountain ranges." Matthew stretched his neck from side to side.

"Right, so why go over a mountain if you can go under it?" Daniel agreed. "You can see what I think is likely a tunnel into Paititi in the photo you have, Matthew."

Matthew looked down at the picture and noticed a darker section that was conceivably a tunnel-shaped void. There was an issue with the anomaly, though: it didn't seem to connect with another, yet larger rectangular void.

He held it for Daniel to see. "What is this?"

"I believe that is the City of Gold."

"But it doesn't seem to connect with what looks like a tunnel," Matthew said.

"It comes close, but it's also possible the tunnel goes deeper and that's where it meets the city. It may be beyond the scope of the technology's ability."

"So the darker it is in this image, the further it is underground?"

"Yes."

"You really think it's underground? It seems strange to me. The Incas loved to be elevated. They established cities on the top of mountains to bring them closer to their sun god," Robyn explained. "You've already mentioned Machu Picchu."

Daniel gave her a knowing smile. "Another reason I believe the city of Paititi is hidden underground. It would be the last place people would look."

The room fell silent. Was it really logical to consider the existence of Paititi? And underground, at that?

Robyn looked around at them. "You know, it does kind of make sense when I really think about it. If the Incas really did shuffle gold back to the city of Paititi, they couldn't have done so aboveground. They would have easily been followed. But if they had a discreet entrance and a tunnel system…"

"People expect Paititi to be elevated," Daniel reiterated. "But positioning the temple in a cavern between two mountain peaks would serve their purposes. The sun would stream in and illuminate the gold to honor their god. You can see it in that photograph you have, Robyn."

She took a look. "There does appear to be an opening between the two mountains. It's really overgrown, though."

"How do we get inside the cavern?" Matthew asked. "By foot through the tunnel system, assuming there is more than one? Or can we climb the mountain and scale down? Maybe we could be lowered in from a plane."

"No offense, sir, but you're not a mountain climber," Daniel said. "Besides, the altitude makes scaling impossible."

"That's too bad because dropping in from a plane sounds fun," Cal said, earning Matthew's approval.

Daniel turned to Cal. "You'd freeze to death. And that would be such a shame."

Cal snarled.

"Okay, so we're back to the tunnel," Matthew said to Daniel.

"That we are."

"Is it possible that the tunnel goes deeper than what was captured in the pictures? Can we know with certainty that it starts here and ends there?" Matthew pointed to the spots on the map. "And the distance between what we think is a tunnel and Paititi looks pretty large."

Daniel smiled. "That is where your sense of adventure comes in."

Matthew had to admit he was getting excited, despite the odds presented with this quest.

"So no one has come close to finding the city?" Cal asked.

"Oh, some people thought they were," Daniel responded, "but they were in the wrong spot or they were killed."

Cal swallowed audibly. "Killed?"

"One example: An explorer went missing and was never found. Rumors ranged from starvation to illness to succumbing to wild animals. In a more recent documentary, a native Indian chief confessed that their ancestors had beaten the man to death. Apparently, he had showed no interest in their culture and had no respect for their way of life."

"Whoa! Hold on." Cal leaned forward. "You're telling me that we also have to worry about natives who are going to beat us with a club?"

"How do you know it was a club?" Matthew smirked.

"A lucky guess."

"Well, this time your guy's right, Matthew," Daniel stated matter-of-factly.

Matthew had nothing to say to that. But he did like Daniel's fresh take on Paititi being underground. "Where exactly were these pictures taken?"

Daniel rattled off the coordinates. "Basically, the heart of Bolivia, in what was the fourth Inca Empire. It was the central location in the Inca Empire and far from Cusco. Even if the capital city was conquered, the gold would remain safe." Daniel rose and indicated the file he had left on the table. "There are more pictures in there. You let me know which way you're leaning with this. I'll bring you the research binder tomorrow, but I have to get back downstairs." With that, he left the room.

The ability to change the world was tempting, but was it at too high a cost? At what point did one decline and leave a discovery for others to make? Explorers and archaeologists had searched for the City of Gold for centuries with no success. What made him believe he'd have better luck? It was ludicrous to even consider that they would meet with a different outcome. But these photographs certainly made him curious. Maybe it was worth checking things out in person.

"What are you thinking, Matthew?" Robyn asked.

"Honestly, I'm not sure."

"Riches beyond imagination," she said.

He recognized the irony in the trap she'd lain before him. She knew he wasn't materialistic. "You know that's not what this is about for me."

"Yes, but can you imagine being the man who discovered the legendary City of Gold? That would be beyond incredible."

"Assuming we find it."

"And if we did, would a fictional archaeologist receive the credit?"

He glared at her. "I know you don't like the alias, but it's necessary."

"I think it's time to come clean with your dad. It would make all our lives easier. Wouldn't it, Cal?"

He didn't respond, and Matthew and Robyn turned to him.

"What is it?" Robyn asked.

"In this day and age, I still can't believe the man hates me because I'm black."

Robyn laughed. "Don't be crazy, Cal, it has nothing to do with that."

CHAPTER 6

MATTHEW'S FEET BEAT THE SIDEWALK mercilessly as he ran. Despite the chilly air, sweat dripped down his back and wet his face. It was the morning after the gala, and he had been at this for over an hour. His body fed on the adrenaline, and the burn in his muscles told him he was alive while his mind released stress and made way for clear thought.

Was he crazy for considering this quest? The city had been assigned legendary status for a reason. Its existence wasn't certain, and as Cal had pointed out, it held a popular place in fiction. From a logical standpoint, going off in search of it was a ridiculous notion. But isn't that what he did? Seek out the unlikely?

He'd set out around the world before, often propelled by nothing more than a notion and a glimmer of faith. But the City of Gold? Was he being sucked into a fairy tale? If so, nothing good would come of it. What came after the happily-ever-afters was never written: the ones where star-crossed lovers broke each other's hearts or the hero died at the hand of a nemesis who'd risen from the ashes were. Sadly, all people wanted was a sweet ending, and that rarely existed in the real world.

Besides, Paititi had been lost in the sixteenth century. Maybe it was supposed to remain that way.

He punched in the security code at the mansion's front gate and the wrought iron gates swung open. He jogged slowly in place for a few minutes to bring his heart rate down and was full of despondency that always came at the end of his runs. He'd keep going if it were possible.

Was he seriously thinking about doing this? He'd have to see if Robyn or Cal were up for the adventure. Even if they were, was he willing to risk their lives again after their quest for the Pandu statue?

His mouth lifted in a smirk. The looks on their faces when he'd pushed them over that ravine had been priceless. Did it make him a bad guy that the memory made him chuckle? Everything had turned out all right.

William's burgundy Jaguar XJR was in the drive, boasting another materialistic achievement for his old man. Matthew was surprised he was still home. At ten in the morning, he should be at his downtown office.

Matthew's sneakers squeaked on the marble entry, and he pulled them off.

"Matthew?" His father wore a designer business suit, which meant he was getting ready to leave. Maybe his late start was due to last night's indulgence in whiskey and cigars.

"Hi."

"How long are you home this time?"

By the way William settled into his stance, Matthew wasn't going to get away with a quick, slingshot answer. "There's another opportunity. This time in Rome." Out of habit, he provided a location for a real archaeological dig. It was best for his father to think him there as opposed to where he really was, should Matthew pursue Paititi. It also created a separation between him and Gideon Barnes, making their meeting up impossible. Matthew hated the lies and deception. What he really didn't care for, though, was the mental knot that came with thinking of, and referring to, himself in third person.

"And what's in Rome?"

Good question. The specifics were fuzzy, but he had remembered reading about it in *Archaeologist Worldwide*. It was a magazine devoted to ongoing and upcoming digs around the globe. They stuck to proven historical finds, not catering to people like him who preferred to chase after legends and folklore.

William intensified his glare and jutted out his jaw. The man had little patience, and it was hard to say which he disliked more, waiting or being ignored. Matthew would say the latter.

"What's in Rome?" Matthew repeated his father's question.

"That's what I asked. I mean, unless you're making it all up." William paused for a beat. "You know, sometimes I wonder where in the hell you run off to."

Matthew's eyes snapped to his father's. He suddenly felt like a teenager. Maybe it was time to move out. "Why? I tell you every time I leave."

William shook his head. "It just doesn't sit well with me."

"You miss me." Matthew smiled, hoping it would come across as lighthearted and even somewhat sincere, but it faltered part way through. Hiding his true feelings wasn't one of his strengths.

"Do you know Gideon Barnes?" William asked, instead of playing along.

"You've asked me that before."

"Yes, and before you said no. I'm asking you again."

Matthew forced himself to keep eye contact. "The answer is still no."

"Hmm. Yet you approached me and zealously requested that I fund his expeditions." William paused a moment, then continued, "One day we're going to sit down and really talk." He took a step toward the door, signaling the end of the conversation.

"Why start now?" The retort came out automatically. If he tried to take it back, his father would deem it a weakness. Besides, Matthew didn't regret it. William's last statement carried a promise that would never see fulfillment. Father and son bonding? In this household? It was hard to imagine. They were more suited to parting ways.

William spun around. "You like to play the victim, don't you, son? I've never been a good enough father for you. Excuse me if I've always valued keeping a roof over your head and food in your belly over long chats about our feelings. Hell, if that makes me a bad father—and a horrible human being—well, then you'll have to suck it up and accept it. Things are the way they are."

"Why would I expect you'd say any different?"

"Like I said, things are the way they are."

William slammed the front door behind him, and instead of Matthew steaming over their recent conflict, he considered his father's inquiry about Gideon. Was it possible he suspected Matthew was involved, or was it just the man's bruised ego that Gideon didn't grace him with his presence last night? It was harder to shake the possible implications than it was to brush off another William Connor confrontation.

Chapter 7

Ian had felt the redhead leave the hotel bed somewhere around two in the morning. When he woke up, she was gone, and he was relieved that he hadn't been forced to give the speech he knew by heart by now. Not that it was so much a speech. It was really only two brief sentences: *It was fun. Time to go.*

Yes, he preferred to be sparse with his words. Why use twenty when six made the point? It wasn't as if he ever gave any of the women he bedded a reason to believe their time together was more than a one-night stand. They both got what they wanted, and that was the end of it.

Beyond satisfying him sexually, being with a woman had a way of clearing his mind. Giving and receiving physical pleasure was instinctual, animalistic. There wasn't time to analyze and contemplate. And that's how his mind worked best. Diversions worked quite well to help him solve problems.

And the redhead had fit his needs perfectly. He wasn't her first tryst. She was worldly, independent, and wealthy. He had sized her up in the first few minutes standing by that statue.

It wasn't the expensive dress, her clutch purse, or even the way she carried herself. It was her hair. So many men failed to consider this attribute. They were too busy ogling women's bodies and basking in the fact they actually might get laid that they were obtuse to the finer details.

Ian had been at this awhile, though. At forty-one, he no longer became caught up in the rapture of possibilities. He created his future. He didn't act the victim or allow someone else to play his cards. No way in hell.

It led him to his chosen profession: a gun for hire. He reported to the highest payer and killed—or tortured—when required. After a job was complete, he moved on to another employer, another job.

But he wasn't so confident about his current employer. They had contacted him through text messages sent from a phone originating in New York City. That and the letter *V* was all he had. And with a population of more than eight million, not to mention more than fifty million in tourists yearly, this did little to narrow things down.

He'd normally reject a job if he didn't have enough information about who was hiring him. This time he'd let himself go in blind. Whoever it was had appealed to his ego, saying he was the man for the job because both he and it were in Toronto. That alone should have sent him running. Working outside of the city made it less likely that things would be tied back to him.

Another tip-off should have been that killing wasn't a requirement of the job. That was what most people paid him to do. He had deceived himself into thinking that not having to kill might be any easy way to earn a wad of cash.

All these signs that something was off, and he had ignored every one of them.

He was entrapped by the seeming simplicity of the job. All he had to do was obtain a stupid Indian statue. When he'd accepted the advance, however, he hadn't known it involved the mayor's son. He also hadn't known that by the time he tracked down the statue, it would be on display behind plate glass. He'd handled home security systems before, but he wasn't egotistical enough to believe he could tackle one at a museum.

His expertise wasn't in breaking and entering. His skill was pulling a trigger. And while killing may not be a requirement with this job, he'd gladly throw it in if necessary to acquire the statue. He considered his options and all the seeming dead ends. And just as he was feeling blocked, clarity came to him. He would have the idol brought to him, and he finally realized how he could manipulate the mayor's son into doing just that. After all, he wasn't paid to try, he was paid to succeed.

CHAPTER 8

WILLIAM CONNOR SAT IN HIS OFFICE doing his best to get through this report. But he'd read the same two sentences at least five times. His mind wasn't on his mayoral responsibilities. It wasn't on the bitter face-to-face he'd had with his son, either. Even though he detested Matthew's utter and apparent disrespect.

No, he dwelled on his doubts about Gideon Barnes's existence. He was credited with many great finds, but was he flesh and blood or an alias? William had never met the man, yet every month he shelled out six figures to fund his expeditions. In repayment, Barnes had never shown his face—not in person, at least. He had seen the pictures, but that didn't mean anything these days. But to dismiss his existence didn't make sense, either. In that case, where did the finds come from?

Barnes's disgusting lack of gratitude was only trumped by the resulting hit William took in the public forum. That was unacceptable. And if the man wasn't real, where was William's money going? Though bleeding money didn't affect him as much as the personal insult.

His phone buzzed, his assistant trying to reach him. He pressed the intercom button on the telephone console. "What is it, Ashlynn?"

"I have Nicholas Hartman on the phone for you, sir."

Hartman was ruthless, and if William had his way, they wouldn't ever speak. But he was a terrific asset to have on a guest list.

"Patch him through." He tossed the report on his desk.

"Certainly. Right away."

Ashlynn's eagerness to please never failed to make him smile. Why couldn't his own son respect him as much? He'd never given him cause to hate him. He was faithful to his wife, Matthew's mother, throughout their entire marriage. The morals of most men—or lack thereof—disgusted him, and it was the one thing, he supposed, that tied him to the standards of a past century. Yet, he'd rather be considered old-fashioned than have a sexually transmitted disease.

He heard the subtle click on the line indicating the transfer went through. "Good morning, Nicholas. To what do I owe this honor?"

"Nicholas? Nick to you, and stuff it, Bill. You're better than all that BS repartee."

The man was a breed all his own. Smiling, William said, "All right, then. What do you want?"

"You sound all too pleased, to phrase it directly."

"Can you blame a man?"

"I can, but I won't. I'm just calling because I wanted to tell you that last night was an enjoyable evening. That woman, Robyn Garcia, is quite a gem."

Leave it to Nick to hone in on one woman who'd never succumb to his charms—if that's how one wanted to see them. The only thing charming about the man was the thickness of his wallet. It was what kept William around. "You know she's like a daughter to me."

"Yes, I know."

There was a rare second of hesitation on Nick's end, but William let it ride. After all, Nick had called him and he was certain it had to do with more than bedding Robyn.

"The gala last night was superb," Nick continued.

Superb wasn't exactly the way William would have described it. An outright disaster, really. A display of public humiliation.

"I must say, however, that I was disappointed Gideon Barnes was a no-show. It's such a shame. Everything was lovely except for that."

William's mood soured with the demotion from *superb* to *lovely*. He cooled his temper through a breathing exercise he'd learned awhile back. It was a necessity for survival in his line of work. Emotions in the political arena led to career suicide. The previous mayor's run testified to this. His had spiraled out of control, leading to drug abuse in the media spotlight, making him more the punch line in a joke than the lead.

"I take it by your silence that you're thinking the same thing."

Another measured inhale followed by a paced exhale. William's heart rate began to slow, and he put on his most diplomatic air. "I agree that it was disappointing the man didn't attend."

"And it wasn't the first time."

Nick had already punctured William's pride, but now he wielded the bloody knife and threatened the jugular. He must not realize with whom he was dealing. It was time to pull out the semiautomatic.

"Yet I managed to pull off the rest of the evening, now, didn't I, Nick? I don't believe I've ever attended one of these galas at your home."

You told me to speak bluntly with you. Well, screw you, Nick.

It may not have been a bullet, but it was a shot to the gut for a man who valued public opinion more than his own sanity.

"I see that we've taken the gloves off."

Well, you threw the first punch…

Childhood banter paraded in William's mind.

"Maybe the next time it will be at my home *and* Mr. Barnes will be in attendance," Nick said.

"Please be sure to invite me." The words, easily subject to sarcasm, came out with a detached professionalism. "Now, if that will be all, I really need to get back to work. The city does need me."

"Yes, I'm sure in your mind, it does."

"Tsk. Now who isn't playing nice?"

"You can handle it." With that, the detestable defense attorney terminated the call.

William sat there holding the receiver, his knuckles turning white from his tightening grip. Of all the people to call him out on Gideon's no-show... Who did that man think he was? Regrettably, he wasn't alone in noticing Barnes's absence from the event. It began with Jacob shouting out at the gala. How many more of these calls could he expect?

He stared at the buttons on the phone, considering the slew of people with whom he was associated. Surely one would be willing to help him track down the man...

He dialed his own home number and the phone rang three times before Lauren answered.

"What have I told you, Miss Hale? The phone is to be answered in two rings."

"Yes, I am sorry, sir. I was—"

"There's no need to elaborate. Please put Daniel on the phone."

"Yes, sir."

The hold music came on. It was a collection he had orchestrated for this purpose. No detail was too small. But instead of appreciating the rises and falls of the compilation, he was concentrated on one thing: Gideon Barnes.

"Mr. Connor, sir, how may I assist?" Daniel answered the phone.

William tapped his fingers on the report he'd cast aside. "I need you to enlist the help of a private investigator."

"An investigator, sir?"

William rolled his eyes. Life was too short for repeating oneself.

"There is a matter that needs to be taken care of. I don't care how much it costs, but I want Gideon Barnes tracked down. I don't want to hear any excuses. I want results, and I want acknowledgment."

"Of course. No problem."

"Damn straight it's no problem." William slammed down the phone, the dam of cool reserve broken. Until this know-it-all archaeologist gave him the respect he was due, he'd turn the world upside down.

Chapter 9

Cal and Sophie were sitting in a Starbucks. Whenever he caught her gaze, he basically burst into flame from the ferocity burning in her irises.

"So you went last night even though I asked you not to?" she asked, although it wasn't really a question. It was an accusation.

"I didn't." That was technically the truth—a white lie. It still parched his throat. He took a sip of his coffee.

"Not even to Matthew's house for the after-event? I tried to reach you. Your phone kept going to voice mail."

"How do you know that I was there and not in bed sleeping, or… You weren't around. Maybe I enjoyed an action flick."

"You watch it, Cal, or you'll have the movie choice all the time." There was more bark to her words than bite to her tone.

He reached for her hand. "Come on, baby, please stop giving me a rough time about all this."

She folded a napkin and then unfolded it. She drew the corners in, dog-earing them, and then straightened them out. She dropped it and reached for his hand. "I might be taking things out on you."

"You what? What's wrong?" He wasn't doing a good job of hiding his shock at her confession.

"You mean, besides the man who is stalking us?"

"Speaking of, have you seen him today?" Cal looked around the packed coffee shop to find a bunch of people in need of caffeine fixes. No familiar faces were in the crowd except for one guy who was Leonardo DiCaprio's doppelganger. There was no

Liam Neeson.

She shook her head, her small dreads flopping from side to side. "It's more than him that has me upset, but don't get me wrong, that whole thing is still unsettling. I just have bigger things to worry about."

"Like what?" He swept his thumb across her skin, trying to calm her.

"Work." She let go of his hand, but instead of going back to the napkin, she toyed with her cup, rotating it until the logo faced her. "I have this house that isn't selling. It's been on the market for three months. That might as well be forever."

"Maybe they need to lower their asking price?"

"It's not that. It's priced right in the sweet spot. The home is immaculate and in a state of excellent repair. If I even suggested a lower price, I might as well confess to being a bad agent." She took a sip from her cup and lowered it, but continued to hold on to it. "Maybe it's just the economy, and I'm overreacting."

"No, I can't imagine that being a remote possibility." Sarcasm. Every word.

Her eyes narrowed, and she lifted her cup toward him. "Do you want to wear this?"

He smiled at her. "Come on, now. Things have been worse. Aren't you always telling me things happen when they're supposed to happen?"

"I love it when what I spew out comes back to bite me in the ass," she grumbled.

"Well, that is what you say, isn't it?"

"It's easier to preach than to believe sometimes."

He leaned across the table and squeezed her hand, taking the one from the cup. Her mood wasn't lightened despite his efforts. He may as well have squeezed a damp towel.

"You want to know what the big deal is? Here it is. If I don't sell this place, I'm looking at the unemployment line."

"What do you mean?"

She pulled her hand back. "I mean exactly what I said. I'll be without a job, unemployed, seeking government assistance."

"Edwin would never let you go. You're one of his best agents. In fact, why don't we go out tonight and celebrate your success?"

"My success hasn't happened yet."

"Your face is on buses."

She laughed. "You think I've made it"—she attributed air quotes to her last two words—"and Ed's going to keep me because my face is on buses? You do remember that I paid for those ads myself, right?"

"You're giving it too much thought. So what? Your face is all around the city…at least this part of it. If Edwin lets you go, you'll get a job somewhere else or go out on your own. The possibilities are endless."

Her eyes softened as they leveled with his.

"Baby, you're unstoppable," he said. "You are going to take over the world of realty."

"Ha, you had me right up until the end." Her phone rang.

"Get it. It could be that offer you're waiting for."

"One can always hope, I guess." She picked up her cell from the table, pressed a button, and held it to an ear. "Sophie Jones… Yes, that is me… You want to see it? I can certainly help you with that." She pointed frantically at the phone and mouthed, *This is it.*

Cal smiled at her and turned away, affording her privacy. The line at the counter had thinned out and he considered getting another coffee, but the execution of his plan stopped when he thought about it hitting his stomach. Maybe he'd get Sophie something.

A few minutes later, when he returned with a strawberry scone and a chai tea, Sophie had finished with her call and was beaming.

"You might have been right, Cal."

"Excuse me? Can you say that part again? *You might have been right, Cal.*"

Sophie laughed. "Someone wants to see the house tonight at nine." Her face fell, and she must have just remembered their plans to go out for drinks. They had discussed it days ago.

"It's all right. We can make it tomorrow night."

"You're sure?"

"Yes, of course. That is late for a showing, though, isn't it?"

"This isn't a nine-to-five job, Cal. Besides, he said that's the only time he could make it."

"He?"

"Don't get like that. I'll be fine. I call it in to the office. They'll know where I am." She smiled. "You could come over to my place afterward."

"Oh, you'd be thinking so."

She shrugged. "Maybe. How about I call you if I'm up for it?"

He leaned across the table and kissed her.

If it weren't for the passing thoughts of being watched, he'd let himself sink into the moment. Pulling back, he took another glance around, but it still didn't reveal any Liam Neeson look-alikes. Maybe he was being paranoid. As for the SUV parked out the front of his house the other day, there had to be thousands in this city just like it.

CHAPTER 10

EVERYTHING WAS ON THE LINE, and making this sale was an opportunity to prove herself. Sophie didn't expect Cal to understand. To him, she was perfect, and everything she did was, too. But it wasn't just about selling the house and netting the tidy commission. It was the resulting sense of accomplishment and fulfillment. It was the largest estate she had taken on, and she was out to show everyone—namely herself—that she had what it took to see it through.

She pulled out a Calvin Klein skirt suit from her closet and slipped it on. She did it terrific justice, if she did say so herself. The skirt was black and the jacket gray, and beneath the latter, she wore a black blouse—streamlined, simple, and elegant. She had to give the impression that she had money when her client no doubt would. She added diamond stud earrings as a final touch, keeping her neck bare. Too much could simply be *too much*.

She sprayed Chanel No 5 on her neck and then her wrists, then watched herself in the mirror as she rubbed them together.

"You've got this, Sophie Jones."

She pumped her fists and grinned. It was a coaching technique she used to combat nagging self-doubt. If she didn't squash the negativity from its roots, it would ruin everything she'd worked for.

She snapped her fingers and made a finger gun at her image. "You can do this!"

One quick tug down on the jacket and she left her reflection behind, her confidence stepping in to take the lead. She'd get there an hour before the showing so she'd have plenty of time to set up. She had her keys in her door when she remembered the tube of premade chocolate chip cookie dough sitting in her fridge.

Her heels clicked across the linoleum as she hurried to her kitchen to grab it. It was a proven trick in the industry that the smell of freshly baked cookies made people feel at home. She always found it ironic as most people never took the time to bake anymore, especially anyone who was financially capable of buying this particular house. They likely had servants who took care of such things. Tonight, it didn't bother her to assume that role. With the amount of debt she carried—which barely ever changed between the interest rate and her minimum payments—she'd do anything it took to make this sale. Well, almost anything.

The evening was brisk, and she exhaled puffs of white fog as she walked from her apartment to her car. The interior of her car had barely warmed by the time she reached the large house she needed to sell. The lights were on inside and landscaping ones bathed the exterior in a soft glow. It was all set on a timer. The owners were vacationing in the Maldives for the winter.

Must be nice...

"Brr," she said as shivers started in her legs and ran through her. Nylons did very little to keep out the cold, but they did make for an elegant final touch. Just as heels hurt like a son of bitch until they were broken in, the benefits outweighed the torture.

She left her stilettos on and hung her coat in the front closet. Every time she entered the place, she became caught up in the rapture of its architectural beauty. It wasn't as if it was the first mansion she'd ever seen. She had been to the Connors' monstrosity on numerous occasions, but one day, she could see herself living in a place like this with its marble flooring, sweeping staircase, tiered chandelier, and crown molding. If she had the time, she could admire the fine touches for hours.

Lord knew she'd visualized herself in this particular house

many times. It was nothing more than a daydream at this point. She'd made the same wage without much variation over the past three years, and while it would have been more than substantial outside the city, she still wanted more.

She headed for the kitchen and got started cutting the cookie dough and setting the slices out on a cookie sheet. She slipped the first batch into the oven. As they cooked, she did a quick walk-through, and by the time, she was on her way back to the kitchen, the sweet smell of chocolate chip cookies warmed the air and quickened her steps. She unloaded them onto a cooling rack and brewed a pot of coffee.

She was ready for her buyer. And, yes, that's how she was going to think of him. He wasn't just a *potential* buyer, he was a *buyer*. This was going to be a piece of cake.

Or a tray of cookies.

She smiled at her silly thinking. But how could it prove difficult when she loved the place so much? She dismissed the internal voice that reminded her it hadn't made a difference so far. Tonight things would change. This man, he was the one. She felt it in her soul.

As if it were divine confirmation, the doorbell rang. She hadn't heard a car pull up, but the kitchen was toward the back of the house.

"All right, girl, it's go time." She pumped her fists again and smoothed out her skirt.

With a fleeting glance in the front mirror, she smiled at herself and whispered, "You've got this."

She opened the door, smiling broadly, but the instant she saw him, she hurried to shut it again. She tried not to scream when the latch didn't cooperate.

He pushed through. "Keep it quiet, Sophie Jones. Back up into the house."

Her racing heartbeat made it difficult to breathe. "Who are you? Why are you doi—"

He drew a gun, cutting off her words. "Move back into the house. Slowly."

Images from the crime shows she loved filled her mind. He wasn't wearing a mask. He wasn't worried about her identifying him. There's only one reason he'd abandon that worry, and her heart sank at the realization. He planned to kill her.

She assessed his hold on the pistol. She didn't know much about guns, but based on his calm demeanor and easy grip, he was experienced at handling one.

Oh God, this is it! I'm going to die in my dream house.

She stepped back, and he slipped inside the house and closed the door behind him. He did it without taking his eyes—or his gun—off her.

"I know you f-followed them from India," she said, trying to be brave.

"My, you think you have it all figured out, don't you?"

"The Pandu is in the museum. You can't get it, and we can't give it to you. I don't even hunt treasure." The last sentence slipped from her lips, and her conscience stabbed her for betraying Cal by demeaning what he loved to do.

"Yes, all that is true, except for my not being able to get it. You see, it's very important that I get my hands on that statue. And you are going to help me do that."

"I don't see how. I told you—"

He pressed the muzzle of the gun to her stomach. "You are going to do exactly as I say."

Her gut twisted, and the sweet aroma of the cookies morphed into an unpleasant coating on her tongue.

"Do you understand what I'm telling you?"

She swallowed roughly, her saliva a thick paste, and nodded.

"All right, then. We should get along just fine."

If she survived this, she was going to kill Cal for getting her involved.

CHAPTER 11

IT WAS TUESDAY, TWO DAYS after the gala, and Matthew was in his office working through Daniel's findings about Paititi. Maybe somewhere in all his research, the historical facts would coincide with the photographs and convince him that it existed.

Not that he was like others in his field, who based their decisions strictly on certifiable fact. Matthew loved discrediting myths and seeing firsthand what was widely perceived as fable. But was he willing to stretch his ideology to include Paititi? Its existence might be too far a stretch.

He refreshed himself first on historical truths. The Incas were extremely intelligent, amassing huge armies from surrounding natives and growing their troops to approximately two hundred thousand warriors. That number was even more impressive when considering it represented approximately 1.5 percent of their population. Comparing the figure to the modern-day US military—and taking into account active and reserve personnel—it meant that the Incas had twice as many of their people serving in a military capacity than the United States did today.

But the Incas weren't a bloodthirsty people. They'd rather reach a diplomatic solution than go to war. Yet they did practice child sacrifice as a gift to their gods. Their firm belief in reincarnation removed their fear of death and elevated their view of passing to a bestowed honor. For some, these conflicting concepts were hard to accept, but how could one judge an ancient civilization based on today's standards?

The Incas accepted the world as being abundant and one family ruled over the rest. Food and goods were brought to that family for distribution. As a result, there was no crime or famine. The gold wasn't even assigned an intrinsic value; it was revered. It brought them closer to their sun god, Inti.

Strategic battle plans commenced with slingers, archers, and spear throwers, and then proceeded to a full-frontal charge that armed Inca troops with maces, clubs, and battle-axes. But it wasn't their head-on assaults that reaped the highest advantage in battles. It was their talent for organization. With one third of the army in hand-to-hand combat and another third attacking the flanks, the final third would be held back in reserve. In fact, their flanking maneuvers were more effective than direct confrontation, and oftentimes they'd feign withdrawal while their enemy was exposed and vulnerable. Discipline defined the Incas' existence and carried over to their combat tactics. It was one reason they had met with so many successes.

But in the sixteenth century, greedy Spanish conquistadors had threatened their peaceful existence. The Spaniards had come at the Incas with smaller numbers but with something they had never seen before—horses.

To the Incas, the beasts were mythical creatures drawn from fantasy. One theory is that the Incas may have seen the horses as demons and the Spanish riding them as coming to put an end to their way of life and to steal their connection with the divine. But it was the Incas' stubbornness—or rigid structure, perhaps—that limited their ability to adapt in warfare. In 1572, this resulted in the Spanish conquest and the last emperor being executed in Cusco.

Matthew looked up when a knock sounded on the door.

Daniel's voice called to him from the hall, and he tore his eyes from the material he was reading, but not because he wanted to. The history of the Incas was fascinating.

"Come in," he said.

Daniel entered and unloaded the tray he was carrying, setting both a cup of coffee and a turkey sandwich on Matthew's desk.

"Ah, reading, I see."

Matthew took a bite of the sandwich. He was aware of it all the way down to the base of his empty stomach. How long had he been in here? He consulted the clock on the wall. Six hours. They do say that time flies when having fun.

He gestured with the sandwich toward Daniel and spoke with his mouth full. "Thank you."

"Don't mention it. So what are your thoughts?" Daniel sat in the chair across from Matthew.

"On the history of Incas of Peru or the alleged city of Paititi?"

"Alleged? Ah, not quite a believer yet, I see."

Matthew swallowed a large piece of bread and turkey, and then shook his head. "I don't really know what to believe, actually. I haven't made up my mind."

"Hmm, well, that's a first. Normally you know right away. You jump in with both feet."

Daniel was right. Normally he did. But maybe he'd had a bit more to go on in the past. Maybe it'd be easier if there were more recorded documents—a difficult task as the Incas had never developed a written language.

"What have you learned so far?" Daniel prompted.

"A lot. I remember studying them in school, but unless I'm using knowledge actively, it's gone. Sadly, that happened with the Incas."

"And now?"

"They fascinate me."

"And the city of Paititi?"

"It's an enigma. Does it exist? Did it ever exist? With the vast territory the Incas took in, the search area is expansive."

Daniel laughed. "I'd have agreed with you before I saw those photographs."

Matthew pulled one from the pile and placed it at the top. It showed the color variations, hinting to something underneath the surface. "It's these images that are most convincing."

"Yet you still hesitate to believe?"

"It's just… What if the Spanish conquistadors took all the gold after they conquered the Incas?"

Daniel pressed his lips together. "It's possible, I suppose." He paused a beat. "So you think the treasure is gone?"

Matthew wasn't ready to resign himself to that assumption, either. "I'm not sure. But I keep thinking about Machu Picchu."

"Why is that?"

"Well, it's believed that the Spanish kept that city's location quiet."

"You're thinking they also kept Paititi's whereabouts hidden?"

Matthew nodded. "I wonder. I mean, think of it this way: You just conquered a large nation. You feel entitled to all the spoils. The Spaniards were not only brutally violent but greedy. Why spread word about finding all this gold? Would it not be better to remain quiet, and maybe many years later, as the story of conquest is retold, throw in a rumor about a City of Gold? Meanwhile, the riches were long gone."

Daniel nodded. "It is definitely possible."

The scenarios, the numerous possibilities, raced through Matthew's mind. "History confirms that the Spaniards recovered some gold, but the quantities were considered insignificant against what the Incas were believed to have had. Expanding on this, some items weren't accounted for."

"You're referring to the gold chain?"

"Yes, that and a gold disc. These items are too large simply to vanish. The chain was six hundred fifty feet long, each link as thick as a man's thumb. It was so heavy that it took two hundred men to lift it. The disc was said to be thirteen feet in diameter and was considered the most precious object of the empire. Termed the holy of holies it was said to be kept in the big temple in Cusco. After 1572, it never resurfaced. Gone." Matthew snapped his fingers. "Just gone? I'm not buying that. I wonder if the Incas hid it in their city. In Paititi."

"Ah, there he is." Daniel smiled. "I find this interesting. The Spaniard Francisco Pizarro held Atahualpa, the last Sapa Inca, or ruler, for ransom. He ordered that a room of eighty-eight cubic meters was to be filled with gold. For months, precious objects were carted in from across the span of the empire—jars, pots, vessels, and golden plates. Over the course of weeks, the gold objects were melted down and the spoils divided among Pizzaro and his men. But Pizzaro ended up killing the ruler anyway. But I have a theory," he said, looking to Matthew, who nodded at him to continue. "Do you really think the Inca people brought Pizzaro all the gold they had, precious items used in worship, knowing they were all going to be destroyed? It was rumored that the Spaniard doubted their trustworthiness. Related to that or not, he killed Atahualpa before the ransom had been completed."

"Good points. It also leads back to the idea that underground tunnels were a viable means of travel and obscurity."

"So you are considering the mission, then?" Daniel asked slowly.

"Hmm," was all Matthew said in response.

Then Daniel fell quiet, and Matthew sensed he had more on his mind than Paititi.

"What is it, Daniel?"

"Gideon Barnes."

"What are you talking about?"

"Your father... He wants me to hire a private investigator to hunt the man down. What am I supposed to do?"

Matthew hadn't anticipated that coming, though maybe he should have. At one time, he had deliberated on hiring a man to play the role—beyond the photographs—but had decided it would be too risky.

"Your father says he wants acknowledgment. Maybe send him a card?" Daniel hitched his brows, and it made Matthew laugh.

"I could do that."

"And in the meantime, what should *I* do?"

"Either stall or get someone you can control? Better yet, pretend to get some—"

Daniel was shaking his head. "Not going to work. He's going to follow up."

"Okay, go with my second suggestion, then: pretend to hire

someone."

"Will do." Daniel stood.

"I'll let you know what I decide to do about Paititi."

"You know, even if the treasure itself isn't there, the temple was rumored to be made of gold. It's not as if the Incas could have carried that back for the Spaniards. And to lay claim to Paititi would be beyond compare."

"Again, assuming that Paititi is even real." Matthew's phone rang, and Daniel excused himself and left the room.

Matthew glanced at the caller ID. An unknown number. He sent the call to voice mail, more interested in getting back to his research than dealing with a telemarketer.

He settled back in his chair, analyzing one of Daniel's photographs.

Are you the legendary Paititi?

The door swung open and Cal came in, Lauren racing behind him, her hands flailing in the air. "He just steamrolled right by me."

"It's all right." Matthew waved her off, and she closed the door behind her.

Cal stood in front of him, heaving for air, hunched over and ragged. "Someone has—"

Matthew's phone rang again, and he pushed it aside.

Cal's hands shot out. "You have to get that and you have to get it now."

Cal hadn't even been this panicked when Matthew had pushed him over the ravine. Matthew accepted the call, keeping his eyes on Cal. "Matthew Connor."

"Meet me in the history section of Indigo Books on Yonge in an hour." It was a man's voice but not one he recognized.

"Who is this?"

"Don't worry about who this is, worry about who I have."

Matthew's eyes shot to Cal.

"He has Sophie," Cal whispered.

Matthew's stomach dropped. "What do you want?" he said into the phone.

"I told you what I want. And no police. You follow directions and your friend gets to live. One hour."

The man hung up.

Matthew continued to hold his phone and tapped his clenched hand against the desk. "What do you mean he has Sophie? He who? How did he get my number?"

"He called me first. That's how he had your number. I gave it to him. Sophie and I had talked about getting together after her showing last night, but she said she'd call. When she didn't, I just assumed she was tired and thought nothing of it. But then I got the call..." Cal was wearing a pattern in the floorboards with his pacing. "Remember the dark SUV? The Liam Neeson look-alike? I think it's him."

"Why?"

"I think it ties back to India."

"Well, if he's after the statue, he's too late."

"It can't be too late." Cal swallowed roughly. "He will kill her, Matt."

Chapter 12

Matthew drove since he was in a better emotional state than Cal, who hadn't stopped shaking since he had entered Matthew's office forty-five minutes prior.

"I think you should stay put," Matthew said, pulling into a spot near Indigo Books.

Cal kept his gaze straight ahead. Matthew let him take time to collect himself, and mere seconds later, Cal turned to Matthew. "You're probably right. I'd kill the son of a bitch. Just get Sophie back."

"I'll do my best."

Cal shook his head, distress written all over his face. "I can't believe I let her get caught up in this mess. She's going to kill me."

"This isn't your fault, but when you put it that way, I almost feel sorry for the guy who has her." Matthew tried to add humor to lessen the impact of their grim situation.

"Damn straight."

Matthew left the keys in the ignition and let it idle to keep Cal warm. It was cold and damp outside, and he didn't know how long he'd be gone.

With each step he took toward the bookstore, Matthew replayed the conversation with the strange caller. His voice was clearly North American but otherwise had no discernable accent. He didn't think this man was the same one from the jungle, though. He'd also debated whether the "no police" demand was something to worry about or not. Was it simply a play for dramatics? A bluff? While he wished it were, he had a bad feeling this man meant business.

A young blonde smiled at him when he entered the bookstore. "Good day. Can I help you find anything?"

She was a cute little thing, and on any other occasion, he might have invented a reason to take her up on her offer of assistance. But this time, he shook his head and kept on walking to the history section.

A man was sitting on one of two sofa chairs situated near each other.

He really does look like Liam Neeson.

The man spotted him, too, and sauntered over to the shelving on a perimeter wall.

Matthew's heart was racing, but he ignored it. Sophie's life was at stake. He followed the man and, once next to him, Matthew pulled out a hardback on the American Civil War. Maybe if he were holding something, he'd be less nervous. Or at least able to hide his emotions better.

The man remained where he was, still facing the shelf. "You're going to get the Pandu."

The Pandu? It's secured in the museum. Impossible.

Besides, he and his friends weren't con men or thieves. They were treasure hunters.

The stranger's head slowly swiveled toward Matthew. "Did you hear me?"

"Yes, I heard you."

"You are going to get the statue, and then—"

"That's not possible." Matthew shoved the book back onto the shelf. "It's already at the Royal Ontario Museum. It's on exhibit. There's no way to get it back."

The man curled his lips. "No statue, no Sophie. Don't tell me that I didn't give you a choice." He turned to leave.

"How do I know she's still alive?" he countered, his gut twisting. Verbalizing the situation made it surreal, like he was in another dimension of reality. These types of things happened to characters in the movies, not to him and his friends.

The man closed the distance between them. He stretched his

neck forward and spoke into Matthew's ear. "What does it matter if you're not going to help me out?"

The Pandu was off the table. He and his friends knew nothing about bypassing security. And even if they could figure out a way into the museum, it would likely take weeks to plan and orchestrate. If they were caught, they'd all go to prison. But maybe he could make another trade…

Daniel's proposed quest flashed through his mind. Was he willing to risk Sophie's life on a legendary city that may not even exist?

His blood pounded in his ears at the prospect of what he was going to bargain with. "There may be something I can offer you instead."

"Now what could that possibly be? I really had my mind set on the man in a dress."

Matthew wasn't going to correct him that it was a jama, not a dress.

"First you show me proof of life." He squared his shoulders and widened his stance, the familiar rush of adrenaline calming his nerves.

The man took a phone from his pocket, pressed some buttons, and held the screen for Matthew to see.

A short video began to play. It showed Sophie gagged and tied to a chair.

Matthew scrutinized the background for any identifying landmarks, but the man had been smart enough to film with his back to a window. The glare cutting across the lens gave that much away.

"Come on. Say hi to the camera."

"Screw you." Sophie's words were mumbled but easy enough to distinguish. Even with her life in danger, the girl was spirited. Maybe Cal had reason to fear her once they rescued her.

"There, you've seen enough." The man pocketed the phone.

"How do I know that you didn't record this and then kill her?"

"Listen, if you want to play games with her life, that is your choice, but you are quickly wearing on my patience."

Matthew's vision was narrowing, his hearing sharpening, and his heart thumping. If he concentrated, he could even hear its beat. Was offering Paititi the right decision? As if the universe was giving him a sign, his eyes landed on a book about the Inca Empire. "Like I said, I have something even bigger to offer you."

The man shrugged and splayed his hands.

"This treasure is estimated to be worth ten billion," he said, borrowing Daniel's summation. "That's well over the estimated value of the statue. But really, this find is priceless. It has the ability to change the world."

"It's not about bettering the planet or the money, Gideon Barnes."

Matthew's eyes shot to meet the man's.

"That's right. I know who you are. *Both* your identities."

It must be a tactic to throw him off, and by God, it was working. His mind was whirring. There was only one other person aware of his alias outside of his circle of friends…Veronica Vincent. And suffice it say, their relationship wasn't a good one. Was she behind Sophie's abduction?

"See, it's not about the money," the man went on. "It's about the Pandu."

"You said that." Confidence veneered Matthew's words.

"Then the next move is yours. Sophie lives or she—"

"What I'm offering you is the City of Gold."

"The City of Gold?" The man laughed, showing a characteristic that was all his own, without any likeness to the actor he so resembled. "As in El Dorado? I would have given you more credit. There is no such thing. It's a myth."

Paititi, actually.

"Are you certain that it doesn't exist?" Matthew said, making his tone and expression serious enough to create doubt.

The laughter stopped. "People have been searching for it a long time. If it were real, don't you think it would have been found by now?"

"I have a reason to believe that it exists," Matthew said. "As I've said, it's on the table."

"And who are you to call the shots?" the man growled.

"I'm the one who knows where to find it."

He scoffed. "You know where it is?"

Matthew just nodded. He hoped that he was coming across with conviction. Inside, he was quaking. It was possible that Daniel's photographs would amount to nothing.

He appeared to be considering the proposal. While he did, Matthew's mind replayed the man's earlier words. *Help me out.* Combining this with the fact that he knew he was Gideon Barnes made it worthy of acting on a hunch. "Maybe you should run the offer past your boss."

"What are you talking about? I'm in charge."

Matthew raised an eyebrow. "If you really were in charge, you would have jumped at the opportunity to stake claim to the City of Gold."

"Maybe I'm attached to the statue."

Maybe you're full of shit was what Matthew wanted to say. He played the silence for a bit longer before walking away and leaving the man with the words, "Check with your boss and let me know."

Out of the corner of his eye, Matthew saw the man ball his hands into fists. Matthew would likely receive a phone call within the next half hour. If it even took that long.

CHAPTER 13

MATTHEW CAME OUT OF THE bookstore reveling in a sense of power, but this mess was far from over. And he had no idea how his friends would react when they found out what he had proposed.

He slammed the driver's-side door and buckled his seat belt. In his peripheral vision, he saw Cal regard him and then angled himself to glance behind the vehicle.

"Are we getting Sophie back? What happened, Matt?"

Matthew gripped the wheel.

"Matt?"

He hated himself right now. He hated the fact that he couldn't bring Sophie back immediately. He hated that he couldn't be certain Sophie was even alive. A lingering darkness in that man's eyes set him ill at ease. He was a killer. And he hated that Vincent was likely pulling the man's strings.

Matthew's silence must have given Cal his answer. Cal smacked the dash and the next second, he was cradling his hand.

"It's not over yet," Matthew said, "but it will be."

"How can you be so sure? What's going on? Is he the guy from India?"

"I don't think so. His voice is different."

"Maybe you're not remembering it clearly. Maybe the stress of being shot at has distorted your memory."

Cal's accusations fell mute when Matthew locked eyes with him. "We need to go see Robyn."

Cal slammed his back against his seat. Hard. "Sure, whatever. We just need to get my girl back."

"We'll get her back." Again, Matthew spoke with more assuredness than he had the right to convey. But if finding Paititi could save Sophie's life, failure wasn't an option.

MATTHEW AND CAL WERE IN Robyn's office, which was streamlined and clutter free. She had personalized the space with framed photographs taken on their past excursions, each one carefully selected so that landmarks were unidentifiable. It was to protect his cover if his father came to visit her, as he did periodically.

"So are we going after the City of Gold?" She was sitting at her desk, grinning. "We're going to do this. Right, Matthew? It would be the find of a lifetime." She let her gaze go back and forth between Matthew and Cal.

Neither man said anything.

"What's wrong? Come to think of it you're both dragging yourselves along like your grandma died." Robyn's eyes widened "She didn't, did she, Cal?"

"Not my grandmother, no." With a quick glance, Cal petitioned Matthew to share the news.

"Sophie's been kidnapped," Matthew said.

"Kidnapped? What are you talking about? Is this some sort of a prank?" Her smile deflated as she absorbed their message and observed their body language. "You're being serious."

Matthew nodded.

"Why? What happened? What do they want? Money?"

Matthew shook his head. "They want the Pandu."

She massaged her temples as if she had a headache setting in. "That's not even possible."

"That's what I told her kidnapper," Matthew said.

"You've been talking to the kidnapper? Have you called the police?"

Matthew shook his head.

"Let me guess. They said no police?"

"Yep." Matthew watched as the situation sank in for Robyn, and he was certain it mirrored his initial reaction. It was a hard concept to accept.

"Well…" Robyn flattened her hands on the desk, her fingers splaying repeatedly in, then out, in, then out. "What are we going to do? We can't get to the Pandu. Even I can't, and I'm the curator. And if we tried to steal it and got caught…" She took a choppy breath. "I'd lose my job, everything I worked so hard for."

"I know," Matthew said. "So I made another proposition. I had to."

"What did you offer up?" Robyn's hands stopped moving. Her eyes locked with his. "No, Matthew, you didn't."

"To get Sophie back, I had to."

Robyn stood and paced a few steps, a hand covering her mouth, then lowering to her chin. "So instead of just losing my career, all of us could be sacrificing our lives? And all we have are photographs and coordinates. We have an *idea* of where to go. What we don't know is if we'll actually find Paititi there. This is crazy." Matthew wasn't going to point out that a moment ago she was fired up to go in search of the city and now she had changed her mind. He consented that there was a lot at stake.

"Wait. You offered the City of Gold?" Cal's head snapped in Matthew's direction. "Indians, Matthew. Indians who beat people with clubs," Cal said, obviously recalling Daniel's example of the missing explorer who met that exact fate.

Robyn stopped pacing. "The easy part is the jungle. We've survived them before," she said, ignoring Cal.

Leave it to Robyn to spin things back to the positive.

"Easy for you to say," Cal muttered. "I'm still having nightmares from the last one, but—" he chewed on his bottom lip "—I guess if it's the only way to get Sophie back…"

Matthew turned to Cal. "You've always been a bit of a—"

"If you say chicken—"

"Guys, can we focus? What if they don't accept the offer? Or worse, what if we can't deliver on—"

Matthew's phone rang. He held it up, and like before, the caller ID was blocked. "Guess this is the moment of truth." He let it ring again. Answering too soon would seem too eager.

Cal bumped Matthew's elbow. "Get it."

Matthew accepted the call but didn't say anything.

"Well, Matthew, it seems our paths have crossed again. I wish I could express disappointment over that."

He recognized this voice immediately. When the kidnapper had called him out as Gideon, he'd suspected she was behind this. "I'd swear you're obsessed with me, Vincent."

"Oh, I do hate it when you call me by my last name. It's so masculine," she sulked.

Her full name was Veronica Vincent. They first met years ago, but that was a trip down memory lane he didn't care to take right now, or ever again for that matter. Matthew had to admit, though, that the woman had bigger cojones than most men, as well as the power and money to back her endless ambitions. She was as dangerous as a viper bite—fatal if left untreated, recoverable if treated soon enough. The latter was his experience.

He aligned his focus to the matter at hand. "I take it that you received my offer?"

"I did, and I can work with it."

"Work with it?"

"Yes, darling, but please don't repeat what I say. You sound like a parrot, and it's unattractive."

This woman possessed the ability to make him tingle, but this time it wasn't from pleasure. It was from adrenaline and rage. He could feel his friends' eyes on him, but he wasn't going to meet either one's gaze.

"What do you want, Vincent?"

"Isn't it more a matter of what you want? I understand we have your friend."

"To the point."

"I will accept your offer on two terms: one, you will take two of my people with you."

"No, that's not going to happen. I'm already offering you an invaluable find."

"You're asking me to trust—"

"Let Sophie go! She has nothing to do with this!" Cal called out, bending closer to Matthew's phone.

Matthew cupped it and shushed his friend. He accompanied his directive with a glare.

"Keep your guy quiet, Matthew."

Cal had received the message as evidenced by the bulging vein in his forehead, his hardened gaze, and his crossed arms.

"You said there were two conditions?"

"Yes, I almost forgot."

As Vincent laid out the other term, Matthew wondered what he'd gotten them into. Failure was a distinct possibility, and there was no way they could adhere to that short of a deadline, as well. He considered Sophie, then the risks. "You've got a deal."

"Most excellent."

"Now that I've agreed to your terms, I have some of my own."

"I love it when you take charge like this, Matthew. It's so sexy."

"Shut up, Vincent."

"Ooh, so nasty," she cooed.

"I'm taking *my* team," he said.

Robyn and Cal were in front of him. Robyn was waving her arms in the air, and both of them were jabbering away. He brushed them aside.

"You can take your team, and by that I assume you mean your two close friends. Hardly a team, Matthew, but whatever works for you."

It wasn't time to celebrate victory yet.

A few beats later, Vincent added, "*My* two friends will keep you honest and make sure that you report it if you find the City of Gold."

"You seem to be forgetting you have Sophie. That is motivation enough."

She smacked her lips. "Consider it an added incentive. Besides, I know you're arrogant enough to think you can have both the City of Gold and your friend. Don't cross me, Matthew. She'll pay the price for your betrayal."

There was a brief lull in the conversation, but Vincent broke the silence. "I will arrange transport. Tell me where you're headed and be at Pearson Airport at oh-six-hundred. And Matthew?

Don't be late. I do hate tardiness. Do we still have a deal?"

"No."

"No?"

"Now who is the parrot? You will have your goons meet us at the airport. You get the plane, but all you need to know to arrange transport is that we'll be landing at Viru Viru Airport in Bolivia." The last thing he needed was her people taking off with the coordinates, staking claim to Paititi themselves, and sealing Sophie's fate. "And another thing, you send video updates every day to confirm Sophie's alive." He gave her Daniel's phone number.

She sighed. "Yes, okay." Then she hung up without another word.

Matthew lowered his phone. Robyn had her neck angled to the left, her eyes bulging. Cal's gaze was fixed on Matthew.

"Did I hear you right? Vincent's behind this? You've got to be kidding me." She crossed her arms and spun so her back was to Matthew.

"Who's Vincent?" Cal asked.

Robyn turned back around. "Vincent is this—"

"Enough." Matthew stood. "We head out for Bolivia tomorrow morning at six." His stomach churned thinking about Vincent's unreasonable condition.

"Tomorrow?" Cal exclaimed.

Matthew continued. Maybe it was best to come out with the stipulation. "We have one week to find—"

"One week? Something like this takes months, if not years, to plan." Robyn was wringing her hands. "What about vaccinations? Permits? Travel arrangements?"

"If we want to save Sophie, we don't have a choice. Daniel has all the information we need." He didn't want to elaborate that the seven-day countdown began immediately.

"And you've had time to go over all of it?" Robyn asked.

He wasn't going to answer that one.

"That's a no," Cal said.

"I've read enough. Daniel has people there who can help us. He and I will get everything organized tonight. Just get yourselves ready."

Robyn looked at him, unblinking. "What else, Matthew?"

Sometimes she was too smart for her own good.

"We have to take two of her people with us," he admitted.

"God, not tagalongs." This was from Cal, who had taken over for Robyn and was pacing the room.

"Call them whatever you like," Matthew said coolly.

Cal stopped moving. "Why do I sense there's more to this Vincent person?"

"Because you'd be spot on, Cal." Robyn responded to Cal with her eyes on Matthew. "Vincent is Veronica Vincent."

"A woman is behind this?" Cal asked, clearly surprised. "What about the Liam look-alike?"

Robyn licked her lips, her eye contact with Matthew not faltering. "Just keep it in your pants, Matt, or we'll all pay the price this time."

"She didn't say anything about coming along with us."

"You better hope that she doesn't."

Anger tapped in his cheeks. The worst part was that Robyn was right. Veronica Vincent was to him what kryptonite was to Superman.

CHAPTER 14

SOPHIE WAS BOUND TO A CHAIR, her legs and arms secured by zip ties. If she broke free, Liam's clone had better run because he'd pay for this. She was certain she hated being restrained more than the average person did. Even commitment in relationships had been a challenge until she'd met Cal. And ironically, the person for whom she had made an exception was the reason she was here, captive and unable to move.

She squinted, trying to block out the setting sun that was streaming in through the wall of windows. This told her two things: one, twenty-four hours had already passed, and two, seeing the CN Tower told her she was in the entertainment district. It was a good thing because of the crowds, but a bad thing with her being so many stories up. Any cries for help would go unheard, but as it was, a gag in her mouth ensured her silence. She had tried jerking her head and contorting to no avail. She wasn't getting out of this chair or free of the gag on her own.

The place she was being held wasn't a hotel room. The large floor vases and sculptures looked too expensive. The paintings on the wall screamed of money, too. Based on location and the obvious wealth of the homeowner, she guessed she was in one of the newer high-rise condominium buildings. And from the angle at which she looked at the CN Tower, she'd guess it was one on Spadina Avenue near Front Street.

The last thing she remembered was being at her dream house and the man showing up. He must have drugged her, though, as a big chunk of her memory was blank. She recalled him coming to the door and holding a gun to her stomach. Next thing she'd known, she had woken up here, a throbbing pain in her head from sleeping with her neck craned to the side. And he had been filming her.

Afterward, he had made two phone calls. The first must have been to Cal, as he had used the words *your girlfriend*. On the second call, he had demanded to meet someone at a local bookstore. She guessed that *someone* was Matthew, and she surmised this all tied back to India as she'd originally thought when she first spotted the man following them.

The condo was silent now. She must be alone.

Hope was the one thing that kept her calm. Somebody was likely to notice she had been taken. The cookies and coffee would both be growing stale on the counter. The homeowners were away, but surely someone checked in on the place. And her purse. It was likely there, too.

Edwin probably wouldn't worry about her, as she'd sometimes go a day or two without speaking to him. But Cal had to know something was wrong even before her kidnapper had called him. He would have been expecting her to call last night. She cursed herself for changing their plans.

It was quite possible no one even knew she was missing yet. And if they did, from what she saw on TV, missing persons reports weren't taken too seriously and a certain amount of time had to pass before one could be filed. She hoped that fictional take wasn't a derivative of real life.

The man hadn't arrived at the mansion in a vehicle. She recalled that now. She had originally concluded she hadn't heard one because she was in the kitchen at the back of the house, but there hadn't been one to hear.

Did that mean the man took her here, to his place, in her car? A glimmer of hope filtered through her. If the police found her car, they'd be close to finding her. But that hope was short-lived. Toronto was a huge city with a considerable geographical footprint. The Liam guy would have had to be pretty stupid to park her car in his spot in the building's underground garage. And what would lead police to his building in the first place? The odds were getting slimmer the more she thought things through.

If, or when, they started looking, how were they going to find her at all? There was nothing at the house to point them here. All this would be enough to drive most people crazy, but she had a fighting spirit and she was just getting fired up. With every moment she was left to stew in this chair, limited in movement, with hard plastic biting into her wrists and ankles, she had a greater sympathy for wild animals in captivity. Like them, she was ineffective at resisting her captor.

Tears filled her eyes, but she refused to give in to the overwhelming sense of hopelessness.

She slowed her breathing and strained her ears as someone shuffled outside the room. A key was inserted into the door, and it opened.

"Help me!" In her mind, it came out as a scream. In reality, it was a garbled whisper behind the gag.

"I see you're still awake. How lovely." The man unwound a scarf from his neck and threw it onto a nearby couch.

Then another thought occurred to her. He must not be worried about company dropping by. He had her positioned in the middle of the living room.

"This whole thing is spiraling out of control." He paced the room and, after a few seconds, turned to her with a pointed finger. "This your fault."

Even her hardheaded nature wasn't going to contest his accusation with the fact that he was the one to blame. If he hadn't kidnapped her, there wouldn't be anything to "spiral out of control."

But for him to kidnap her, obviously hold her for ransom, and to contact Matthew, this had to involve some stupid treasure. At least she could find solace in knowing that if her freedom— and her life—depended on Matthew, Cal, and Robyn securing treasure for this man, they would deliver. She just hoped that she wasn't living on a prayer.

CHAPTER 15

IAN BRIDGES STUDIED THE WOMAN. She had deep-brown eyes, the kind one could get lost in. But his lack of discretion wasn't on her. This was all on him.

He hated the fact that Matthew had seen right through him and had known he wasn't in charge. Was it all because of his hesitancy to jump at the City of Gold? It had to be more than that… Something he had or hadn't said. He'd likely never know.

He pried his eyes from the woman. He should have walked away from this job at the beginning, but now he was in too deep. A hostage? He really hadn't thought things through before he'd acted. It was a slight miracle that he had even pulled off the ruse that she was a drunk girlfriend when he brought her up the building's elevator.

He resumed pacing the room, seeking solutions with each stride.

He was a professional. A gun for hire. What the hell was he doing abducting someone and holding them for ransom? Was he that desperate? A whimsical fancy had him running away overseas, but there would be no place on earth to hide if he did that. The people who hired him were scarier sons of bitches than he was. And they didn't tolerate failure.

He looked toward the entrance when there was a knock on the door. He hunched down in front of the woman and whispered, "Keep quiet or you and your boyfriend will both eat bullets."

A tear fell down her cheek. If she was seeking someone with a conscience, she was looking at the wrong guy.

He punched the wall behind her, barely missing her face.

Shit! He never should have gotten involved with this contract. Murder was easy. It was in, *pop*, out. Job complete.

But this mission was strange from the start, even beyond the lack of information on his employer. He should have just accepted his limitations. Securing a relic? That wasn't his world. What the hell did he even know about fine art? He chose the pieces in his home for their beauty, nothing more.

"Who is it?" he called through the closed door. He looked through the peephole. The nausea that had started to chew on his stomach receded. It was the redhead from last night. How had she found him? They had gone to a hotel. "It was just a one-nighter, baby."

She pounded on the door.

Crazy broad. Guess she just wants more of me.

"Now's not a good time," he said.

"You can open this door or I can. Your choice."

This chick was certifiably nuts. It was probably best not to broach the subject of how she had tracked him down.

"Come on, it was a fun evening, but let's leave it in our memor—"

The woman pulled back her white fur coat to reveal the pearl handle of a handgun. "I know you're watching me through the peephole. Now open up. Last warning."

Now she was threatening to shoot him through the door? The ice in her eyes told him she was fully capable of following through on her words. He recognized it in her eyes now, one killer to another. He must have been blind not to see it two nights ago.

"Opening up." He pulled his gun from his waistband, undid the chain on the door, and then unlocked the bolt.

She opened the door, came inside, and rushed past him. He'd dealt with his share of crazies, but this one took the cake. He held the gun on her. "Listen, baby, we had fun, but it's over. Okay?"

She gestured toward the door, not showing any concern about the barrel aimed on her. "Close it. Now."

Again, her voice was level and cool.

"Listen. Veronica, is it?"

"You're quickly losing your appeal." She drew her weapon to match his. "Close. The. Door."

He put his hands up. "All right."

"Now lock it."

Why was she here? What did she want from him?

"My name is Veronica Vincent," she began.

"Yes, I believe we've met."

She kept eye contact with him until it clicked into place. His employer's name was V. He pulled out on his shirt collar. "V?"

"Yes." A sly smile. "I see that you understand now. I can put this away?" She let her eyes trail over him, and he figured she was assessing any potential risk to herself.

His earlier thought that he worked for scary sons of bitches struck him then. In this case, it wasn't a son of a bitch, just a bitch, but he was certain she came with an army of "sons."

He nodded and holstered his gun.

"Good." She put hers away and took a few steps. "It seems that a simple job has become complicated."

Her words laid a trap. There was nothing to gain by opening his mouth. He waited it out for her to continue.

"You couldn't secure the statue. You failed."

Again, another attempt to get him to argue, to defend himself. He remained silent.

She smirked. "Your self-restraint is good, I'll give you that. You came highly recommended, but I must say I am disappointed. I had my heart set on the Pandu. I had a considerable investment in that endeavor." She snaked around him, brushing her fingertip over his clothes as she circled. She stopped and pressed her finger into his chest. "But you are brilliant."

If he spoke now, he risked stammering, but remaining quiet was no longer an option. She was waiting on him to speak.

"Brilliant," he reiterated.

"Yes, of course. Because of you, I will have the City of Gold."

A tingle ran down his spine. He didn't like the way she was

presenting this. *Because of you.*

"Well, I accepted their offer. And you"—she drew her hand from his chest up to his chin, her fingertips a whisper against his skin—"are going to help them find it."

"I'm going to what? No way. I'm not a treasure hunter." He removed her hand from his chest.

"You work for me," she said.

"Nope, no, not anymore. I'll give back the advance."

"I think you're forgetting some things, Ian Bridges."

He winced. She had said his name loud enough that his hostage would have heard her. The options were bloody but doable. Kill the girl, kill Veronica, and run.

"Now, I see it in your eyes. You are scheming. How adorable. But you don't have the resources to run from me. See, I have people on my payroll all over the world. I have killers even better than you. I mean, well, obviously."

"You never hired me to kill. You hired me to get a statue back." He almost spat out *stupid statue.* The tingles in his spine intensified, which was a telltale sign that bad news was imminent. If she had all these men working for her, why did she involve him in the first place?

She continued. "I do give you kudos on the whole kidnapping approach, by the way. Hostages are better motivators than dead victims. It was fresh thinking and, given the circumstances, not entirely stupid. And I am willing to dismiss the entire thing on one condition."

"And what's that?"

"You are going on a little excursion, Mr. Bridges."

The hairs on the back of his neck rose, signaling his rage at her saying his name again. "What about the girl?"

"She will be safe with me. Speaking of, where is she?"

Ian waved toward the living area and watched Veronica—V—saunter off. How the hell had he gotten himself into this mess? He should have listened to that little voice in his head that had told him not to accept the job proposal in the first place. On the upside, if the City of Gold did exist, maybe time machines did, as well, and he could go back and reverse all this.

CHAPTER 16

IT WAS ELEVEN O'CLOCK by the time Matthew returned home. There were only a few lights on inside the house, but the outside was lit up as if it were the White House. The amount his father had paid for the display cost well over the average yearly household income in Ontario. Just another show for William Connor.

Matthew knocked on Daniel's door. He had called Daniel hours earlier to have him start making the arrangements.

"There you are," Daniel said, ushering Matthew inside.

The man's quarters testified to his love of history and fondness for collectibles. With dull lighting, dark furniture, and built-in bookshelves, it held the noir feel of a private investigator's office. One almost expected a burning pipe to be resting in an ashtray, but Daniel was not a smoker. He had a pine desk in one corner that stood in contrast to the mahogany walls. It was the lightest accent in the room. Even the tapestries were a wild, dark pattern that matched the chair and ottoman in front of the fireplace.

"Do you have everything under control?" Matthew asked.

"As far as Bolivia is concerned, you are there for a holiday."

"Daniel, that's not going to work. When we find it—"

"It will all be fine. Even as a tourist, you'd get the credit. I'm not going to lie that there won't be a lot of red tape involved, but we can manage that afterward."

Matthew preferred to remain positive. They were going to find Paititi, rescue Sophie, and lay stake on the City of Gold.

"I must say I don't like the circumstances or the rushed nature of this expedition. Are you sure this is the only way to save the girl?" The look in Daniel's eyes right then was like a grandfather's, loving and soft. He put a hand on Matthew's shoulders and peered into his eyes.

Matthew bobbed his head and let out a deep sigh. "Yeah, it's the only way. They wanted the Pandu, but obviously that's not an option."

"And you're sure breaking into a museum wouldn't be easier?"

"Maybe it would be easier." Matthew shrugged. "I did give it consideration, but it's not what we do, Daniel." Matthew had no qualms about retrieving treasures from centuries ago, but stealing them and risking prison time wasn't in his life plan.

"I know." The man sighed. "And Sophie? Where is she going to be while you're in Bolivia?"

"I don't know." Matthew backed up and opened his hands. "I have no idea."

"We need to involve the police."

"We've discussed this already and you know it's not an option. We've specifically been told to keep this from them."

"Bah, of course you have, but that doesn't mean—"

"It does, Daniel."

They locked eyes for a moment before Daniel nodded.

"But it doesn't mean we do nothing," Matthew said.

Daniel looked at him quizzically. "I don't understand what you mean."

"I made some terms of my own."

One side of Daniel's mouth rose. Matthew loved to see that he had impressed the man.

"They will be sending proof of life videos at the end of each day."

"Videos? But how on earth are you supposed to be looking at those? You'll be in the jungle, fighting for your life—" He paused. "I'm sorry, sir."

"Don't worry about it." The sentiment was true. Matthew was worried enough for all of them. Robyn was right when she had said it took months, at the very least, to pull off an expedition of this size. He was hopping on plane based on a potential find and completely relying on a few images. He witnessed the question in Daniel's eyes. "You'll be getting the videos to your phone."

"And what am I supposed to do with the videos?"

"You're going to investigate them."

"Now you've lost me. I'm not a detective, sir."

"At some point they have to mess up, and it will provide a clue as to her location."

"At least you hope so. And let's say they do slip up and I manage to pinpoint where she is, then what am I supposed to do? You specifically said a moment ago, we're not supposed to involve the police."

"We're not."

"I don't understand."

"If we can figure out where Sophie is being held, we can free her ourselves when we get back."

"Oh, Matthew, are you sure that—"

"I am trusting you to take care of this, Daniel. Is my faith misplaced?" Matthew hated putting the man on the spot. After all, if it weren't for his hard work in researching Paititi, they wouldn't have had anything to barter with. Then where would they be? Where would Sophie be? "I'm sorry, but it's the only way."

"No, no, it's all right. I will figure it out."

Matthew clapped the man on the shoulder. "Just be careful. Hopefully everything will come together and we'll be able to secure both Paititi and Sophie." Matthew refused to entertain a different outcome.

"I've never seen you leave for an adventure so ill-prepared."

"I know and I hope it doesn't cost us dearly."

"Juan and Lewis—my contacts in Bolivia—will be waiting for you at the Viru Viru Airport. When you get there it will be night, so I suggest you start your trek at the crack of dawn. But tonight, they'll drive you sixty-five miles along a local highway. In the morning, they'll accompany you downriver for nine miles. From there, it will be a hike of ten miles through jungle and mountain terrain."

"Thank you for everything, Daniel."

The man dipped his head in recognition, and Matthew turned to leave but spun around halfway to the door.

"One more thing." Matthew pulled a card from his jacket pocket. "Please give this to my father."

"Why not give it to him your—" Daniel skimmed the card. "Ah, I see."

"You said the old man wanted acknowledgment from Gideon, that even a card would do." Matthew shrugged. "I had Cal write it out in case my father recognized my handwriting."

Daniel tapped it against the palm of his other hand. "When shall I give it to him?"

"Tomorrow evening should be good. Maybe tell him that Gideon dropped it off in person when my father wasn't home."

"Do you think that's wise?"

Matthew laughed. "Well, it's not far from the truth."

He headed out of Daniel's room, shut the door behind him, and leaned against it from the other side, considering if he should act on his thought to see his father. He'd only had that brief conversation with his father yesterday morning about going on a dig in Rome, and now he was turning around and leaving tomorrow morning. With William's recent curiosity about Gideon, he'd better update him. He doubted his father would worry, but he didn't need any more going on than there already was.

Matthew made his way to William's den. Hopefully the old man was still up. He rapped on the door, but despite the light, no one was in there. That left one other place. His father was boringly predictable. He had a ritual before bed that involved laps in the pool, followed by reading in his den.

He took the stairs to the basement in the east wing of the house. His father had installed the saltwater lap pool not long after they had moved in. His father swore that the salt water was just as healing and therapeutic as the exercise. Matthew had yet to take so much as a dip in it.

William's arms cut through the water, and Matthew took

position at the end where his father was headed.

William reached the edge, stopped, and looked up. He must have sensed he had a visitor.

"Are you finally going to take a swim?" William regarded Matthew's wardrobe. "Where is your suit?"

"Dad, I'm not here to—"

"Excuse me, but did you just call me *Dad*? Wow, did the market crash? Have we lost everything?"

Matthew noticed how his father's concerns went straight to material things, as always. "I'm going to be heading off earlier than I had expected."

"Are you going to Rome?" William asked.

"Ah, yeah. Rome."

"The discovery of a road system or some such thing?"

Matthew hadn't provided him the details about Rome. What was going on? First, his questions about Gideon and now he was researching archeological digs? "Yes."

"And when will you be back?" William swiped his hands down his face to drain the water.

"About a week."

"A week? That's a short stint."

"That's why I have to go now."

"All right, I see. Well, we'll talk when you get back, then." William pushed off the side of the pool, and his strokes chewed up the water.

"Yeah, we'll talk later," he muttered to himself. "If I survive…"

CHAPTER 17

MATTHEW CRAWLED INTO BED, and after a few hours, he wasn't sure why he had bothered. Sleep wasn't going to happen with so much on his mind—the city of Paititi, concern over Sophie, and his father's sudden interest in Gideon.

Maybe the research he did before trying to sleep was partially to blame. He had explored some of the perils that existed in Bolivia—wild animals, poisonous snakes and insects, rough terrain, and unpredictable weather—and his mind kept coming back to the jaguars. One translation of Paititi was "the city of the jaguar." It was unlikely they'd spot one, though, due to the shy nature of the animal. The big cats hunted at night and rarely revealed themselves to humans. He remembered a documentary that showed one man trying to spot one for thirty days before it had actually happened.

He also studied the photographs taken by Daniel's contacts, Juan and Lewis. There seemed to be about two miles from the point where the tunnel-shaped anomaly showed to the large rectangular area.

Shaking his head, he did his best to dismiss his own terminology. *Anomaly*. That's possibly all it was, yet they were wagering everything on it being *something*.

He gave up on the illusion that sleep was going to happen and pulled himself from bed at four thirty. The plane was set to leave at six, and he was actually thankful the flight was a long one. Hopefully he'd be able to catch some shut-eye.

Once they touched down in Bolivia, they'd spend the night

in a hotel near to where they'd set off down the river. At first light, the real trek would begin. Not only did they have to find a centuries-old hidden city but they had only a week to complete the mission. Actually even less. Six days now, and with one day eaten up by travel, that would go down to five.

Stepping outside into the brisk early-morning air, Matthew watched his breath leave him in wispy clouds.

He unlocked his Jeep Patriot and threw his hiking bag into the back. It held only the essentials, including water, food, clothing, a sleeping bag, a first aid kit, some flares, and a tent. There was also a switchblade and a machete for clearing terrain. What the typical hiker didn't carry was a Smith & Wesson. He and his friends all had their own. Treasure hunting wasn't a safe business by any means, and it didn't hurt to be prepared. With Vincent's men accompanying them, there was even more reason to be armed.

With one final look at the house, he shifted his vehicle into gear and pulled out of the driveway.

"We'll talk when I get back, Dad. I promise."

Even though his words fell on an empty vehicle, with no way for William to hear them, saying them aloud bolstered Matthew's confidence. After all, if he had made a promise, he couldn't break it.

THE THREE OF THEM WERE walking toward the private lounge areas of Toronto Pearson International Airport. VIPs who came through there wore everything from business suits to casual wear. Being loaded down with hiking backpacks wasn't a common sight, though, and it garnered some attention. Still, the place required decorum, and out of respect for their privacy, nothing was said to them and people were quick to look away.

"I just can't believe we're doing this." Robyn's eyes were bloodshot and testified to little sleep.

Cal didn't appear rested, either. "Do you really trust this woman's guys to take us where we need to go? What's to say they don't crash the plane to kill us?" Cal said.

"They want the City of Gold," Matthew answered.

"But in *Indiana Jones and the Temple of*—"

"You're pulling in the movies? At a time like this?" Robyn raised her takeout coffee cup to her lips. She lowered it after taking a sip. "This is nothing like the movies. I don't understand how you can even bring it up right—" She stopped talking, and Matthew hoped she received his silent communication. Cal was going through a lot more than the two of them, so they should give him some room to breathe. "I guess if you want to talk about the movies we can." Robyn pressed the cup back to her lips.

Cal glared at her. "In *Temple of Doom*, the pilots parachuted out, leaving Indiana Jones, Short Round, and Willie to die in a crash."

"I'm sure we'll be fine," Robyn asserted.

"We'll be fine? We have a week to find this City of Gold. And while we're in Bolivia, Sophie's being held by a killer."

Six days but who was counting? Matthew wasn't going to point that out. He'd worry about the schedule, and he certainly didn't need Cal's summation. He was well aware of the situation and offered the only reassurance he could. "If they want Paititi, Sophie will go unharmed." He held Cal's gaze until his friend nodded. Matthew continued. "We have to stick together and keep alert. Do you understand?"

Robyn saluted and winked at Matthew.

"And you?" Matthew turned to Cal.

"I understand. It's just—" Cal ran a hand over his bald head. "I just keep thinking about her, ya know? Like if she's okay, if we're going to get her back…"

Matthew put both his hands on Cal's shoulders. "We've got this. Piece of cake."

"Hmm…piece of something. But it ain't cake," Cal replied.

"Cal, he's trying to help you here, but he's right." Robyn tossed her coffee cup into a waste receptacle. "We can do this. We can do anything we put our minds to."

Matthew jacked his thumb toward Robyn. "She knows what she's talking about."

"She's agreeing with you, so of course, you're going to say that. But do you notice how she drinks her caffeine and transforms into a sweet little thing?"

Robyn hissed at their friend playfully and clawed at the air.

Cal laughed and Matthew smiled. They had this.

If he thought it enough times, he might actually convince himself that it was true.

Matthew spotted Vincent's plane—he'd been on it before—through the window; the morning sun gleamed off its silver fuselage. Bringing his focus back inside the lounge, he noticed a tall man who was in good physical shape standing by the door to the tarmac. His hair was spiky, and he had an extended goatee. His eyebrows were thin and his eyes deeply set. Beside him was the Liam Neeson look-alike.

"You've got to be kidding me. I'm going to kill him myself." Cal charged, but Matthew reined him in, holding one arm while Robyn took the other.

"If he's here, where is Sophie?"

"Good question," Robyn said.

Matthew and Robyn caught each other's eyes. They let go of Cal, and Matthew was pleased that Cal somehow managed to stay put.

Liam Neeson seemed more miserable than the day before. Apparently no one had slept. Matthew suspected this part of the arrangement wasn't included in his original deal with Vincent.

"Where's Sophie, you son of a bitch?" Cal spat out the question.

Liam held up his hand. "She's being taken care of."

"Taken care of? What does that mean, exactly?"

Instinctively, both Matthew and Robyn clutched Cal's arms.

"You get us to this City of Gold, and we'll all be happy." Liam turned to walk toward the plane.

"Do you think I give a shit about your happiness? You're a killer!" Cal broke free of his friends' grips and tore after Liam.

The man stopped moving and twisted at the hip. He drove his fist into Cal's nose with starling force and accuracy.

"Holy sh—" Cal cradled his nose. Robyn handed him a wad of

tissues and rubbed his back.

Adrenaline raced through Matthew. It took all his focus not to reciprocate with a well-aimed blow himself. And, there was a millisecond there when he actually thought he'd fought the urge. But then his fist caught Liam in the jaw.

Liam's eyes widened, and Matthew anticipated retaliation. Instead, Liam left through the spinning doors, mumbling, "This so isn't worth this shit."

The other man remained silent.

"Guess we're stuck working together on this," Matthew said to him.

"Guess so. Name's Kevin."

There was that voice—the one he had heard in the jungles of India, directing the herd of men to pursue them with gunfire. A quick glance at his friends told Matthew they recognized it, as well.

"Are you sure we haven't met already?" Matthew asked.

"Not officially anyhow."

This was the guy. Matthew was certain. He made the introductions, and Kevin nodded. "And who's the other guy?" Matthew asked.

"Ian."

"Well, it's best that he keep his face outta mine." Cal spoke from behind his hands. The tissues were soaked with blood.

Kevin nodded again—apparently, he was a man of few words—and then led the way out to the plane.

Matthew gave another glance over his team. It definitely wasn't the ideal start to their quest for Paititi. Robyn consoling Cal, Cal hurting over Sophie and sporting a bloody nose. At least it wasn't broken.

Matthew looked at his own knuckles. They were raw and tender from meeting Ian's jawbone. This was shaping up to be just *great*.

CHAPTER 18

THE LIAM NEESON LOOK-ALIKE HAD LEFT, and Sophie didn't think he was coming back. But now she had his real name—Ian Bridges. A woman remained behind at the condo and her name was Veronica Vincent. She had cut the zip ties from Sophie's wrists and ankles. For that, Sophie was thankful. Red marks and bruising had already begun, but she figured they were the least of her worries.

The woman had also moved Sophie to a bedroom. It obviously belonged to Ian, as numerous frames on the bed's bookcase headboard displayed photographs of him. Expensive-looking sculptures accented the space, and windows encompassed a full wall. The bed was a king, and the bedding was smooth to Sophie's touch. She'd guess Egyptian cotton, at least 1,500 thread count.

She may not be tied to a chair anymore, but she was in a makeshift prison cell. A man guarded her door, gifted with the face of a baboon—and that was being mean to the primate—and wearing a holstered gun. She'd wager he knew how to draw it in a hurry given the right provocation.

She had withdrawn into the room and had lain down on the bed, trying not to give any more thought to the fact that Ian slept there. Exhausted, her body had shut down for a while.

Her eyes didn't open again until it was a little after five.

This was her second morning in captivity. She recalculated her options, as she had been doing since she came to yesterday. Even the windows offered no opportunity to plead for help. She was at least thirty stories aboveground. There weren't any buildings across from where she was and below were train tracks. Farther out, sidewalks. Even if she flailed her arms in the window, it was unlikely anyone would see her, let alone pay her any attention. So despite the fact she was on display, she might as well be invisible. Her mind shifted from her desperate situation to the woman.

She was a beautiful woman—Matthew's one weakness. It wasn't a stretch to place Matthew and this Veronica chick together at one point, and possibly on more than one occasion. Thinking about their paths intersecting made sense, even now, because Matthew had somehow managed to make a deal with the devil.

The City of Gold in exchange for her release?

Veronica had looked stoically on Sophie when she had delivered the message. It was ludicrous to think that her friends even stood a chance. There was no way the place existed. It was a poor man's dream fueled by a greedy man's hunger.

Veronica had told her they'd have time to become acquainted. She also added that if her terms weren't met within a deadline of six more days, Sophie was dead. Veronica had laughed at that prospect. This woman was physically beautiful, but she was a scary bitch.

Being a real estate agent made Sophie good at reading people. Veronica was wealthy, as evidenced by her wardrobe, her jewelry, and the way she carried herself. But more importantly, she had influence. She utilized her looks to get whatever she wanted and she had that skill crafted into an art form. She also had a way about her that lured people in. Sophie wouldn't exactly label it as charm. Charisma, maybe? A fine line divided the two, but the latter inspired devotion. Veronica likely valued and greatly rewarded loyalty.

Sophie turned the door handle and found the baboon on the other side. "I need to use the washroom."

Vincent's man stepped to the side and dipped his head.

She walked past him down the hall, checking behind her diligently at short intervals. She latched the door and rummaged through the cabinets and drawers, wishing she were in a woman's home. If she found a tube of lipstick, maybe she'd be able to take advantage of that large window after all. Still it was a reach that anyone would see the writing.

Her endeavors were not rewarded. Braced on the counter, she looked at her reflection in the mirror. She peered into her eyes. She didn't really know who was in more danger of losing their life—her or her friends.

CHAPTER 19

VINCENT'S PLANE WAS BUILT FOR luxury and didn't exactly mirror the purpose for the trip. It was a means to get them to Bolivia. Nothing more.

Matthew, Robyn, and Cal sat at a table while Kevin slept in a seat next to a window and Ian watched TV with earbuds. Matthew spread out a map on which he'd drawn out their approach to the supposed city of Paititi and noted the distances. He flattened it out, and Robyn and Cal each held a corner down. He ran through it for them, as Daniel had for him.

"I keep thinking of that guy who was beaten to death with a club," Cal said. "My damn nose hurts enough."

"Don't worry, Cal. If you're dead, you won't feel anything." Robyn smirked.

"Didn't you dump her ass in college? What is she still do—"

Robyn shoved him in the shoulder.

"Hey!"

"Well you deserved it. And for your information, it was mutual."

"Come on, guys. I know this situation is shit, but it's where we are and Sophie's life depends on us succeeding." Matthew, constantly the mediator.

Cal became sullen, but he nodded. "Let's look at those pictures again."

"Yeah, of course." Matthew pulled out the aerial photographs that Daniel's contacts had taken.

Cal leaned across the table and spoke quietly. "These might be nothing more than a cave."

Robyn put her hand on Cal's forearm. "We have to keep positive."

Matthew traced his fingertip from the tunnel to the large rectangular space. "It seems it's just over two miles from where the passageway starts to Paititi."

"They don't even look connected. Let's hope there is a direct pathway that the technology didn't pick up," Robyn said.

"I hate to always be the negative one in the group, but what if there's no entrance to this void? What if it's not even a tunnel?" Cal asked.

Matthew looked between his friends. "Then we'll need to walk through more jungle and climb a mountain and find another way in."

Cal sank back in his chair, his hand still holding his corner of the unraveled map so it wouldn't curl. "Huh. But as your male maid kindly pointed out, we're not mountain climbers."

"You know, this might be why he hates you," Robyn chimed in.

Cal pressed his lips. "And this spot between the mountain peaks, we're pretty confident it's Paititi?"

Matthew shook his head. "We won't know anything for sure until we get there."

"But I mean, obviously someone feels positive about this being the location or we wouldn't have bartered with Sophie's life." Cal's eyes moved from Matthew to Robyn and back to Matthew. "Right?"

"This is our best bet, Cal," Matthew said. "I know that's not what you want to hear, but it's the best I can offer. And since none of us got much sleep last night, I suggest we rest up for the remainder of the flight. We won't be getting in until about eight tonight, and it will take some time to drive down the highway and get set up in a motel. We'll head out for the jungle tomorrow at first light. If you need to sleep, get it now."

IAN FEIGNED INTEREST IN THE stupid television program, but he was really listening in to what Matthew was saying. The thirteen years between them age-wise was enough to make him view Matthew as a child when it came to world experience, but he had a feeling the kid knew what he was talking about when it came to this Paititi.

Not a second had passed that Ian hadn't cursed his unconventional means of attempting to secure the Indian idol. He certainly never imagined the kidnapping ending with him headed to the jungle.

Eavesdropping on the three friends discussing the trek made failing Vincent an appealing option. A bullet to the brain, even if preceded by torture, might be better than running into God knows what in the wild terrain of Bolivia.

He glanced over and caught Matthew's eye.

A dull ache had taken up residence in Ian's jaw since the man had punched him. Just looking at Matthew conjured feelings of rage. But he'd have to swallow the emotion if he was going to survive this. Based on the way his friends listened to him, and by the way he carried himself, Matthew had things under control, even though the underlying connotation to his words revealed doubt.

Ian had figured this mission was put together in more haste than other excursions Matthew's team had taken. Recognizing this fact only settled uneasiness and fear into the pit of his stomach. It was a feeling he wasn't used to experiencing, and he didn't like it.

He hated the concept of being immersed in nature. He never liked camping as a kid, and as an adult, he never found a reason to subject himself to a wilderness experience. It was for other people. It didn't suit him with his expensive taste and love for the finer things. He'd rather stay at a ritzy hotel than rough it in some tent.

"Hey."

Great, Matthew had made eye contact with him again.

"What?" Ian pulled out the earbuds.

"Since we're stuck with one another, you guys should know what you're in for, too."

Ian didn't miss the look the woman gave him. It was obvious she didn't much care whether he or Kevin survived the ordeal or not. Buried beneath a professional job and her prestigious friends, Ian had no doubt that she possessed the ability to kill. The same really went for all three of them, and he'd keep a close eye on them. He was armed, but he suspected they were, as well. There's no way they would enter the jungle without weapons. Unless he was giving them more credit than they deserved.

"Just talk to us from where we're sitting," Kevin said, rubbing at his eyes like a damn baby waking up from sleeping. Being paired with this man was another penance for deviating off course. Never again.

"Just tell us what we're in for," Ian said.

"All right, well, you want the Sunday school version? Here it is: Jaguars, alligators, piranhas, pumas, and that's just a bit about the wildlife. Then you have jellyfish-infested rivers and mosquitoes that can infect you with malaria. You have waterfalls and lagoons. You have steep climbs and then…well, then you have the weather. It can be sunny one moment and you can be freezing from a torrential downpour the next."

"So basically, we're headed to hell." Despite the severity of Kevin's summation, his tone gave no indication he feared what lay ahead. Ian got the feeling Kevin had done this type of thing before.

"And you're certain we're going to find this City of Gold?" Ian asked, testing him. He had heard Cal's earlier question to Matthew despite his efforts to keep his voice low.

"There are no certainties with this, just as there aren't with anything else in life," the woman said dryly.

This was just great. They were headed for godforsaken terrain and he had some bitch preaching about life's uncertainties. He was the living embodiment of that truth. He just hoped to walk away from it.

CHAPTER 20

THE PLANE BUCKED IN THE air currents as the pilot brought it in for a landing. Robyn sat there, unable to pry her eyes from Vincent's men. How dare Matthew get that woman involved with such an important mission? Finding Paititi held the power to transform myth into reality. It had the ability to reshape people's thinking on the Incas of Peru. And what made for even greater impact, as Daniel had mentioned, was that people would start to believe again. Believe in life, in purpose, that anything they put their mind to was possible.

Robyn had faith that Paititi did exist. Yet so many people had gone in search of it. So many had sacrificed their lives, both in research and actuality. To think that she and her two closest friends were going to make the find moved her on a spiritual level.

With all the reasons to succumb to doubt and fear, she opted to remain positive. No one else had investigated this particular area for the City of Gold before. Others had concentrated their searches on northeastern Peru, close to Cusco. She initially understood their reasoning, but after scrutinizing the different versions of the legends, she saw the potential in where they were now going.

She gave credence to the Incas traveling by means of underground tunnels. It made sense given their mountainous landscape, and they more than possessed the intelligence and expertise to structure such an undertaking.

While the boys slept, she read a letter written by a Catholic missionary that dated back to the early seventh century. He spoke of being taken to Paititi and described it as "a ten-day march far away from Peru." Yet, despite him having provided the location of the city, it lay in obscurity, shrouded behind myth and legend. Allegedly, the Society of Jesus never revealed the location to avoid a gold rush.

Add to that the many accounts that contradicted one another, leading explorers in opposite directions of the Inca Empire. One account even mentioned that Paititi was in the grasslands. This version didn't resonate with Robyn.

When she consulted the photographs that Daniel's contacts had taken, though, she saw it. The child inside of her, the one who believed in Paititi's existence, had sparked to life and sizzled with expectation. There was definitely something under the ground.

The plane touched the runway then, and she took a deep breath.

This is it.

Matthew and Cal stirred awake almost in sync.

"We're here," she said, nudging them. She attempted a smile, but the nerves fluttering through her system made it difficult to complete the expression.

"No turning back now." Matthew's words mirrored her thinking.

"Are you ready, Cal?" Robyn asked.

Cal stretched, and his six-foot-five frame made it possible for him to touch the cabin's ceiling without much effort. "Yeah, let's do this thing."

They unloaded, and Robyn wished there were some way to ditch Vincent's men. She didn't want to accept that she, Cal, and Matthew had ended up caught in that awful woman's web. A draw remained between Vincent and Matthew, despite his protestations otherwise. Every time Matthew came into direct contact with her, metaphorical brimstone rained down from the sky destroying life as they knew it.

Cal slipped his camera strap over his head, securing his

gear. One thing Robyn had learned by being friends with a photographer was that every event belonged on film, or digital file as it was these days.

As they entered the airport, she spotted two Bolivian men holding signs with Matthew's name scrawled on them. Both men were short in stature and had wide, round faces. Their eyes were dark and deep.

They smiled at the three of them as they approached but then scowled at Ian and Kevin. Robyn knew how they felt. Daniel must have explained the situation when he'd arranged the escort from the airport.

Robyn held out her hand to the man closest to her. "Robyn Garcia."

"Ah, *bonita*." He took her hand and kissed the back of it before flashing a toothy grin. "My name is Juan Sanchez."

Robyn smiled at him. He wasn't handsome in a typical sense, but he had a softness about his nature.

"This is Lewis Blanco." Juan gestured to his companion. Matthew, Cal, and the two Bolivian men shook hands.

"I see you have baggage." Lewis jerked his head toward Ian and Kevin, who had hung back.

Vincent's men weren't talking to each other, and they were facing opposite directions, their energies mirrored. Kevin's shoulders were relaxed, and his arms hung at his sides. His one thumb was latched on a belt loop. Ian's jaw was tight, and he tapped his thigh.

"Do you mind if I take your picture?" Cal asked Juan and Lewis while motioning for them to get closer to each other.

"Why not take everyone?" Juan suggested.

"Good idea." Robyn headed for Matthew, but Juan reached for her arm and pulled her toward him.

"You will stand by me if that's all right."

Another toothy grin.

Robyn laughed.

Matthew stood on the other side of Juan, Lewis was to Robyn's left, and Cal lifted the camera to take the shot.

"No! No! Get one of them to take it." Juan brushed his hand toward Vincent's men.

Kevin was staring straight at them now but made no movement. Ian rolled his eyes and trudged over.

"This isn't an effin' holiday. Give me the damn camera." Ian snatched it from Cal's hands.

"You break that, you son of a bitch, you bought it." Cal sidled up next to Lewis and threw his arm around the man. "Okay, take—"

"Done," Ian said.

Cal rolled his eyes. "Again. This time wait for us to smile."

"For shit's sake."

Seconds passed.

"Take the shot. Anytime now," Cal directed.

"Say cheese." Sarcasm dripped from Ian's words. The camera shutter clicked.

Cal snatched his camera back from Ian.

Robyn understood Cal's hatred for the man. If a touch of humanity didn't exist within her, she'd be tempted to lose him, and Kevin, out in the jungle somewhere.

CHAPTER 21

THE BOLIVIANS TOOK THEM TO a motel along the highway. Cal was sitting under a covered picnic area and staring at the heavy downpour. His mind was thousands of miles away, back in Canada.

If it wasn't for him craving excitement and chasing the resultant high like a drug addict, Sophie wouldn't be in this position. How could he ever forgive himself if she was hurt? Even if her captors never laid a hand on her, she detested confinement. She was surely having waking nightmares without him there to soothe her. He hated that he was responsible.

He gulped some pop, wishing for something stronger. But the real trek would begin at the crack of dawn, and he needed to be in top form.

What Matthew and Robyn didn't know was he had also researched the area and legends on Paititi. He had even scoured the vicinity on Google Earth. One point was tagged as INTO THE UNKNOWN. That wasn't reassuring.

He looked at the shared photographs, some of which showed waterfalls and lagoons near where they were headed. Both elements were included in Paititi legend. But that could describe many places in Peru, Brazil, and Bolivia.

But Matthew was right: this was their best bet for bringing Sophie back alive. It was their *only* bet.

"Mind if I join you?" Matthew was jogging toward him, holding a jacket over his head, which did little to shelter him from the torrential rain. He shook the jacket once he was under the overhang and didn't say a word as he sat next to Cal.

Both friends sat in silence for a long while with only the sound of the beating rain and the lush smell of greenery as a backdrop.

"You're thinking about Sophie, aren't you?" Matthew asked.

"It's my fault she's in this position. Hell, it's why *we're* in this position." Cal squeezed his empty pop can. "If I had just believed her sooner. Maybe we could have gotten the police involved. All this could have been prevented."

"If you want to fault anyone for this, blame me. I'm the one who offered up Paititi."

"We're not thieves, Matt, and I'm not going to prison trying to steal that statue." His words struck his own ears and hurt his heart. He wasn't willing to sacrifice his freedom for his girlfriend. What kind of scum was he?

"You're risking even more than prison, Cal. You are putting your life on the line. She's lucky to have you."

Cal spun to face Matthew. "Lucky to have me? You're kidding, right? If it weren't for all this treasure hunting shit, we'd all be back home doing whatever. It would certainly be a better time than this. I guarantee you that."

Matthew waited for a few seconds before he spoke. "Listen, maybe none of this is any of our faults. Maybe it doesn't even matter who's to blame. We're in this predicament because… Well, we just are. We do what we've come to do. Then we go home and get Sophie."

"I still don't like it."

"You don't have to, but let's get it over with."

"Yeah."

"You okay? We should hit the sack. Tomorrow starts early."

Cal nodded and crushed the pop can in his hand even more. He'd have to come to terms with all this somehow. Right now, he needed to see it through and be strong—for his own sake and, more importantly, for Sophie's.

CHAPTER 22

VERONICA VINCENT WAS USED TO getting her way with very little effort on her part. She had employees at her disposal—men who considered it an honor to be at her service. The fact that she paid handsomely may have had some bearing on their attitudes, but she preferred to believe her interest in them was flattering for them.

Before she came into their lives, they were men without a charted course in life. She provided them purpose. In return, she expected—no, demanded—that she be treated like royalty. Whatever she desired was to be delivered with no questions asked. But then there were times in life, like now, where things seemed to enter a twilight zone of sorts, where everything upended.

And she had one person to blame for this—Ian Bridges. She should have known better than to go out of house for this job. Initially, it had seemed like a good thing to do. Matthew wouldn't identify him as one of hers, but somehow he still managed to call the man out. If only Ian had taken care of things himself.

Now she was imprisoned in Ian's condo. She was used to her mansion in Manhattan with its spacious floor plan, its vaulted ceilings, and wainscoting, not to mention her grand kitchen. Ian's scullery, however, was in the space as if it had been an afterthought. While the appliances and counters were top-of-the-line, the size of the room limited her enjoyment. Cooking normally calmed her agitated nerves, but doing so here would likely have the opposite effect.

At least he had a collection of wine and impressive taste. She helped herself to a Ridge Monte Bello red and poured a glass. Swirling it, she appreciated the way the wine coated the glass, and then she took a small sip. It had a robust flavor and woodsy undertones, with hints of plum and peppercorn. Exquisite.

She dropped onto the plush, black leather couch and took in the cityscape. It wasn't as vast as it was at home, but nowhere compared to New York.

The CN Tower was lit with various colors, traffic on the streets a blur of red and white. Still, as she let her gaze fall over the city, her mind wasn't on the people below, on the fancies of what they were doing or where they were heading. Her mind was on Ian Bridges.

His previous employer, a man whom Veronica respected for his own tenacity, had praised him, but Ian had failed her thus far, or at the very least complicated the situation. While he was unsuccessful in obtaining what she had originally contracted him for, it was because of him that she was on the cusp of staking claim to something much more valuable.

A smile smeared across her lips before she took another drink of her wine.

Maybe all wasn't lost. While she'd had a buyer lined up for the Indian statue, his disappointment eased with some expert negotiating on her part regarding the offer of Incan treasure. She had trumped up the sale with the assertion that her team was on the verge of the greatest discovery of humankind. It may be an exaggerated point of view, but she favored optimism. And for good reason. Her entire life had been about getting what she desired, and Ian wouldn't be the one to teach her the brutal lesson of want.

Without disclosing specifics of the find, she had promised her buyer a pick of artifacts and said she'd extend him a deal. A price was bartered and haggled upon, its value inflated, the price reduced, and everyone walked away pleased. Everyone, that is, except for Ian Bridges. She had Kevin Porter in place to take care of things. He was a cocky son of a bitch, but he was reliable.

She had received his call earlier confirming they had touched down and that so far things were "going." When she had asked how specifically, he had disclosed Ian's failure to keep his temper in check and how he had hit one of Matthew's friends. Rage had fired through her upon hearing the report. Now that she'd had time to absorb the situation, it might not be that horrible.

She had sent him—a city man to the jungle. That in itself was a death sentence. And if nature didn't kill him, Kevin had his directive. After all, it was a lot easier to dispose of a body in the wilderness than in civilization.

Veronica snapped her fingers, and Don, who was guarding the girl's door, came to her. "I want you to send out for a gourmet meal. Surely, there's a healthy restaurant that delivers. Make sure you get enough for the girl, too."

"You got it, boss."

She didn't let her pleasure show but inside her heart pulsated. Being obeyed never grew old. "But before you do that, take a video of the girl."

Don remained standing there.

"Now." She dismissed him with a wave of her hand and a shake of her head.

SOPHIE WAS HUNGRY, AND HER mouth was dry. Seconds were morphing into minutes, minutes into hours, hours into days. Two full days had already passed, and in that time, her hope was already slipping.

A shiver of fear lanced through her. In this place of captivity, her rights were violated and stripped from her. She didn't have freedom to eat or drink as her body dictated or to come and go as she pleased.

Her strong nature forced her from the bed. She'd demand an audience with the woman and get more answers. She deserved that much, didn't she? She was almost to the door when it opened.

It was the baboon.

His size dwarfed her. His pumped biceps probably measured

the same circumference as her thigh.

She backed up, only to realize that she was drawing him toward the bed.

He followed her strides, matching the distance she moved until she had nowhere else to go. She fell back onto the mattress when it pressed against the back of her legs.

Was the woman still here? She'd somehow feel safer if she were.

All the things she had learned about self-defense raced through her mind. But the lessons were buried so deep in her past that she'd have to trust her instincts, her will to survive, and her resolve not to be defiled.

Her thoughts traced to Cal. God help this man if he even tried to do anything to her. If she lived through all this and Cal ever found out, this man, despite his giant structure, would die.

She closed her eyes, and warm tears slid down her cheeks.

The man loomed over her, his shadow casting a darkness she could sense. Her eyes popped open, and she saw he held the gag that she'd been forced to wear before.

She struggled against him, trying free herself from his grasp, but he was too powerful. All she wanted to do was yell, but the woman had made the consequence of her doing so very clear. She would be shot, and her friends would die. Any helpful Samaritans would also be killed.

The man's hands encircled her wrists as if they were small twigs, and he tugged on her, pulling her up the bed.

She kicked her legs and bucked against him to no avail. He secured her by one wrist to the bedframe and took out a smartphone.

Tears poured down her cheeks now, and a bawl hurled from her throat. He laid his hand over her mouth, adding another sound barrier to the gag he had put in place.

She calmed, and their eyes locked.

"I'm going to record you."

Her eyes widened more, and it was then that he seemed to recognize her primal fear. "No, no, I'm not going to—" He wiggled his fingers, indicating her body.

He held up the phone, and she continued to fight against him, twisting her body like a worm, drawing up her legs and bucking outward. Her heels found purchase in a sweet spot, and he howled.

She drew deep breaths in through her nose, her exhales meeting the cloth in her mouth and flooding her face with hot air.

As he was keeled over, cradling his manhood, Veronica rushed into the room. It was almost as if she glided in, her movements were so crisp and quick.

Veronica gave the man a look over. "You stupid shit." She snatched the phone from the man's hands and held it aimed on Sophie. "Say hello."

Sophie blinked slowly, her lashes brushing the skin beneath her eyes. When she opened them again, her gag had been removed, but the camera was in her face.

"Speak or you and your friends are dead."

To support the woman's words, the man had gathered himself enough to draw his gun. He pressed its muzzle against Sophie's forehead. "She said to say hello."

More tears fell, and as Sophie struggled to give life to the words, she fell apart. Her body shook and she cried deep, heaving, painful sobs.

CHAPTER 23

THE ENTIRE DAY HAD BEEN a montage of faces, some important, others easily fading into the background. But they all equated to one thing for William Connor: they were his meal tickets. Without the public, he'd be of no importance. Life as he knew it would implode. In fact, he'd rather not draw breath if he wasn't making a difference or at the center of attention. Really, that's where he thrived. And most people respected him for his achievements.

Pleasantries were always spoken, generosities extended. It was the life he'd been born to live, and despite it all, one man didn't have the decency to yield to him: Gideon Barnes.

With back-to-back meetings, William had no time to follow up with Daniel on his progress in securing a private investigator to track the mysterious explorer. His day was occupied with other matters. Political grandstanding took up a great deal of his energy, and Hartman had brought up Gideon's no-show again. Everything from that point had turned to shit, and it was beyond fixing at this point. He had tried.

He had attempted to find solace in the sanctuary of his home office last night. But after Matthew had come to him with his last-minute expedition, it was impossible. The boy had no set schedule at all.

William wasn't blind to the fact that his son preferred to live his life that way. Flying by the seat of his pants, as the saying goes. He didn't have any responsibilities pinning him down. If Matthew had only married Robyn years ago, William would have grandchildren by now and Matthew would have stability. But, again, that's not what his son wanted.

A trace thought of envy over his son's freedom appeared and was dismissed just as quickly. William required grounding to remain focused. The opposite of order was disorder.

Walking into his house at eight thirty, Daniel greeted him with a smile.

"Good evening, sir." Daniel took William's coat and draped it over his arm.

"You tell me if it is." Only a few words were needed for Daniel to get the implication.

"I have hired an investigator to find Gideon Barnes."

"His name?"

"Justin Scott."

"And you trust his work ethic and discretion?"

"Certainly, sir. I'm not sure if we'll need his services, however." Daniel reached into his pocket and extended him an envelope. "It is from Gideon Barnes."

William accepted it. It was the size of a greeting card. "Gideon?"

"Yes, sir. He stopped by today. He was awfully regretful that he had missed you."

"You should have sent him to my office."

"I did call, but you were in a meeting at the time."

William maintained eye contact with his servant as he slipped his thumb under the seal. He wasn't impressed with Daniel. The man was aware of how badly William wanted to meet Gideon. And for the money he shoveled Gideon's way, waiting around for a meeting to end shouldn't have sent him on his way. Surely he could have waited for a few minutes. An hour or more, even.

William read the sentiment, a brief and impersonal thank-you, at best. It wasn't that he required some touching piece, but this only fanned his fuming anger. "I assume he's in the city for a while."

"Um, actually, sir…"

William waved the card in Daniel's face. "This is utterly

ridiculous and unacceptable."

"You said that if—"

His glare quieted his employee. He clearly recalled what he had said: all that he needed was an acknowledgment. Yet to receive a card so soon after the gala struck him as a mocking gesture. And that was to say nothing of the fact that Gideon showed up so soon after the event.

"You make sure that Justin Scott gets on this right away. I want to know where Gideon lives. I want to know where he's going to be before he knows where he's going to be. Do you understand?"

"Yes, sir."

"All right, then." He pressed the card to Daniel's chest before turning to leave. He was surrounded by idiots. And apparently, he funded them, too.

CHAPTER 24

MATTHEW HATED HIS WORDS FROM the other night, the ones that expressed his true feelings on this entire scenario. *Let's get it over with.*

It wasn't how he imagined ever feeling about treasure hunting, let alone a discovery of this magnitude.

The sun wasn't even up yet, and the landscape was covered in darkness. He had woken Cal, and then the two of them headed for Robyn's room.

The scent of coffee wafted from beneath her door. She was already awake. She always took that portable machine with her. It operated on a small propane tank, making it the caffeine addict's best friend when roughing it.

Matthew knocked.

"I'm up. I'm up."

Matthew heard her steps coming toward the door, and then she opened it. Already dressed for the day, she wore beige khakis with a matching long-sleeved shirt. She'd left the first few buttons undone, exposing the curve-hugging white tank she had on underneath.

"Don't look at me like that, Matthew." Her eyes flashed to Cal. "Morning."

"Yep, it is."

She smirked and shook her head. She spoke to Matthew. "Looks like someone's not in a good mood."

Cal interjected. "Do you blame me? My girlfriend is being held against her will and her life is being threatened."

She watched as Cal helped himself to her coffee, but she didn't say anything about it. "You're right," she said in a serious tone. "The situation sucks, but somehow, we have to stop letting it get to us. Otherwise, it will weigh us down and blind us."

Cal set down the small cup. "I wish I could turn it off like that."

"Matt, will you help me out here?"

He wished he could, but he was at a loss for words. While he had a feeling he knew where she was going with this, he was having a hard time detaching from how Cal must've felt. But they were all friends with Sophie, even Robyn. He had heard that the women had shared a bottle of wine on more than one occasion.

"Sophie and I are friends, Cal," Robyn reminded him.

"Well, you're not acting like you're too upset about all this."

"What am I supposed to do? Sulk and be grumpy about it? We need to keep our heads for Sophie. We're not going to succeed in saving her if we don't."

Her speech resulted in her and Cal locking eyes. Seconds passed in silence before Cal nodded.

Matthew noticed the dark bruise on Cal's nose. At least it wasn't broken.

Robyn glanced from Cal to Matthew. "All right, let's do this. For Sophie."

Matthew witnessed it then, the sorrow that lay buried within her eyes. Her portrayed strength was for Cal's benefit, for Matthew's benefit, and maybe even for her own. Whether the courage was genuine mattered little. It was enough to latch onto.

JUAN AND LEWIS TOOK THEM to the river where two motorized canoes sat on the bank.

It had been an hour since Matthew, Cal, and Robyn were in her hotel room mentally preparing themselves—yet again—for this mission.

The early-morning air hung heavy with humidity, hinting that another downpour was possible.

Kevin and Ian were dressed as if they were on a pleasure-camping trip rather than an expedition through the jungle. Their clothing was generic, as if from any random department store, and their bags were just slightly glorified backpacks, like the ones high school students strapped on their backs.

Ian glowered, his mouth set in a tight frown, but his eyes were beady and focused. If it was even possible, he looked more miserable than he'd been the day before. The spot on his jaw where Matthew had cuffed him was a dull red and starting to bruise.

Kevin appeared just as indifferent as yesterday. Like his apparel, he gave no indication that he thought their outing at all risky.

Cal was the first to trudge through the long grass and sit in one of the canoes. Lewis joined him and then so did Kevin.

"Ian, you go with them." Kevin gestured toward Robyn, Matthew, and Juan.

As the motors rumbled to life, Matthew experienced the buzz of excitement. And so their quest for the City of Gold was underway.

CHAPTER 25

DANIEL HAD WATCHED THE PROOF-OF-LIFE video an hour ago and didn't imagine the upset feeling that had settled in his stomach would go away anytime soon. Technology should be used for good, to find cures for diseases, to unite nations, but sadly, it also supported the perils inherent to an imperfect and greedy society. It dispensed knowledge on how to achieve global annihilation, how to build bigger and better weapons. It brought together terrorist networks. And even when science wasn't taken that far, the Internet was a stomping ground for pedophiles and a hotbed for pornography. He had come across plenty of these sites when carrying out research for expeditions. For the most advanced species on the planet, humans dedicated an awful lot of their resources to extinction.

But today, technology had brought him something new. The video of a frightened young woman being held against her will and forced to talk to the camera. What made it worse was that he knew her.

He connected his phone to his desktop computer and copied the file. He'd have an easier time analyzing background images on the larger monitor. His hand hovered over his mouse as he gathered the courage to watch it all play out again. With a quick blink of his eyes and a deep breath, he clicked "play."

Sophie appeared to be confined to the bed. Maybe she was strapped to a leg of the bedframe. The headboard had built-in shelving. But with the dim light in the room, it was hard to make out what was on the shelf in much detail. There were picture frames, but the artwork or photographs they held were impossible to see through the reflection on the glass.

He paused the footage and enlarged it. He wasn't the most technical person, possessing only basic computer and Internet knowledge. He was still learning to use his smartphone. But he'd try for Sophie's sake. The poor girl.

He took another deep inhale and exhale, detaching himself from the images. This was a movie, not real life, he tried to convince himself. The leading actress just resembled someone he knew.

There, that was better. He felt his heart rate come down and his breathing even out.

He angled his head left, then right, stretching it out, as if by doing so he'd find clarity and the image on-screen would come into focus. And it worked. He noticed a reflection in the glass of one of the frames that revealed a pinpointed light. Probably just the light from the camera phone. It made him realize he'd been thinking about this too hard.

He pulled up the video message on his phone. The sender's number was blocked.

He gripped his cell tightly. What did he expect? The caller ID to be right there for him?

He turned back to the screen and saw that Sophie was only bound by one wrist. He zoomed out to the video's natural resolution.

He enlarged the frame he had analyzed seconds earlier in an effort to discern more around the pinpoint of light, but it was just darkness. He let the video play in slow motion next, placing his attention on each corner of the frame. Then he caught a reflection. He hit "pause."

He angled his head again, this time to the left. His eye caught two shadows. It was difficult to assign them proportions, but one was significantly smaller than the other. And one was a woman.

His left fist balled while his right remained poised over the mouse. He'd bet anything it was Veronica Vincent. He never disliked anyone as much as he did her, especially one he had never met in the flesh. But he had heard enough from Matthew, and what he had failed to tell Daniel, Robyn had filled in. It came down to one summation: Veronica had caused Matthew a lot of pain.

Daniel pulled back from the shot, with nothing striking him as useful in helping him determine Sophie's location. She could be anywhere in the world.

As he watched the video play through again, his stomach knotted. Any earlier self-advisement to detach was forgotten.

About fifty seconds in, a flash of colored light shone across the room. He rewound the video and watched it again. The source wasn't from inside the room, but rather, from outside. It wasn't clear enough to discern anything else, though.

He slumped back in his chair. "Wow, good job narrowing things down, Daniel. The girl's in a bedroom that has a window."

CHAPTER 26

ROBYN PULLED OFF HER LONG-SLEEVED shirt and tied it around her waist as she prepared herself mentally, once again, for what lay ahead. There was no way to forget that this wasn't a vacation. It wasn't even a fun expedition. Despite being on the verge of a remarkable find, suffocating threats hung over them.

She tried to keep positive, to speak courageously to Cal and Matthew. She sensed that Matthew had seen through her attempts but appreciated her efforts nonetheless.

She sat toward the back of Juan's canoe. Matthew sat at the front, next was Ian, then her, and finally, Juan. She watched as the gentle breeze, which beckoned a whisper of relief from the heat, teased Matthew's dark hair. It brought her back to the past when her fingers used to do the teasing. She abruptly stopped the walk down memory lane. Nothing good came from rehashing what had been.

She looked around at the beautiful landscape. Tall grass, grand trees, and all types of flora lined the shore on both sides. Here, the river wasn't very wide, maybe a hundred feet at the most. The water would have tempted her for a dip if it weren't for the hazards that lurked everywhere.

Alligators watched lazily from the riverbanks, their eyes like windows to the past. Was it true the species dated back to the dinosaur era, and if so, what had they witnessed?

The boat jerked as it came to a stop and she turned to Juan, who was showing off his toothy grin again. He yelled something to Lewis in Spanish.

"*Si*," the man replied.

"What's going on?" Ian asked.

"We're grounded," Juan said.

"What does that mean?"

Juan leaned in toward Robyn. "The guy's not too bright, is he?" He straightened up. "It means we have to push the boat."

Her eyes widened. She was just thinking about the water and the— "We have to push the boat?"

"Yes." Now Juan was giving her a look that questioned her intelligence.

"There's nothing else that can be done?"

"You stay in the boat, Robyn. The guys have this." Matthew winked at her and jumped out.

The man had a constitution of steel, but he was also aware of how she didn't like being treated as if she were fragile. And that wink he'd just pulled...

"I'm fine, thank you," she said, stepping out of the boat.

"Suit yourself." Matthew flashed her a dimpled smirk.

She grimaced at him, but the expression met only the back of his head.

Her feet reached the river bottom quickly. She figured it best not to analyze the water or contemplate and imagine what was lying in wait beneath the surface.

The four of them unloaded. Ian was the last to take the plunge. Cal, Lewis, and Kevin also had to get out of their boat.

"What about the alligators?" Ian asked.

"Nah, they won't hurt you if you don't bug them. It's the poisonous jellyfish you have to worry about." Juan started whistling a tune.

Despite her own fears, she found it amusing how a "tough guy" like Ian could be such a wuss.

CHAPTER 27

IAN CAUGHT THE LOOK THE woman gave him, and he didn't like it one bit. But it didn't matter whether he liked it or not. It was impossible to reverse time. If he could, he never would have touched Bolivian soil.

Hell, if he really had the ability to reverse time, he'd have rejected Vincent's proposal in the first place. This job was more of a headache than the compensation was worth. And it wasn't as if he was being paid any more to risk his life in the jungle.

It was then that he felt a brushing against his ankles. Instinctively, he stopped moving.

"Move it, Ian!" Kevin barked.

He hated the guy almost as much as he hated this country. But Ian was confident that in a face-off with Kevin, he'd be the victor. And as far as he was concerned, this entire venture only heightened his awareness of self-preservation.

"There's something touching me," Ian said, again catching the look in the woman's eyes and perhaps the hint of a smirk on her lips. The message she sent him, the lack of fear in her, didn't suit him at all. Somehow, he'd have to establish himself as a killer. But for some reason, being out here had muted what he really was. He was letting his anxiety over the unknown get to him, and that was uncharacteristic. Maybe it was the fact that every bit of this jungle concealed killers. He sensed their eyes on him. He was used to being the hunter, not the prey.

Juan laughed. "It's probably just a fish."

Again with the ridicule from this squat man.

Matthew, Gideon, whoever he was, might have made a speech about all of them needing to have one another's backs, but as far as Ian was concerned, he only had one to worry about: his own.

MATTHEW GLANCED BACK AT ROBYN. She seemed to be moving along without concern. He figured her determination would counterbalance any fear she may have had over being stung by a jellyfish.

"We can probably walk from here." Juan bobbed his head toward the shore. The riverbank appeared clear of alligators, but it was thick with lush greenery.

"We? You're joining us?" From what Matthew had understood, their guides were going to bring them to this point and then turn back.

"Sorry, there must have been a misunderstanding. Daniel made it sound as if we would be coming along. We were the ones to fly overhead and take the photos," Lewis said.

Matthew took in one man and then the next and wondered if he was overreacting. The more people on this expedition the better. With hired guns sent by Vincent, they needed all the help they could get, so at least he'd have two more men on his side.

"I don't care who comes as long as we find this thing," Cal said, readying his camera.

Juan and Lewis were still watching Matthew.

"He's right. The more the merrier." Matthew gripped Juan's shoulder.

Juan showcased a toothy grin. "All right, then. Let's go."

"Look!" Robyn pointed to the mountain ranges that peaked above the jungle canopy. Fog clung to the treetops surrounding it, covering the area in an eerie haze that intrigued more than frightened. "We're getting closer." Excitement laced each of her words. There was no hesitancy or apprehension.

Matthew couldn't help but smile. Despite all the tension among them, he lived for this kind of discovery. To put one's hands on something that had been buried for centuries, to walk where no man had in just as long. They had quite a distance to go still, with untold obstacles ahead, but he was ready and so were his friends.

They maneuvered the boats to the riverbank, and Juan and Lewis took one and hid it in the dense growth. They did the same with the other.

Foliage towered overhead and all around, robbing them of their view of the mountains. They'd need to use their machetes to clear a path. But rather than fear his surroundings, Matthew felt as though he was returning home. It was another reason why he was suited for a lifestyle that had him traveling to remote regions of the globe.

"How's it looking, Cal?" Matthew turned to his friend, who was taking photographs.

Cal lowered the camera and exchanged it for a GPS. Their destinations had already been keyed into it to ensure they were headed in the right direction.

"Are you sure he should be the one doing this?" Robyn laughed. "You do remember India?"

"Oh, be quiet, woman…" Cal flashed her a smirk and returned his focus to the screen. "All right, so we have ten miles of jungle ahead of us."

"Ten miles?" Ian asked.

Everyone turned to face Ian.

"If you were listening earlier, you'd know this. If the distance is too much for you, you can wait by the boats," Cal offered.

Ian shook his head and looked away. Matthew was sure the man was having many regrets. Maybe next time he'd consider the consequences of his actions beforehand. Not that Matthew had any empathy for the guy. He deserved what he had coming to him.

"All right, let's get going." Robyn withdrew a machete from her bag and swung it in wide, even arcs.

Matthew stepped to her side, and the two of them worked to make a path.

He never would have dreamed years ago that he and Robyn would be seeing the world together in this way. When he had been ready to propose marriage, the timing hadn't been right. She had just received a job offer, and he'd always known what her career meant to her. He had refused to hold her back. She'd needed to devote endless hours to the job in order to build her reputation and succeed in her field. Truth was, he'd loved her too much to see her give up on her dreams.

"You know, ten miles in the jungle isn't like a leisurely Sunday stroll," Kevin said to Ian.

If the two men despised each other as much as they seemed to, Matthew and his friends could use it to their advantage. If they managed to divide the men, they could conquer them. Like most things, it was all about timing.

CHAPTER 28

PAITITI WAS OUT THERE WAITING to be discovered. Matthew sensed it. Some called it intuition, others a sixth sense. Whatever it was, it spoke to him now. A hidden treasure of this magnitude would bring untold dangers. This fact brought up a deeper question: was the city meant to be found? Not only did the legendary city carry the stigmatism of whether it even existed, it brought intrigue and mysticism.

While the Incas never developed a written language, they were well ahead of their time scientifically. There may even be curses or other such deterrents protecting the city. His studies hadn't revealed any ancient rumor as to hexes laid upon the City of Gold, but for it to remain undiscovered made Matthew wonder if it was simply due to the wrong geographical search area or something more.

He knew one thing for sure: those who'd set out with real intent to find Paititi in the past had sacrificed their lives in the search. Native Indians, disease, starvation, or an unknown factor? It made sense to him that fortifications could secure the city against capture and discovery.

He continued to swing the machete wide, Robyn working in harmony with his swipes.

"How far have we gone?" Matthew asked Cal.

"Is that your way of asking, 'Are we there yet?'"

"Sounds like it." Matthew stopped to catch his breath.

Cal consulted the GPS. "We've gone a quarter of a mile."

Matthew wiped his brow. His skin was slick with sweat that

had soaked through his clothing. The one saving grace was the cover of the trees that protected them from direct sunlight. He took out his canteen and swigged back a healthy mouthful of water. The rest of them followed his lead and drank from their own containers.

"Look at this." Robyn indicated a butterfly, its wings like glass. The leaf it rested on showed through the clear wings.

"Beautiful." Matthew smiled at Robyn, and she returned it and nodded.

Their eyes locked, and he was catapulted to the past. He was waking up beside her in bed. Her brown eyes were full of love and wistfulness.

Back in Bolivia, he turned away from Robyn. "We better get mov—"

"No!" Juan shoved Cal away from a tree he was about to lean against.

Cal stumbled a bit, catching his balance. "What are you—"

Juan pointed to an insect on the bark. It was about an inch long and of fusiform shape with patterned wings on its back.

"It's a kissing bug, and they can be deadly."

"They are also known as vinchucas. Correct?" Robyn asked.

"Yes. They are bloodsucking and known to spread Chagas' disease."

"Chagas' disease?" Cal's Adam's apple bobbed with a rough swallow.

"Yes. It causes skin disorders, brain toxicity, digestive system irritation, and heart damage. If left untreated it can be deadly. Some people don't even realize they are infected until it is too late."

Cal winced and then twitched as obvious shivers crawled through his body.

"You want to find relics, yes? Not become one?" Juan asked. "Because if you become infected, it's possible we'll be burying you in this jungle."

Cal nodded. "Thanks."

"Don't mention it."

Just when there had been the possibility of a calmness settling over the group, a blood-sucking bug had managed to upset things. But with it, any hesitation about having the two extra men, dissolved. They had already potentially saved Cal's life, and their intimate knowledge of the land and its creatures was certainly advantageous.

"We still have a long way to go, and it would be nice to get at least halfway before nightfall," Matthew said, expecting a comment from Ian about spending a night in the jungle. None came. Maybe he was finally learning how to keep his mouth shut. In fact, Matthew was impressed that the man had remained silent through everything that just happened with the kissing bug. Or perhaps he was too terrified to speak.

Chapter 29

Detective Brody Fuller would have preferred to make better use of his time than be looking into an abandoned car. But until his investigation concluded otherwise—this particular car was being viewed as a crime scene.

He pulled the department sedan up beside the tow truck and took in the area. This part of the city was stereotypical for vehicle dumps. There weren't many people down here except for homeless people and drug dealers, both of which came out at night. Not that they weren't out there now, too, but they were pros at blending in.

Drums full of burned debris spotted the area. Ratty comforters littered the streets, and shopping carts packed with garbage, likely to feed the fires, sat nearby.

Brody had been called down here more times than he could count for everything from drug overdoses to murder. Then there were cases like this one—a vehicle with a missing driver. But usually the cars were run-down pieces of shit.

In this case, it was a new model Hyundai Accent in pristine condition and it was behind the tow truck, not yet hooked up. It didn't appear to have been taken for a joyride.

Brody ambled over to the truck driver who stood beside the car. The man was balding, middle-aged, and had an expansive belly. He wore overalls and his winter coat was unzipped, giving Brody more than an ample view of the man's pear-shaped torso.

"Did you touch the car?" Brody asked.

"Nope." The man crossed his arms, and by doing so drew

Brody's eye to an embroidered name patch announcing him as McKenzie.

"Good." Brody pulled out a pair of latex gloves and took a step toward the vehicle. "And you found it unlocked?"

"Yeah, it—"

"But you never touched it?"

McKenzie rolled his eyes and headed to the cab of his truck. Brody remained aware of the man's movements. He didn't know why he was on the move. Was he getting a gun? Maybe the dislike had been instantaneous for him, too. It wasn't uncommon for a cop to be shot down in the line of duty. Sadly, these days, it happened on a regular basis. It was a risk assumed by those who donned the badge. And it was better to border on paranoia than be dead.

When Brody assessed that it was safe, he carried on. He first peered through the front passenger's-side window, holding his hand to his forehead to cut out the glare from the sun. No blood or weapons on any of the seats. There were no clear indicators that a crime even took place here. That was what stirred his gut. It was too pristine. Too immaculate.

He looked in the back. No garbage on the floor, front or back.

He lifted the handle on the front passenger door.

Brody heard McKenzie's boots scraping over the gravel. He'd probably returned to watch. Without acknowledging the man, Brody continued his quick search and crouched to look under the seat. Afterward, he walked around the car and repeated the process on the driver's seat. He found nothing.

His fingers traced the steering wheel—without making contact—dropping to the ignition. No keys. Not an uncommon find. The person who took the car could have tossed them anywhere.

The plate would be run for a few reasons. First, to obtain the owner's identity. Second, to see if the vehicle was reported stolen. And third, to find out if it was reported in conjunction with a crime.

He opened the glove box and like the rest of the car, it was organized and tidy. An accordion-style folder seemed to hold maintenance receipts, he noticed with a quick glance. He reached beneath the folder and pulled out the car's registration. He could mark off the car's owner.

"Who is it?" McKenzie asked, yanking Brody from his contemplation.

Nosy driver, but he'd appease his curiosity.

"Some chick named Sophie Jones." Saying her name aloud, Brody recognized it, but couldn't remember why.

"Isn't that the girl from the buses? The real estate agent?"

Ah, that's where he'd seen it. Maybe this guy wasn't useless after all. "Yeah, I think it is."

Chapter 30

Matthew tucked his water canteen back into his bag. "Are you good to clear again?" he asked Robyn.

"Absolutely."

They took over for Cal and Ian, resuming their swipes, once again moving in perfect sync.

The seven of them made good time, eating up miles of jungle, each taking turns at cutting down the foliage, but the sun streaming through the canopy was getting dim.

"We should set up camp for the night," Matthew suggested, sheathing his machete.

Robyn secured hers, as well. "I agree. Night falls quickly. We'll need to get a fire going and our tents set up."

"Wait, do you hear that?" Cal held up his finger, summoning everyone to remain quiet.

"A waterfall?" Lewis said.

"Yeah, I think so." Cal pulled out his machete and swiped at the foliage, heading in the direction of the sound.

After about fifty swipes, they reached a small clearing. Sheltered by overhanging trees, there was a bit of a flat space, perfect for setting up camp. It was next to a lagoon with a small waterfall rolling over its back edge.

"Great job," Matthew said.

Cal turned to Robyn. "And you still probably think I have no sense of direction."

She laughed. "You got lucky."

"So a waterfall and a lagoon… We are getting close." Juan

flashed his toothy smile.

Matthew sensed Juan was trying to encourage the group. Being a native, Juan would have known there were many waterfalls and lagoons in Bolivia. But it was best to leave them invigorated and thinking that they were almost there. Of course, *almost there* was a relative term. Distance-wise, as Juan had noted earlier in the day, a total of ten miles wasn't that far. It was the terrain that made it feel more like a thousand-mile trip.

"How are we making out?" Matthew asked Cal, nodding toward the GPS.

"First things first…" Cal started snapping photographs of the lagoon and the falls, and then he took a couple of Matthew and Robyn. She moved in close to Matthew and held up her hand behind his head. He surmised she was giving him bunny ears with her fingers. Some things would never change.

Cal turned and swept his camera around and included shots of Juan and Lewis. Ian and Kevin denied permission to have their photos taken. Not that it came as a surprise.

"You about done there?" Matthew waved his fingers toward the camera.

"Yeah, I— Whoa, look at him." Cal directed their attention to a low-hanging branch. On it, camouflaged to near perfection, was a large iguana.

"Oh wow. He's awesome." Robyn jogged to Cal's side, as he was closer to the reptile. "You have to take his picture."

"Already did," Cal said and then put his camera away. "All right, back to business." He consulted the GPS.

"Thank God," Ian groaned.

Is it too much to ask for the man to keep his mouth shut for the rest of the trip? Matthew thought.

Cal didn't give any indication that he'd heard Ian say anything, though. "According to this thingy, we're just a bit over halfway."

"Excellent." Matthew spun to take in the area. "We'll set up here."

If being in the jungle wasn't punishment enough, he was stuck there with this team of misfits. Ian recognized he was part of that collective label, but he accepted it. He'd rather be that than other things. Like dead.

He looked over at Cal. The guy was a true pain in the ass. He was acting like a damned tourist, snapping off pictures here and there. This wasn't some sightseeing tour they were on, for God's sake. They were assembled to accomplish a mission. One in which the stakes were of the highest caliber. Yet here this guy was, acting like he was oblivious to the danger. All of them acted as if this was perfectly normal, aside from when the short Bolivian man pointed out that bug.

Ian felt a pinch on his neck and swatted at it. This whole damn place gave him the heebie-jeebies and made his skin crawl. It was quite possible that nothing had bitten him except his imagination. But on the flip side, it was just as possible something had and that he might not make it till morning.

CHAPTER 31

BRODY FULLER REALIZED HE'D BE on scene a little longer. Calls to Sophie Jones's phone met with voice mail, and uniformed officers had visited her apartment to find no one was home. At this point, she was considered missing and the possible victim of a crime.

Brody sent McKenzie on his way after taking the driver's statement. His griping about losing towing fares by sticking around had gotten on Brody's last nerve. Once Crime Scene finished processing the area, the guy would be called back.

Investigators scoured the vehicle with microscopic intensity while Brody tried to secure witness accounts. If he found someone who'd seen the Accent dropped off, he'd be closer to finding out exactly what was going on.

At times like this he wished for a junior partner. Otherwise, he was more than happy to work solo. There was no small talk or bonding required. Attachment to another person wasn't necessary to get the job done. In fact, emotional connection complicated things and just left a vulnerability for criminals to take advantage of.

If he had a lackey, the poor schmuck would be the one scouting for vagrants amid garbage and makeshift shelters of tattered blankets, tarps, fishing rods, and broomsticks. Brody would be at Sophie's apartment, which was no doubt a Ritz-Carlton compared to this area of the city, even if discarded clothes covered her floors and dirty dishes lined her counters.

Brody focused elsewhere, summoning up the imagery of him

lounging on his leather couch, a football game on TV, a whiskey on the rocks in his hand, and chicken wings on his plate. They were his one true vice. As the conjured smell of honey garlic teased his sinuses, he was hit with the onslaught of…rotting meat?

He gagged and coughed. Tears welled, hindering his vision, but he caught the vagrant quickly shutting his eyes, pretending to still be asleep.

"Hey, you! Get up." Brody kept his attention on the man and watched his eyes flutter open, at first only to a slit. "I know you're awake. I need to talk to you."

The man let out a deep moan, keeping up the pretense of being roused from a deep sleep.

"Get up." Brody barked the directive this time and clapped his hands.

The man's eyes opened wide, and he stood up. He was tall and had Brody by three or four inches. He was dressed in a plaid wool coat that had seen better days two decades ago. His hair was a knotted mess of silver, both on the top of his head and on his face.

The shiver that laced down Brody's spine was involuntarily, but he fought the urge to curl his lips. Hygiene was one thing Brody held sacred.

"We've got a car over there." Brody jacked a thumb over his shoulder toward the Hyundai. He never took his eyes off the man, despite the overwhelming desire to do just that. "Did you see when it was left there?"

The man was walking away.

"Hey, get back here." Brody followed him.

The man turned, blinked deliberately, and stayed still, standing about five feet away from Brody.

He was good with the distance. Even from here, the man's movements wafted the aroma of cheap booze, ripe underarm odor, and urine.

"Did you see anyone around the car?" he asked again.

As Brody kept a connection with the man's eyes, he realized

what he should have noticed right away. The man was hammered, drunk out of his mind.

Brody took a few steps back to seek another candidate. "Never mind."

"I saw a man," the vagrant said.

Brody stopped. "A man?"

"Yes."

"Can you describe him?"

"It was late at night."

"Was he alone?"

The vagrant nodded. "Yes."

Brody took a deep breath, and he recited the mental mantra he repeated more often than he cared to acknowledge: *patience is a virtue.*

"What did the man look like?"

The vagrant shrugged. "I dunno. A man."

"White? Black?" Brody hated to categorize human beings by skin color, but it was necessary in his line of work.

"White." The man belched, renewing the strong scent of alcohol.

Brody twisted his head to the side, wishing for fresh air, but received nostrils full of rotting garbage for his trouble.

"When was he here?" Brody asked. He hoped that rewording one of his original questions might spark a useful response.

"I dunno."

"Well, thanks."

"It's not like I have appointments to keep, son," the homeless man added.

Brody waved his hand in a pacifying effort to tell him it was fine, he'd move on.

"I said, *son.*"

"Yes, I heard you."

"Don't they teach you to respect your elders anymore?"

Brody studied the man's appearance. A rebuttal would have Brody responding with something along the lines of respect needing to be earned. The odd thing was, despite this man's

CAROLYN ARNOLD

stench, obvious dependency on the bottle, haggard wardrobe, and detestable living conditions, Brody found some respect arousing within him. "Yeah, they do."

"Then listen to me, boy."

"I will if there's anything else you can tell me."

"I drank a bottle of Jack last night."

Brody steadied himself. He tried to walk away from this man twice and was stopped. He'd wait out this tangent before wasting the energy a third time.

"The night before I had Skol."

"And your point, *sir*?"

"I may not need to know the days, but I know what I drink. I tell the day by the drink. Sometimes I catch the date on the newspapers at the stand…when I can get close enough. Or I'll see it on a TV in a coffee shop window before I'm shooed away."

Who cared if this man tracked his days like that Bon Jovi song *Wanted Dead or Alive* if he had information. "So do know when the car was dropped off?"

The man nodded. "I do. And my point is that it woulda been three days ago. At night. I was drinking Bacardi. It's actually my favorite. The gold stuff, not the clear. Yum, yum." He let out a whistle.

"What did the man do after getting out of the car?"

"If I recall right, he just walked away, not even like he was in a hurry."

Not in a hurry. This denoted self-assuredness, confidence. And the fact that he left on foot might mean he was headed someplace nearby. Then again, not necessarily. He could have taken public transportation or had his own vehicle somewhere close-by.

"For your help, I owe you a bottle." The words slipped out and surprised Brody. With this man, he could look past what the eye saw. He imagined him being a father. And maybe he was.

"Brody?" Dawn, a female investigator, approached him. She was a pretty little thing—dark hair and blue eyes, a small, upturned nose, and a slim figure. They'd had drinks one night that resulted in more fun than either had intended. Their relationship had snapped back to a professional one quickly the next day, and neither of them had spoken of the tryst since.

"We've finished up," Dawn said. "The car was pretty clean, but we took a bunch of pictures, of course, and we were able to pull some prints from the wheel and handles." With her message delivered, she turned to leave.

"Let me know as soon as results come back."

She waved over her head as she walked away.

When Brody turned back to the vagrant, he was gone. Just like a shadow—there or imagined, it was hard to say. Brody shook his head and walked toward the department sedan. Crime Scene would have the Hyundai towed to the police impound lot. He, however, was going to take a look at Sophie Jones's apartment and hopefully find a clue not only as to her whereabouts, but also to see if he could figure out if she left of her own free will or if her life was, in fact, in danger.

Chapter 32

Sophie's stomach rumbled at the smell of steamed vegetables, garlic, and onion. It was nine thirty at night and the last thing she ate had been a muffin at noon. While it was true that she wasn't moving around much, her body still chewed through the calories. She used to frequent a gym and was aware that a limited number were required for bodily functions, and she didn't think she was getting enough to even cover those. She didn't need to lose weight, but if she had, captivity wouldn't have been the program she'd go with.

After they tied her to the bedframe last night, she was freed only for bathroom breaks and then restrained again. At least she was afforded privacy when it came to that, but she was desperate for a hot shower. She'd been wearing the same clothes for three days now. The pantyhose had long since been abandoned for the sake of comfort.

Her gag had been removed under threat that if she screamed they'd kill her, her friends, and anyone else who got involved. The man assured her that collateral damage didn't bother him, and Sophie believed him.

The door swung open, and the man entered the bedroom. He stepped toward her, holding up his phone. "It's time to record you again. Just say hello. I don't really care. Just breathe and move a little."

The light on the smartphone brightened. He had started recording. She spent many of the past hours thinking about how to work these sessions to her advantage, but she had to be careful not to make any of those efforts obvious.

"Why are you doing this?" she asked.

He didn't respond.

"Where did that other man go?" She asked, knowing she probably shouldn't push it and say Ian's name. "Is this his place?"

Still, she was met with silence.

"And where is the wom—"

The blow struck her hard across the face. It came so fast that she hadn't even seen Veronica enter the room. Veronica must have figured out that Sophie was trying to lay some clues as to her whereabouts.

"You are a damn idiot!" Her arms flailed and her hired gun sheepishly retreated a few steps. The phone lowered, and the light dulled.

Sophie cupped her cheek with her free hand. It stung and burned to the touch, and it was already beginning to welt.

The woman turned her attention to Sophie. "You think you're so smart. Maybe because you are friends with Matt, but I have news for you. He only is who he is because of me. I made him. Do you hear me?" The wildfire in her eyes tamed, licked by another side of the woman. She coolly took in Sophie's face, and then let her gaze lower. "Maybe you are more than his friend."

Sophie shook her head. The woman almost sounded jealous. She didn't know what Veronica was thinking, obviously, but there was a flicker of jealousy and curiosity in her eyes.

"We are just friends." Sophie's voice slid from her throat, barely more than a whisper.

"Well, he seems very confident that he's going to find this Paititi."

"Matthew doesn't know failure." It was only a feeling, but there was something in the way the woman's gaze left hers briefly, combined with the flash of emotion in her eyes. Unfortunately, to find out, she'd have to rouse the woman's anger. A well-timed throb in her cheek warned her but went unheeded. "He left you for dead, didn't he?"

Veronica's nostrils flared, and her eyes fired.

Based on her reaction, Sophie's words struck close to the truth. She had to press further. "He did. Your life was at risk, and he was willing to leave it that way."

"What the hell do you know, you stupid bitch?"

"That's it, isn't it? You loved him…well, as much you are capable of such a thing. He turned his back on you. He broke your heart."

"Shut up." Veronica charged at Sophie, but the man held her back. She attempted to shrug him off, but he didn't release his grip. She glared back at him. If looks could kill…

He held up his hands in surrender. "I'm sorry, boss, but you told me not to let you hurt the girl."

Veronica glared at Sophie and snorted before shirking from the man's hold and leaving the room. The man slipped out of the room afterward. Sophie wondered if that meant she'd go to bed hungry. The first thing Cal was going to do when he got back was take her to an all-you-can-eat buffet. It was the least he could do after getting her into this mess.

Chapter 33

Sophie Jones lived in a one-bedroom apartment that she kept tidy and meticulously organized. Her closet was sorted by color and her dresser drawers were organized by function—casual, semiformal, pants, long-sleeved shirts, and short-sleeved shirts.

Brody wasn't surprised by this. What the woman presented on the bus ads was a professional and put-together real estate agent. That image was just confirmed by her home.

As he worked over the apartment, nothing stood out to indicate that she had any enemies. In fact, it was the opposite.

Framed photographs on the walls and tables showed a socially active woman. In numerous poses, she was with a man Brody had concluded was her boyfriend. With her arms wrapped around him in one picture, her lips pressed to his in another, it was an easy assumption to make.

Her counters were bare with the exception of a coffeemaker, kettle, and toaster. There was also a picture frame and a vase holding a dozen long-stemmed red roses. Beside the flowers was a card signed, *Love, Cal.*

A first name wasn't a major development in the case, but it was a start. Brody would hunt this guy down and see what he knew about Sophie, how close they were, et cetera. Maybe he would finally be able to make the conclusion that Sophie was, in fact, taken. It was possible she had run off with some other guy, but why have him dump the car? Based on the way she lived, she was a responsible and organized person and those factors didn't support her dropping off the face of the earth intentionally.

No, Sophie was made to disappear. The question remained: by whom?

There was a huge flaw to assuming the boyfriend was involved, though. His skin was mocha, and the vagrant had said the man ditching the car was white.

Brody was standing in Sophie's kitchen, thinking everything over. At first, his focus wasn't on anything. Then his eyes narrowed in on a framed photograph. He picked it up for a closer look and recognized one man right away. Matthew Connor.

The mayor's son?

He studied the face. It was definitely him.

Scanning the rest of the photograph, Brody spotted another familiar face. He only knew it because an ex-girlfriend was fond of history and had taken him to the ROM every week of their six-week relationship. The woman in the photo was Robyn Garcia, a curator at the museum.

He dialed the museum's main number on his cell and was connected seconds later.

"This is Detective Brody Fuller, and I'm looking to speak with Robyn Garcia."

"One moment, please."

Instead of hold music or silence, he listened to news on the latest exhibits while impatiently tapping his foot.

Two minutes later, the same woman who had placed him on hold picked back up. "I'm sorry, but Miss Garcia is not in the office today."

"When will she be back?" Brody sensed the woman's hesitation and reminded her of his position. "I am a police detective."

"She's on holiday, *Detective*."

"Holiday? Where?"

"I don't know, and even if I did, I'm sorry, but I'm not at liberty to say. I hope you understand."

"Yes, of course." He hung up slightly discouraged but far from feeling defeated.

His eyes fell to the photograph again. The same black man from the other photos had his arm around Sophie's waist. He surmised, based on his gut feeling, he was the Cal from the card. And if they were as close as the photos indicated, his full name had to be in this apartment somewhere.

He worked through the space again and found a shoebox full of postcards. All of them were from a Cal Myers.

A QUICK BACKGROUND CHECK ON Cal Myers showed his employment as a freelance travel photographer. There wouldn't be an office to check with, but Brody obtained the man's address.

His high expectation that he'd find the man at home was met with disappointment.

He had a couple of options left, but first he'd speak with a superior and a friend. He knocked on Chief Snyder's office door. Despite it being almost nine at night, the chief didn't adhere to strict office hours, and Brody expected he'd still be at work.

"Come in."

Brody entered.

"Ah, Brody. What's up?"

Brody had always appreciated the chief's laid-back approach to things. It actually threw new people off because, despite that first impression, the man was tenacious and had no issue backstabbing both professionally and personally if the need arose. He and Brody had a history and got along well. In fact, better than well. They'd gotten drinks together on many occasions and were on a first-name basis unless they were around their colleagues.

"Please, sit." The chief directed him to the chair across from his desk.

Brody closed the door before sitting. "Erik, there was an abandoned car left down at the harbor."

"That's exciting news," he said sarcastically. He laughed, and it shook the man's taut frame. He was in his midfifties, but he could probably bench press more than some men in their twenties.

"Normally I'd agree, but it's not your run-of-the-mill ditching. It wasn't taken on a joy ride. I believe it was involved in an abduction. The vehicle is registered to a Sophie Jones." He caught the brooding look on Erik's face as he tried to place the name. Brody eliminated the guesswork. "She's the real estate agent plastered on the buses."

"Ah, yes."

"Well, there's no sign of her or a struggle. The car was clean, no blood. Crime Scene was able to lift some prints so I'm waiting on the results. In the meantime, I checked out her apartment and had a good look around. I even spoke to her employer, and they haven't heard from her for three days. He said that it wasn't unusual for her lately. She's been obsessing over selling this one property." He had made the quick call to Sophie's boss while driving from Cal's apartment to the station. "Apparently, when agents show a house, they call into the office for safety reasons. I have the address for the last house she showed. It was the night her car was dumped, as verified by an eyewitness. I drove by the place but need to get inside to have a closer look at things."

"Sounds like a good lead."

What he needed to say next was where hesitation crept in. Brody's strength had never included politics and diplomacy. "There's something else."

Erik leaned forward, clasping his hands on his desk. "And why do I get the feeling I'm not going to like it?"

"Because you have good instincts. There was a photograph of Jones with the mayor's son."

"Matthew Connor?"

"Yes, sir."

He waved his hand, dismissing the more formal address. "Erik."

"I trust that you know what I'm asking?"

"You want to make sure I'm on board with you questioning the mayor's son?"

"I do."

Erik let out a deep breath. "Let me talk to his father first."

"You're sure?"

The chief bobbed his head side to side. "I'll handle this."

"Thanks, and in the meantime, I'll see if I can get inside that house."

CHAPTER 34

THE ENVIRONMENT MIGHT HAVE SOFTENED Ian's dangerous nature, but Matthew didn't trust that he was harmless. And multiply that threat by two when factoring in Vincent's other man, Kevin. He'd been the one ordering a cavalry of men after them in India.

Juan got a large fire going, and it instantly removed the shadows from the immediate area so they would be able to see when darkness fell. But more importantly, it would keep the wildlife to the outskirts of their camp.

Matthew and his friends, along with the Bolivians, favored one side of the clearing while Kevin and Ian pitched Kevin's tent—Ian didn't bring one—across from them on the other side of the fire. Watching them set it up was painful and time-consuming. Dusk had sunk its teeth into the sky before they had finished.

Matthew called Robyn and Cal over to him. They were standing by their tents, which were about ten feet away from the fire where the Bolivians sat with Vincent's men.

With the crackling of the fire, the hum of insects, and the distant cries of animals, he trusted no one would overhear what he had to say to them, but he still spoke at a low volume. "One of us has to be up at all times. We'll take turns."

"Good idea," Robyn said.

"We can't risk them doing anything. Now, I don't think they will, but you never know."

"And if they try anything?" Cal asked.

"Then whoever is up wakes the rest of us."

Cal nodded. "Too bad because I'd love a shot at that asshole."

Matthew knew Cal was referring to Ian, and Matthew couldn't blame him. It had felt good to hit the man at the airport, but they weren't here to start fights. They were here to find Paititi and save Sophie. "Self-control, Cal. Got it?"

"It's not fair that you got to hit him."

Matthew put his hand on his friend's shoulder and squeezed. "I'm not going to lie and say I didn't enjoy it."

Cal was smiling when he shrugged Matthew off him.

"All right, so you guys good with it? I'll go first if you like."

"Let me do it, Matt," Cal began, "I'm not sleeping much anyhow."

"Robyn, do you want to go first, then?" Matthew hated asking her to do this, and his protective nature overwhelmed him. What if she was hurt because he had left her alone?

"I can see it your eyes, you know," Robyn said, calling him out. "I'm a grown woman. I can handle myself, and I can handle them."

"You know my concern has nothing to do with the fact you're a woman," he said softly.

"I'll be fine. Besides, I do have a gun." Robyn pulled her weapon from the waistband of her pants, just enough that the firelight caught the metal.

Matthew nodded. "Just be careful."

Robyn rolled her eyes.

He understood her side. She frequented the gun range to keep up her shooting skills, but at the same time, he knew how she felt about violence. It was necessary only when there was no other option. And that equated to kill or be killed. She hadn't yet taken a life, and he didn't look forward to the day when it happened. As confident as she came across, she was fragile.

"You got this, then?" He tossed in a smirk.

"Yes. Go. Get some rest. I'll tag you in a few hours."

Running on minimal sleep out in the jungle wasn't ideal, but in this case, it was necessary. Matthew nodded to Robyn, and then he and Cal went into their respective tents.

Chapter 35

IF IT WERE POSSIBLE TO conjure something from nothing, it would have happened hours ago. Instead, all Daniel had to show for his efforts was a twitching eyeball from the strain of staring at the video. He pinched the bridge of his nose and shut his eyes. Still, in the darkness, the images played out. He watched the footage enough times that it was logical to expect a perfect instant replay of it in his head.

A mild headache had lodged behind his eye sockets, but he didn't have the time to succumb to any physical hindrances. He needed to keep at this until something gave him a clear indication as to Sophie's whereabouts.

This was necessary not so much because he was going to perform some sort of rogue rescue mission, but so they were armed with intel.

The extent of what Veronica Vincent was capable of wouldn't shock him. She was ruthless and vindictive and used to getting her way. A double cross wasn't out of the realm of possibility. In fact, Daniel could foresee Matthew and his team finding Paititi and her going back on her promise not to harm Sophie. Veronica always had the upper hand, or she created one to suit the circumstances. She did have one weakness, though. She was blind when it came to Matthew, and Daniel believed she underestimated him.

He willed his eyes to open. There was much to do. A second video had just come in, and he hoped that between the two, he'd be able to gather some more clues. The fact that Sophie was in a bedroom with a window was hardly enough.

He hit "play" on the new video when a solution presented itself. How could he have been so blind? It must have been his ardent focus on the video itself rather than its source.

He was getting ready to plug the phone into his desktop computer to transfer the file when his eyes caught "unknown number."

There must be a way to ascertain the sender's origin, with or without a number. It was, after all, the twenty-first century. There were means to obtain almost anything. Not that he possessed the expertise to attempt such a thing.

He realized it was also possible that the sender was using a burner phone. Rumored untraceable. But he saw enough movies to know GPS could be used to ping—at least he thought that was the term—a phone's location.

Suddenly experiencing a little uneasiness, he looked at the phone he held in his hand. It wasn't even a burner phone. But he let the fear go. If Vincent wanted him, she likely knew where to find him anyway. Surely, she wouldn't be so bold as to come here for any reason.

His mind went back to tracing the sender's phone. How was he supposed to manage that? He had no idea how to do it. He couldn't involve the police or Sophie would pay with her life.

"They've got you by the short hairs," he mumbled as he completed the transfer process and opened the file on his computer.

The footage on this latest video was brief but telling. Sophie was obviously trying to give him a clue. Only she did a poor job of it—or he was being obtuse—and her words were cut short by a slap across the face.

Daniel slowed the frames and was able to tell it was a woman who had struck her. The nails were manicured. Rings adorned most fingers. Veronica had hit Sophie.

Rage fired within him. She was already failing to hold up to her side of the deal by leaving Sophie unharmed.

Daniel had never been one for violence, detesting action

movies and the like simply because his emotional fortitude couldn't handle such things. Watching the evening news or CNN were two other things he avoided. While he knew evil existed in the world, he didn't need a front-row seat.

The abruptness and strength behind the blow served to do more than simply outrage him, though. It cleared his mind. The headache that had been threatening to turn all his thought processes into vapor receded.

He paused the feed, focusing on what he had in the first video: the headboard and the framed photographs behind Sophie.

The room was slightly brighter this time, and a definite blur of lights streamed into the room from an outside source. If only the camera were angled just a little more to the left…

He resumed playing the video.

Then there it was. Just after Veronica had slapped Sophie, the cameraman's aim faltered slightly, dipping to the ground and to the left.

While there wasn't enough to derive their location, it was enough to confirm Daniel's suspicions. The colored lights weren't indoor Christmas decorations leftover from the holiday; they were coming from outside.

He rewound the video and paused in that frame. His fingers traced the image on the screen. He angled his head and studied it for a few minutes.

Sophie was in a high-rise. The lights weren't from traffic; they were from a building or buildings.

Elation fluttered in his heart even though he realized this still left him miles away from Sophie's location. Even assuming she was being held in Toronto, there was a multitude of tall buildings in the city.

He went back to the frame that showed the headboard again and zoomed in. Just as it had in the first video, glare cut across the glass, making it almost impossible to make out the image behind.

He enlarged it further, and this time it revealed the more obvious outline of a person. Features remained indistinguishable.

Daniel balled his fists and leaned back in his chair. The headache intensified with a vengeance as he tried to think everything through.

Before Veronica had slapped Sophie, Sophie had confirmed that she was being held in a man's home. This eliminated her being held in a hotel, and that made sense because housekeeping couldn't be kept out forever.

Second, she was in a high-rise, and based on the first clue, likely a condominium.

Third, this video verified that Veronica was crumbling. Her emotions must have been at a peak for her to react so swiftly to Sophie's words. Along with Daniel's earlier conclusion that the woman was capable of anything, he realized that she took pleasure in violence. If push came to shove, she would kill Sophie, without hesitation or regret.

Taking a deep breath, he rested his eyes again. Three clues out of a total six minutes of video. He may be a genius sleuth when it came to uncovering details for Matthew's expeditions, but he wouldn't be getting his detective badge anytime soon.

Then an idea struck.

He snapped his fingers and bolted to his feet. They were told not to involve the police. But if he had an expert enhance the video feed who also happened to be able to track the location of the phone…

His lips curved into a smile. Nothing was said about obtaining help from a private investigator.

CHAPTER 36

THERE WERE MANY THINGS TO occupy him, yet William Connor kept coming back the one thing that was bothering him. It was a thorn in his side, an encumbrance that limited his attention to other matters at hand. These days, he wasn't carrying out his mayoral duties as efficiently as he normally did. He was too focused on finding Gideon Barnes.

He trusted Daniel to handle the matter with the PI and realized he had better things to do than to get personally involved. But meeting Gideon face-to-face had become a personal mission.

It was after ten, and William was ahead of his nightly ritual. He was in his home office, wrapped in his silk robe, sitting behind his desk. He had already swum his laps, and his muscles were purring from the exertion. He loved that feeling—the satisfaction that came with knowing he was taking care of his body.

He was reviewing some financial report that he should have handled during office hours, but really, his position wasn't one of a set schedule. His concentration wasn't on the numbers, though. Hartman's phone call from the other day kept repeating in his mind. And if that wasn't enough, another VIP from the gala had mentioned Gideon's absence in passing, too. Though it may as well have been a pointed finger.

Was this going to become his legacy? Instead of people seeing him as the man who changed history in the greater Toronto area, he would be the man who gave away his money recklessly. Really, he was risking a lot more by *not* making the matter a personal one. From an outsider's perspective, Gideon Barnes could be a front for illegal activity. This was not an overreaction on his part. He only hoped that his failure to be attentive to the matter sooner wouldn't cost him everything he held so dear.

He used the intercom system to buzz through to Daniel's bedroom. Despite the hour, the man was always accessible to him. For this, he was compensated generously.

"Yes, sir?" Daniel answered, sounding perplexed, perhaps preoccupied.

"I need you to come to my office."

"Certainly. I'll be right there."

William hung up first, and as he waited for Daniel to make his way from the west wing to the north, he ruminated on Gideon Barnes and why it seemed to be so hard to track him down. What was so difficult about finding one man?

There was a faint knock on his office door before it opened.

Why was Daniel being so quiet? It's not as if he had to worry about waking anyone. Lauren had retired to her quarters for the evening, and she was in the east wing, anyway.

Daniel took a seat across from him.

"I need to know how things are coming with the PI. Has he found Gideon Barnes?"

Daniel's brow furrowed, and his mouth fell into a straight line. If William were to guess, the man had a headache.

"Daniel?"

He exhaled a sharp breath. "I am sure that Mr. Scott is working on it."

"Working on it? I'm starting to think that Santa Claus might be more real than this Gideon Barnes."

"Maybe he just likes his privacy, sir. He did drop off that card for you the other day."

"Yes, and conveniently, I was at the office. That, he should have known. And a card, Daniel? In exchange for how many years of funding his digs? I demand answers. I deserve them!"

The phone on his desk rang, but it wasn't notifying of an incoming call. It was the tone for the front gate. After seven at night, it was set to ring on all the phones in the home. William's thinking had always been that only bad news came unannounced or after the dinner hour.

William clasped his hands in his lap, and Daniel got up, walked around the desk, and answered the call.

Seconds later, he cupped the mouthpiece. His face was pale when he said, "It's Chief Snyder."

William's gut sank. This was a precursor to what was to follow—bad news. His generalization about news in the evening was about to be proven true once again. He could feel it. "Let him in immediately."

Daniel hit the appropriate code on the phone to release the gates.

"Bring him up here," William directed.

"As you wish." Daniel excused himself from the room to answer the main door.

Minutes later, the chief of police was being shown into William's office.

He studied the chief's face and his saunter. His shoulders were slightly hunched, and William sensed it had to do with more than the hour.

He got out from behind his desk and gestured toward a seating area that had deep-green leather sofas and chairs. "Chief Snyder, to what do I owe this visit?"

"I'm sorry to bother you late at night like this, sir."

"I'm certain it must be for an urgent matter."

Snyder nodded. "I was debating whether to come tonight or wait until the morning."

William let his eyes trace the man's face, but he didn't say anything. Their relationship had been built upon mutual respect and friendship. While they didn't always see eye to eye, Snyder was a worthy opponent and a man who kept William honest.

Snyder dropped into a chair. "I don't know how to say this other than to come out with it."

William sat on the couch across from him. He hated delays. His patience had been tested enough.

"Do you know a Sophie Jones?"

"Sophie? Yes, of course. She's a friend of Matthew's."

Snyder grimaced. "I was afraid you were going to confirm that."

William leaned forward in his chair, the tone of the conversation shifting suddenly. "What's happened, Erik?"

Erik rubbed the top of his thighs. "Her car was found near the harbor. It's a popular location for vehicle dumps used in crimes."

"Is she alive?" William's mouth was thick with saliva.

"We don't know."

"You don't know? How can you *not* know?"

"There was no sign of a struggle in the vehicle. An eyewitness says they saw a man walking away from her car but no sign of her."

"So, what? You think my son is involved with this?"

"Of course not, but we're wondering if it's possible to talk to him, ask him some questions, see if he's aware of anyone who might have something against her."

Being a politician for most of his life, William recognized when people withheld information. It was in the eyes, and Erik was holding back. "What aren't you telling me?"

"We were able to track down the lady's boyfriend. A—"

"Cal Myers?"

"Yes, that's right."

"He's also a friend of Matthew's."

"Well, Cal Myers seems to be missing, too. At least my detective hasn't been able to track him down."

Now it was William who needed to decide what information to provide and what to withhold. If he told him that his son had left the country, and rather quickly, he would appear suspect.

"When was she last seen?" he asked first.

"Three days ago."

William's shirt suddenly felt constricting, despite having a scooped neck that fell to his collarbone. Matthew had made his departure for Rome yesterday. As for his friend, Cal, who knew where the hell he was.

"I know all this must come as quite the shock to you, but if my detective could speak with Matthew—"

"He's not in the country," William interrupted.

"Where is he?"

"He was called away, urgently, to a dig in Rome."

"Hmm."

"Don't say it like you believe he is wrapped up in this. My son would not be involved with this at all. What about Cal? You said he's missing, too? What's to say that he didn't do something to her?" William didn't like putting the kid in the line of fire, but if it took the focus off his son, he'd make the exception.

Erik's eyes fell briefly to the floor. "The eyewitness said it was a white man."

William shot to his feet. "You do think it was my son!"

"No, no, I am not implying that." The man waved his hands frantically. "Not at all."

"My son would never lay his hand on a woman, let alone do God knows what to her and dump her car. I will not listen to these absurd accusations anymore. Get out of my home."

Both men held eye contact for seconds before Chief Snyder consented and stood.

"I apologize, William. Good night."

William was left staring at the wall as he listened for the door to shut behind the chief. There was no way his son was involved with this. Why would he be?

Still, a knot settled in his gut and grinded in a churning motion. First, Matthew hadn't been planning to leave for weeks, but then he'd made a sudden departure. No, there had to be another explanation.

CHAPTER 37

IAN STARED AT THE CEILING of the tent, his eyes searching the darkness, darting across the canvas in search of anything that didn't belong. His mind conjured up scurrying critters parading overhead and tried not to shudder. It was bad enough that he was in a sleeping bag and anything that wanted to could find its way through an opening and cozy up next to him, like creepy, poisonous insects. There was no chance he'd be closing his eyes tonight. The only way he'd get any sleep was if his body simply gave out on him. Really, the tent wasn't much of an upgrade from outside, only now Ian couldn't see what was going on around him.

Despite the constant drone of insects, he heard the crackling and popping of the fire. One of the three friends would be watching over it, but he knew their real interest was him and Kevin. They didn't trust them, and with good reason. But Kevin was the only one they really needed to worry about. Until Ian was back safely on Canadian soil, the three twentysomethings were his ticket out of this place.

Ian still didn't understand why Kevin had offered his tent to him, but he was certain it had to fit into the man's agenda somehow. It certainly wasn't out of the goodness of his heart or concern for Ian's welfare. It was what he was up to that remained a mystery. Maybe Ian should just go outside and see for himself what was going on.

He had crawled out of the sleeping bag and made it to the flap of the tent when Kevin pulled it back.

Kevin seemed surprised to see him up and paused in the opening. "You're awake?"

"I'm not sure how the hell I'm supposed to sleep."

Kevin laughed, and Ian recognized it for what it was—mockery.

"I'm just not tired."

"Yeah, sure, that's what it is."

"Listen, asshole, I don't care if you believe me." Ian brushed past Kevin. Assuming his full height, he breathed in deeply, appreciating the space around him. He hadn't realized how the confines of the tent had been suffocating him.

Ian turned to look at Kevin, and he had a smirk on his face.

"What?" Ian snapped.

"You. You're apparently this big bad killer but a little jungle scares the living shit out of you."

"It's called respect for my surroundings."

"Bullshit."

There was no point in carrying on with this meaningless banter. Suddenly, Ian's heart started pounding. There was a sinking feeling in the pit of his gut, the one that foretold bad news. Kevin was deflecting.

"What have you done?" Ian asked.

Kevin continued smirking like some sort of satanic doll.

"Did you…?" This couldn't be happening. Kevin wouldn't have killed them before they delivered on the City of Gold, would he? What benefit would there be in that?

Ian raced toward the fire, spotting the silhouette lying out on a blanket next to it. The form wasn't moving. Shouldn't it be poking the fire or sitting up or something?

Kevin pulled back on his shoulder, slowing Ian's forward momentum.

Ian stopped and faced him. "Let the fuck go of me."

"Or what?" Kevin did let go and shook his hands in mimicry as if he were trembling in fear.

As Ian got closer, he heard the snores. "You didn't kill him."

"And why would I do that?"

Ian studied Kevin's eyes in the limited light. "What were you doing out here?"

"You're on a need-to-know. And you don't need to know."

CHAPTER 38

THEY BROKE DOWN CAMP AT DAWN. Robyn's coffee was a tease at civilization in the jungle setting. At least she was generous enough to share with Matthew and Cal. Even Juan and Lewis were given some. Vincent's men, on the other hand, had forced her at gunpoint. Even then she'd hesitated, only conceding when Matthew intervened and convinced her the situation wasn't worth bloodshed.

But all this had been hours and at least five miles ago. They were pretty much on top of the mountains that had taunted them at the start of their journey. They were taking a break at the base of one of them.

"Cal? Update?" Matthew asked.

"According to this…" Cal studied the screen. "Well, it says we're here."

Matthew's eyes widened. "Here, as in where the tunnel appears to start?"

"Yeah. I mean, like, right here."

"All right, everyone, branch out. See if you spot an opening."

Cal and Robyn spread out, as did Juan and Lewis. Kevin paced around uselessly, and Ian stood still.

Matthew brushed past Ian. "Be careful of your steps," he warned the group. "We don't want the ground disappearing beneath our feet." He noticed the look Cal shot him and remembered his friend's dream. Maybe he shouldn't have phrased it that way.

Matthew moved some of the leaves around on the ground, brushing them to the side with his feet as he kept an eye out for any blood-sucking insects. He wasn't finding anything noteworthy.

He glanced around at the others, who seemed to be meeting with the same result.

After twenty minutes or so of investigating the area, Cal pulled out his camera and started taking shots.

"ARE YOU SERIOUS?" Ian didn't regret his words even when everyone stopped moving and the dark eyes of the black man fixed on him. He took him on at the airport and was more than willing to do so again.

"What is your problem?"

"What is my—" Ian paced two feet and stopped. Matthew's warning about being sucked into a sinkhole or some such thing stalled his movements. Of all the hazards that came with this place, now he imagined being swallowed by the earth.

"Yeah, that's what I said. What's. Your. Problem?" Cal was staring him down.

Ian narrowed his eyes in return. He was a damn killer, and before all this crap, he had been a damn good one. He used to be highly sought after. One bad employment decision and he'd been relegated to babysitting Indiana Jones. "What's my issue? My problem?" Ian elongated the word *problem*. "My issue is you." He pressed a fingertip into Cal's chest.

"Well, mine is you." Cal reciprocated by poking his finger at Ian's chest.

"You go around taking pictures like you're a damned tourist," Ian spat. "We're not here to take in the scenery."

"You're one to talk. You're such a chickenshit, you're not even moving. Are you afraid?"

Ian's fist connected with the sweet spot of Cal's jaw socket.

Cal's retaliating jab struck Ian in the gut, doubling him over. Cal grabbed his head, and Ian swore the guy was trying to tear it off. Through the lightheadedness, he heard Cal's friends telling him to stop, that it wasn't worth it.

Ian let his resistance fall a trace, just enough to deceive the black guy into thinking he was surrendering. When Cal's grip loosened and he straightened up, Ian charged him, slamming into his torso. Both men barreled across the landscape.

Hands pulled him back and more shouting made it through, but nothing was stopping Ian short of this guy's death.

As they jostled and fought for dominance, Ian twisted his ankle, and it proved to be just enough for his opponent to gain the upper hand.

The black guy, supercharged, his grip on him stronger, shoved Ian back in the direction of the mountain.

He anticipated meeting the rock with a wrenching blow. Instead, Ian watched helplessly as the distance grew between him and Cal. Ian was falling backward, *through* the mountain, into it. When he reached the ground, the wind gushed out of him.

What the hell just happened?

His mind tried to process it all. Their struggle and the final ram into the side of the mountain. A mountain that wasn't solid?

It was then that he felt movement. On his neck. On his face. Following it was an intense pain and then a burning sensation. He didn't dare move and was too paralyzed with fear to scream.

CHAPTER 39

EVERYTHING HAD HAPPENED SO QUICKLY Matthew hadn't had time to get involved, let alone intervene. He saw the agitation building in his friend, and when Ian had started pressing, he'd figured the physical confrontation was inevitable.

Matthew stood behind Cal now, both hands on his shoulders. Somehow he had managed to prevent him from going down with Ian.

Now they all stood there, looking at where Ian had fallen.

The briar patch of greenery and vines had broken to reveal an opening in the side of the mountain. There was darkness beyond the immediate couple of feet where the sun's light shone in.

Careful not to cut himself on a thistle vine, Matthew ducked down and aimed his flashlight into the hole.

Juan hustled forward, coming up beside him, while Robyn and the others hung back.

Ian was sprawled out on the floor not too far inside the cave. When the beam of light first caught him, Matthew thought his eyes were playing tricks on him, but there was movement all over the man. As he fixed the shaft of light on Ian, he realized it wasn't an illusion.

Furry caterpillars were wriggling all over him. A quick sweep of the light revealed that the cave was full of them.

"Smile." Cal must've snuck up behind Matthew. The shutter of his camera sounded as he took a photograph of Ian.

The scowl on Ian's face deepened, but Matthew sensed it was in response to more than having his picture taken. His eyes were open wide, and his jaw was rigid. The man seemed frozen by fear and in great pain.

"Burros." Juan made the sign of a cross on his chest and stood to his full height.

Lewis shimmied his body, moving like one of the caterpillars. "Jungle donkeys."

"What are jungle donkeys?" Robyn asked.

Juan stepped inside the cave, treading carefully, and swept the bugs off Ian with a handkerchief. "Come out. Now. Be careful."

Ian got up and hunched over, lower than necessary to clear the entrance, came into the light of day.

"Holy shit! Holy shit!" Ian was stomping his feet like a madman, and Matthew didn't blame him.

It seemed wherever the crawlies had made contact, his skin had turned a glowing red.

Lewis dumped some water onto the ground and scooped up some of the mud. He smeared it on the affected areas of Ian's flesh while Juan repeatedly made the sign of a cross.

"This will help with the sting," Lewis explained.

Ian managed to keep still long enough to be plastered with mud.

"You were lucky," Lewis said.

"Lucky?" Ian scoffed.

"Yes. It could have been much, much worse."

"Am I going to die?"

"What are jungle donkeys?" Robyn repeated her question.

Juan glanced at Robyn but spoke to Ian. "They are a type of caterpillar, as you can see, but they have poison sacs at the ends of their long hairs. They cause a burning sensation that—"

"It makes death feel like a welcome release." Ian attempted to massage his shoulder, an injury likely incurred from the fall, but he winced every time he made contact with his flesh.

"Yes, like that." Juan bobbed his head wildly, like one of those dolls people put in their cars.

"Aw, it looks like you're going to live after all." Cal smiled smugly and raised his camera again. "Say cheese."

"I'm going to kill you, you son of a bitch, I swear."

The two Bolivians held Ian back from throwing another punch.

Cal continued to add insult to injury. "At least you're good for something. I think you just found the road that leads to the City of Gold."

Chapter 40

THE PRINTS HAD COME BACK from Sophie's Accent. They weren't in the system, but when compared to personal items in her apartment, it was determined that they were hers. There was one lead, though, that needed to be followed up immediately.

Sophie Jones's employer, Edwin Briggs, had said that she was an exceptional real estate agent and one of his best up until recently. Her fixation on selling one particular property apparently had led to the neglect of all else. He'd said that he hated to say it given the fact she was missing, but if she didn't pull in a sale soon, he'd have to let her go.

Edwin said that the homeowners were vacationing for months in the Maldives so if any evidence was left in the house to support that Sophie was taken against her will, no one would have noticed as of yet.

Brody arranged to meet Edwin at the estate and when he pulled up, his mouth literally gaped open. To think that some people lived in such opulent luxury while the majority struggled paycheck to paycheck just reconfirmed for Detective Fuller that life wasn't fair.

The gated entrance and stone driveway of the Gracens' property set the tone for what awaited beyond. A gray brick, two-story structure stood regally on a professionally manicured lawn. The large boulders used in the landscaping design were aesthetically pleasing, but they must have cost a fortune. Brody never understood why people spent such exorbitant amounts. He summed it up as some people having more money than common sense.

Brody's requested backup sat in a squad car at the curve of the circular drive. Both it and Brody's department-issued sedan stuck out here. Such a residence begged for a Lamborghini or Porsche as an accent. For now, Edwin's Mercedes would have to suffice.

Before going in, Brody observed the shrubbery around the front of the house. Small trees that may have bloomed during the summer months were now wrapped in burlap cocoons. As his gaze went beyond the gardens and up the side of the brick, he spotted it right away. There was a security camera positioned beside a window shutter. For an untrained eye, it may have been hard to spot, but not for Brody.

"I got you, you bastard."

He'd call in for the footage from the security company, but first, he'd check out the interior of the house. He motioned for Edwin to punch in the security access code for the front door.

The stench of burned coffee assaulted him the moment the door opened and he stepped into the entry. With it, there was a faint sweet aroma—a baked good of some sort.

He followed his nose to a large chef's kitchen. On the counter was a cooling rack full of chocolate chip cookies. He lifted one and tapped it against the marble. It knocked back. Stale as hell. He let go of it, brushed his gloved hands together to rid them of the crumbs, and went to the coffee machine, which was the kind designed to turn off after a certain amount of time.

And there on the floor next to the counter was a red satchel and a cloth grocery bag. He went for the purse first, pulled out the wallet and confirmed it belonged to Sophie Jones. Inside the bag, he found a wrapper for premade cookie dough.

So what he knew for sure was that Sophie Jones had shown up, baked the cookies, and made coffee, probably all while waiting for her buyer. She'd had no idea she'd really been waiting for her abductor.

CHAPTER 41

NIGHT WOULD BE FALLING SOON, not that it mattered once they'd entered the cave. Darkness there wasn't dependent on the time of day. And it wasn't as if resting was an option now anyhow. The City of Paititi could be just steps away. How could any of them sleep?

Robyn ducked inside to get a clear picture for herself. Anything to serve as a reprieve from the level of testosterone suffocating her in the jungle. She wished Cal would drop the matter with Ian and focus on their mission. She understood why he hated the man. She did, too—for what he did to Sophie, for what he was putting them through, and for robbing the pure zeal and adventure from this expedition.

She let her eyes skim over the caterpillars. They were slithering away from the light and receding farther into the cave. If she didn't know better, she'd have described them as beautiful. The tunnel itself appeared to be manmade and ancient, with hewn stones lining the walls. The space where Ian had fallen was about ten feet by five feet.

She moved her flashlight to the right, and the beam of light revealed an opening. "There's another tunnel feeding out from here." It made complete sense that this would lead somewhere.

Matthew shuffled in beside her. "She's right."

She straightened up, her hands going to her hips. "You had to see it with your own eyes to believe it?"

"It's not that I didn't believe you."

"Uh-huh. Why is it that a man can never take a woman's word

for it?"

"No way in hell am I going back in there," Ian said from the cave opening. He was rubbing his neck, and the welts from where the caterpillars had burned his skin appeared to be tender. Shivers of pain ran through Robyn simply from looking at them.

Cal stood beside him. "The choice is yours. You come with us, or you spend the night out here alone."

"Yes, and if you stay out here, all by yourself, you'll be jaguar poop." Juan laughed.

Ian scowled. "This sucks."

Kevin brushed past him. "Well, whine all you want, Ian, but it's time to find the City of Gold."

As all the men advanced on her position, Robyn had two choices—go first or move to the side. After seeing what had happened to Ian, she wasn't eager to take the lead.

She gestured for Matthew to go ahead of her. "By all means, after you."

He gave her a knowing smile, and she instantly regretted her decision. Just because she was a tad apprehensive didn't mean he needed to acknowledge it.

Matthew put his hand to the wall as he moved forward. "This is definitely Incan in origin. Just the way the stones are fit together so tightly."

Robyn followed him. She touched the stone, too. To be here, where people hadn't walked for centuries, was more intense than words could describe. Her heart raced with both excitement and fear. Her stomach swirled with the possibilities. Had humankind really searched all this time in the wrong place? Were they actually on the doorstep of the City of Gold?

They entered the tunnel that branched off to the right. All of them had their flashlights out now. Since the entrance to the tunnel, none of them had seen any more caterpillars.

After about twenty feet, the tunnel turned left.

"If we're on the right path, shouldn't there be markings on the wall or something?" Kevin asked.

"The Incas never had a written language," Matthew answered.

"Yes, but what about drawings? It's possible we're not in the right place."

"Oh, we're in the right place all right. Besides it's not like they would have put up flashing neon lights to point out the path to Paititi." Matthew smirked at Robyn as they led the way together now. Cal was a few steps behind them, and the others came after him.

"I find it strange that the photos only showed what looked like one tunnel, though. This one snakes a bit," Cal said.

"You're sure we were in the right place according to the GPS?" Robyn asked Cal.

"Yes, Robyn."

"Maybe the pictures penetrated the ground farther down, then?" She wasn't totally convinced yet, either, with the discrepancy.

"Shouldn't there be booby traps? Wouldn't they have protected the city from people who may have stumbled upon it? You know, like Ian did," Kevin said.

Robyn glanced back and saw Ian give Kevin the finger. While she was amused by Kevin's sense of humor, and Ian's lack thereof, she realized Kevin had a made a valid point. Things shouldn't be this easy.

"How far did you say it was from the tunnel to where the crack in the mountain peak was, Cal?" she asked.

"Two miles."

They quickly came to a section where the tunnel forked, and this time, there was even a third path continuing straight ahead. Two miles could house a lot of danger, especially if they went the wrong way. No one could know what was ahead of them.

Robyn turned to Matthew. "Now what?"

HE LOVED HOW WHEN A decision was needed, Robyn immediately requested his input. Matthew loved to pretend he had all the answers, but out here, his choices were only best guesses.

His gut was telling him there was nothing wrong with the path they were on already, so why divert left or right when there was an option to continue straight? With the absence of any "booby traps," as Kevin had put it, Matthew was apprehensive, though.

While being placed on the spot to make a judgment call, an overwhelming sensation swept over him. To think that no one had been in this spot for hundreds of years gave him the sickly sense of trespassing, yet he beheld the surroundings in reverent awe. The excitement of being here was enough to turn his legs to tingling jelly and shoot adrenaline through his body and extremities.

He moved his flashlight right, then left, then back straight ahead. He bobbed his head in that direction. "Let's just keep going."

"Are you sure?" Robyn's dark eyes questioned him along with her words.

"You asked me to make a decision. I did. We go straight."

"All right."

They both took their next step at the same time.

The floor of the tunnel was dirt, and the walls themselves had a thick coating of earth on them, as well. The passage of time had been kind to the space overall and had left the rocks in good shape.

They carried on for at least ten minutes before reaching another fork. This time their only choices were left and right. Straight ahead was a dead end.

"You can't just pick straight this time, Matthew," Cal called out.

"Thanks for stating the obvious, buddy," Matthew replied. Sometimes he hated being the one to decide. But he'd assume responsibility for the outcome. He hated to admit that it was his idea to risk Sophie's life for this mission. He just had to hope it would all end well.

CHAPTER 42

DANIEL SET UP THE MEETING with Justin Scott for that afternoon. He was the son of an old friend, but as the years went on, their lives had taken them in different directions. Daniel hadn't seen Justin since his father's funeral ten years ago. Justin had been seventeen at the time.

Daniel scanned the Starbucks and spotted him in a sofa chair near the fireplace. Justin hadn't changed much since he was a kid, other than filling out.

Justin had a laptop balanced on his knees, and he was pecking away between furtive glances upward. He looked as if he'd suit the profession of an accountant more than a hardened investigator. Maybe it was why he hadn't lasted as a police detective. But Daniel didn't question the young man's gift to dig into areas of people's lives that they preferred remained secret. He also never doubted Justin's ability to net answers in a short period of time. The man was actually a genius, but as Matthew had advised Daniel do, the man was also controllable.

"Justin."

He looked up, pushed back his glasses, and flashed an awkward grin. "Yes, and you are Mr. Iverson."

"Daniel is fine." He rubbed his hands together and peered around. There was an empty chair next to Justin, and he sat down.

"Ah, I haven't been able to find anything out on Gideon—" Justin placed his laptop on the table in front of him and, in the process, knocked over his drink. "Oh, crap." He rushed to grab his computer, and he tucked it between him and the arm of the chair. At the same time, his other hand righted the cup.

Daniel jumped up, retrieved a bunch of napkins, and returned with them.

"Oh, I'm sorry. I'm such a klutz sometimes." Justin extended his hand for the napkins, but Daniel smiled and cleaned up the mess.

The kid really needed to work on his self-esteem. Here he was apologizing when it was his coffee spilled and his laptop.

Daniel pointed to the cup. "Would you like another one?"

"Ah, sure, if it's not too much trouble. A grande double-double with milk and sweetener." Justin maneuvered in the chair, angling himself on his left hip as he dug into his back pocket, presumably for a wallet.

"It's all right. I've got this." Daniel left before Justin straightened out.

Five minutes later, he returned with Justin's large coffee with two milk and two sweeteners and a black coffee for himself. He took a seat in his chair and faced Justin, briefly wondering how the kid had survived puberty, let alone made it to his late twenties.

"I'm sorry, Mr. Iver—Daniel."

The kid was still apologizing? It was for reasons like this that Canadians got the reputation for saying they were sorry for everything.

"Nothing to apologize for. Enjoy." Daniel took a sip of his coffee. "I need to talk to you about—"

"I knew it," Justin interrupted. "You do want an update. I don't have one for you yet. This Gideon Barnes is elusive as hell. I apologize for swearing."

Daniel waved his hand. "I actually have another job for you."

"Another? But I haven't finished this one. I haven't got any real answers yet."

Daniel wanted to say, *And you won't find any*, but he bit his tongue. As he prepared to present this kid with the new proposal, his heart bumped off course. *No police.* The warning had been clear, but the implication could have been that third parties were not to become involved. Maybe this was a bad idea. But as the hesitation struck, determination erased it. The anger he had experienced at seeing Sophie get slapped, at knowing she was being held hostage, pushed him forward.

"This project needs to be held in absolute confidence, as well. Can you guarantee me that?"

Justin scrunched up his nose as he pushed his glasses up again. "Yes, of course."

Daniel glanced around the coffee shop and was pleased it wasn't too crowded. Most people were taking their beverages to go, and those who remained were absorbed in their own worlds. "And you cannot involve the police, no matter what."

"Okay." Justin dragged out the word. "Does this involve something illegal?"

It was a tough question, and Daniel wasn't sure how to answer.

Justin pinched back the tab on the lid of his cup. "You know what, never mind. You were a friend of my father's."

"Yes." Daniel's eyes traced Justin's face.

"So, what is it, Daniel?"

Careful to speak at a low and inconspicuous volume, Daniel told him about Sophie, how he needed help in analyzing the videos, and that he needed a phone's location tracked. By the time he was finished, Justin was mostly pale with a splash of color high in his cheeks, as if he was going to be sick.

"Can you handle this, Justin? Like I said, I need absolute confidentiality."

Justin didn't respond right away but then slowly nodded.

"This is your chance to save a life. You're making the right decision." Daniel had overheard the police chief talking to William, but he wasn't going to tell Justin that the police were looking into the matter now, too. There was no sense in shaking him up. His father was prone to overreacting, and if that gave any indication about his son, he'd probably fret, thinking that he was interfering with a police matter. He didn't need Justin telling him to turn the videos into law enforcement. His conscience had questioned that enough already.

Daniel stood and put a hand on the kid's shoulder. "Your father would have been proud of you."

Justin's gaze glazed over.

Daniel felt a tad guilty over bringing up the kid's dead father, but it wasn't because the statement wasn't true. It was because his father would have been livid with Daniel for getting Justin involved with this.

CHAPTER 43

MATTHEW HAD CHOSEN TO GO right despite Robyn protesting that they go left. Splitting up was discussed as an option, with one of Vincent's men going with each group. Matthew thought it best they stick together. But after walking for at least forty minutes, they came to another crossroads. They could go left, right, or straight. They continued going straight.

After another thirty minutes, another fork presented the options of right or straight.

"This is ridiculous. We just keep walking and walking," Ian said.

Cal scowled at him. "It's not like we've been here before."

"I knew we should have gone left." Robyn crossed her arms.

"I'm not sure it would have mattered," Ian said.

"What do you mean?" Robyn shifted her focus to Ian.

Ian pointed to the ground. There were footprints in the dirt. *Their* footprints.

"Ah, son of a bitch," Kevin cried out.

Juan and Lewis started laughing.

Cal pulled out his camera. "We're right back to where we began."

This was entirely his fault, or at least Matthew was taking the blame. He was the one who headed up this expedition. His guilt was only offset by what Cal had said earlier: It's not like they had been here before. This was all as new to him just as it was to the others. How could he expect to have all the answers?

"Smile." Cal held up his camera.

"Cal, it's not a good—" The flash blinded Matthew and spotted his vision. But his eyes picked up a wink of light as if it had reflected off metal. He quickly scanned the area. Maybe he had imagined it?

"Would you just put that damn camera away," Ian said, "before I make you put it away?"

"You saw how that worked earlier. You can't make me do much of anything." Cal was back in Ian's face, literally mere inches away, the camera wedged between their torsos.

"For heaven's sake will you just cut out the macho bullshit? It's getting old," Robyn said.

Matthew's vision was coming back, but orbs of light were popping up here and there, as he blinked. Even at the risk of reverting the progress, he couldn't get his mind off what he swore he saw. "Cal."

"What do you want, Matt? I'm getting ready to kick this guy's ass again."

"Take my picture."

"Oh my god, Matt." Maybe the tight quarters were getting to Robyn, and claustrophobia was wreaking havoc on her otherwise easygoing personality.

"Just one more." Matthew faced her when he spoke.

Robyn drank from her canteen.

"Fine." Cal snapped the picture.

The flash went off again, but Matthew was ready for it. He averted his eyes from the light and caught what he'd seen before. "Again. Just one more."

Cal appeased him, and this time, Matthew's gaze was in the perfect direction. He took a few steps toward it. Everyone was quiet, their eyes on him.

He explained. "The camera flash reflected off—" He ran his hand along the stone wall, clearing the dirt. He stopped when his fingers felt a carved relief.

Robyn hurried up behind him, positioning her flashlight's beam to see it clearly. "It's gold. And it's the symbol of their sun god. It looks like a seal or something."

"It does." Matthew didn't take his eyes off it. This was more confirmation that they were on the right track. He ran his hand over it, and as his fingers dipped into its ridges, the emblem pushed inward.

"What—"

Matthew held his finger to his lips to silence Robyn. He didn't know what he expected to hear, but there wasn't any sound in the tunnel except for their breathing. "All right, spread out and see if you can find more of them."

They split up, a few going right, others going left. Cal stuck with him.

"There's one in here," Robyn called out from the left path.

"Push it," Matthew responded.

Again, it was unspoken but all of them remained quiet, assuming that they'd hear something. Yet there was only silence.

Matthew urged them to continue. "Keep looking."

"I found one. I'm pushing it," Cal said.

Again, no sound.

"What are we missing?" Robyn called out.

Matthew noticed her voice was coming closer.

They all met back in front of the wall where the path forked left and right.

"Uh, guys…"

They all turned toward Ian. Matthew expected he was going to complain.

"I think I found—" He bent down and rubbed away dirt from a spot on the floor. It was beneath the first emblem they had found.

"It's the fourth." Robyn dropped to her knees. "Why the floor?"

Matthew knew the answer before she asked. "Remember the legend about Cápac?"

Robyn smiled. "He was supposed to sink the golden staff into the ground. You're thinking this has something to do with that?" She didn't wait for a response and pushed on the emblem. "It's not moving."

"Let me try." Ian hunched next to Robyn, brushing her hands

aside. "I can't get it to budge, either," Ian said.

"Wow, really?" Robyn wiped her hands together to clear the dirt.

"Stand up." Kevin hoisted her up by the arm and aimed his gun at her head.

Ian straightened and followed suit by pulling out his weapon.

"What the hell is going on?" Matthew approached Kevin and slowly drew his own firearm.

Cal and the Bolivians did, too. Matthew noticed how Ian had maneuvered closer to Kevin, using him for shelter.

"It's not looking like the odds are in your favor, Kevin. Don't be stupid."

"You, don't be stupid. Feel anything different about your guns perhaps? Like the fact they aren't loaded?" Kevin laughed. "While you were all sleeping last night, I took all your bullets. Well, everyone's but Ian's. He and I, we are kind of on the same team."

They were *all* sleeping? Matthew turned to Cal.

"I'm sorry, Matthew, I must have nodded off," Cal said.

Matthew returned his gun to its holster and took a deep breath. His mind picking up on Kevin's wording "kind of." Matthew translated that to mean Ian was going to be a dead man by the end of this, just like the rest of them. He swallowed roughly. He had promised his dad they'd talk when he got back. "Listen, maybe we're overreacting a bit? It's tight down here. There's probably less oxygen."

"That's why you have to get us out of here. Now." Kevin nudged his gun against Robyn's head.

It was the movement, though, that sparked the solution. Matthew was four feet from the emblem in the floor. "I have an idea, but I need you to trust me."

Kevin nodded.

With each step Matthew took forward, Kevin and Ian stepped back, taking Robyn with them.

Matthew drew his gun again and pressed the muzzle down on the emblem. Nothing happened. Maybe he had given his idea too much merit. He was just thinking that if pressure was centralized over the emblem, as it would be with a staff, it might work. He tried again with as much force as he could muster. Like the first attempt, the emblem didn't budge, but then it began to give way. "It's work—"

The mountain shook, and Matthew, Cal, and Robyn looked at one another.

Ian gripped the wall. "There's a reason this place should have stayed hidden."

The rumbles intensified, quaking the ground and making their footing unsure.

"What's going on?" Kevin leaned against the wall, his gun no longer aimed at Robyn's head but it was aimed on them as a group.

It was then that Matthew noticed that the wall in front of them was lowering into the ground.

CHAPTER 44

THEY FLASHED THEIR LIGHTS INTO the space where the wall had receded into the ground. It was another tunnel with stone brick walls and a dirt floor. But the ground wasn't as smooth.

"What the hell are we waiting for?" Kevin pushed through the group.

Matthew tried to reach him, to stop him, to pull him back, but he flew past.

Kevin's scream was nightmarish—and short. There was no way to save him. His body spasmed against the long spear that skewered his center, its tip sticking out of his throat. The twitching lasted long enough for Matthew's eyes to meet Kevin's and witness the light extinguish from them.

Robyn and Cal turned away. Matthew wanted to, but he remained fixed on Kevin.

"God, what the hell just happened?" Ian's hands alternated between cupping his head and gesturing toward Kevin's body. "Seriously, what the hell?" Ian came to within a few feet of Matthew.

Matthew glanced at the Bolivians, who looked as shocked as Robyn and Cal, but not to the extent that Ian was.

"Simple answer. A trap," Matthew said.

"No shit, Sherlock. I mean, what the hell." Ian thrust out his arm, pointing at Kevin.

"When the Spanish conquistadors came after the Incas, they made these types of traps to swallow man and horse," Matthew answered.

"The stupid idiot had to bring up booby traps. What, aren't you going to take his picture?" Ian verbally jabbed Cal, who didn't give him the satisfaction of acknowledgment.

Beyond Kevin, the tunnel's safety fell into question. Matthew wagered more traps would be staggered without a predictable layout. One false step and someone else could die.

Matthew leaned over the hole, thinking about retrieving Kevin's gun, but he couldn't see it. The weapon must have fallen to the bottom of the pit. It would have to be left behind.

Straightening up, a subtle breeze swept across Matthew's skin. But it wasn't coming from the opened tunnel ahead of them. It was hitting the right side of his neck.

He took off down the tunnel on the right.

"Matthew?" Robyn followed him, as did the others.

"I feel a draft. Something else must have opened up when this wall did. We never would have heard it, either."

"You think it's another tunnel?" Cal asked.

"I don't know," Matthew said. He reached the point where the tunnel took another sharp turn to the right and spotted a rectangular opening in the wall. It hadn't been there before the other wall had lowered into the floor. He shone a light inside and saw a rope. He reached in and yanked on it.

Another tunnel opened in front of them with fewer dramatics than the other had.

"I don't have to remind any of you what happened the last time someone went running ahead." Matthew received a smug glare from Robyn for his trouble.

"I don't think I'll ever forget," Robyn lamented.

"I might need counseling," Cal added.

Their flashlight beams showed nothing immediately dangerous. Again, the floor was dirt and the walls were made of the same brickwork.

"I'll go in first," Matthew said.

Robyn touched his arm, as if to stop him.

"I'll be fine," he said softly. It was another promise he hoped he could keep. If he were a religious man, this would have been another good opportunity to pray. Instead, he took his first step inside, bracing himself—for the floor to fall out from beneath him, for the walls to shoot poisonous darts, for anything, really. But nothing happened. "Looks good."

Robyn came in next, then Cal, followed by the Bolivians with Ian at their flanks.

Cal let out a deep breath and Matthew glanced back at him.

They took each step slowly, deliberately. But not precisely enough, Matthew realized, when about twenty feet in, the floor shifted under his feet and his hands shot out to the walls to steady himself.

"What was that?" Ian asked.

The mountain shook again, and Matthew spun, realizing what it meant.

"The door! We have to get to—" He plowed into the others, urging them to get out, but it was too late.

Their way out was sealed shut. No doubt it was masterful engineering and design that was responsible for putting the pressure switch at the location it had been placed.

Matthew went back to where he had inadvertently activated the switch. He remembered the feeling of it under his boot. Maybe if he could push it again, the door would reopen.

But no such luck. He found the switch—a rectangular button about five inches long by three inches wide. It was still depressed, sunken into the ground. There'd be no reversing what had happened.

Ian slammed his palms against the stone blockade. "Now we're going to die in here."

Matthew was thinking the exact same thing but phrased it less dramatically and placed a positive spin on their predicament. "Well, there's no turning back now."

"Yeah," Cal said. "Literally."

CHAPTER 45

DANIEL'S CELL PHONE RANG AND jarred him, but it wasn't because he was sleeping. A third video had come in somewhere around one in the morning. He glanced at the clock on his desk before answering his cell phone. It was now five. Not that it seemed to matter. The hours had blurred together ever since all this had begun.

He massaged his forehead as he answered. "Hello."

"Daniel?"

"Yes, Justin. Who else would it be?" Daniel shook his head as if the kid could witness the mockery.

"You did tell me to call you any time of day—morning, noon, or night. Right?"

"Yes." Maybe it was the combined effects of little rest and redundancies, but Daniel's mood was sour. "What is it?"

There was a pause on the other end, as if Justin was taken aback by Daniel's cool reaction.

"I was able to isolate the man's face in the photograph. I haven't gotten any further than that, but I—"

"Justin, send the picture over."

"It should be flying to you through cyberspace as we speak." Justin paused to chuckle and cleared his throat when he realized Daniel wasn't amused. "I just thought maybe if you saw the man's face, there might be a chance you'd recognize him."

Daniel opened his e-mail program and clicked SEND/RECEIVE ALL FOLDERS. He wasn't waiting a second longer than necessary.

E-mails filtered into his in-box, including spam, but it was easy to spot the one from Justin. The subject was Important Information.

Justin was still droning on when Daniel double-clicked to open the message.

"...Liam Neeson," the kid said.

The name seemed to come out of the blue, but when Daniel opened the attachment, he understood the correlation. He could have sworn he was looking at a photograph of the actor himself.

"What do you think?" Justin asked. "Have you seen—"

"Assuming this isn't the guy from the movies—"

"Yeah, see? I told you. He looks a lot like him."

"What about his identity?"

"Sadly, I will need more than a picture to determine that."

"All right. And what about identifying the lights outside the window?" Daniel inquired. "Are we anywhere with that?"

"Not yet." The bit of confidence that had rung through Justin's voice at isolating the man's face had disappeared.

"And the GPS on the phone?"

"No luck yet."

Daniel hesitated to forward Justin the latest video. Maybe he shouldn't have dragged the kid into this after all. What if the police found out that Daniel had been in possession of these videos all this time? He shook the notion aside. Surely any well-intentioned cop would understand following the directive of a killer.

"I got another video," Daniel said.

"Send it over, and I'll get to work on it right away."

"Will do."

"And Mr. Iver—Daniel?"

"Yeah, kid?" he said with a sigh.

"It sounds like you could use some sleep."

"I'm pretty certain you're right about that." At the admission, his body sagged a little deeper into the chair and his eyelids grew heavier. "'Night."

He ended the call and exchanged the chair for his bed. There were many things to be done around the house, but they'd have to wait.

As soon as he shut his eyes, the images from the videos appeared again. But this time it didn't take long for them to disappear from his consciousness as he drifted into a deep sleep.

CHAPTER 46

ROBYN WAS DOING HER BEST to keep pace with Matthew. Cal was behind her. They were going on twenty-four hours. Her watch read 6:10, the exact time they had left camp yesterday morning. She was the type of person who thrived on eight to ten hours of sleep a night. Her eyelids were gritty like sandpaper, but there was too much going on for her to sleep now. With Kevin having succumbed to the spear trap, it was enough to keep her eyes open and her legs moving. It confirmed they were the first ones here since the Incas had built the tunnel system.

Their flashlights revealed nothing ahead but more tunnel.

"This is feeling too easy again," she said.

Her comment received moans from the men.

"You know what happens whenever people say things like that, right? The opposite comes at them." It was Cal giving her the lesson, but all she did was look back at him and smile in response. "Anyone else getting tired?" he asked.

"God, yes," Matthew said.

Robyn looked forward again and ran right into Matthew's back.

Her body formed to his, and her cheeks heated. "Maybe you could warn a girl the next time you decide to just stop moving."

Matthew smirked over a shoulder. "And why would I do that?"

She narrowed her eyes, but she couldn't fight what she was feeling. She was too tired to play mad, and he would see through the pretense anyway. Even in the dim light, fire sparked between them.

"Hey, lovebirds, let's get to the City of Gold, shall we?" Ian called out from the very back of the line. Ever since he'd realized he was armed and none of them were, it seemed as though the status quo returned to his favor, and it had gone to his head.

"We're not lovebirds," she voiced.

"I don't really give a shit. Let's get this over with."

She really disliked that man. If it wasn't enough that he had kidnapped their friend and was responsible for this expedited mission to Bolivia, now he was prying into even more personal territory.

Robyn brushed past Matthew, and he yanked back on her arm.

Two small spears shot out of the walls, missing her by the fraction of an inch.

"Holy shit!" Robyn cried out.

He pulled her to him. It seemed that he realized how close they were at the same moment she did, and he released his hold on her.

"More traps," Matthew said.

"This means we are on the right path." Any tiredness that had threatened to claim her washed away with the realization.

"What did you do?" Cal asked, pushing between her and Matthew.

"All I did was take a step," Robyn said.

"There must be more pressure switches." Matthew took off his backpack and tossed it onto the floor in front of them.

Numerous spears shot out of the walls, heading from left to right, right to left.

"Here. Give me your pack." He turned to her. She was already working on getting it off.

When she did, he tossed hers a bit farther than he had his and more deadly spears fired from the stone bricks. Then he took Cal's pack and repeated the process. It happened again.

Next was Juan's pack, but when it landed past Cal's nothing shot from the walls.

"We must have made it to the end of the gauntlet," Robyn said.

"Just to be sure. One more." Matthew pitched Lewis's bag and it too met with no reaction. "All right, I think we're safe to go."

He took a step, and Robyn took his hand and squeezed. She couldn't lose him like this. He nodded as if he had received her silent message to be careful.

He'd just made it to Cal's pack when he said, "It's safe. Come on."

The rest followed his lead, Robyn first, then the others.

They all reclaimed their packs, careful to keep to the area where they had landed to avoid setting off any more flying spears.

With all of them geared up again, they proceeded for about ten feet before the ground swallowed them whole.

CHAPTER 47

WILLIAM HAD MADE IT INTO the office by eight, but again, his mind wandered from his responsibilities. He was starting to bear the guilt of being what the masses accused politicians of being: paid suits executing their personal agendas from behind a podium.

What the public failed to understand, though, was what it took to keep a city running, to keep everything moving along smoothly. They weren't aware of the long hours sacrificed at the expense of a personal life. Maybe if he had spent more time caring for such things, he and Matthew would have a better relationship. So in a way he was due some time to concern himself with other matters.

Even though the house was sufficient with its twenty-six thousand square feet, when his boy was home, the walls felt as if they constricted and pressed them together. It was as if a stranger were residing in his house, roaming the halls, eating breakfast and dinner at his table. And in essence, that's what his son was to him—a stranger, an enigma. In response, William's tendency was to flee and pour himself more heavily into the obligations of his mayoral position.

But to have the police chief approach him as if Matthew were involved in a crime, or had knowledge of a crime, was an insult. Matthew was his blood and, thereby, incapable of such things. And to harm a friend? There was no way Matthew possessed the ability to hurt anyone physically, let alone someone he considered a friend.

William tried numerous times to reach Matthew on his cell

phone without luck. Each of the five attempts resulted in him being sent straight to voice mail. Defeated, he settled for leaving a sternly worded message.

While he might assign innocence to his son, he demanded an explanation. Having the police chief show up at his house was enough to start the rumor mills rolling and swirl the consternation in his gut. The most important things to a politician were reputation and image. He didn't need his name associated with a police investigation and, as his predecessor had, have it smeared across page one of the *Toronto Star*.

His phone buzzed. It was Ashlynn.

"Mr. Connor, I made that connection that you had asked for."

"Patch them through."

"Yes, sir."

A moment later, he was connected with a man named Marshall Abbott. He was the head of the archaeological dig in Rome.

"Mr. Abbott, this is William Connor. I am the mayor of Toronto." He paused, expecting the man to respond in some manner. Instead, he was met with silence. "I'm trying to reach my son, Matthew, in regards to an urgent family matter." Really, that wasn't much of a stretch.

"Mr. Connor, you said?"

"Yes." William adjusted his tie and moved around some items on his desk.

"And you said Matthew was your son?"

"Yes." William was quickly losing his patience.

"Well, there's not a Matthew on this dig. Are you sure you have the right one?"

"Rome, Italy, correct? In search of lost Roman roads?"

"Yes."

William didn't appreciate the derision that echoed back at him. "Well, you must be mistaken. My son headed out there three days ago."

"And I tell you for a fact that he's not here."

William's neck tingled and his skin heated.

Mr. Abbott continued. "We're just getting organized. It's

possible he'll be coming with the rest of the team in a few months, though I highly doubt it. I review every applicant and I have a pristine memory, and he doesn't sound familiar."

"You know, from memory, after looking at a long list of archaeologists, that there's not a single Matthew?" Mr. Abbott was obviously delirious.

"No Matthew. No Matthew Connor."

William was being beyond diplomatic. Until now. He slammed down the receiver, the sound so loud and sharp he may have cracked the plastic. Not that he cared enough to look.

Where the hell was Matthew?

It was as if William was living someone else's life right now. A scandal was being born and taking its first breath. He had to suffocate it before it caused real damage.

He picked up the phone again and dialed the number he had found for Justin Scott. There was no need to get Ashlynn involved any more that he already had.

"Good day, Justin Scott speaking."

He plastered on a huge smile before he spoke. "This is William Connor."

"Oh, Mr. Connor. I was speaking with—"

"Yes, and that's fine."

"You're not calling about Gideon Barnes?"

Hearing the name poured more salt on his proverbial wound. It pained him to answer. "No, I'm not."

When Justin continued, his tone was lighter. "All right, then, whatever you would like, Mr. Connor?"

"I need you to locate my son."

His request was met with silence, and William imagined Justin thinking, *You don't know where your son is?* He gave it another few seconds. "Are you there?"

"Yes, yes, of course. I'm sorry. You were saying that you need help finding Matthew?"

"*Locating* Matthew." *Finding* made it sound too much like he was lost, and that implication was worse.

"Okay."

"I believe there is a way to track a phone?"

"Yes."

William chose to disregard the lack of conviction that seeped from the single-worded answer. He gave him Matthew's number. "You got that?"

"Yes, I—"

"Good. Call me the minute you know."

"I will."

The conversation ended more favorably than the one before it had, but William's unease continued to mount. What the hell was going on? How did things get so out of hand that his own son was missing? He wasn't sure whether he should be angry or worried.

Chapter 48

THE GROUND GAVE WAY SO suddenly that Matthew didn't have a chance to brace himself. He doubted any of them could have prepared for the fall.

Robyn's scream and those of the others echoed as they continued to drop. The strobes of their flashlights gave off the only illumination. Without them, it would be pitch-black.

Matthew's stomach heaved, the weightlessness making him lightheaded. A wet coolness enveloped him then, but he didn't stop falling.

Water? Were they were cascading down a waterfall? The sound was thunderous.

He looked down, angling to see beneath him, but it was shrouded in darkness.

Matthew's speed picked up as gravity propelled him like a fired bullet. His life flashed before his eyes, and with it, his regrets. He should have kissed Robyn before he made his way through the tunnel.

"It's a laaaagoooooonn—" Cal's last word was elongated, but then cut short as his friend must have plunged beneath the surface.

Matthew braced for impact, and when his body submerged, it felt like a thousand spikes jabbing through him. The water was ice cold against his hot skin. To say it stole his breath wasn't an exaggeration. His heart hammered in his chest, its beat an irregular rhythm.

It seemed like he was diving down quite a long way, and he

stretched out his legs in an effort to reach the bottom. His feet met with nothing but more water.

With his forward momentum now slowing, he managed to regain control of his legs and kicked in steady, even strokes. The exertion made his chest tighten even more, making its demands for oxygen known, yet he had no way of satisfying its pleas. The bag on his back felt like a stone weight, but he dared not break free unless absolutely necessary. He pushed on, kicking and kicking. Just when he didn't think he had any more in him, he broke the surface, heaving for air.

Cal burst up beside him. "You all right?"

"Yeah, I think so… Yeah."

Cal swam to the edge of the lagoon where he hoisted himself out of the water, took off his backpack, and started rummaging through it. He pulled out his camera.

"Aw, will this mean no more photographs?" Ian lifted himself up onto the land near Cal. "What a shame."

Cal took the time to glare at him but didn't say anything. Matthew was surprised at his restraint because, if he were Cal, he would have decked Ian—again.

Matthew raised himself out of the water around the same time Robyn and the Bolivians did. His backpack was heavier than before and threatened to topple him over. He took it off, set it on the ground beside him.

They were in some kind of tropical labyrinth stories beneath the ground. There was a crevice above them, and the morning sky showed through.

The land mass was at least the size of an American football field, the lagoon the size of an Olympic swimming pool.

Looking up, beyond the waterfall they'd come down on, were shadows and darkness.

Around them, the cavern walls were lush and alive with dense growth. Flowers came in a spectrum of color, shapes, and sizes, and the fragrances from the assorted flora overwhelmed Matthew's sinuses.

Closer to the lagoon, the grass was shorter than the five or six feet it was elsewhere. Leaves on some of the plants were larger than the span of his two hands spread out thumb to thumb.

Brown clay, about five feet wide, lined the perimeter of the lagoon, begging to be followed.

"This is unbelievable. Are you seeing this, Matt?" Robyn came up next to him.

The question was rhetorical, but he smiled at her and nodded.

"I still don't see any gold." Ian had pulled off his shirt and was wringing it out.

Cal was perched on a rock, grieving over his camera. "It's destroyed. No doubt the memory card's ruined, too."

"Shouldn't that thing be waterproof?" Robyn asked.

"The camera? Well, it's water *resistant* anyway. Or was…"

"What about the GPS tracker?" Matthew asked.

"What about it?" Cal met his eyes and held contact briefly before going into his bag for the tracker. He pushed a button on gadget. "It seems to be working." Then he muttered, "Figures."

"Where are we in relation to the peak of the mountain? Are we there?"

"We sure as hell better not be. There's no damn City of Gold here." Ian chimed in, but Matthew and Cal gave no indication they heard him. Ignoring him was becoming the common thing to do. Maybe if they did it enough he'd disappear. Unfortunately, that was just wishful thinking.

Cal consulted the screen on the unit and let out a deep breath. "According to this, we're close, but we want to be about a mile northeast."

Matthew clapped his hands together. "Good, so we're still on track."

"What the hell is it with you guys and all the positivity?" Ian hissed, incredulous. "Kevin was killed by some ancient booby trap—not that I really care—and then we get confined to a tunnel where spears shot out of a wall at us. And, then, just because we're special, the ground opened up, sending us for a ride down a waterfall." He scoffed. "And finally, we land in a damn lagoon that's cold enough to freeze the nuts off a brass monkey. But here you are, all 'oh, we're still on track.' Your optimism is disgusting."

"I'll tell you what's disgusting," Matthew said, walking toward the man. "Your attitude." Ian had him by a couple of inches, but as fired up as Matthew was, he was ready to take him.

"My attitude?" He mocked laughing. "You probably believe in fairies, the way you like to see everything through rose-colored glasses. We're in the middle of a damn jungle"—he gestured upward—"underneath a mountain with no way out. It's not like we can scale these walls." Then he pointed to the blackness above them. "Or swim up the falls to reach where we were. And even if that were possible, we'd be stuck with nowhere to go, anyway. Excuse me if I can't be positive." Ian stepped back a few feet from Matthew and pulled his still-wet shirt back on, a scowl etched on his mouth.

Matthew understood Ian's point. He really did. In light of that quick recap, maybe he was ridiculous for holding on to any optimism. But there was a driving force inside of him that told him this was far from over, and that in the end, it would all be worth the effort.

Robyn came up behind him and touched his arm. "What now, Matt?"

He shook his head. "I don't know."

Matthew caught Ian's glance.

"It's obviously a new day," Robyn started. "We've been on the go for twenty-four hours, or the better part thereof. I'm sure I speak for everyone when I say we could use a little rest."

"Oh yes." Juan waved his hand in the air.

"Even just a couple hours," Lewis added.

As Matthew assessed them, he realized the validity of the request. They had no idea what lie ahead or how long the journey would take.

Ian was sitting on a rock, cupping his bent neck. Cal let the GPS dangle from his hand. Robyn's eyes were puffy, and Juan and Lewis were already on the ground.

Matthew's eyelids grew heavy, too. "All right. We need to build a fire, though, just in case wildlife can get in here."

"I'll do it," Juan volunteered. He had a makeshift fire pit built and a fire going in a few minutes. He and Lewis offered to take turns watching it.

"All right, but let's only rest for a few hours. Then we're on the move."

"Amen." Robyn found a spot on the ground and lay down, using her rolled-up sleeping bag as a pillow. She didn't seem to care that it was soaking wet.

Matthew settled on a patch of grass next to the clay, lay down, and stretched out. But his eyes didn't shut. He took in the cavern walls, his mind firmly on the City of Gold. They were so close. This wasn't the time for sleeping. But just as quickly as the thought entered his mind, his eyes fell shut.

CHAPTER 49

ANOTHER DAY OF WAKING UP in a stranger's bedroom took Sophie from feeling like a caged animal to feeling like a criminal awaiting a death sentence. Despite this, every morning she opened her eyes, she held hope in her heart that today she'd be released. Only, every day that hope was squashed, her faith revisited and questioned. She contemplated how her life had taken such a cruel twist of fate. How days ago her chief concern had been losing her job.

Even worse than losing her life was the distinct possibility she would live out her final days here—captive. While they no longer forced her to wear a gag, she had received their message clearly. Any effort to escape would result in her death and that of anyone who tried to help her. This threat was the only thing preventing her from screaming at the top of her lungs.

Last night, the man guarding her door recorded another video. And this time she was fortunate enough not to be slapped by Veronica.

Sophie hoped she had managed to get some clues out as to her whereabouts this time. When the man had come close enough to her, she had swung out her legs. He had reacted as she'd intended by swerving his body to the left. The camera would have—or should have—followed that arc. If it had, then it would have caught a snippet of the CN Tower.

Her memories halted there as she heard the condo's door open and close. High heels clicked across the floor and stopped outside the door. Sophie could hear every word being spoken.

"THE IDIOT ISN'T PICKING UP his phone." Veronica studied the dazed expression on Don's face.

Little could bring her comfort right now. Kevin being in the middle of a jungle was no excuse for not being accessible. He was equipped with a satellite phone and he was supposed to check in midway through the week, and they had left four days ago. She should have heard from him last night and when she hadn't, she tried him—despite hating playing the role of babysitter.

She even included her dislike of such things in the speech she gave to new recruits. They were responsible for making things happen. She wasn't going to hold their hands and coddle them. She wasn't a mother for a reason. Still, circumstances placed her in the position where she had to do just that sometimes. If she didn't step in when necessary, nothing would get done.

But for the amount she paid these men, it was ludicrous and unacceptable. Even Kevin, who she considered one of her best, had disappointed her. There was no way she'd accept that her standards were too high. She adhered to them herself.

"Maybe he's not in a position to answer?" Don suggested.

"Not in a position to…" She paced a few feet, made a circle, and came back to Don. "If he's not answering, he better be dead."

She witnessed the flash in Don's eyes. He was thinking it was entirely feasible that Kevin was dead. She refused to resign herself to that possibility. Kevin was too good to die. Surely there was another reason she was unable to reach him.

CHAPTER 50

MATTHEW OPENED HIS EYES TO find Robyn bent over him. He felt like his eyes had just closed. His head was groggy, and he instantly regretted making the decision to rest. He wasn't a person who took naps. Whenever he had tried, he only woke up moody, unless he was sick. And even though this wasn't a nap per se, on the flip side of staying up for twenty-four hours, it might as well have been. He should have forgone sleep and investigated the immediate area, but his body had given in, so exhausted that he'd found comfort in the clay and grass.

He sat up and tried to get his eyes to focus on his watch. Noon.

"Come on, Matt," she said. "We should get moving."

How was she so awake? He didn't smell coffee in the air.

He had just fallen into a dream before he'd woken, too. His eyes widened when he realized the carnal nature of it and the identity of his partner. He turned away and rose to his feet.

"Why aren't you looking at me when I'm talking to you?" Robyn demanded.

"I am… What do you mean?" He was sputtering.

"Never mind. Matt, we found a cave. Everyone's over there."

"Where?"

Robyn hoofed it to the far end of the cavern. They had cleared the grass into a path, and Matthew saw the entrance to the cave before they were on top of it. Their bags were outside the door, including his.

"Does it seem to go anywhere?" He glanced at Cal, Juan, Lewis, and Ian, who were standing there.

"It goes somewhere anyway." Robyn shrugged and laughed as she put her pack on. "It looks like the other tunnels. Stone walls. Dirt floor. We haven't run into any spears shooting out of walls yet, but we thought we should get you before we went too far."

"Ya think?" Matthew snapped. He was actually pretty miffed the choice was even considered and not an automatic response. Yeah, moodiness was a definite reason he should be banned from sleeping in any interval less than eight hours.

He stepped inside and flashed his light down the tunnel. "It goes on an upward angle?"

"Yes." She followed him but then moved ahead of him.

Cal brushed by the two of them, but just barely given his broad shoulders and backpack. "According to the GPS, it's heading the right direction."

"What's this?" Ian asked. He had remained in the cavern with the Bolivians. "It looks like another gold emblem."

"No!" Matthew moved as fast as his sleepy legs would take him, which wasn't very fast. It was as if his legs were bogged down in quicksand.

Ian must have pushed the emblem because a door was sealing the cave.

"Hurry," Matthew cried as he grabbed Robyn's arm while she reached out for Cal. The three of them were a mess of arms and legs, trying to scurry quickly enough to escape the tunnel. But the door was coming down at a swift pace.

They were four feet away, and there was a gap of two feet high between the base of the door and ground.

"Go, Matt!" Robyn pulled free of him and retreated.

"I'm not leaving you."

"Go!"

They held eye contact, his gaze taking her in as she did him. She put her hands on his chest and shoved him forward. "Please, Matt. You can save us if you get out of here."

He caressed her cheek and kissed her forehead.

The gap was a foot high.

He dropped to the ground and slipped underneath the door.

The stone licked his body, but he arrived on the other side in one piece. He shot to his feet and pounded his fists on the door. "I will get you out of there!"

CHAPTER 51

BRODY FELT AS LUCKY AS a gambler at his first roulette table. Beginner's luck was responsible in the gambler's case, but skill and deduction paired to yield results for Brody now.

The camera at the mansion was set up in the ideal location. Just small enough and far enough out of reach that even if it was noticed it would be near impossible to disable.

Brody was in Bob Lambert's office. He was their technological go-to guy.

Obtaining the video from the security company ceased being a hassle when he explained that a woman was abducted from the house. Pretending that he was the homeowner may have moved things along faster, too.

"All right, what are we seeing?" Brody swung the swivel chair around and sat down, straddling it backward.

In front of him was a sixty-inch monitor. On it, the video was paused.

Bob was next to him chewing on a straw. He had recently decided to quit smoking, but that was like a fat man saying he'd quit food.

The sound of the sucking and chomping was just too much.

Brody's eyes shot to Bob's mouth. "Maybe you should pick up smoking again." He wasn't normally the type to encourage the habit, but it seemed to make the man happy, so who was he to argue?

Bob withdrew the straw, dragging it through his clenched teeth. "Are you kidding me? I haven't had a cigarette since last night."

"Last night? Wow," Brody mocked him.

"That's right. It's been fourteen hours"—he consulted the bottom right-hand corner of the screen—"twenty-three minutes. Somewhere in there anyway. I don't have the second count." He faced Brody with pride on his face.

"Hmm."

"Hey, it might not sound like much, but it's a start."

Brody's gaze fell to Bob's shirt pocket. Something rectangular bulged out about a half an inch. He reached for the man's pocket and was slapped.

"Hey now. That's a man's personal space."

"You know, you'd have a better chance of quitting if you didn't have them on you all the time."

"It's to prove the strength of my willpower. They are there and I'm not smoking them."

"Uh-huh."

"Don't say that like you don't believe me, Fuller." Bob shook his head, grumbled something, and hit "play" to start the video.

Brody smirked and turned his attention to the screen. It was nighttime, but the Gracens' landscaping bathed the monstrosity of a home in light, including the front walk and the curve of the driveway.

The bottom of the screen was time-stamped 8:10.

Headlights came into view. It was Sophie's Accent. The car lights went out, and Sophie walked around the front of the vehicle toward the front door. She was carrying a satchel—the one he had found in the kitchen—over her shoulder and the cloth grocery bag dangled from her hand.

Sophie let herself inside without any delays. She was confident and standing tall. She didn't give any fleeting looks over her shoulder or seem to sense any danger.

With her out of the camera's view, nothing was going on in the frame.

"Forward. Slowly," Brody directed Bob.

Then a man entered the feed.

"Stop. Go back a bit."

He entered the screen from the right, and no vehicle had pulled up. This man had planned to abduct Sophie and take her in her car.

Brody sat up straighter. The time stamp now read 9:02.

"Pause it and get in closer. Enhance the picture."

Bob followed his directions, and Brody's suspicions were confirmed. The emblem on the right arm of the man's coat confirmed the brand as Canada Goose. While an interesting choice for a name, their coats went for around a thousand dollars. Needless to say, the average earner didn't invest that much in outerwear. So the man had money...

Brody's eyes traveled to the man's face. The image was grainy. "Can you clear it up?"

"Working on it." Bob clicked the mouse here and there, and after a few seconds, the picture was of good enough quality to make some distinctions. "My God, he looks like—"

"Liam Neeson."

Bob turned to face Brody. "Yeah, that's what I was going to say. Either the actor kidnaps women as a hobby or it's his doppelganger."

"I'd wager it's the latter."

Bob almost had the straw back in his mouth but lowered his hand under Brody's watchful eye.

"Can you take that picture and run it through facial recognition? I'm thinking our guy is in the system somewhere. At least, I hope so." The arrogant swagger on the man, the expensive clothing, and the premeditation told Brody this guy was a professional. Sadly, most professional criminals didn't have a background. They were too good to be caught.

"Sure thing. It will take a couple days to come back, though. I'll have to send it out of house."

Brody nodded. He knew these things took time, but he didn't have to like it. Two days could be too late for Sophie Jones; it could be too late already. "Let's watch the rest."

Bob resumed playing the feed.

Liam Neeson reached the door and pulled out a gun.

"Son of a bitch. He's right there, and we can't do a thing about it." The words escaped Brody's lips without thought. He hated this part of playing cat and mouse, the part where the cat saw the mouse but was powerless to swat at it.

Back on the screen, the door cracked open, and there seemed to be a brief interaction before the man entered the house. Within five minutes, he was guiding Sophie by an elbow toward the Accent. She was struggling against him, but he tossed her into the passenger seat.

He leaned over her as she flailed her arms out the side of the car, but then they dropped, still. The bastard must have drugged her.

With her rendered motionless, the man walked around the back of the car, going offscreen temporarily, before getting behind the wheel.

By 9:20, Sophie Jones had been swept away into the darkness.

CHAPTER 52

"YOU SON OF A BITCH!" Matthew's fist connected with Ian's eye socket.

Fired by adrenaline, bone on bone went unnoticed to Matthew, who drew his arm back to throw another punch.

Ian jerked to the right and countered with a jab to Matthew's side. Matthew stared at Ian, daring him to come at him again. Ian rose to the challenge, and Matthew kneed him in the gut, doubling him over. As he was hunched, Matthew brought his elbow down between Ian's shoulder blades.

Ian howled in pain, wound his arms around Matthew's torso, and tried to bring him to the ground. The sustained pressure won out and both men hit the dirt hard.

Rolling and twisting, each fought for dominance but neither was able to sustain it. Torquing his head left and right beneath Ian, Matthew avoided the man's blows and then managed to get on top of him.

A well-placed knee had Ian arching his shoulders and neck back. This reprieve was all Matthew needed. He lifted his arm and punched, his fist slamming against Ian's cheekbone.

Ian spewed blood, and Matthew tasted his own. It only fueled him more.

He took advantage of Ian's weakness and shifted their positions. Now Ian was below him. Matthew pulled his arm back, preparing to strike again, but met with resistance.

He glanced quickly over his shoulder to see Juan and Lewis gripping his forearm.

"Stop," Juan called out.

Matthew tugged against their hold, determined to plow his fist through Ian's skull. But as the Bolivians persistently clung to him, his self-control began to return.

Ian's face was covered with blood. Matthew felt the sticky substance dripping down his own face, too. He'd need to pull from a place deep inside to move away.

As if sensing this, Juan yanked on him again. "We have to focus, Matthew. There will be another way out. We must have faith."

Matthew reluctantly lifted himself off Ian. As far as he was concerned, this fight was to be continued.

He banged on the door that closed off the entrance to the tunnel. "Can you hear me?"

"Yes, Matthew," Robyn responded.

He detected fear in her voice. "Do you have a flashlight?" It was a throwaway question. He already knew the answer.

"We each have one."

He took a second to breathe. He had to stay positive. They needed him to. "Follow the tunnel, okay? We'll meet up again."

"And if we don't?" Cal asked.

Matthew's heart palpitated. The pain that would result from that situation bore down on him. He wished not to dwell on it. Screw Ian and his issue with staying optimistic. "We will."

"We have to," Robyn added.

Her voice sounded as if she might be crying. He wouldn't blame her if she was. Tears gathered in the corners of even his eyes, and it wasn't from the wounds Ian had inflicted. "Just be careful."

"You too," Robyn and Cal responded in unison.

Back home, one of them would have proceeded with, *You owe me a beer.*

Matthew closed his eyes briefly, aligning his mental focus, before opening them again and turning around to face the rest of the cavern.

There was nothing here except for the mountain wall, lush

vegetation, waterfall, and lagoon.

Were Juan's words about there being another way out even a reasonable possibility? Or did Matthew just make a promise he couldn't keep?

CHAPTER 53

"WE'RE GOING TO DIE." Cal directed his light toward Robyn's face, careful not to shine it in her eyes.

"Shh, would you keep it down? If Matthew hears you say that—"

"Well, it's true. And I never even had the chance to marry Sophie. I never told Matthew how much his friendship means to me."

"Stop talking like that, all right? It's self-defeating, and the last thing you want to do is create a self-fulfilling prophecy with that outcome."

He wished he could garner the confidence Robyn had. But he also recognized that finding the rose in a shit pile was one of her gifts.

Cal tried to suck in a breath. Claustrophobia was setting in after spending so much time confined to tunnels in the last twenty-four hours. His lungs had to work harder as the walls and ceiling started to close in on him. But he had to somehow pull himself out of the spiral that threatened to dissolve his strength.

Tight quarters didn't usually bother him, but he'd never been squeezed into such a small space for so long before. The short rest in the cavern had done little to help him. He was probably the only one in the group who was actually relieved when the floor opened up. He recognized the irony as his nightmares had him fearing that exact possibility. But at least as he fell, his arms and legs could spread without touching anything. Of course, it was easier to appreciate that fact now that his life wasn't flashing before his eyes.

He bent over, placing his hands on his knees, fighting the urge to faint.

Robyn put her hand on his back. "Are you going to be okay?"

He glanced up at her and nodded his head.

"All right, then. We'll do as Matt said and follow the tunnel to see where it goes. According to your thingy there—"

"My thingy? You make it sound perverse." Cal laughed for the first time in a while.

"Hey, you took it there," she said with a smirk.

The ache in his chest settled with this interaction, the familiarity of it, but then a piercing pain struck his heart. He missed Sophie. God, he hoped she was okay. Would she ever be able to forgive him for getting her involved with this? She had asked him to stop treasure hunting many times. She'd said he needed to grow up and work in a more traditional field. While she preferred he did something other than provide photographs for travel magazines, she appreciated his passion for seeing life through the lens of a camera.

His camera… He couldn't believe it was destroyed. He had spent thousands of dollars on it over the years, and it had survived rough times before, including time in the jungle. All it took was bathing in a lagoon to give it wings.

It was funny how one thought connected to another, and another. Thinking of his camera dying brought everything back around to him, to his friends, to Sophie. They had to survive this.

"Are you coming?" Robyn asked from about ten feet ahead of him.

"Yeah." With one more glance at the walls and the ceiling, he summoned the courage to trudge on, if for no other reason than those three people.

He caught up to her and was about to mention the absence of booby traps but chose to remain silent. Why attract them? Sophie had spent hours talking to him about the law of attraction, so he knew the importance of keeping positive. And if it got through to him, the subject must have come up a lot. For better or worse, he had the stereotypical male quality of being a poor listener.

Keeping optimistic, he said, "On the upside, we're definitely heading in the right direct—"

Her flashlight beam exposed a sharp turn to the right. They continued on to where it headed downhill. "So much for your sense of direction."

CHAPTER 54

DANIEL WAS ANXIOUS. HE REALIZED Justin had only had the latest video for about six hours. He also appreciated that he'd given the kid more to do than simply analyze the feed. There was the matter of tracking down the phone that was sending the videos, and that couldn't be an easy task seeing as there wasn't even a number to use as a starting point. All Daniel could do was hope that the video was imprinted with that information. It was probably a big leap and the kid was being too nice to come out and say it because he was aware of the stakes.

Daniel dialed Justin, and he answered after the fourth ring. He sounded out of breath and haggard.

"It's Daniel."

"Oh, yes, hello. I'm working on it, but no luck yet."

"The videos or the phone?"

"Well, both actually." Justin fell silent, but his tone of voice made Daniel question if he was holding back.

"What is it?" It seemed like this question was becoming a common staple of their conversations already.

"Mayor Connor called."

Daniel straightened up. His employer was likely growing impatient about finding Gideon Barnes. "And?"

"And he wants me to track down his son. What's going on? I mean, I know—"

"Not another word over the phone."

"Sorry, yes. While I know what the situation is in part, I do wonder if I should know more."

"No, absolutely not. You already know more than you should." Daniel paused for a second as he digested William Connor's request of Justin. He was looking for Matthew? Why?

The second Daniel asked the internal question, the answer sparked in his brain. It had to tie back to his visit from the police chief and the news he'd brought. William likely felt he deserved an explanation from his son. Matthew did leave rather hastily, not that it could have been prevented. It would, however, be enough to pique the mayor's interest. In William's world, reputation meant everything, and for Matthew to be unreachable at a time such as this… Well, it didn't look great.

"I have been able to determine Matthew's general location."

"You—" It was the only word that would come out. The rest constricted in his throat. A clammy sweat covered his forehead. "Please tell me you haven't said anything to Mr. Connor about this."

"I was just about to call him before you—"

"No."

"No?"

"Yes, no. You can't tell him."

"But he's paying me to do this."

"And I'll double it from his other pocket. Listen, you know only a bit of the picture, but for your safety, I can't elaborate any further."

Silence.

"Do you understand me?" Daniel asked.

"Yes. I will respect your wishes, but what am I supposed to do if Mr. Connor calls to follow up? I mean, he is the mayor."

Daniel noted the tone of respect in Justin's voice, as if William were the prime minister. "I am aware of his position, but it has no bearing on this particular situation. You do know what's at risk with the woman. I will tell you that it, in a roundabout way, involves William's son."

There was a gasp. "The mayor's son was abducted, too?"

Daniel steadied his breath and tried to stay calm and cool. "Did you look at the latest video yet?"

"Yes, of course. There was definitely a moment there where I believe the CN Tower is visible out the window. Actually, I have that frame frozen and in front of me now. I would say it definitely is the CN Tower."

"Great!"

"I hate to be the bearer of bad news, but that still doesn't tell us a lot. There are many condo buildings with similar views. Of course, I can narrow it down more, but it will take time."

"One thing we don't have."

"I understand that, but please, try to understand. I am just one man. I don't have an office or employees. I have an accountant who does my books, but that's about the extent of my staff. I have three jobs for you and Mr. Connor alone. That does not include my other clients."

If it were anyone else giving this speech, Daniel would have countered quickly with not wanting to hear excuses. Instead, he felt something like pride for the boy sticking up for himself.

"Keep me updated," was all he said in the end.

"I will."

Daniel hung up, not feeling much further along in identifying Sophie's location, and there was a queasiness settling into his gut over William's request to locate Matthew. The man couldn't possibly harbor doubts as to his son's innocence when it came to Sophie's disappearance.

CHAPTER 55

MATTHEW'S FOCUS KEPT GOING BACK to the lagoon. His brain was unable to formulate any other plan but to return there. The notion that they could get out that way was ludicrous. Impossible, even. But what other choice did they have? Scaling the side of the mountain wasn't feasible, as Ian had mentioned earlier. No, the solution had to do with the lagoon, no matter how crazy it might sound aloud.

"What are you thinking?" Juan asked. He stood beside Matthew, his foot braced on a rock, his leg bent, looking serious.

Matthew took in the man's brown eyes and remembered the toothy grin he had shown more at the beginning of the expedition than he had recently. Matthew let his gaze go to Lewis and then to Ian. He almost preferred not to give voice to his thought, but the minute he dove into the waters, he'd only leave behind confusion.

"We have to go down," Matthew said.

"Down?" Juan repeated.

"Yeah, I think something might be at the bottom of the lagoon, some way out, maybe."

"You believe Paititi is under the water?" Ian asked.

Matthew shrugged before going into his bag and pulling out a pair of goggles. "I believe it might lead us there."

"Haven't you had enough swimming for one day?" Ian asked, his snark more apparent than ever.

Regardless, Matthew's chest recalled the cold water. Given the right circumstances, a drastic temperature change could bring on a heart attack. He considered his father's history and hoped they weren't caused by a genetic predisposition.

"I'm going to do this. The rest of you stay here. I'll let you know what I find." Matthew took large strides toward the lagoon.

Ian hurried after him. "Assuming you find something. And that you survive!"

Matthew was sick of the man's attitude, but short of duking it out until one of them died, he chose to ignore him and focus on the task at hand. The sooner they found the City of Gold, the sooner he'd be free of this man.

Matthew approached the edge of the lagoon, his heart hammering in his chest. There wasn't time to stand around and second-guess everything. He tightened the rope connected to his waterproof flashlight around his wrist, put on his goggles, steepled his hands over his head, and dove in.

The water stung like a thousand spikes, but he pushed through. He kicked his feet and headed down. Even with the flashlight on, his eyes took in hazy shadows and shapes. There were definitely fish down here. For an instant, slight panic set in. Bolivia was known to have an abundance of piranhas and poisonous jellyfish.

If he were on land, he'd take a deep breath to steady himself. Underwater, he was left with sheer willpower. *Mind over matter.*

He continued to swim deeper, and the rock formations became more dominant. But as he neared one, he caught a glimpse of a crack between two large rocks.

Could it be?

He was about ten feet away when his brain petitioned him to return to the surface, but he was almost there. He felt the draw and focused on his movements, not his fears. He picked up speed.

He reached his destination and touched the rock with his free hand. Again, his mind screamed at him to return to the surface, but he ignored its pleas. His flashlight caught a dark void, and he maneuvered between the rocks, his lungs yearning for oxygen.

Inside the void, he swam upward and broke the surface of

the water. He found himself in an underwater cavity. He lifted himself onto the small amount of land and hungrily sucked in air.

As he looked around, it was easy to see that he had made the right choice. Opposite where he'd come up, there was a tunnel.

The landmass down here was about eleven feet long by seven feet wide, and the space was about ten feet high.

He took a few deep breaths and headed back to get the others. He realized there was one sacrifice they'd have to make, though, and he wasn't sure he liked it. But it didn't really matter whether he liked it or not. This was their only ticket to salvation.

He swam back until he resurfaced in the lagoon, the water not as cold as it had been initially, as he had acclimated to it.

"Matthew!" Juan came to the edge and extended an arm to help him out.

"I found another tunnel." He noticed the three men's eyes light up with hope. "We'll have to leave most of our belongings here. Our packs won't fit where we need to go. Grab only the essentials."

"What do you mean it won't fit?" Lewis asked.

"At the bottom of the lagoon, there's a crack between two rocks. The space is tight, but more than passable for any of us." His eyes traveled over Ian, who was the largest of the four of them. Matthew suspected even he'd fit through. But none would fit with the bulk of a pack on his back.

The men rummaged through their belongings to get out what they saw fit to take. Matthew grabbed his machete, and he already had his flashlight.

"When you're all ready, follow me."

Less than two minutes later, the men were all gathered at the edge of the lagoon, each wearing goggles. The fact Ian had a pair surprised Matthew. He also noticed that Ian had a satellite phone in a waterproof case attached to a pants belt loop now, and the Bolivians had their machetes.

"Now it's down and to the left. It is a ways down so take a big breath to hold before you dive in. Also, remember how cold the water is. Prepare your brain for that."

Juan nodded. "We can do this." There was his toothy grin.

Ian simply scowled.

"All right. Ready?" Matthew asked.

"Ready." Juan and Lewis gave the go-ahead.

Ian was quiet, but when Matthew looked at him, he nodded.

Matthew observed the water, not really looking forward to plunging beneath the surface again, but there was no other option. He dove in as he had before and gave the odd glance back to ensure the rest were following as he swam.

Once inside the cavern, Matthew was quick to get himself onto the land to allow space for whoever came next.

Juan surfaced first, then Lewis.

Three seconds passed. Five seconds. Then ten.

"Where's Ian?" Matthew asked, heart racing for a new reason now.

Both Bolivians pointed to the water, neither giving any impression he was willing to leave land.

Matthew dove back in, not considering why he was going to save a man he had recently thought about killing.

CHAPTER 56

IAN'S HEART WAS SEIZING. Was he having a heart attack? The water was colder than he remembered it being when he'd fallen down the waterfall.

As he plunged beneath the surface, his childhood flashed before his eyes. His older brother had found it all fun and games to push him under the water and hold him there until he pitched enough of a fit that he was released. No sooner would Ian gulp a lungful of air than he was pushed back under.

All of it came rushing back to him with such stark clarity. More clarity than he cared to recall. And right now the fact that he had gotten even and murdered his brother while he'd slept, did little to compensate for the trauma induced when his brother had tormented him. It was a buried wound that would never scab over. A scar that remained sealed within his soul. It wasn't visible to others. It was worse than physical wounds.

As he kicked his legs, he tried to get himself to swim to where the others were, sensing it was the only course of survival. Yet the haunting memories from his childhood consumed him. They constricted his lungs, squeezing, squeezing… Instinct had him wanting to go up, not down.

He made out the faint glow of light first and then felt the grip on his arms. He was being pulled to the surface of the lagoon.

No, that's the wrong way!

He fought against the hold on him, imagining the face of his brother at thirteen years old. He heard the mocking laughter and saw the arrogant contortion of his face.

He shimmied and bucked, trying to free himself, but to no avail. He was ascending. He was moving away from where he was supposed to be going. With arms flailing, he broke the surface of the water. His vision cleared, and he realized it wasn't his brother. It was Matthew.

"What the hell are you doing? Are you trying to kill us both?"

Ian blinked as the images lay one over the other, and eventually, his brother's face disappeared, leaving only Matthew's behind.

"Did you hear me? That was just damn stupid. I was trying to help you." Matthew breathed heavily as he spoke, each word labored from exertion.

"I didn't know."

Matthew screwed up his brow, and it was enough to snap Ian out of his unpleasant reverie. He gathered a few gasps of air, filling his lungs.

"I'm ready when you are."

"Are you sure about that?"

Ian hated the way Matthew was looking at him like some kind of emotional freak. "Let's go."

Matthew shot off a derisive look before slipping beneath the surface.

Ian followed him. The past threatened yet again to sabotage him, to drag him down to death's abyss, but he wasn't ready to reunite with his brother just yet. He had come this close to the City of Gold; he sure as hell was finishing the job.

This time he stayed close to Matthew's feet, keeping back just enough not to be kicked.

Matthew's flashlight and pointing finger directed Ian to the crack in the rocks. He followed through the opening, and Matthew had been right. The fit was tight, but with some twisting and contorting, Matthew made it through. He disappeared, and Ian hoped it meant what he thought it did.

As Ian followed Matthew's movements, he noticed light above him now and realized he was about to surface.

Thank God!

He pulled himself to land, his legs shaking like jelly while doing his best to present himself as a man composed. Somehow he managed to find his voice. "Tell me we found it."

As he looked around the space, it was nothing more than a small cavern. As panic began to set in, he noticed the entrance to a cave or tunnel. Not that he'd ever say it aloud, but whoever said grown men don't cry was full of shit.

CHAPTER 57

WILLIAM KNEW THE BEST WAY TO get answers was face-to-face. Over the phone, it was easy to smear on a smile, bury your attitude in a tone—if you'd mastered the art—and feign interest in the subject matter. It was even easier to divert a touchy subject. Plainly put, talking without seeing the other person was a conversation of a single dimension. There was no body language to analyze, no telltale signs to detect, no posturing. It's why William preferred to speak in person. At least when he wasn't utilizing the benefits of a phone call himself. But today he had nothing to hide and neither did his son.

His stomach churned as an iota of doubt seeped in with his conviction. While it wasn't common for him to experience uncertainty, when it did arise, it had the tendency to settle into his system.

He had his driver take him to Chief Snyder's office and directed that he wait at the curb with the car running.

"You can go in now, Mr. Connor." The receptionist, who was probably around twenty years old and had model-like good looks, smiled at him. The expression struck William as sincere, but he also noticed the flirtatious glint in her eyes and the way she angled her head, elongating her neck.

Women had always found him attractive, but this girl was younger than his son. He just smiled back and said, "Thank you."

Erik was perched behind his desk, his hands clasped together, torso leaning forward. His body language was a mixed bag. He communicated openness by the forward tilt, so he was willing to accommodate William, but he was also guarded, as disclosed by the hands.

"Please, sit," Erik said with a smile.

William gauged the expression as professional. And again, the word *accommodating* came to mind. He tugged down on his jacket and undid its buttons before taking a seat. He sat, relaxing his posture, a technique he had mastered even when under attack from opposing parties. It was necessary for a politician to appear composed, emotionally stable, and clear minded at all times.

"What can I do for you?" Erik asked.

An obvious throwaway question as a man of his intelligence would know full well what he wanted. William held eye contact. "I just want to know if you've made any progress with Sophie's case. I assume if you found her, I would have been notified."

"Of course, you would have been."

There was an underlying suspicion to Erik's words, and William recognized it as being a potential land mine. But he needed to be as close to this investigation as possible just in case it blew up in his face. There were two options available to him at this time, and that was to fish for information or lie. He chose the former, for now.

"I am just heartbroken by this tragedy. I pray for her family and that she will return home safely. I can't imagine anyone plotting this against her. Do you think it was possibly a random act?"

Erik rubbed his jaw. "It could be, but it's unlikely. If someone spotted her and took her, I'd expect some violent indicators. At least signs of a struggle. Her disappearance seems planned and well orchestrated." The man attempted to temper his words with a flair of diplomacy, but the fact remained: until Erik or his detective spoke with Matthew, he was a potential suspect.

Now came the time to stretch the truth. "I do have word in for Matthew. But you know what it can be like when he's on-site." Of course, the man had no idea.

"Yes, I can imagine."

"All right, then." William stood, did up his jacket, and extended his hand to Erik. "Please keep me updated, and the moment I hear from Matthew, I will have him call you."

"I appreciate it."

William left feeling good about having put in an appearance. It wasn't that he didn't care about the safe return of the girl, but he had a career to protect. To others that may sound like a harsh statement, but it was fact. He had sacrificed everything for this life, and he wasn't about to let it burst into flame.

He walked to his waiting town car, and the driver tipped his hat before he opened the door. As he did, an idea struck hot and bright. Matthew was close to Daniel, so maybe Daniel could provide him with other information. The two did talk.

William realized the answer was one of two things: either Matthew was involved with Sophie's abduction, or he was working to provide ransom for her freedom. Both scenarios circled back to the missing girl, and knowing his son, even the little he did, William found it easier to believe the latter. Hopefully Daniel would be able to provide some clarity. He wondered why he hadn't thought of talking to Daniel about Matthew sooner.

Chapter 58

Matthew, Juan, Lewis, and Ian entered the tunnel that led away from the underwater cavern. It was approximately the same height as the tunnels before the waterfall but narrower. Maybe the Incas had tired of making passageways by this point. If that was the case, Matthew took it as a good sign. Normally exhaustion comes at the end of a journey.

This tunnel moved downward. And as their flashlights hit the dirt floor and the stone walls, it was apparent it was about to get steeper.

All four men traveled in silence, and that suited Matthew just fine. He was worried about his friends. They had to be okay because…well, they just had to be.

People always spoke bravely of facing death until it was theirs to face. Or when loved ones passed away, suddenly the world took on a profound intensity. It was then that the larger questions were asked.

Matthew had learned this when he'd lost his mother. But right now, he wanted to avoid the philosophical riddles about what came after death. He needed to realign his mind and create a positive outcome. At least faith in the law of attraction dictated that sinking oneself into a vision made it come true. And, given the circumstances, Matthew was willing to give it a try.

"Let's just stick close. Keep the light on the floor, doing interval sweeps to the walls," he said to the group.

"*Si*, Matthew. I don't want any spears spiking me through the head," Juan replied. "Especially when we're so close."

The tunnel shrunk as they walked, and Matthew eventually had to hunch over. A pain shot through the back of his neck, but he pushed on.

The ground started to level off after a while, and Matthew heard something. Of course, with everyone's footsteps and so little sleep, Matthew wasn't sure if he had truly heard it or imagined it. But then it came again. This time it was unmistakable.

ROBYN WAS TIRED OF THE shadowed pathways that led them this way and that. Even though she'd insisted on putting faith in the fact they would find Paititi, with each passing minute, fatigue threatened to overpower her resolve. The little bit of shut-eye she had gotten earlier wasn't enough to offset the hours her body craved. She wished that treasure hunting were easier, but at the same time, she knew it wouldn't be nearly as enjoyable if it were.

She glanced back at Cal, who was trudging along behind her. He was stooped over, and it was only then that she noticed how the tunnel's height had pressed in on them. It was a good few inches shorter than it had been in other sections.

"How are you making out?" she asked.

"Oh, hunky-dory."

She laughed. If she had to be stuck with someone, Cal made good company. He made her glimpses of negativity seem minute by comparison.

"Well, Mr. Hunky-Dory, I'm good to get out of here anytime now."

"Don't even get me started."

She laughed again.

When she looked forward, the tunnel seemed like it went on forever. The only sounds in the space were their labored breathing and their boots scuffing the dirt with each stride. At least those were the sounds she could recognize. She swore she heard something else.

The beam of her flashlight hit the path ahead, and it seemed like the ground was leveling out. They were no longer going downhill.

"Do you hear that, Robyn?"

She turned to Cal. At first it had seemed like a trick her mind was playing on her, but that didn't explain his hearing it, too.

"I do," she confirmed.

They both stopped walking.

"It sounds like…" Cal pressed his head to the wall and then pulled back. "I'd say a waterfall."

"It can't be." That wasn't what she had originally heard. She put her ear toward the wall. "It sure does sound like it, though." She paused a beat. "Now what?"

"Shh. There's—"

"Don't *shh* me. I hear it, too." Her heart leaped at the sound of Matthew's voice. It seemed she hadn't imagined it.

THEIR VOICES DIDN'T SOUND TOO far away. Matthew shot into a run, moving as fast as he could bent over. "Robyn? Cal?"

He didn't look back while he ran, but he could hear the others picking up their paces, too. As he moved along, the tunnel leveled out even more. When he saw them, they struck him as an apparition, his imagination at work, but when they both took turns hugging him, he knew they were real.

"Thank God you're okay," Robyn said.

"Me? You guys were the ones trapped in a tunnel."

"How did you end up here?" Cal asked.

"Long story. We'll get into it eventually but not right now." Matthew's words stalled as he considered what all this meant. They had gone one way, and Robyn and Cal had gone another, but they had met up. Was it all one big labyrinth meant to keep treasure hunters away from the gold and, ultimately, lead them to their deaths? One couldn't claim the fortune when one was a rotting pile of bones. Maybe the Incas didn't need booby traps after that early stretch of tunnel. Instead, they played mind games, making people think they were almost there, when *boom!* The tunnel takes another direction, and around and around she goes. It would make sense given the Incas' battle tactics of feigning withdrawal and then attacking from the flank.

"I take it nothing remarkable your way?" Matthew asked.

"No, but listen." Robyn pointed to the wall.

Matthew heard it without much effort. "A waterfall."

"Yeah." Her eyes brightened. "That's what Cal and I thought."

Matthew spun and did a few paces, turned back around. "So two tunnels meet up in one place? Now, there's a waterfall. Maybe we're back where we started."

"Don't even say that," Robyn moaned.

"Everyone spread out. Check the walls. Look for more of those gold emblems."

"Are you sure that's the way you want to go?" Robyn asked.

Ian barreled his way past Juan and Lewis. "The girl's got a point," he said. "Who knows what the hell's gonna happen if we push one of those again."

Robyn glared at Ian. "You should know."

Matthew caught the contempt in Robyn's eyes. It was twofold: first, Ian closed off her and Cal in a tunnel, and second, she hated being called a *girl*. He'd have missed her so much if something had happened to her. Matthew smirked subtly to her, and when they made eye contact, he somehow knew that she'd realized he was reading her mind.

"Who's to say that if we found another emblem and pushed it, this whole place wouldn't flood or something? We'd drown," Ian said.

"Or…" Cal dragged out the word. "We come out behind a waterfall and find the City of Gold."

Robyn glowered at Ian. "We sure as hell can't just stay here forever."

Matthew began searching for an emblem to open another passageway. At least he hoped to God that's what it would do and nothing more. Robyn was right, though. They couldn't stand here forever. Both tunnels led back to dead ends. Literally.

"I found something," Lewis called out. "Should I push it?"

Matthew worked his way around the group, locking eyes with each of them. Then he nodded to Lewis. "Do it."

CHAPTER 59

LEWIS PUSHED THE GOLD EMBLEM. At first, nothing happened, but then the mountain shook.

"We're going to drown." Ian's voice came out flat, as if he had resigned himself to death.

Matthew shook his head. Veronica Vincent had always struck him as capable, but this hired hand was a joke. His respect for the woman would have fallen a few notches if he'd had any respect for her in the first place. Her greed and hunger had put them in this position. Or did the blame really rest with Ian? Matthew had never encountered him before so he must have been a new hire. Vincent must have a weeding-out process, but somehow, Ian had slipped through. It made Matthew think there must have been more to Ian than met the eye. And that was a dangerous prospect.

The wall in front of them opened up. A refreshingly cool mist sprayed Matthew's face, and along with it, the heady aroma of myriad foliage enveloped him. When the stone wall retreated into the floor, it was replaced by another waterfall.

"You were right!" Robyn whooped and slapped Cal on the back.

A pathway of hewn stone went to the right, its surface slick with algae.

Matthew let all the others go ahead of him. Robyn was just in front of him.

She glanced over her shoulder and spoke to him, but it came to him as a whisper with the thunderous rush of falling water.

"There must have been a direct route that we missed along the way. Maybe if we had gone left when I said, you know, *Let's go left*."

Cal must have managed to hear her, because he yelled back to them, "She's probably right. When you pulled that rope latch, who's to say a door didn't open up in the left tunnel?"

"Hey, whose side are you on?" Matthew started laughing, confident the city lay before them. The past no longer mattered.

Along the path, lush vegetation grew from the rock walls once more. Matthew placed his hand on the wall to steady his steps, cognizant of where he came in contact with it. Warnings about poisonous insects entered his mind.

His fingertips brushed a leaf, and it curled shut. He smiled. Everything here was teeming with life.

Matthew had lost sight of the Bolivians and Ian, but they must have made it out from behind the falls because one of them called out, "This is paradise."

With the crashing of the water, he couldn't make out who had said it but the message was in line with what he was already thinking. Its meaning held more impact when Matthew stepped out from behind the veil of water, though. Its cool mist still on his skin, its moisture in the air.

At the sight before him, his heart was beating so fast he thought it might simply cease pumping.

At the base of the waterfall was a huge lagoon about the size of half a football field. And the cavern itself was three or four times the size of that. Much larger than any of the other caves they'd found thus far. The walls were shrouded in every imaginable shade of green as plant life sprouted from the cracks. Their leaves shimmered, iridescent in the sunlight that streamed in from above. A rainbow of colors made it seem as if the world had suddenly gone from black-and-white to Technicolor.

The entire space had a Jurassic Park–feel to it. It was apparent that all had forgotten this place except Mother Nature. Nothing was stopping her down here.

Matthew looked at a flower next to him. It was a bright yellow, its form one he had never seen before in all his travels. It was three feet tall with its petals splayed out, exposing a pink center. Its stem was a quarter inch around, and its leaves were the size of his palm.

Even the grass was supersized. It was taller than he was, its height reaching at least seven or eight feet. There were trees down here, too, that seemed to bask in the sun's radiance. Vines dangled from their trunks.

The waterfall fed into the lagoon that flourished with aquatic life. Fish that resembled koi the size of scooters, and others in hues of red and blue, dimpled the surface of the water. Their large mouths opened here and there for bits of green that floated on the top. He could've sworn the water had a golden hue.

Dragging his eyes from the lagoon, he surveyed the rest of his surroundings. The lagoon didn't reach the back wall of the cavern, and beyond it, there seemed to be dense growth. Similar to the other cavern, brown clay lined most of the perimeter of the lagoon like a path.

With the water now on his left, he noticed what appeared to be manmade structures to his right.

Buildings...

He was certain his heart jumped a few beats. This was it. Paititi. They were standing where no one had stood for centuries, in a city that belonged to what was now an extinct people.

"We did it!" Robyn's voice was a squeal.

The Bolivians high-fived each other and were jumping up and down.

Cal was speechless as he pointed in the direction of the buildings.

Matthew felt as if he were standing at a distance observing, having something like an out-of-body experience. The intensity of the emotion was sublime, whimsical. Daniel's claims about the power of the place were officially confirmed.

But if this was Paititi, where was the temple? It had to be here.

He stepped around the lagoon, and aligning himself with the waterfall, he observed a smaller waterfall to its right. Both emerged from the wall, moss dangled at their entrances, and darkness loomed beyond that. Ferns sprouted along their rocky ledges.

As Matthew headed toward the left of the space, he got a better look at the dense growth against the side of the cavern. He'd guess there was a structure underneath, but unlike the freestanding buildings, it was rather large and its profile unique. Despite the centuries of organic growth, it was tiered and pyramid shaped, except for toward its left side where the vegetation took on mysterious contours. To the front, there was a dock. This was a building and it was the length of the lagoon.

Could it be?

Matthew set off in a run, following the clay path until it ended. From this vantage point, he saw where the structure met the lagoon.

Robyn kept pace beside him. "Look near the water."

He did as she said and saw it immediately. Supports for the dock glittered in the sunlight. "Gold."

"We did it, Matthew! We did it!" Robyn threw her arms around him, and he lifted her up and spun her.

Everyone started laughing and yelling. Reality was sinking in. The City of Gold, known by many different names—including that of Paititi—really did exist, and they had discovered it.

His smile took over his face, but he reined in his excitement. "We still have to be cautious. We don't know what's waiting for us."

He sensed Ian moving closer behind him. "Lead the way."

Matthew stood straighter. But it wasn't Ian's tone that had his attention. It was the muzzle of the gun being pressed into his lower back. The weapon had been submersed in water, but Matthew knew it would take more to stop it from working.

Matthew nodded and the gun was removed from his body. At least for now.

With a quick look over his shoulder at Ian, Matthew pulled out his machete. The grass was tall and dense. The bulk of this space would be impassable without a blade. He made the first swipe, and his gaze fell to the ground. It was just as the jungle had been, all grass and dirt. But while it was definitely a thriving atrium down here, Matthew sensed eyes on him.

Butterflies of all colors fluttered through the air. They were as large as watermelons, but their size had no apparent impact on their ability to fly. As if curious of their visitors, one paused next to Matthew, its wings pulsing together as it hovered there. Matthew studied its eyes as it observed him. They were the size of marbles.

He turned around to see if anyone else was catching this and was met with Robyn's smile. When Matthew shifted his attention back to the butterfly, it was gone. But as he was about to make another pass with the machete, the air surrounding them filled with butterflies. In this quantity, their pulsing wings made a soft humming sound.

What a magical place...

Then something that sounded like the screech of abrading metal echoed through the space before ending with a crescendo and directing Matthew's attention upward. Perched on a vine feeding off the cavern wall was a macaw looking down on them. Two others came to join him. They had flown through the opening above and landed on vines near their friend.

Though Matthew had his face turned up to the birds, he felt something move across the toe of his boot. Glancing down, a snake about three inches around was slithering over him. He didn't catch its full length as he had looked down with only enough time to see the back end of it. It was headed toward the lagoon.

This really was an ecosystem all its own, and Matthew was caught up in absorbing its many marvels. It still teemed with life, even though it had been sheltered from humankind for centuries.

He swung his machete again, and Robyn joined in beside him. "We did it, Matt. We did it."

He nodded. Acknowledging that fact would never grow old. "I think we just might have."

Yet, despite their seeming success, something told him to be more cautious than ever.

CHAPTER 60

WILLIAM COULDN'T WAIT TO GET home and confront Daniel. The man had to know more than he let on. He spoke with his son quite frequently. William had observed that, despite their seeming efforts to keep their interactions clandestine, Matthew often needed Daniel's services for some reason. But Lauren could have handled anything that Matthew requested of Daniel. She was, after all, there to feed them and take care of their needs. Daniel was more of an overseer to ensure the property was maintained and functioning well.

Until recently, William hadn't thought anything more of Daniel and Matthew's relationship. Why would the two of them be keeping anything from him anyway? The concept was ridiculous.

William's town car pulled up to the front of his estate. The driver came for his door, opened it, and said, "Good evening, sir."

William tipped his head forward and got out. The truth of his employee's statement had yet to be ascertained.

Inside the front entrance, Lauren greeted him with a glass of scotch. It was his favorite beverage and one that he periodically sipped on in the evening between time spent in his study and bedtime. Tonight, he'd had his driver call ahead to ensure that two shots on the rocks in a crystal tumbler were ready for him upon arrival.

"Here you go, sir." She extended the drink and exchanged it for his coat.

Lauren had been around when William's wife, Ann, had died ten years ago. She had been consoling and comforting, and she always respected his privacy and showed genuine interest when he spoke. As a politician, he had the ears of many people, but he rarely had their hearts.

With her dark hair, brown eyes, and pale skin, Lauren was a plain woman. She didn't waste time painting her face. There were times he noticed faint lipstick on her mouth, but she was uncomplicated. Down-to-earth. It was the most attractive quality about her, and it had the power to override all others, including her sensitivity. But because of her warm and compassionate nature, she bruised easily. A word spoken out of turn, or even the wrong look, could hurt her. He had inflicted these wounds more than once and he had regretted it each time. Maybe one day he'd learn to harness his moods so he didn't take them out on her.

He lifted his glass to her. "Thank you, Lauren."

In another lifetime, perhaps, they would have been lovers, but too much of Ann existed in his heart to release his inhibitions. Unlike other men in his career field, he valued morals and monogamy. It led to loneliness at times, but William always made it through those low periods. Usually because he'd spend afternoons talking with Lauren. It was safe to say that she held more intimate knowledge of the real him than any previous lovers. They may have had his body, but they never possessed his soul.

Shortly after his wife had passed, he'd sought comfort in the arms of women, before he'd known any better. Even when with other women, bitter emptiness had stabbed his heart. Ann was irreplaceable. But the damage was already done. William was certain this had driven the wedge between him and Matthew. Maybe someday his son would understand. He hoped Matthew never experienced that pain and motivation, though. As for Lauren, she deserved someone willing to commit to her. And ever since those first early trysts, he realized that part of him had died along with his wife.

"Daniel's in the den," Lauren said.

He didn't respond. He simply appreciated the slight hue in her cheeks when she smiled.

He took a deep breath, knowing his evening was about to take a drastic turn. With his back now to Lauren, he walked toward the den and took a sip of his drink. Its heat blazed a trail down his throat to his stomach, which was already churning.

While he had never relished being the tough guy, Daniel owed him some explanations. It was just a matter of how far William was willing to take things. Was he prepared to let Daniel go?

The door creaked when he opened it. Daniel was sitting in a beige wingback chair.

This room of the house was the most compact, and it had been his wife's favorite. What he'd seen as tiny, she'd viewed as intimate. What he'd found suffocating, she'd thought cozy. Since her passing, it had become the place where he'd have serious discussions. Beyond holding the memory of his wife, the room's charm was nonexistent, and nothing was capable of changing his initial opinion.

Three large arched windows, now hidden behind plum drapes that were drawn, made the room feel closed off from the outside world and compressed the space even further than the floor plan. And despite the towering height of the ceiling, the antiquated wooden beams managed to shrink the room. A matching chair sat beside the one Daniel occupied. A sofa sat on each side of the rectangular room, as well. In the center were nesting coffee tables. At the far end, a wood-burning fireplace with a handcrafted mantle boasted a fire. One Daniel must have started.

William loosened his tie, laid his suit jacket over the other chair, and took a seat on a couch. He didn't say a word as he did this. Smartly, Daniel didn't say anything, either.

Once seated, William took another sip, smacked his lips, and prepared to sink his teeth into this much-needed discussion.

"I want to talk to you about Matthew."

"What about him, sir?"

"Do you know where he is?"

"He's on a dig in Italy, is he not?"

"*Is he not* would be accurate. Do you want to try again?"

Daniel's eyes drifted to the fire. The action said it all.

William set his glass on the table in front of him. "He's not in Rome, but I think you know that. Where is he?"

Daniel didn't speak, his jaw clenched tight.

"I understand that you must have some sort of confidentiality arrangement with him, but need I remind you that I pay your salary?"

"No, sir."

William hated having to bring up the topic of money, but if it worked… "Unfortunately, you are forcing my hand, Daniel."

"You would fire me?" Daniel's eyes widened, and he sat straighter.

William shrugged. "I need answers. I cannot have conspiracy under my roof. I am the mayor of Toronto." His voice rose with each word. His anger was becoming an all-consuming fire more powerful than the one that burned in the hearth.

And the following silence was more deafening than his roar.

Daniel cleared his throat. "I am not at liberty to say, sir. I apologize for that. But you hired me to maintain this household, and by withholding this information, that is what I am doing."

William studied the man. There was fear in Daniel's eyes, but more significantly, there was determination. He kept glancing away, too, indicating he did know more than he was saying.

"Did you know that one of Matthew's friends is missing? Matthew may also be in danger. Do you want something to happen to him?"

"Of course not."

William slammed his fist against the table. His glass jumped, and the ice clinked against the sides. "Then where is he?" At seeing the look on Daniel's face, William regained his composure, taking his drink and settling back into the sofa. "You do know…"

"Yes, I know about Miss Jones. But beyond that, sir, I would suggest you speak with your son directly."

"That's the point. I can't reach him. His friend is missing and it turns out two other friends of Matthew's are also missing, in the wind, whatever. I have no idea what to believe about anything anymore."

Daniel proceeded, his voice checked, tone modulated. "I can't assure you of Matthew's safety, but I can assure you that he isn't involved with what happened to Sophie."

"What do you know?"

Daniel stood. "May I be excused?"

"No, you may not."

Daniel clasped his hands behind his back, and William shot to his feet. "Tell me," he demanded.

"Sir, fire me if you have to, but I cannot say any more. It's a matter of life and death. Please take my word on this."

"Life and death? Matthew's?"

Daniel met his eyes now. "It could be. Please, sir, I have worked with you for how many years?"

Stuck on the horrendous possibility that Daniel's speaking could somehow lead to Matthew's death, William stepped back.

"Thank you, sir."

Daniel left the room, leaving William standing there. In shock. Rendered speechless. How was he supposed to stay out of it while his only child was involved with something that could get him killed?

Chapter 61

THE FOLIAGE BECAME THICKER AS they neared the structure, resulting in more swipes with the machete to clear a path. It was frustrating to be so close yet have their progress impeded. The sun coming through the aperture above had dimmed, indicating it was early evening. It wouldn't be much longer before darkness fell. But none of them would stop this close to their destination.

After an hour, they reached the building, and what they had thought to be gold was, in fact, just that. Matthew touched the vegetation-covered pyramid, paying attention to where he placed his hand as he had earlier.

Cal and Robyn started ripping vines and roots from the building. Their thoughts were obviously far removed from any poisonous insects.

"Damn! We really did it!" Cal screamed and turned to shake Matthew's shoulders.

"It's not even tarnished underneath here. It's pure gold," Robyn observed. "Do you have any idea what this building alone would be worth?"

"Priceless comes to mind," Cal said.

"Where is all the treasure?" Ian asked.

"You mean besides the entire building being made of gold?" Matthew sneered at Ian, then said, "It's likely inside."

"Well, if the treasure's inside, let's get in there and move on," Ian said.

Cal scowled and faced Ian. "Finding the entrance might help."

Ian lifted his gun.

"Cal, come on." Robyn yanked on a patch of briar and tossed it behind her.

Matthew had to make the call, and it was better to do so sooner rather than later. "I hate to be the bearer of bad news, but I think we'll have to wait until tomorrow for that."

"Why?" she asked.

He indicated the fading sun. "It's going to be dark soon, and the temple is covered. It will take a long time to clear it enough to find an entrance."

The way her eyes fell told him she recognized the truth in his assessment, even though she didn't want to accept it.

Juan and Lewis had stopped moving and Matthew found Ian off to the side, picking at some leaf the size of an elephant ear.

"I wouldn't touch that if I were you," Matthew said.

Ian quickly pulled his hand back. "Why?"

Matthew shrugged. "You never know." On past endeavors, he had encountered Venus flytraps that could rival those of Hollywood's creation. What could seem an innocent plant could mean death.

Ian swept some tall grass aside with his gun, then headed away from the temple. Seconds later, he called out, "Look what I found."

The rest of them stopped what they were doing and went to Ian. In front of him was a golden staff stuck into the earth. It was to the right of the temple, past where they had cleared a path.

Robyn looked at Matthew. "This must be the rod that Cápac was said to have put in the ground where he planned to build a temple in Inti's honor."

She threw her arms around his neck, and when she pulled back, she did so slowly. Their eyes traced each other's lips. Matthew had the urge to follow through, recalling his earlier regrets for not doing just that, but Cal punched both their arms.

"Hey, we've saved Sophie's life." He grinned and blinked back tears.

"All I want to know is why no one has found this before now." Ian gestured toward the crevice above.

Matthew took in the overgrown foliage, figuring that the Incas likely kept it trimmed back to allow direct sunlight. He imagined the temple cleared and sparkling as the sun streamed down on it. It must have filled the entire cavern with a golden glow. This thought brought his mind back to the golden hue of the lagoon. He glanced back at the water. Was it gold due to the fish or something else?

Ian raised his brows at Matthew, impatiently waiting for a response. The memory of the gun pressing into his lower back was a vivid one, so he answered. "Planes weren't invented until the early nineteen hundreds, and as for treasure hunters, most concentrate their efforts in Peru, Brazil, and northern Bolivia."

"So we got lucky?"

"If that's how you want to see it," Matthew said. "Either way, we found it."

"I'm not satisfied until we find treasure that we can hold in our hands." Ian pulled the golden staff from the ground.

"No!" Robyn's cry came too late.

The mountain started to shake around them, and the macaws that had serenaded them for most of the day flew away with wild flaps of their wings. They weren't the only ones who were spooked, either. What was happening now?

CHAPTER 62

THE SNAPPING OF ROOTS AND branches filled the air, mixing with the calls of more birds than Matthew had known were there. They had blended into their surroundings so well before, but now they flew away in droves, filling the air with thunderous applause. They all fluttered out the opening of the cavern.

"Put that damn thing back into the ground!" Robyn snatched the golden staff from Ian, who stood there, frozen in place. She tried to return the rod from where he had taken it, but it wouldn't go back into the spot. It was as if the hole had sealed up.

Just as fast as the quaking had started, it stopped. The calm before the storm?

Robyn pushed the staff hard into the ground, shoving it back into position. "There."

Nothing happened. But what Matthew guessed was supposed to happen had already occurred.

The greenery was mostly cleared away from the temple. The entire thing was gold, and it butted up against the side of the cavern with its front face meeting the lagoon. There were docks made of gold connecting it to the water. Upon one dock were four figures that resembled Incas with headdresses, and it seemed as though they were standing guard. There was also a lone water mill; it, too, was made of gold.

The tiers of the ziggurat were smooth on the top and sides. There were no carvings of any kind. It must have been so that the sun could better reflect the gold.

It appeared as if half of the building was the temple while the other was full of residences.

"The Sapa Inca and the high priest would have lived here with their families," Robyn commented. "Sapa was the title of their emperor."

No one responded to her, but a reply wasn't necessary.

Matthew was enthralled by the brilliant and intriguing architecture—pointed, steepled roofs adorned the dwellings, similar to those of Cambodian construction. Each had windows of darkness that beckoned to him, taunting him to investigate. But his feet remained fixed on the earth.

Matthew scanned the temple again. Fourteen layered tiers—each looked to be two feet tall—made it possible to walk up the temple's side. The roof of the temple area was flat, but to its left was a square, vaulted room.

Then he saw it. Up the center of the temple were three panels. Like an engaged garage door system, the bottom panel now overlaid the one above it, and the temple door gaped open.

The positioning of the building made it necessary to either cross the lagoon on a boat or climb up from the side, as Matthew intended to do.

He took the first step up, carefully balancing, and made it to the first flattened section where he walked around to the center of the structure.

He heard the others following him but continued with his focus straight ahead. As he neared the temple door, he saw steps going down inside the structure.

His heart was pounding, and his stomach was churning. Adrenaline pumped through his system at an alarming speed. He was standing on the temple of Paititi. The intensity of this monumental discovery washed over him, drowning him in emotion.

"Damn, I wish my camera worked," Cal said.

"And we're all happy it doesn't," Ian moaned.

"Shut the hell up."

Ian spoke through clenched teeth. "Listen, this isn't some fun excursion. Let's just get this over with. We go inside, see the treasure, get the hell out of here, and then let Vincent know where and how to collect it."

CHAPTER 63

DANIEL LEFT WILLIAM AND RETREATED to the privacy of his own room. He had Lauren bring him a bowl of soup to calm his queasy stomach, but he wasn't sure it would truly help. For William to approach him like that and so blatantly demand answers—answers that he wasn't in the place to provide—was hurtful. Daniel loved him because he saw who William was outside of the media light, but the man who'd just confronted him was not the William he knew. Behind the closed doors of his home—a mansion, no less—he was simply made of flesh and blood. Like anyone else, William did what was necessary to provide for his own. Daniel had thought for sure that William was going to let him go. Instead, he'd witnessed in the man what he knew was there all along, a sense of humanity.

While his chicken noodle soup cooled in the bowl, Daniel waited for the next proof-of-life video to come through. Sleep was elusive these days anyhow. Until Matthew and the others returned safely and Sophie was rescued, he didn't have time to rest.

As if on cue, his phone vibrated with the incoming message. He opened the video and took a few deep breaths before hitting "play." He found it best to prepare himself. Even though he had already seen three videos of Sophie's confinement, they didn't get any easier to watch.

This one had her confined to the bed as the others had, but her eyelids sagged as if she had surrendered to her situation. The spark of hope seemed to have left her.

After being held five days already, Daniel was impressed that her captivity was only just starting to show its wear on her. He assumed she was being physically provided for but surmised sleep was elusive to her, as well.

Since Vincent had slapped her, Sophie hadn't opened her mouth in any of the videos again. The image of her sitting there gazing into the camera lens in silence was deafening, though.

Daniel watched the video and then replayed it frame by frame. Nothing in it seemed to provide any clues this time. He hoped that Justin had made some progress trying to track the phone via GPS, at least, but the way things seemed to be going, it was unlikely.

CHAPTER 64

As HE STEPPED THROUGH THE entrance, the hairs on the back of Matthew's neck and arms rose. He was trespassing on sacred ground. It felt as if the spirits of a lost civilization remained, instilling both fear and a reverential awe.

He flashed his light into the cavernous space. Ten stairs led down to a flat surface. As he swept the beam around the rest of the interior, it reflected back as a spotlight, bouncing off the gold.

Cal had been right when he'd said this place was priceless. First, the structure was made of gold. Second, the building was centuries old and belonged to an extinct people. It was impossible to put a price tag on it.

With each step, his chest tightened a little more. An earthy smell lingered in the air, as if sealed inside. His gaze traced over the walls, then the floor, on his next step. He searched for any indicators that traps had been laid in case outsiders made it this far. Despite the unlikelihood that traps might await them inside the temple, he wasn't going to let his guard down. Doing so could mean the difference between life and death.

He found his imagination skipping ahead to what they might find down here, including treasure beyond human comprehension. His soul longed to investigate the dwellings, too—the ones on the other side of the temple and those across the lagoon.

Matthew reached the bottom of the stairs, the others still close behind, and their flashlights revealed an area of about twenty feet by twenty feet, but there was no treasure to be seen.

"There's nothing down here," he said, and he made a note of how his voice echoed in the space. It truly was empty.

"What do you mean there's—" Ian brushed past him. His flashlight beam moved in wild arcs, crisscrossing the space. "Where's the gold? The treasure? It's not like we can walk off with the temple in our pockets." Ian raised his gun and pointed it at each of them in turn. "Is this some sort of fucking joke? I will kill all of you right now."

Matthew wasn't in the mood to deal with Ian, even if he was armed. "It has to be here somewhere. Everyone spread out but be careful."

"I'm holding a gun on you and you still think you're in charge?" Ian cocked his head.

Matthew saw desperation in the man's eyes, and desperation was the root of most tragedies. Matthew didn't need Ian making a demonstration of it here. He raised his hands in surrender. "What do you suggest?"

"That's more like it." Ian's jaw jutted outward. He remained silent for seconds, as if he contemplated suggesting another course of action than what Matthew already had. At least a minute later, he said, "Spread out. Don't think of doing anything stupid, though."

"What are we going to do?" Cal asked Ian as he walked past him.

Matthew relaxed when Ian lowered his weapon. He started to search straight ahead, as did Cal. Robyn headed to the right, the Bolivians stayed in the middle of the room, and Ian went left.

Matthew looked up, noticing an aperture in the middle of the pyramid. What appeared flat from outside was, in fact, an opening. The floor was made of stone blocks, larger than those the Incas used for building the tunnel walls and came in at approximately three feet by four feet. They'd been laid out in an offset pattern with the ends of the bricks centered at the middle of the bricks beside them.

The walls were gold and smoother than drywall.

As Matthew's hand came into contact with the gold wall here, the past rushed over him. All the research he had conducted on the city of Paititi summoned up images of the people, their gods, their battles, their victories, and then their destruction. He pulled his hand back as if it had been burned. He hesitated, then touched the wall again, anticipating to be thrust back into the past, but that didn't happen. This time he simply felt the cool temperature of the gold.

He glanced at the others in the room. They all seemed to be as caught up as he was in the architecture and history.

"I found something," Robyn called out. "Should I push it?"

Matthew took a deep breath and walked over to her. The others followed his lead. It was round and engraved with what looked like a man's face with a headdress on his head. Apprehension and excitement swirled through him. This was different from the emblems they had found in the tunnels and so far pushing those were responsible for good and bad luck. Who knew what activating this one would mean.

"It could open up the treasure room." Cal smirked.

"It could also seal us inside," Ian countered.

Cal rolled his eyes at Ian. "You're always so positive."

"Let's just get the damn treasure," Ian hissed.

"Matt, what do you think?" Robyn asked.

Matthew assessed the Bolivians. Juan and Lewis met his gaze.

"It's up to you, Mr. Connor. We trust you," said Juan.

There it was again—the weight of a life-and-death decision on his shoulders. He glanced at the open temple door. Then back to the group. Each of them watched him, awaiting his decision. "We have no choice. Push it."

"Push it? Just fabulous. Now we're going to die in here," Ian muttered.

"Do it, Robyn," Matthew directed.

She nodded at him and pushed the seal.

The ground shook again, a result that was becoming an expected reaction to initializing the emblems.

Their flashlights cast light in the direction of the entrance.

"Good news. It's not shutting," Robyn said.

The back wall slid open like a pocket door, revealing an angled golden disc. It was mounted to a type of trolley and came out to the middle of the room on a ratcheting system. The disc was then placed on an angle. It was at least thirteen feet in diameter and was now positioned beneath the opening in the ceiling. In this location, it would reflect sunlight from above into the city.

"It's just as the legends claim," Matthew said. "It's probably the one that was in the Big Temple of Cusco. They must have moved it here to protect it."

Robyn rushed to his side, her hand covering her mouth. "It's beautiful. Can you imagine how bright it would have been in the cavern with the precipice of the mountain fully cleared away of overgrowth? Just the thought takes my breath away."

"I can hardly wait to see it in the morning light," Matthew added.

"God help us. You're all losing sight of why you're here in the first place." Ian's hand grazed his gun, but he didn't raise it.

"We are well aware of why we're here," Cal snapped.

"Shut up." Ian leveled the gun on Cal.

"Go ahead."

"Don't tempt me."

Matthew had to step in before something horrible and irreversible happened. Ian was getting impatient, and he was way too comfortable behind a gun.

"The treasure is hidden somewhere else," Matthew blurted out.

"Somewhere else?" Ian took his eyes off Cal to look at Matthew.

"In all the legends, it's said that there's also a gold chain that is six hundred and fifty feet long. Its links are said to be made of gold and the thickness of a man's thumb. It weighed so much that it took two hundred men to carry it. I'm not giving up hope unless we find the chain and nothing else."

"So where is it, then?" Ian asked.

"That's a good question, but I'm guessing once we've found it, we'll have found the rest of the treasure."

CHAPTER 65

THEY FOUND SMALL CARVINGS ON the temple's interior walls, and while they looked like buttons, nothing happened when they were pushed. It was time for Matthew and the others to get some rest. They considered sleeping in the temple but it was too unsettling. Sleep wouldn't come with them lying in the belly of a sacred building. They didn't belong here in the first place.

"How are we supposed to sleep when we just found the City of Gold?" Cal asked.

"I know we're all excited. I am, too, but it's not logical to think we'll be able to explore all this and leave tonight." Sometimes Matthew hated being the voice of reason. He wanted nothing more than to search every inch right away, but they needed rest. Otherwise, they'd risk missing important clues while operating on as little sleep as they were.

Robyn crossed her arms. "We shouldn't build a fire down here, though, Matt."

He understood her standpoint. This was revered ground and likely a sanctuary for untold wildlife, including species that might not even exist elsewhere if those large butterflies were any indication. Besides, they hadn't had time to scout out the cavern in the daylight, and Matthew was certain there would be a direct opening somewhere that permitted jungle life to wander in freely. The rich vegetation of the atrium would surely draw some in, and in turn, the prey would draw in their hunters. And Matthew worried about those carnivores. It made staying inside the temple appealing, but it wasn't a true option.

"We have to build a fire. I'm sorry, Rob—"

She shook her head. "You're making a mistake."

The sound of wings slapped above them as a colony of bats descended through the mountain crevice.

Poisonous insects, spiders, snakes—all those Matthew could handle. But these wretched creatures with their beady eyes, pointed ears, and noses? Give him anything else. They were rats with wings.

These specific bats were the size of dachshunds. Everything seemed to be larger here. He tried to steady his breath while his heart thumped in his chest. A deep inhale. A staggered exhale. He recited a silent prayer that they be vegetarian. He wasn't willing to offer up his blood. Yet, he'd be powerless against them if they tried anything. He was rendered paralyzed, even from this distance. If they came closer the condition might become permanent.

"Build a fire. Now." The words scraped from his throat. He identified it as his voice but he wasn't sure where he'd found the ability to speak.

Bats were nocturnal and preferred the darkness. The light of a fire might send them on their way. He realized it was a distant dream given the height of the cavern, but the others did as he said. Juan and Lewis cut down a couple of branches from a nearby tree and put them to the side of a cleared section on the ground. Then they found some dead, dry leaves and put them down. Juan struck a match. As the leaves were consumed in flame, the Bolivians added small twigs and built up to the larger pieces of wood.

Matthew's gaze kept going from the growing fire back to the bats that were darting around overhead. If only he could keep his mind off their forms.

He tried to relax as the group surrounded the fire. They shared food from Cal's backpack, and each found a spot around the fire to lie down.

He rolled up one of Cal's shirts and positioned it under the nape of his neck. Above him were the dark silhouettes. There was much nicer scenery he'd prefer to see before he closed his eyes. But as the darkness washed over him, his mind was no longer on them but on the treasure.

There was no doubt this was Paititi, the city of legends. The gold disc was in the temple. But where was all the treasure? He didn't want to accept that the Incas had handed all of it over to the Spanish conquistador in exchange for Atahualpa's life. And even so, the conquistador executed Atahualpa before the ransom amount was fulfilled. That right there dictated that gold and treasure remained, didn't it?

He fell asleep thinking about the lagoon and its golden glow. Was it just the sun refracting off the large koi or was there gold down there? He'd have to wait until morning to find out.

CHAPTER 66

"Look, Matthew." Robyn nudged his shoulder with her foot, and he struggled to open his eyes.

He adjusted to the light slowly, wondering how long he had slept. He sat up. Then he remembered. *The bats.* He jerked his gaze upward and was temporarily blinded by the morning sun. But once he stopped seeing spots, he sighed with relief. The flying rodents had evacuated. "Is everything okay?"

"Look." She bobbed her head toward the temple.

Golden light spilled out of the temple's entrance and reached over the water. The disc looked like the sun itself, and it wouldn't even have been as bright as it would be if the aperture were cleared of all growth.

"Beautiful, isn't it?"

He was certain his mouth gaped open. Words were incapable of describing how amazing the scene in front of him was. The last civilization to witness this magnificence was now extinct. Yet here he was, bathing in its splendor. Here the five of them were.

With this observation, he was fired up to find the treasure, to place his hands on what hadn't been touched since the Incas had left this world. He looked around the cavern, suddenly remembering his thoughts from before he'd fallen asleep.

The water in the lagoon...

He let his gaze travel there. Was it possible his imagination was getting away from him? It was likely a combination of the temple's glow and the fish giving the water that color. Surely, he was succumbing to the whims of a child who in earnest wished Santa Claus or the Easter Bunny were real. Still, the water's hue was too intense to ignore.

"Matthew?" Robyn nudged him with her elbow this time.

He glanced over at her, and without saying a word to anyone, pulled his goggles from his pocket and put them on. He ran to the lagoon and dove in. The cold water shocked his system, despite his mental preparation for it. He was already well beneath the surface before he considered the possibilities of what else might lurk beneath.

Fish brushed against his legs, slamming into him with more force than he expected. One knocked him to the left and another bopped him right. They were volleying him back and forth, but he never sensed evil intent. They were just playing with him.

He started to participate, moving his body to the right to meet the first fish, then moving left to meet another. Seemingly no longer amused now that their toy was joining in, the fish scattered, leaving him alone.

An iota of fear slipped in. Were they simply bored of him or was danger coming that made them leave?

His heart rate increased as he descended, considering various theories. But now a golden glow was definitely coming from the bottom of the lagoon.

CHAPTER 67

"WHAT THE HELL IS HE DOING?"

This came from one of the Bolivians. If Ian remembered correctly, his name was Juan.

Juan moved over to Robyn and stared up at her. His height made that the only option as he came in at easily three to five inches shorter than the woman.

"Your guess is as good as mine." She looked to Cal, but Ian didn't follow along with her line of sight.

There was a tingling feeling in Ian's spine, distracting him. He was experienced when it came to killing, and the air carried that veil of death. And it wasn't coming from him.

A scream escaped the woman's throat.

Juan was holding the tip of a machete to her neck while his other little friend had one against Cal. It was unexpected, but Ian liked seeing him in that position. Maybe he'd learn to shut up now.

Now Juan was staring straight at Ian. "Give me your gun."

Was this really how the midget was going to play things? He thought he could control the situation by threatening to harm someone Ian didn't even care about? He'd pay to see Cal bleed out, and he'd be lying if he said he hadn't dreamed about cutting out the guy's tongue. Then they'd see what smart-assed remarks he made.

"Did you hear me? Give me your gun." Juan poked the tip of the machete into the woman's throat enough that a small stream of blood trickled down her neck.

"And why should I care if you kill them both? I'm the one with the gun." He had faith in his Glock's working order, despite its submersions underwater. The gun was loaded and fire ready. He thought about shooting both Bolivians. It was a shot he could pull off, and it would happen so quickly that neither of them would even see the bullet coming. But would they kill Robyn and Cal before going down? If so, Matthew would leave Ian to die in this jungle. He just knew it.

"I see you're scheming," Juan said. "You're thinking about shooting us both. I caution you not to."

"And why shouldn't I?"

Juan laughed and showcased that ridiculous grin of his.

Ian splayed his palms. "Go ahead. Kill them."

"Go to hell, Ian," Cal yelled.

"I believe that's where you're going, actually." Ian tossed him a smug smile. The situation was, after all, good from where he stood. But he considered Matthew again. Shouldn't he be resurfacing soon? He'd been under the water for a while already.

"If you let me kill them, you'll have to kill us," Juan said. "You kill us, and you'll be left with Matthew. He's going to believe that you killed all of us. He will find a way to exact retribution. He may kill you or simply leave you here to die. Maybe you are coming to like the jungle?"

"Ian, please, do something," Robyn pleaded.

He let his eyes go to the woman. She was beautiful when she was begging for help. He felt the heat growing in his pants.

"Give me the gun," Juan demanded again. He readjusted his hold on the machete, and the action seemed to emphasize his small stature, as if the weapon were bigger than he was.

Ian ruminated over what Juan had said. He wasn't afraid to take on Matthew, in theory, but where would that leave him in reality? Neither scenario would end well for him.

Then he dwelled on the order of the Bolivian's words. *If you let me kill them, you'll have to kill us.*

If he killed the Bolivians first, though, it was a win-win. But his confidence was starting to waver. The doubt was fostered by the envisioned possibility of being left in the jungle by himself.

"I will give you my gun...slowly." He pulled the Glock from his waistband.

"Now place it on the ground between us and then stand back up again."

Ian complied with Juan's stipulations and held his hands over his head when he returned to his place. His heart thumped in his chest as a new but distinct possibility came to him. What was to stop the Bolivians from shooting *him*?

The jungle was really messing with his head.

CHAPTER 68

MATTHEW'S CHEST BURNED, BEGGING FOR OXYGEN. But he couldn't go back up yet. He was certain the treasure was on the bottom of the lagoon. He was still a good five feet away, and despite yearning to reach it, he would have to attempt doing so on the next dive. He had to surface. It was then that he caught movement out the corner of his eye.

His body froze as he made sense of what he'd seen. It wasn't a fish, and instead of swimming forward, it swayed side to side like a snake. Its shadow had been large, too...

Oh shit!

He kicked his legs as hard as he could and spotted it again. It was circling him.

Focus. Focus.

The lungs that yearned for breath were now competing with the screaming alarms sounding in his head from his overexerted muscles.

The shadow lurked off to the side again. This time Matthew got a better look. It was definitely a snake. Its body was easily ten inches around, but its length was indeterminable by the way it maneuvered through the water. He'd guess at least twenty or thirty feet.

Matthew burst out of the water, sputtering, and made wide arcs with his arms to reach the edge. He hoisted himself up and straightened to a stand. "I know where—" He stopped abruptly. The rush of adrenaline ebbed enough to restore clear focus, though his eyes hadn't fully adjusted, and he could hardly believe what he was seeing. He stuffed his goggles into his pants pocket.

"Please, by all means, continue." Juan held a gun on Robyn, Cal, and Ian. Lewis was at Juan's side.

"What are you doing?"

"What am I doing? What does it look like I'm doing? This is our country." He tilted his head left to indicate Lewis without taking his eyes off Matthew. "And technically, we found this place. It was our plane and our photographs."

"Funded by my money."

Juan's toothy grin twisted Matthew's stomach. "Your father's money, actually. But it doesn't matter. Though I'm sure he'd disagree."

His father... Matthew had a promise to fulfill, he realized. He'd said that they'd talk when he returned. That meant he had to survive. His eyes went from the machete in Lewis's hand to the gun in Juan's.

"I still don't understand what you think you're going to accomplish," Robyn said, a pleading tone in her voice.

"Be quiet. I'm talking to Matthew." Juan paced a few feet while keeping the weapon aimed at Robyn, Cal, and Ian. "You are going to find that treasure or all your bodies will be left down here."

If Matthew came clean about what he was certain he had seen, the situation would lean further in Juan's favor. If he held it back, he risked making a fatal mistake. "Even if we find the treasure, how do you suppose you're going to get away with it?"

Juan flashed another grin. "See, that's the beautiful part. When you find it, we'll still kill you."

Not very intelligent for the Bolivian to reveal his hand. How was death to serve as motivation?

"I don't understand why I should help, then." Matthew said. He had an idea, but it was a risk. The shadow in the lagoon had to be an anaconda. It was possible he could use it to even things out. While it was true that there were only two Bolivians and four of them, Juan was holding a gun. One pull of the trigger and... Well, Matthew didn't want think about it.

Then it struck him. Kevin had admitted to emptying everyone's guns of ammunition except for his and Ian's. He glanced at Ian, who subtly shook his head. The gun Juan held was Ian's.

Shit! Could it get any worse?

He had to stall. "We don't even have a way out of here. If we find the treasure here—"

"Don't you worry about that. We'll scour every inch of this cavern until the answer presents itself. Or should I say, the exit."

Matthew glanced at Robyn. Her expression was pained, as if she were siding with surrender, but he knew her better. She was a fighter. Cal's eyes indicated he was ready to fight, too, given the word. Ian looked angrier than a raging bull.

"I found the treasure," Matthew blurted out.

Robyn and Cal let out gasps, and Ian stared at him. Juan gave another grin and Lewis appeared to be in shock.

"You found it?" Lewis asked.

"Mm-hmm."

"Where?"

"At the bottom of lagoon."

"You're just saying that to stay alive a little longer," Juan said.

"No, honestly. If you don't trust me, let me go down with Lewis. He'll confirm." Matthew had no real intention of going back in the water.

Juan passed a glance to Lewis, who shrugged. "All right. But any funny business and I'll shoot the woman first. I see you have a soft spot for her."

It was hard to ignore Robyn's gaze, but Matthew settled his on Juan. "I am being serious. The treasure is down there."

"Oh, did you hear that, Lewis? We're rich."

Lewis was chuckling as he sheathed his machete, his eyes taking on the look of a deranged man.

Juan nudged the gun toward Matthew. "You go in with Lewis and— Wait, no. Ah, I see. You're going to drown him down there."

Lewis looked like he had swallowed his saliva the wrong way. His eyes bulged, and he coughed.

"No, I'm not—"

"See, I am smarter than you," Juan interrupted, pointing a finger at Matthew.

It was no time to smear on an arrogant smirk, but boy, did Matthew want to. The Bolivian was feeding right into his hands. He just hoped that the anaconda was hungry.

"Whatever you like, Juan. You're the one holding the gun." Appealing to his ego could help calm the situation, he thought.

"Go, Lewis," Juan commanded. He turned to Matthew. "So where is it?"

"Just straight down. It appears to cover most of the bottom. At least as far as I could see."

"All gold?"

"Yes, and piled up. It's hard to say how high as I needed to come up for air." Matthew glanced back at the water for any indication of the deadly reptile. Not even a ripple on the surface.

Lewis was already at the edge of the lagoon, his goggles on. "Want me to go in now?"

"No, I want you to stand around for a while first." Juan rolled his eyes. "Of course, I want you to go in now, you idiot."

Matthew dared to turn his back on Juan and watched as Lewis dove into the water.

CHAPTER 69

ROBYN NOTICED HOW MATTHEW KEPT looking at the lagoon. What had he seen down there? She didn't sense that he had lied about seeing the treasure. Still, she set her gaze on him, hoping that he would feel her watching him and make eye contact. It wasn't working.

Glancing at the others, they too were all watching the surface, but more out of curiosity than with the intensity Matthew was giving it. She studied Matthew's body language. He was standing back from the water's edge.

Assuming the treasure was under the water, the Incas wouldn't have just tossed it in there without protection. Even if someone had made it this far, it was possible they may still miss out on the vast fortune.

Then she recalled the way he had shot out of the water and onto the land, how out of breath he had been. Matthew was an excellent swimmer and in great physical shape. He wasn't heaving for breath from exhaustion. He was afraid. Something dangerous was down there.

As if on cue, Lewis shot to surface. He was flailing his arms and treading water, but for the exertion, he wasn't making any forward movement.

Her eyes darted to Matthew. He just stood there. Although he was the closest to the lagoon, he wasn't moving. He had sent Lewis in there knowing that it could mean the man's life.

She wasn't sure how this made her feel about him. Sure enough, he wasn't the one pulling a trigger, and she knew that he had killed before in self-defense, but this seemed more contemplated.

Juan had a gun, yes, and Lewis was his partner, for the lack of a better term, but she wasn't willing to concede to their tactical advantage. She had chosen to remain positive that they could overpower the Bolivians given the right timing and maneuvers.

Another thing nagging at her was why Ian had handed over his weapon in the first place. It was hard to believe that he did so out of the goodness of his heart. People who worked for Vincent didn't have hearts, did they? There had to be a selfish motive, and it probably boiled down to the threat Juan had made to Ian's life versus the idea of being left in the jungle to die.

All these thoughts fired quickly as she watched Lewis struggle to stay above water. Whatever he had seen down there frightened the hell out of him, taking away the man's ability to swim.

"Help him," Juan yelled to Matthew.

Matthew remained still.

"Help me!" Lewis's voice was full of panic.

More sweeps of his arms, trying to close the distance to land, were brought to a halt when a large snake shot up out of the water next to him. Its head and neck arched back, reaching the height of at least four feet. Its body was easily ten to twelve inches around.

At lightning-fast speed, it lunged at Lewis, catapulting itself across the water. His screams pierced the air in a deafening pitch.

Robyn's instinct had her wanting to turn away, to close her eyes, but her gaze was fixed to the situation unfolding before her.

"Do something!" Juan shouted. He no longer seemed concerned about holding them at gunpoint. He had left the group and nudged Matthew's back. "Get in there. Save him."

Another slew of screams and then all fell silent.

The snake coiled around Lewis's body. And reminiscent of a Hollywood movie bearing the name of the snake, Lewis watched them helplessly. The constriction of the anaconda must have been too tight for him to make a sound now, and with that, the snake slipped beneath the water, taking Lewis with it.

Robyn looked away, her hand to her mouth and tears beaded in her eyes. She understood why Matthew stood there, but she didn't have to like it.

CHAPTER 70

BRODY HUNG AROUND THE STATION, waiting for the results of the facial recognition scan to come back. There was nowhere else for him to go right now. His priority was Sophie Jones, and he could only hope that there would be a living woman to find when they tracked their perp. The statistics weren't stacked in her favor. Kidnapping victims, especially those without any ransom calls, were usually dead within twenty-four hours of disappearing. And that was after the abductor performed unsaid horrors on the victim first.

He dropped into his chair and propped his feet on his desk. As soon as he got comfortable, his phone rang.

"Fuller here."

"Bob here."

Brody smirked. The man might have a nasty habit to shake, but he was amusing. "Tell me you've got a hit."

"I've got a hit."

"And you're not just saying that because I told you to say that?" Brody teased.

"No, I'm not just saying that."

Brody straightened and grabbed a pen. He held his hand poised over a notepad. The top sheet was already filled with his messy handwriting, and there wasn't a clear spot to squeak in a few more characters. He tore the paper from the cardboard backer to realize that's all he was left with. Whatever. It would work. "Shoot."

"The guy's name is Ian Bridges. He lives here in Toronto. The entertainment district."

"So it's not the actor. Address?"

Bob rattled it off.

"Thanks, Bobby. Reward yourself with a ciggy. You did good."

"I was just thinking the same— Hey, you almost had me."

Brody laughed, hung up, and grabbed his coat from the back of his chair. Out of habit, his hands prepared to tear off the piece of paper to take with him, but cardboard didn't work as well. He took the whole backer.

CHAPTER 71

IAN SAW HIS OPPORTUNITY. The remaining Bolivian was at the edge of the lagoon, in shock and mourning his friend. He was vulnerable.

Ian shoved aside what he had just seen, assigning it to a compartment in his brain that he never cared to access again. The memory would be stored there along with so many other things from this expedition—the poisonous insects, the fiery caterpillars, the trap that shish-kebabed Kevin, the disappearing ground, the shooting spears, the plunge into an underwater cavern, almost drowning. All those memories needed to be purged. At this point, he couldn't have cared less if Vincent paid him a dime. He just wanted this trip behind him. And he needed to get out of this damn country while he still could.

With these thoughts firing in rapid succession, he hurried next to Juan and landed a roundhouse kick in the Bolivian's face, dropping him to the ground.

Ian bent down for the gun. Matthew went for it, too, but his reaction was a tad slow.

"I'd rethink your plan." Ian straightened to a standing position in time with Matthew, but Ian held the Glock. Suddenly aware of the vulnerable position he was in by standing where Juan had, he moved so he could see the three friends and Juan. Based on the loud snapping noise he had heard just before the Bolivian went down, Ian had likely broken his neck, but he wasn't going to take any chances by exposing his back to the man.

"Tie him up," Ian directed Matthew. He didn't need Juan to

wake up and come flying at him with a machete.

"With what?"

"Here, Matt." The woman handed him some zip ties from her backpack, clearly cautious of each step she took.

She and Ian locked eyes for a split second. She wasn't as innocent as she liked to make people believe. She glared at him, and he knew the zip ties must have originally been intended for him and Kevin.

Matthew lowered to his haunches.

"Around his wrists and ankles," Ian directed.

Matthew lifted one of Juan's wrists and let it drop. As if looking straight through Ian, he spoke to his friends. "He's dead."

"God," Robyn said, starting to pace. "Three deaths?"

"Get over there with your friends," Ian told Matthew.

He rose and walked past Ian, never taking his gaze off him. He was cocky, Ian gave him that.

Robyn slipped her arm through Matthew's and then opted to put it around his back. Matthew reciprocated.

Ah, how sweet. The lovers reunited.

Really, it made him sick. Monogamy was for people who didn't know better.

"Why did you give him your gun?" Robyn asked.

Of all the questions, he hadn't anticipated her asking this one first. He saw hopefulness in her eyes, as if she were ready to see the good in him. It reminded him of the look she gave him when this expedition started out and they had to push the boats down the river. He hated it.

"Don't mistake my actions for interest in your lives. I personally don't give a shit about any of them."

"At least you're honest," Cal said.

"What are you going to do to us?" This from Matthew, always playing the leader.

"None of you are worth my bullets. Just get me out of this damn country."

CHAPTER 72

BRODY CALLED IT. THIS SITUATION required the Emergency Task Force and he was on his way to them now. There was no way the backup of a few officers would be enough. While it was likely they were going after one man, he seemed to be a professional. But had he simply kidnapped her or had he murdered her? If it was simply an abduction, Brody was certain that the kidnapper's motivation was powerful and tactical. He also had the gut suspicion that there was a lot more going on and that it did, in fact, somehow involve the mayor's son and his friends.

Cal hadn't shown up at his apartment, according to the surveillance they'd put in place. If you could call it "surveillance." Given budget restraints, Brody drove by a few times a day and knocked on Cal's door each time. He'd also managed to track down the building manager, who'd said that Cal had been planning to go away for a week. He'd asked the man to collect his mail from the box.

This lined up, at least relatively, with Robyn Garcia's absence. She was supposedly on holiday from the museum, except they still wouldn't tell him how long she was going to be gone. It could be a week like Cal, or nothing more than a coincidence.

Then there was Matthew Connor. The man was famous more because of who his father was than for making his own headlines. There weren't many straight-arrow kids anymore. It was apparent that William either had control over his household or the ability to ensure things were kept from the public. It would involve many key players to keep things quiet, but inevitably, tidbits always leaked out. With Matthew, nothing ever had. He really was the city's golden child.

But Erik had said that William had visited him at his office—a highly unusual move on the part of the city's mayor. He was known to be catered to, not to do the catering. Erik had told him that he had the distinct impression that William had no idea where his son was, even though on their first meeting, he had mentioned Matthew being in Rome.

Brody had his resources, too, and was able to track down the dig there. He even managed to get Marshall Abbott, the site's manager, on the phone. He was a cantankerous man who was still mumbling Matthew's name up to the point when he abruptly hung up. It seemed Brody wasn't the first one to make the call. He wagered that William had been there before him. So wherever Matthew was and whatever he was doing there was outside of the mayor's knowledge. He was just as in the dark as the rest of them were.

All this had brought him to this point. Today, they would rescue Sophie, hopefully, and find out how Matthew and his friends tied in, if at all.

Lance Tucker was an ETF team leader and a man Brody had great respect for. His track record alone was enough to inspire awe from any law officer. He had the most successful ops with minimal casualties. Sometimes deaths couldn't be helped, but Tucker was a man who didn't accept the standards. He did everything to avoid casualties. He had fired men for being trigger-happy. There wasn't room for a dismissive attitude on Tucker's team.

Brody watched as they each geared up with vests, AR-15s, two pistol mags, two AR-15 mags, one flashbang, pepper spray, flashlights, handcuffs, a radio, and a small personal medical pouch. What most people didn't realize was that they wore anywhere between thirty-five and fifty pounds around their torsos alone. There were another three or four pounds for their helmets, and some members also wore face shields. If that wasn't enough artillery, they each had a thigh rig on one leg with a pistol, another magazine, and a multi-tool. On the other leg, each of them had a gas mask. And of course, it didn't end there. They also wore tactical boots with steel shanks and toes. Essentially, they were prepared for war.

And that's what Brody needed on his side—warriors. As he watched them getting ready, he noted their movements were precise yet fluid. There was haste to their actions as dictated by the situations they were called in for, but they were organized and mechanical. Professional. Just like the man they hunted today.

Brody left them and headed to Ian Bridges's condo building. He'd made the call to cordon off the area, a block in each direction around the building. It was quite possible Ian Bridges wasn't in this alone, so they had to be ready. Brody didn't want to consider the possibility that Bridges wasn't holding her in his home. At least this was a starting point.

He stopped the department car so quickly the nose dipped and then raised. He went to the first officer he saw. "Everything in place?"

"Yes, Detective. Officers are stationed inside the building to ensure that anyone who comes down is taken to a safe room."

"Good. And no one is let go until everyone provides—"

"A name and full address."

Brody didn't much care for being interrupted, but he let it go this time. He nodded and stood there, squinting in the setting sun and looking up at the building that housed Ian Bridges's condo.

Brody just needed Sophie Jones to hang on a bit longer, assuming she was still alive.

CHAPTER 73

IAN'S DEMAND THAT THEY TAKE him home surprised Matthew. What about the treasure? Maybe there was a part of the man that no longer cared. And maybe they should have spread out to explore the cavern for an exit. But Matthew needed to get inside those dwellings. It was a pull he could no longer ignore as the archaeologist and the explorer in him battled for dominance. But he'd have to appeal to Ian's greed first. He just hoped that the man's fear of the jungle hadn't completely eradicated his earlier vision. While he was certain that gold lay on the bottom of the lagoon, he had yet to see the gold chain.

"It's possible there's more treasure to be found," he tried.

The callous expression on Ian's face made Matthew question his resolve. He refused to put Robyn's and Cal's lives at stake again, just to satisfy his whim.

"And what makes you think I care about that anymore? I just want out of this godforsaken country."

Matthew wasn't sure how to approach it. He no longer felt like Ian was concerned about pleasing Vincent. He was now on a solo mission, and it was one that hinged entirely on survival.

"There's no telling what we could find," Matthew said, hoping to appeal to Ian's greed.

The gun Ian was holding lowered slightly.

"We could split the profits," Matthew went on. "We might even find a way out in the process."

He watched as Ian chewed on the proposition. Seconds later, the man bobbed his head. "Whatever, just get me out of here."

Ian snarled and turned his back on them, tucking his gun into
the waist of his pants.

"Thank God," Robyn whispered. "I didn't think we'd ever get
in those dwellings." He followed her gaze, which was focused on
Ian walking away.

Watching after the man Matthew came to realize the sacrifices
made thus far, the lives lost. First Kevin and then Lewis and
Juan. He shouldn't have been surprised by the double cross
of the latter two. What he cursed himself for was not seeing it
sooner. Daniel had told him Juan and Lewis were only going
to take them down the river and no farther. He shouldn't have
let himself believe the Bolivians' statement that there must have
been a misunderstanding in that regard.

Now both men were dead. One in a way Matthew summed up
as the thing of a nightmare, and the other was brought down by
a single kick and a well-placed foot.

Considering the latter, it was possible that Matthew had
underestimated Ian. Witnessing his moments of cowardice on
this journey managed to overshadow what he was capable of—
what he did—back in the real world. Or at least what Matthew
surmised he did when he wasn't abducting women.

Ian put his satellite phone to his ear—its waterproof case had
obviously protected it—and Matthew could make out some
of the conversation. Enough to know that he was reporting to
Vincent.

Matthew continued to listen. Ian had mentioned everything
going sideways. There was a bad feeling in the pit of Matthew's
gut that told him the original plan had been to kill them once
they'd found the City of Gold. It made sense from Vincent's
standpoint. It meant fewer witnesses to point fingers at her. After
all, how could she ensure their silence when they returned to
Canada?

But Vincent wasn't a person who was driven by fear. She would
swerve to encounter it, not dodge it. It was like an aphrodisiac to
her, a drug providing a high like no other.

And she had the means and power to live life like that. She

didn't worry about being handed over to the law. She didn't quake in trepidation of the justice system. She would have them killed to protect the find and to keep it hers. With no one to contest her, she'd be free to flaunt the greatest discovery of the twenty-first century to the world. No one even needed know that Matthew—or Gideon Barnes—and his friends had been the ones who'd actually found it.

Still, Vincent didn't do things for the glory. Although she'd never turn away from the limelight, she did things for money, for cold hard cash. It didn't matter if her riches were bloodstained. It was all currency whether in the form of electronic digits or wads of bills. That was Vincent's motivation in life. She was in love with money, and it had been her greed that had almost cost him his life years ago.

"Matt?" Robyn called out to him.

He was so lost in his thoughts that it was possible she'd said his name more than once. Given the emphasis and pitch to her voice, he'd guess that had been the case.

"What?"

She curled her finger to draw him closer. When he reached her side, she leaned in and whispered, "He's going to kill us."

"I know." As he heard himself respond, he wasn't so sure that he was as good at keeping quiet as she was.

The finger she pressed to her pursed lips confirmed his suspicion. She lowered her hand. "We have to get his gun somehow."

He gestured with his hands and arms as if playing a game of charades, filling in the odd word. "Tonight…asleep."

CHAPTER 74

KEVIN HAD OWED HER A call days ago. What could have possibly happened for him not to follow through on his orders? He was someone who she trusted to carry out everything to the letter. He wasn't prone to giving in to independent thought. Unlike that Ian Bridges fool. But mistakes could be remedied and smoothed over. In fact, it was already arranged. Kevin would be the only one returning from Bolivia.

While she regretted Matthew's loss, it was unavoidable. He surely wouldn't give up the City of Gold as easily as he'd led her to believe. As a man of both principle and archaeology, he made that outcome unlikely. He was probably working things behind the scenes to get away with both the woman and the find. But no, Vincent was not going to let that happen. It wasn't even a remote possibility. Not if she had anything to say about it. And she most certainly did.

Her phone rang and she answered. It was as if the dead were talking from beyond the grave. "Ian, where's Kevin?" she asked, despite the bad feeling in her gut.

"He's dead," Ian replied without fanfare. "Listen, everything went sideways."

"You're damn straight it did. Ever since I hired you, I've been a glorified babysitter." What she didn't say was that because of him, her best man was dead. To continue her rant struck her as pouting, and she wasn't going to be reduced to that. She had people who righted wrongs, and while Ian might make it back to Canada, he wasn't going to return to the life he'd had before her. No way in hell. She'd never let that happen. In fact, it was his fault Kevin was dead. If Ian hadn't kidnapped that girl, they wouldn't even be in this mess. "Aren't you going to say anything? Defend yourself?"

"We'll talk when I get back."

Oh, you keep thinking that, was what she wanted to say, but she realized the prudence of biting her tongue this time. "When are you coming back?"

"I'll call with an update on that."

"An update? What the hell? Are you—"

"Yes, still in the damn jungle."

She sighed. "Did you find the city?"

"Yes."

Now, he had her attention. "Send me the coordinates."

There was silence on his end.

"You don't have them? Well, get them," she huffed.

"I'll call you when I'm ready for your plane."

With that, he hung up. The silence of the dead line resonated through her. This man could have been her undoing, but at least the City of Gold was real. That was something to celebrate. But first, she had things that needed taking care of.

"Don." She snapped her fingers. He was loyal, and as Kevin had been, he was reliable because he wasn't an independent thinker. She didn't pay her people to think. She paid them for results. The results she wanted.

He sauntered over to her, his head slightly lowered in a display of submission. She smirked at the power she held over him. Here he was, bulky at six foot four, and she was all of five foot six and trim. He could have snapped her like a twig, and that wasn't even considering the fact he was also armed.

"I'm leaving," she told him. "This is over."

"I'll wipe the place down. What about the girl?"

She laid her hand on Don's cheek, the way a passionate lover would, sending him affection and receiving deepened loyalty from him in return. "Ah, that's the best part, my dear... Kill her."

CHAPTER 75

SOPHIE DIDN'T LIKE THE ENERGY swirling around her—nervous, excited, unpredictable. Something had happened, and it was hard to tell whether it was in her favor or not.

She hadn't harmed physically, except for when Vincent had slapped her days ago, but Sophie wouldn't put murder past either of them. The baboon who guarded her door was carrying, and she was sure the woman was, too.

She heard Vincent's heels clacking against the wood flooring outside the bedroom door. She'd been talking away and then paused before speaking again. She must have been on the phone. What she was saying sounded promising one minute and dire the next, further mixing up the signals Sophie was getting.

If she had to guess, there wasn't anger in Vincent's words so much as disappointment. Sophie tended to believe she heard from her contact about Matthew and everyone's progress.

The footsteps stopped.

"I'll wipe the place down. What about the girl?" This came from the man.

Sophie didn't hear the woman's response. She must have lowered her voice, but Sophie felt the implication. Regardless of what had or hadn't happened in Bolivia, it meant the same result for her. They were going to kill her.

She bucked against the restraint that secured her to the bedframe. Right now she didn't care if she ripped her hand from her wrist. If she didn't get out of here and find a way to defend herself, she'd be meeting her grandma in heaven.

Vincent's heels started clacking against the floor again. They were getting quieter, heading for the condo door. She was leaving her goon to do the dirty work.

Shit! Shit! Shit!

The zip tie cut into her flesh, the hard plastic burrowing its way toward bone.

Then the handle on the bedroom door twisted…

CHAPTER 76

DETECTIVE FULLER WAS IN FRONT of Ian's condo building and looked inside a lobby window. He should be standing back and letting the ETF handle everything, but he wasn't a wait-and-see type of person.

The officers inside recognized him and some shook their heads, while others motioned for him to leave.

His cell phone rang, and he knew who it would be. Call it a sixth sense, intuition, whatever, but Brody based his guess on a calculated likelihood. "Tucker, I will stay out of the way when the time comes."

"That time is now. Damn it, Fuller."

"Sorry, Tucker, you're breaking up." Brody didn't bother making fake static. He just hung up. Tucker was probably cursing him right now, but he must have also called his men off. One of them opened the building's door for Brody, a smug smirk in place. Brody sensed respect coming from him. Someone had stood up to Tucker and survived.

Brody entered the building, noticing immediately that the concierge desk and security guard posts were already vacated. Instead, there was an officer stationed just inside the front doors, another toward the back of the space, and by the way he was standing there, it was likely where they were routing anyone who came down the elevator. There was another officer in front of the elevator bank.

Brody looked past the officers and at the space itself. This place was posh. Everything was dark wood and chromes, slick lines and modern touches. It was easy to understand, from the lobby alone, how the place was able to garner millions for each living space the size of a postage stamp. For Brody, this cemented his suspicions about Ian being involved with illegal activities, possibly even being a hit man.

A small ping indicated the arrival of an elevator. The unmarked silver doors parted and revealed a woman of striking beauty. She wore a white fur coat—it was definitely not faux, which was ballsy these days—and she carried herself like royalty. Her long red hair flowed in loose curls over her shoulders, and she smiled demurely at the officer who greeted her. It was her eyes that struck Brody. They had a way of looking through him. Combining this quality with her showy wardrobe and silky hair, given where she was in, she fit in. He watched as she walked across the lobby. Brody wasn't sure why he was so fixated on her. It had to be her looks. He could certainly imagine the toned body beneath that coat.

As if she'd sensed his eyes on her, she smiled at him. Her smile lacked the innocence of the one given to the other officer. This one carried a predatory hunger. She let it linger, even turning her head to look back over her shoulder as the officer directed her down the side hallway. The officer there gestured for her to go into the room. Their gaze only broke when she exited Brody's line of sight.

If he were Spider-Man, his Spidey sense would be tingling. When most people were confronted with a police presence, they retreated either from fabricated guilt or fear. Some made eye contact to portray their innocence, as it was generally accepted that looking someone in the eye demonstrated forthrightness. But this woman was overcompensating. She had fixed her gaze on him too strongly.

He'd question her personally.

CHAPTER 77

MATTHEW CHOSE THE DWELLING CLOSEST to the temple's entrance on the lower level. Cal had hopped up the tiers of the structure, and Robyn went past the one Matthew had taken to explore another on her own.

He paused at the entrance, as if hesitating. He had already been in the temple, but felt as if going inside what had been someone's living space would cement the fact that he didn't belong here, that Paititi should have remained lost. Yet, the discoverer in him wouldn't accept that.

Still, did he have the right to breach this private dwelling? The debate only lasted a few seconds, possibly a minute, before he could no longer resist the temptation. A discovery of this magnitude should be appreciated, should be shared with the world.

The windows and doorways yawned before him, the darkness within haunting, and he took a deep breath before stepping over the threshold. Almost as if someone had just gone out for the afternoon, the articles inside seemed mostly untouched by the passage of time. The only indication was the thick layers of dust on everything. And he wouldn't tempt fate by sitting on any of the furniture or touching any of the fabric.

It was a one-room dwelling and there was a bed against the wall ahead of him. A quilt that lay over it was handwoven in bright colors and a bold pattern. There was a leather storage chest at the end of the bed with Inca drawings carved into the leather. Its latch was gold.

In another corner of the room was a small round table with four stools. While the Incas were small people, he imagined that even they would be squished around this table. A wooden vase was placed in the corner of the room, painted with bright colors in Navaho-like patterns.

On the wall hung a quipu. Unbelievable. He had read about such things in literature and only seen them in museums. While the Incas never developed a written language, they used these to record numbers. Also nicknamed "talking knots," a quipu was an accounting device made of ropes and knots.

Depending on the placement of the knots on the string, it either signified units of 1, 10, 100, 1,000, or more. With the one in front of him, following the string from the top to the bottom, the knots were in groups of three, two, nine, and four. This was a four-digit number, therefore, 3,294.

He walked closer to it, allowing his fingers to hover over the string, feeling it through its energy and nothing more. Again, he feared touching it in case the oils from his hand damaged it after all this time.

He did, however, carefully run his hand across the top of the leather trunk, clearing it of dust, and then he lifted the lid, unable to fight the compulsion. Inside were several wooden pots and another quilt. He didn't pick up anything, again, afraid that his touch possessed the ability to turn it to ash. But just being in this room, this close to an ancient people, was surreal. A mixture of emotion swirled through him, ranging from excitement and awe to something that made his eyes mist with tears.

He knew that he needed to find a way out of this city, but his legs remained frozen in place. As much as he considered himself a trespasser, he also felt at home, as though he belonged here. He didn't want to leave, but unfortunately, life had different plans for this trip.

Ian had afforded them the time to explore and probe each corner of the dwellings, but it was a means to an end for him. At some point, his patience, his leniency, would expire, and he'd press to leave. But it wasn't Ian who made Matthew feel any true urgency. It was Sophie. The longer they were here, the longer she was being held against her will.

They had to go. He placed his hand on the dwelling's wall and took a longing look back on the room before setting out to gather the others.

CHAPTER 78

THE CONFERENCE ROOM COULD SEAT TWENTY to thirty people. Currently, only seven sat around the dark oak table. Similar in tone to the lobby, this room was opulent, from its marble flooring to the three oval chandeliers that hung over the table. Ten fabric-covered chairs lined the table's flanks—five on each side—and there was one on each end. Along one wall was a long bench upholstered in material that matched the chairs. It would accommodate another ten bodies easily.

Brody analyzed the small crowd as he entered the room. It was easy to pick out the concierge and security guard. The others would have come from the higher floors.

Two women were casually dressed in jeans, their hair pulled back into ponytails and they smelled of cleaner. Brody sized them up as hired help leaving for the day.

Even though it was early evening, most of the people who lived here were likely still at their corporate jobs earning the money necessary to pay their mortgages, maintenance fees, and property taxes.

The two other men could have been models for *GQ Magazine* with their trendy slacks and designer jackets. Despite the differences in the coloring and styles of their clothing, the men struck Brody as identical.

Both men were attentive to the last person—the redhead. She was the only one Brody had any interest in, but he had a very different agenda. Maybe if he had met her at a bar and warning bells hadn't been going off all over the place, he'd be able to see her from a strictly male point of view. She wasn't paying the models any attention, though. Her gaze had been on Brody from the second he'd entered the room. Maybe the badge had something to offer in its favor after all.

She crossed her legs as he approached. He knew her type. She was too young to categorize as a cougar, but she was nonetheless carnivorous, preying on a man's attraction to manipulate him to her advantage. Brody imagined that when she did succumb to their advances, it was always her choice.

"Detective," she purred.

"Good instinct."

She slightly ticked her head to the right. "I know men."

He had no doubt that she did.

She gestured to the chair on her left. "Why don't you sit down? Get comfortable?"

Brody took off his jacket, laid it over the back of a chair, and got comfortable, per the lady's suggestion. The shirt he wore accented his muscular frame well. Two could play the game of sexual prowess, and he was not one to back down. His daily fitness regimen gave his body the form of a man ten years younger than he was, and his healthy diet, combined with no filthy habits, kept him in peak physical condition. Ever since he hit the big three-oh six years ago, he had promised never to let himself go. Too many people used that excuse, as if assigning their level of fitness—or lack thereof—to a number mattered at all.

His move seemed to work as he caught her giving him the once-over. The corner of her mouth lifted when their gazes met, and she narrowed her eyes.

"My name is Brody Fuller."

"Nice to meet you, Detective Brody Fuller." She extended her hand. Her long fingers were adorned with jewelry, and her nails were manicured.

He noticed that she didn't offer her name. "Sorry to inconvenience you like this," he said.

"Things happen." She was cool and calm. Maybe too composed.

Most people didn't care for interruptions in their days, and she was acting as if it was no problem at all.

This combined with the steady eye contact made his suspicions ratchet up. He didn't have any real basis for these hunches, except for these small indicators.

"Do you live in the building or are you visiting?" he asked her.

"Visiting."

"Nice building, that's for sure."

"Yes. I might get a condo here one day." Her eyelids lowered slightly—an indicator that she was telling an outright lie.

"Who were you visiting?"

A sly smile. "Are you jealous, Detective?"

"No, not at all."

He watched as the smile faded from her lips.

Her features took on hard edges, and her energy became cold. "I do know my rights."

"Only those who have something to hide worry about their rights." He had her trapped.

Her features softened again as she tucked a strand of hair behind an ear, a move that struck him as more strategic than habit. "Oh, I apologize. I get nervous around cops."

"Is that why you haven't given me your name yet?"

"My name is Amber Watts."

"Amber suits you well."

Her head dipped forward in a thank-you. "When can I go?"

"Shortly. You will have to provide all your information to the officer first."

"Something horrible has obviously happened. In the building, I mean. All this police presence and ETF?"

"It's an open investigation, and I cannot discuss it."

She placed her hand on his forearm. "I understand."

He nodded. She made a huge mistake touching him. Humans were given more than five senses. There was a sixth, whether people wanted to accept it or not. It was intuition, and based on the fact that people were energy beings, with her touch, this sixth sense set off sirens. Any suspicions he had were confirmed.

Of course, he'd have to let her go. It wasn't like he could prove any of this. At least not yet.

CHAPTER 79

AFTER ACCEPTING THAT THEY DIDN'T have the luxury of exploring every inch of the dwellings, Matthew and the others split up to cover more ground and worked their way around the perimeter of the cavern, hacking through the overgrown grasses. The other houses that still hid below the foliage would have to be left for a second visit. The sunlight was fading fast.

Matthew was exhausted from all the machete swinging. His muscles took the brunt of it. His abs, his arms, and even his legs ached with each swipe of the blade. He stopped to catch his breath, finding irony in the fact that they had sought Paititi with such passion and now needed to get away from it as fast as they could.

"We need to call it a day," he shouted.

"You stop once you find a way out," Ian yelled back.

"The sun is setting. We might not even find a way out tonight. Besides, we are safer in here than out there," Matthew responded.

"We keep going."

Matthew's lungs heaved, anger swirling in his chest. He thought of his friends' welfares. The man had a gun, but Matthew had to call the shots. "We're done for the day."

"Matthew?" Cal's voice was a mixture of panic and excitement.

Despite his tired body, Matthew jogged in the direction of his friend's voice and came to a Banyan tree. It was as if it had missed the memo about keeping its roots beneath the ground and, instead, were a tangle along the tree's trunk.

"Where are you?" Matthew asked.

"Over here."

Matthew rolled his eyes as if Cal could see him. "And where is 'over here'?"

"By the temple."

Matthew hadn't thought to look near or inside the temple. He'd figured that if there were a way in, it would be at the opposite side of the cavern so that when visitors arrived, or the Incas entered for worship, they would be instantly struck with awe.

"Do you think you found a way out?"

"I'm coming," Robyn shouted.

Matthew heard Robyn breaking stalks as she approached quickly. There were no audible indications as to where Ian was, which surprised Matthew given the announcement they might have found the way out.

Matthew went around the tree and lifted himself onto the structure. Robyn caught up with him.

Her eyes said she was thinking the same thing he was: if Ian was nowhere around, and Cal had found a way out, they could make a run for it. If only there were somewhere to actually *run*. And even if they had found a way out, Ian could catch up, and when he did, at least one of them would pay with his or her life.

"Call out again," Matthew shouted to Cal.

"The other side of the temple."

Robyn glanced at Matthew. "The other side?"

Cal must have heard her, or developed a mind-reading ability, because he answered her question. "Yes. Past the dwellings."

"We're coming," she said.

They kept walking across the front of the structure, past the residences to the far side. Over here, the building was tiered as it was on the temple side. Matthew stepped up onto the first tier and turned to help Robyn.

She looked from his hand to his face. "Being all chivalrous I see."

"All in a day's work."

"Uh-huh." She slapped her hand into his, and he hoisted her up.

They made quick work to move along the end of the structure despite the tiers being narrow, two feet wide at the most, forcing them to walk single file. Matthew imagined the petite Incas wouldn't have had an issue traversing the structure.

"Call out a—"

Cal was against the cavern wall, up on the structure's first tier. "See me now?" He did a quirky little wave.

"Of course we do, dumbass." Robyn laughed.

"Hey."

"Well, you say something stupid, and…" She shrugged.

There were many reasons Matthew liked her, but her sense of humor was definitely one of them. He periodically had to remind himself that they were better off as friends, though.

Cal gestured for them to hurry, as if they weren't already moving as fast as they could. "It's back here."

Staying on the first tier, Matthew led the way.

Ahead of Matthew, the blocks were slightly set in from the surrounding brickwork, in a pattern roughly the size of a door. Matthew laid his palms against it and pushed left, then right.

"I already tried that," Cal said. "It doesn't budge. But you agree? It looks like a door, right?"

"Yeah, absolutely."

Robyn had gone up to the next level to see it, as Matthew was otherwise blocking her view. Cal moved up one more tier.

"So how do we open it?" Cal asked.

Matthew surveyed the area. "This is definitely a door." Then he gasped. "Do you feel that?"

Cal leaned down and put his hand near Matthew's. "A draft."

"Did you look around for any of the gold emblems?"

"Yeah, I did, but I didn't find anything," he reported. "Hey, where is Ian?"

Matthew turned, and Robyn waved her hand in the air. Now was the time to share their plan with Cal.

"Tonight when Ian falls asleep, we're making a move for his gun," Matthew said.

"Making a move?" Robyn used his words against him. "You

better sure as hell hope the *move* is successful because if it's not—"

Matthew put a hand on hers to stop the wild gesturing. "We *will* get his gun. Is that better?"

"Much."

Matthew run his hands along the stone, then around the framework. "First it would be nice to figure out how to open this thing. The trigger mechanism has to be around here somewhere."

CHAPTER 80

CAL CLIMBED UP THE TIERS, inspecting every crack. Robyn did the same.

Matthew stayed in front of the door. There were no gold emblems nearby. If only it were as easy as the modern day keyless entry.

Wait… That was it!

He raced past the dwellings and into the temple. The only illumination now was his flashlight and the faint glow of the moon. He directed the beam to the left wall, and there was one of the symbols they'd found earlier that looked like a button. Efforts to push this one and the others had resulted in nothing happening. The symbols must need to be pushed in sequential order.

It had to be connected, and with the Incas love of misdirection, it was actually possible. Matthew looked at the symbol carefully. What he had failed to identify previously was now blatantly obvious: the number three thousand depicted as it would appear on a quipu. So it was a vertical line—representing the string—with three circles, representing the knots, drawn toward the top with an empty space beneath them.

The gold disc remained in the center of the room where it had settled after emerging from the wall. He considered pressing the gold seal to make it retreat, but would check out something first. He maneuvered into the space where the disc would be concealed when the wall was closed.

His light revealed his suspicion as fact. On the inside wall, where the disc would retreat against, was the number two. Two knots in the hundreds position, with a blank line coming out beneath it.

His heart was racing as he searched for the symbol representing the number nine. He found it on the right wall.

Now, he needed to find the fourth symbol, which also needed to be the number four. Where was it?

"Cal! Robyn!" He cried out for them, not caring if Ian heard, and when they found him in the temple, they gave him a quizzical look.

"Shouldn't we be finding a way out of here?" Robyn said.

"I think I might have found something. I'm not sure if it's the way out or not, but it's worth a try."

"What is it?" she asked, moving toward him.

He swept his light around, starting with the first symbol and making his way around the room. "When I was in the first dwelling, a quipu was hanging on the wall. You both know what that is?"

"Yeah."

"Not a clue," Cal said.

"It's a device that the Incas used to record numbers," Matthew explained.

"Okay."

Matthew smirked. Cal's ignorance was amusing, especially when Matthew was on an adrenaline high. "The number on the quipu was three-two-nine-four."

"We pushed the symbols when we first got in here," Robyn said.

"Yes, but not in the right order."

"Okay, well, that sounds worth a shot, but we only found three symbols. If you're right, there needs to be a fourth, and it needs to depict the number four as it would on a quipu."

"Right. That's where I'm stuck. I'm open to ideas, guys." It was by saying it aloud that he realized what he'd missed. When Robyn had pushed the gold seal that brought the disk out of the wall, it had been such a quick discovery that it had sidetracked him. But if he remembered correctly...

He walked to the gold seal in question. "Stand back, guys."

He pressed it, and the gold disc made its way back and was concealed behind the wall.

Robyn crouched down in the center of the room, exactly beneath where the disc had been. "The number four."

"So, it's not a four-digit combo. It's actually six, if you count the gold seal as a digit." Matthew paced. There were a couple of variations they could try. For example, they could press the three, then the gold seal to reveal the number two, then the two, then the nine, then the gold seal again to put the disc away and reveal the four, then the four. Or it could go gold seal, three, two, nine, gold seal again, four. There were more variables, but it all seemed to come down to the timing of pushing the gold seal.

"Matt?"

He explained to them what he was thinking. "I say we just keep trying until we get it right and hope there aren't any penalties if we get it wrong."

"Do you think this will open the door we found?" Cal asked.

"Your guess is as good as mine, but it's an idea."

Cal nodded. "All right, well, let's try it."

The three of them stood there, taking deep breaths.

Matthew pushed the gold seal to bring the disc out again. "Okay, Cal, push the three on the left wall."

He pushed it.

"Robyn, push the two on the back wall."

"Okay."

"Now, I'm going to push the gold seal again." They waited for the disc to return to its hiding spot. Robyn was now in front of the nine. "Press it." She did. Then he took a deep breath. "Are you guys ready?"

He walked over to the symbol on the floor and pushed it. The sound of stone grating against stone, shifting, echoed through the temple, and the ground beneath them began to shake.

Matthew jumped back as the floor to the left of the number-four symbol parted. Much like the pocket wall that concealed the disc, the floor gave way, but nothing was coming up. Instead, there were stairs leading down. They had guessed the right sequence the first time.

"You weren't thinking about leaving me behind, I hope."

They turned to find Ian, his gun leveled on them.

"Would you put that thing away?" Robyn advanced toward Ian. Matthew was able to reach her to stop her from moving any closer to him.

"Now, now," Ian said. "Take your boyfriend's advice."

"He's not my boy—"

"I don't really give a rat's ass. Is this the way out?"

"Not sure about that, but we definitely found something. Why don't you lead the way?" Matthew secretly hoped there were more traps waiting inside, and he was more than happy to let Ian clear the path.

Ian studied Matthew's face. "You must think I'm really stupid." He waved the gun at Robyn. "Ladies first."

CHAPTER 81

SOPHIE WATCHED THE KNOB TURN, and then the door opened. The man entered, his gun pointed at her, and she pinched her eyes shut.

Seconds passed as she anticipated the bullet, crime shows playing through her mind. The bullets would fire and the video would continue in slow motion, frame by frame, until the bullet met its target... She couldn't finish the thought. It was her head she was thinking about here, her life.

Why hadn't he done it already? Was he delaying to drag out this torture even longer? It wasn't enough that she'd been held here for days, against her will, tied to a bed, given just enough food and water to survive, and no opportunity at all to bathe. Her human rights had been reduced to basic necessities and nothing more.

She took a deep, staggered breath and opened her eyes. "Please, don't kill me."

He smiled at her, and it chilled her to the bone. He had more on his agenda than simply following orders. The woman was gone, and here she was alone with this man.

He holstered his gun, and she almost wanted it back in her face. A quick death would be more welcome than what he obviously had in mind.

As he approached the bed, he unbuttoned his jeans and then unzipped his fly. He leered at her, the corners of his mouth lifting. "You are going to get a gift before you leave this world."

The coldness in his eyes froze her insides. The scream bubbled up in her throat, longing to be expelled. She had nothing more to lose anymore, did she? With the woman gone and this man with his pants almost literally around his ankles, he'd be impeded if he tried to carry out his earlier promise to kill anyone who dared help her.

He unclasped his harness and holster and set it on the end of the bed.

She heaved for oxygen, her chest visibly expanding. His smirk filled out as if her terror turned him on more. He was truly mad.

If only she could somehow get her hands on the gun. If she did, though, was she ready and willing to kill a man? She'd have to be.

As her conscience struggled with the moral implications, her instinct responded with a resounding affirmative. If it meant the difference between life and death for *her*, she could justify it, couldn't she?

He needed to get closer if she was going to pull this off.

God give me strength.

As he lowered himself to the edge of bed, his fingers sought out her flesh. He caressed the base of her neck, tracing down to her collarbone. She wanted to vomit.

But she tried to focus. She needed to fix her foot around the harness and maneuver so she could reach the gun.

"I've never been with a black woman before."

She fought to make herself smile at him, to be seductive, to distract him from any movement she made with her legs. "There's a first time for everything." Acid roiled in her stomach as she said the words.

"Yes, there is." He leaned down and pressed his mouth to hers.

His tongue pushed into her mouth, hungrily and greedily trying to possess her. She tried to allow the situation, to place herself out of body, but it was getting harder and harder to do so.

Her foot found the loop of the harness, then, and she was lifting it up the bed. She had to open her legs to do so, and he took it as an invitation to place his hand on her thigh. He seemed oblivious to the fact she was bringing the gun closer with her movements.

She forced out a moan, and it encouraged him further. She'd never be able to shower enough to wash this man's touch off her.

Her one free hand brushed his cheek. She opened her eyes and was sickened by this man's intentions. His eyes were shut as if savoring every second of violating her.

Her hand fell to the harness that wound around her heel. Just another couple of inches and she'd be able to get a grip on it. She moved quickly now, in a jerky motion. Her strength was almost depleted. Enough was enough.

She pulled the gun free of the harness and pressed it to the side of his skull. The weapon was heavy in her hand, her adrenaline all that made it possible to hold it there.

He stopped raping her mouth immediately and pulled back.

All he'd have to do is swipe the gun away, her wrist felt so weak… But would he chance that when she could just pull the trigger?

He smiled.

What kind of a maniac smiles with a gun to his head?

He sat back, and she moved with him, as far as her restrained wrist would allow, and kept the muzzle on him. He flashed another smile as he reached for the gun.

The moment had come. Did she have what it took to kill a man?

In a split-second decision, she pulled the trigger. And nothing happened. She squeezed it again.

He was laughing as he snatched the weapon from her. "You didn't think I'd leave the safety off did you?" He rose from the bed, the gun settling into his grip. "And here I thought I'd give you a little fun before you left this world." He shrugged. "Your loss."

This time she did scream, preparing for the bullet to take her life. Instead, the condo's door was rammed through, and a bunch of men dressed in ETF gear stormed into the bedroom. They had the man secured and disarmed in seconds.

Sophie had seen these kinds of scenes in movies and on TV,

but it was nothing like experiencing it in real life. Even though she knew they were the good guys, they scared the shit out of her.

"Are you okay?" a man's voice asked.

She heard the officer speaking to her, but it was as if he were somewhere distant. He cut the zip tie from her wrist, and she rubbed at her flesh.

"Miss?"

"Yeah, yes, I'm… There's a woman."

"A woman?"

"She was here. She just left. Red hair. Beautiful. Her name is Veronica Vincent."

She listened as the officer communicated they had secured the hostage.

It was over. She was free.

CHAPTER 82

ROBYN'S HEART WAS BEATING FAST as she anticipated entering the belly of the temple.

"Don't make her do this," Matthew pleaded. "I'll go first."

Ian shifted his gun's aim to Matthew. "If you want to live, I suggest you start listening to me." Back to Robyn. "Go."

She glared at him. She wasn't afraid of his gun, even though she knew she should be. What she feared more was what might be lying beneath them. She imagined more shooting spears and disappearing floors, poisonous insects and caterpillars.

She pointed her flashlight down the stairs, and with no sign of obvious danger, she gave a quick look back to Matthew and Cal and stepped inside.

She made it to the base of the stairs without trouble. There was a room at the bottom, easily twenty feet by twenty feet. As her light filled the space, it reflected off the gold walls. They had set out looking for an exit, but they had found more treasure. They had found *the* treasure.

"Get down here," she yelled.

Her light beam traced over necklaces, coins, chests, rings, gems, jeweled goblets, and statues. All gold. But lying in the corner was the greatest treasure of all. The gold chain. Its links really were the thickness of a man's thumb.

Footsteps sounded behind her, and she turned to see Matthew. "If this is the treasure, what was at the bottom of the lagoon?" she asked him.

"More of it probably."

"You didn't make that part up?"

"You should know me better than that." His tone confirmed he was offended.

Cal and Ian were moving around the room, picking up trinkets and looking at them.

Ian shoved some coins into his pockets. "It's the least I'm due."

"It's what you're due?" Robyn felt the heat creep up her neck and settle in her earlobes. She closed the distance between her and Ian. "You are due nothing. Do you hear me, you shit? It's because of you that we've been forced to rush the greatest find of this century. It's because of you that Sophie is being held hostage and in who knows what state of health at this point. It's because of you that we are stuck in here without a way out. What is here belongs in a museum for the world to enjoy. Not for you to fill your pockets because you feel you des—"

The bullet kissed her skin so fast it was as if she had imagined it. If not for the shock taking over her body and Matthew's and Cal's screams, if not for the blood draining from the wound, she might have been able to dismiss it as fiction. That was before the searing pain burrowed in, worse than she had ever experienced as her legs buckled, and she crumpled to the ground.

CHAPTER 83

THE PEOPLE FROM THE CONFERENCE room were just being released when the news came. The mission was successful. They had Sophie Jones, and she was alive. It was a win from that perspective, but Brody wouldn't be fully satisfied until those responsible were behind bars.

Amber Watts was coming toward him. They had her information, and with the all clear, she was free to go.

"Good day, Detective." She smiled at him as she walked past.

Brody wasn't sure if that was her normal stride, but her hips swayed side to side as if trying to tempt men to chase after her. She most certainly knew how to take care of herself. Brody had to give her that.

The elevator chimed its arrival then, and four ETF officers stepped out with a large man who was cuffed behind his back. The cop-to-criminal ratio may have seemed like overkill to the average observer, but Brody knew that men like this, hopped up on adrenaline, in fear of facing jail time, were capable of anything. It was also at this point that they had no fear and no longer thought about repercussions to their actions. This combined to make them a lethal threat. So four-to-one was a logical decision.

But what had Brody's attention was the fact that the man wasn't Ian Bridges.

He watched as this man was carted through the front doors to the street. When he disappeared from sight, the second elevator arrived in the lobby.

Sophie Jones stepped out with two officers. Her eyes were a swirling mess—full of conflict, fear, and confusion, but also determination.

"Did you get her?" she asked the officers as they walked by him.

"We're working on it," one officer answered.

Her?

"Stop."

The three of them followed Brody's directive.

Brody went around and stood in front of Sophie. "You said her? Her who?"

His directness seemed to scare her. She blinked her wet lashes. "There was a woman who—"

He suddenly felt peaked. "What did she look like?"

"She has red hair, and she—"

"Shit!" Brody turned and ran out to the street. Turning left, then right, there was no sign of her. She had vanished.

CHAPTER 84

"ROBYN!" MATTHEW DROPPED BESIDE HER. Ian's gun held no power over him now. With Robyn shot, the man might as well fire a bullet at him while he was at it.

Cal crouched down on the other side of Robyn.

"Keep her awake, Cal. Get her to talk." Matthew's heart was hammering. He tore off his shirt to stanch the blood flow. The bullet pierced through the meat of her upper chest, off to the left. It was hard to tell with all the blood exactly where it had hit her. A part of him actually feared looking any closer. "What the hell—" He couldn't speak or even formulate sentences in his mind. She deserved so much better than this. This wasn't the end for Robyn. This wasn't how it was going to go down.

"Robyn, talk to us." Cal touched her face, lightly slapping it to keep her awake.

She moaned and slowly her eyes fluttered open.

"Thank God!" Matthew's insides liquefied. He refused to lose her—now or ever. Naive maybe, but he couldn't bear the thought of not having her in his life.

"What…" It was the only word that broke through from her lips.

"You were shot. But you're going to be okay." Matthew caught the glance Cal gave him, the one that asked if he should be promising something he might not be able to deliver. It was all about staying positive, right? If one just managed to do that, nothing bad would ever happen. That's what Robyn always said.

Maybe if he recited that as a mantra…

"Where did he…?" She sounded so weak, so vulnerable.

Matthew's soul ached, and he looked over at Ian, who had given them space. His face was stoic, and he registered no feelings at all about having shot her. No regret. No empathy. It took all Matthew's willpower not to face off with the man. But if he did, it wouldn't get them anywhere. Robyn needed him.

"Bet you'll find that damn exit now!" Ian moved two feet toward Matthew. "Get us the hell out of here!"

Matthew ignored Ian and reached for Robyn's hand. She gripped it, and he squeezed hers. "You're going to make it, baby." The word came out naturally, without thought to context or meaning. It was a true reflection of how he felt about her. If he lost her, he would be full of regrets for not taking the chance. Life was short. Isn't that what they said? Faced with tragedy it seemed to hold even more truth.

He couldn't stand seeing her like this, bleeding and in pain, tears streaming down her cheeks. He lifted her hand and kissed the back of it, then the palm. He held her hand to his face.

Ian thrust the gun into Cal's face. "I said get me the hell out of here!"

Cal held up his hands and slowly rose to his feet. "We might have found a way, but we're not sure."

They had one hope, and they truly were living on a prayer. What they had tried opened the treasure room. Was it too much to ask that it also opened the door Cal had found and that it was their way out? Robyn needed medical attention immediately.

CHAPTER 85

SOPHIE WAITED OUT IN THE HALLWAY with two police officers while the detective cleared her apartment. She wasn't sure exactly what he suspected but if they hadn't found Vincent… The thought of her being free sent chills through Sophie's core. But she was safe now, wasn't she?

She found it ironic that all she longed for was solitude even though that was all she had for the last six days. But here she was protected, and more importantly, she was home.

"It's all clear," the detective said to the officers. He had a way of talking over and around her. Maybe he was uncomfortable with making eye contact, but Sophie had a feeling there was another reason. To him, she must have been an apparition. He probably hadn't expected to find her alive, and the fact that he had, made her the equivalent of a ghost. She still sensed that he was relieved by the outcome. Despite any seeming discomfort he had around her, he had a gentle nature.

Maybe he just felt deeply for what she had gone through. Maybe she reminded him of a girlfriend or a sister.

"You can go in, but we'll need to talk with you, Miss Jones."

She expected this, but the idea of discussing all she had been through was exhausting. Her mind skipped to Cal, Matthew, and Robyn. "Have you heard from my friends?"

The detective's eyes met hers now. "Why do you ask? Is there something I should know about them?"

The glint in his eyes was accusatory, questioning. Did he think her abduction was connected with them?

"Please forget I said anything." She knew it was a desperate wish. She'd watched enough crime shows to know how cops sank their teeth into any morsel they deemed important to their cases.

He didn't let his eye contact waver, but his features softened. She didn't take it as a sign that he was letting her off, but she didn't see condemnation there, either.

"I'll be back in an hour, and we'll talk, okay?"

She nodded and bit down on her lip. She had to hold herself together at least until they left, at least until she was alone.

"I should be taking your statement now." He stopped talking. His mouth twitched as if he wanted to say more, but he didn't need to finish for her to receive the message: he felt bad for her.

To her, she had become the helpless victim in need of rescue. He probably saw her as pitiable and was extending her mercy.

To realize that's what she had become tore at her insides. Before all this she was hardheaded and even stronger willed. She had no doubt she'd return to her normal self, but it would take time.

"One hour," the detective repeated before walking off.

She envied his freedom, his ability to move on wherever and whenever he saw fit. Being able to exercise that basic human right had been far too long for her.

"You can go in, Miss Jones." One of the officers smiled at her, a tender expression that carried the underlying connotation that he felt sorry for her. She wished never to have that directed at her again. She didn't need their sympathy. She was self-sufficient. She was free.

She entered her apartment and had her hand on the door ready to shut it behind her.

"We'll be right out here for you, Miss Jones."

She barely nodded. She was still a prisoner. She had simply exchanged an armed criminal for two armed law enforcement officers. She closed the door, slipping into the sacred cocoon of her private sanctuary. She locked the dead bolt and slipped the chain across.

It was then that her legs became unsteady. She leaned against the door, steadying her weight on one leg, then the next, as she pulled off her heels.

Her hands started to shake, slowly at first and then faster. Her dam of resolve, the one of a fighter, the one she had somehow managed to keep erect, broke apart in a flood of tears. The sobs heaved from her chest and racked her frame. The reality was setting in and not with ease. The emotion crashed into her, stealing her breath, threatening her sanity. She could have died. She was almost raped. And the one person she needed, wanted, was God knows where.

CHAPTER 86

IF VERONICA HAD THE ABILITY to feel regret, she might have experienced it for that detective. His suspicion of her was obvious. It had been written all over his face and clear in the way he talked to her, in the manner his eyes studied her.

She settled into the backseat of the town car as she was driven to a hotel.

She was happy to have made it out of there when she had. If it had taken any longer, she could have been carted off like Don.

It was too bad that she'd lost him, but her people knew the risks of working for her. She defended no one. They were paid as independent contractors, and if they were going down, it was solo. She always ensured that she had no paper trail connecting her to them. Even payment was routed through so many offshore accounts, it would keep a forensic accountant busy for years trying to follow the money.

What infuriated her was the fact that her leverage for the City of Gold was gone. With Sophie alive and under police protection and Don arrested, this entire mess had just gotten a whole lot messier. Sophie knew her name. She reassured herself if any of this tied back to her, she'd find a way to beat the charges. She always did.

Ian Bridges was to blame for all this. She should have just terminated her contract with him when he refused to steal the statue, but no, she had fallen into temptation with the offer of Paititi. She had allowed herself to buy into the legend as fact. She had taken a bite of the juicy, red apple.

Even knowing that they had found the City of Gold did her no good.

People said control of any kind was an illusion, but for her, up until now, she'd held it within her grasp. Whenever it had threatened to fall out of reach, she'd adjusted to ensure she kept it.

In this case, she resigned herself to the fact that Ian Bridges may have been overpowered. With Matthew and his two friends, that was three against one, and what's to say they didn't assume that authority?

It would explain the police. Otherwise how did they know where to look? Yes, the blame lay completely with Ian Bridges. He never should have abducted the girl in the first place. She hired him to use his persuasive powers as a killer, not to turn around and make her a babysitter.

No, Ian Bridges deserved to die for what he had put her through, but she couldn't risk going after him when he returned. The police were already involved, and with that girl alive—another disappointment by one of her own—she was starting to feel like she could rely on no one but herself.

Somehow she needed to obtain the exact coordinates of the find. Her buyer would soon grow impatient, and letting down others was not what she did. She provided results.

Her cell phone rang, and she answered without acknowledgment. After a second, Ian said, "Vincent?"

"Yes?"

"Arrange the plane for two days from now."

She hung up without saying a word, a smirk on her lips.

Once in the privacy of her hotel, she popped a couple of ice cubes into a glass and poured herself a double scotch. She then dropped into a chair and dialed a man she could rely on. Ian had missed his chance to give her the coordinates. When he answered, she said, "It's time." She then told him where and when.

Lowering the receiver with one hand, she raised her drink with the other. She swirled the amber liquid, the ice clinking against the glass, and took a sip. As it burned its way down her throat, a solution came to mind. What she contemplated was a risk. She'd lie low for a day or two, but since when did she shy away from a challenge?

CHAPTER 87

SOPHIE STAYED UNDER THE HOT water of her shower until it ran cold. Even then, she remained there, leaning against the tiles, tears streaming down her face, down her body, down the drain. If only it were that easy to purge herself of all that she had undergone. But she had to pull herself together. The spark within her, her fighting nature, told her that much.

Yes, she had come close to being killed, to being raped, but neither had happened. She was one of the lucky ones.

She wrapped herself in her terry cloth robe, preferring the texture and warmth of cotton over silk. Hugging herself, she continued to suppress the tears, but they would be subdued no longer. She let them flow again. It was healthier to let emotion out than to hold it back, she supposed.

She cried until no moisture was left. Her tear ducts were tender, her eyes no doubt bloodshot. Utter exhaustion was on the cusp of swallowing her whole.

Then a knock came on her door. The detective was back with his questions, with his inquiries, maybe even with his accusations.

She peered through the peephole, more out of habit than anything. It was him. He wasn't facing the door, but was speaking at a low volume to one of the officers, his head turned to the side.

She unlocked the dead bolt and unlatched the chain. Her fingers pinched around the little knob on the chain. For some reason she found security in touching it. She took a deep breath and opened the door.

The detective spun toward her and nodded his hello, before entering. He was holding a brown paper bag, its bottom soiled from its contents, and her purse. She took the latter from him and put her hands around her cell phone as if it somehow brought her closer to Cal.

"This is for you, too." He extended the bag to her.

The sight and the smell of food washed over her like a tidal wave. Her stomach growled and reminded her that she hadn't eaten for hours, and before that, she'd barely had anything for six days.

She took the bag from him. "Thank you."

"It's chicken wings. Honey garlic. I hope you like them."

Comfort food. She could have kissed him. Okay, maybe not, but she most certainly could have fallen into him for a hug. To feel a safe connection with another human being, to come into contact… Her soul longed for it. But life didn't always operate by instinct. It operated by protocol, and it wouldn't have been appropriate.

"Would you like tea? Coffee?"

"You don't have to worry about me." He stood there, as if he was lost, thrown into her apartment and released.

"I was going to make tea for myself."

"Sure, in that case, I will take some." He pressed his lips together. His attempt at a smile?

"Is chai all right?"

"Yes. Fine."

Was he irritated now? Was she not talking to him fast enough? If so, too bad. He'd have to wait. She wasn't going to talk without tea, or food, in her stomach. Maybe he sensed her thought process, though, as he made himself comfortable on her couch.

Sophie smiled awkwardly at him. It was strange having another man in her apartment and being alone with him, even though it wasn't for any impure reason. She filled up the kettle and flicked the switch, then grabbed two cups and two tea bags and set them on the counter.

She tore into the brown take-out bag and pulled out a

Styrofoam container. The aroma of the wings made her salivate before she even opened the package. She emptied them onto a plate from her cupboard. Whoever had made the wings had done a great job. They were meaty and coated with sauce. She couldn't even wait to sit down before digging in.

She tore a chunk of meat off the bone, and then she took another bite and another until she realized she had carried on as if he weren't there. She had eaten three wings before she came up for air. Self-conscious, she ripped off a piece of paper towel and dabbed the corners of her mouth and then scrunched it up in her hand.

The kettle clicked, and she set the wings aside to pour the boiling water over the tea bags. "I usually let it sit for five minutes."

"Sure."

Was he impatient with her? Did he have better things to do? Or did he only want answers? For all this, she still found that she couldn't fault him. Or maybe she was just being paranoid.

She sat across from him, her plate on her lap and her mind and her stomach on the food. She picked up another wing and took a bite, studying his appearance as she did so. She wouldn't have pegged him for a wing man. He was lean and handsome, in a chiseled sort of way. Too thin for her preference. Not that she was thinking of him like that. These were simply observations.

"Thank you again." She lifted the remains of a wing, essentially saluting him with the bones.

"Don't mention it." He leaned forward, clasping his hands between his legs. "I do have some questions for you, Miss Jones."

"Yes, I know." It had only been three minutes, but she had to move again.

She finished preparing their tea, making his with two sugars the way he had responded to her inquiry.

She handed him the cup and sat back down. The chicken wings begged her to return, but she let them sit on the coffee table in front of her. She would have plenty of time to eat. It's the least she could do after all this man had done for her, for his kindness, for doing his job and rescuing her. "What would you like to know?"

"I want to know everything from the beginning. First, did you know your abductor?"

She shook her head.

"But you had mentioned a Veronica Vincent."

"Yes. And you know about Ian Bridges?" She paused and retracted her question. "I mean obviously since you found me at his place, you do." She looked away, embarrassed. She just needed some time to relax and to collect her thoughts.

She blew on her tea and then took a small sip. Instantly she was catapulted back to the coffee shop, the last time she was with Cal when he brought her a strawberry scone and a chai tea. She'd give anything to go back in time. She wouldn't have let herself become so blinded. She would have realized there were more important things than selling a house.

"So you want to know everything?" The question was rhetorical, a rise to pique his interest, even though it wasn't necessary based on the way he sat perched on the edge of the sofa cushion.

"Please."

CHAPTER 88

THE BULLET WAS A THROUGH and through. The door that Cal had found was the way out and it must have opened when they'd accessed the basement of the temple. Despite the fact it had been night, they'd set out right away. Robyn's health had been of the utmost importance.

Robyn was treated in a Bolivian hospital, given a bunch of painkillers and the go-ahead to fly. They didn't hang around to question the doctors but rather boarded the plane the first chance they'd gotten.

Ian had lost his power when Cal and Matthew had assumed strength in numbers. Surprisingly and blessedly, a stray bullet never so much as fired during that altercation, and they'd successfully disarmed him.

They had made Ian call Vincent to arrange for her plane to be ready for them. Matthew and Cal took turns holding the gun on him, while the other helped Robyn. She'd told them that she wasn't an invalid. The recollection of her words, her attitude, hadn't gotten old by even the next day. It still brought a smile to Matthew's face.

They had found a way to seal the door to Paititi from the outside. Their find was safe. They buried Juan in the location where he had died. Then they had maneuvered through the jungle all night and all the next day, taking periodic rests. The canoes had been exactly where they had hidden them, and the four of them had loaded into one. The trek back had been smooth considering all they had been through, all Robyn had been through. They'd reached civilization twenty-four hours, give or take, after Robyn had been shot. She'd been treated and the next night, they boarded the plane.

Now they were on the plane heading home, and they couldn't touch down in Canada fast enough. They were hours into the flight, and the sun was starting to rise, flooding the plane's cabin with natural light.

Matthew was sitting at the table reading more on the Inca Empire. Cal was across from him, sleeping with his chin resting on his chest. Matthew could only imagine the neck pain he'd have when he woke up. Ian was zip-tied to a side table and wore a permanent scowl.

Robyn was asleep on the couch but then stirred, as if she had felt his eyes on her. She yawned and wiped her eyes. "I could sleep for a month."

"Me too."

"Me three," Cal grumbled as he rubbed the length of his neck.

Cal had been asleep when Matthew had called Daniel with an estimated ETA. It was then that Daniel shared news of his own. But after the limited sleep they had during this quest, he let Cal rest with the intention to tell him as soon as he woke up. Matthew had also had a number of missed calls and a voice mail from his father.

"How are we getting Sophie back?" Cal asked.

Matthew smiled. "She's safe and she's home." He went on to explain how her rescue had all played out.

"Thank God." Cal steepled his hands and gazed upward.

About a minute later, Matthew went to open his mouth, but Cal spoke instead. "What is the deal between you and Vincent anyway?"

"Yeah, Matt. I think he deserves to hear about it." Robyn rose from the couch and took a seat beside Cal at the table.

"It was a long time ago. Water under the bridge."

"You didn't just say that." Cal turned to Robyn. "Did he just say that?"

Matthew took a deep breath. "We first met in South Africa.

Have you heard of the missing Krugerrands?"

"Yeah," Cal said.

"Well, they're not exactly missing."

Cal angled his head. "What do you mean?"

"Vincent took possession of them."

Robyn raised an eyebrow at him. "You're being awful cryptic here, Matt. Do you want to actually tell the story or should I?"

"Fine, fine. I found them—"

"But she seduced them out from under him. When he woke up in the morning, he was tied to the bed. The 'rands—and Vincent—were gone." The hint of a smile dusted Robyn's lips.

"Why do you find such amusement in this?" Matthew asked. "And shouldn't you be sleeping?"

"It just proves that men are easily distracted by a good-looking woman."

"So you lost the treasure and the woman?" Cal asked for clarification.

Robyn answered. "He thought he had. Then the door to the hotel room opened and it was Vincent."

"She came back?"

"Not by choice."

Matthew rolled his eyes. "Why am I even here?"

Robyn snickered and continued. "Turned out two guys with guns had cornered her and forced her back to the room."

Cal looked at Matthew. "So you were tied to a bed and two armed men came in?"

"Yep. Why don't you continue, Robyn? You're doing an excellent job." He settled back into his chair, lacing his fingers behind his head.

"Don't mind if I do. So here he is, naked and tied to the bedpost, and—"

Matthew sighed. "You had to add the naked part."

Cal let out a chuckle, and then Robyn went on.

"These men turned out to be Vincent's buyers. See, she doesn't hunt treasure for fame. She does it all for the money."

"So that's why she took Sophie?" Cal asked.

"You actually have that idiot over there to thank for that." Robyn jacked a thumb toward Ian.

"But to answer your question," Matthew began, "she would have had a buyer lined up for the Pandu statue. She missed the window of opportunity, though. So when I offered her the City of Gold, she likely offered that to her buyers, instead."

"All right, back to the story." Cal rubbed his hands together. "You're naked and tied to a bedpost."

Matthew shook his head.

Robyn picked up where she had left off. "Vincent tries to use her charm on the buyers, but it doesn't work. There's a struggle and the gun goes off."

"I still have nightmares about that," Matthew interjected.

"The bullet just missed him, but it got the rope. It frayed enough that while the three of them were involved in an altercation, Matthew got free."

"You're like an action hero," Cal said with a laugh.

Matthew rolled his eyes. "It sounds so much better looking back. At the time it was kind of horrifying."

"Kind of? I would have been shitting my pants. Oh, wait you weren't wearing any." Cal's statement had both him and Robyn doubling over.

"Knock it off," Matthew said without conviction.

Robyn held up her hand. "So…sorry, Matt. Ouch, it hurts to laugh."

Matthew made a vee with his fingers and drew it from his eyes to her. Their history made the message discernable. He'd once joked that he'd put a voodoo spell on her for being a smartass.

"Then what happened?" Cal asked.

"He jumped out the window."

Obviously, after taking a real bullet, she didn't fear a fictional spell.

"Naked?"

Robyn was smiling. "Yep."

"Then what?"

"He lowered himself onto my balcony and banged on the

window."

"You got more than you bargained for."

Robyn's cheeks flushed.

Seeming to sense the awkwardness, Cal said, "And Vincent?"

Matthew shrugged. "I didn't really care anymore."

"Oh, you're cold."

"I'm cold? She's the one who left me tied to a bed."

"True." Cal seemed to ruminate on all he had been told. "So that's why it's so personal between you two? You heated the sheets, she stole the 'rands from you, and you left her for dead?"

"Yeah, but instead of being like any normal woman who would be pissed off at being left to die, she became more attracted to me."

"She's an interesting woman," Cal responded.

"You can say that again. I still remem—"

Robyn slapped his arm. "Enough trips down memory lane for one day."

Slicing through the tension, Cal's cell phone rang. "Caller ID says it's Sophie!" He answered. "Sophie? Oh, thank God." To the rest of them, he said, "She's all right." Back into the phone. "Did they hurt you? God, I love you so much."

As Matthew listened to his friend, he glanced over at Robyn. She was rubbing her bad arm, and while it could have been to ease pain, he sensed it had to do with comforting herself emotionally. He remembered what it was like to be in a loving relationship and to care about the other person as much as his own soul. He had—at one time—had the love of his life, like Cal had with Sophie. Now she sat across from him, seemingly as haunted by the memories of their time together as he was. Maybe one day things would change again. Calling her "baby" sure had seemed natural.

Cal lowered his phone. "They got the man who was in the room with Sophie." He choked back on his words. "He was going to rape her."

Robyn put her hand on his shoulder. "I'm sorry."

"The police showed up just in time." He took a deep breath.

"Bad news, though. Vincent's in the wind."

Chapter 89

Sophie had been returned safely and while that mattered, it was far from all that mattered. William adjusted his tie in the mirror, his mind far from the image reflecting back at him. The other day, the PI had said he still hadn't tracked Matthew down and there was no progress on connecting with Gideon Barnes, either. Both of which he sensed were lies.

William hated the lack of results more than he hated pointless updates. His time was far too valuable to spend following up with people. He paid them to take care of things. He shouldn't have to hold their hands as they searched for answers. He shouldn't have to check in with them to see how they were making out. They should be keeping him apprised of any current developments, no matter how small.

He may just have to swallow his pride and make the call, though. To be visited by the detective and told they had found Sophie was a fishing expedition. William recognized them from a mile away. He had to be proactive and know when someone was searching for the latest scoop on the mayor of Toronto. Despite the peace and love that some people preached, negativity and self-advancement were what ruled society. People didn't want to see others succeed; they wanted to be the ones who succeeded. Most didn't care if they reached this by ethical methods or not. Anything was a go when it came to getting ahead.

With William in the media spotlight at all times, he had to stay one step ahead of people like that. He had to ensure he was professional and diplomatic at all times. While he was known to lose his temper now and again, those episodes had to be few and far between. The reputation he demanded of himself required as much.

The phone on his dresser rang. It was an internal call, meaning it was either Daniel or Lauren.

"Hello?"

"There's a woman at the front door for you," Lauren said on the other end of the line. "She says it's about Matthew."

"Let her in." He hurried out of his room, uncertain if he even returned the receiver to its cradle in his haste.

Standing in the entry was a woman in her midthirties. Her beauty was striking. Her red hair was curly and flowed over her shoulders, but her good looks mattered less than her message.

"You know something about my son?"

"I do. Is there somewhere we could talk in private?"

It was an odd request, but whatever it took to get her to speak. "Lauren, please take her coat."

"No, if it's all the same to you, I'll keep it."

William waved Lauren away. To the woman, he said, "This way."

He led her to the den where he had questioned Daniel a few nights ago. He gestured to a wingback chair. "Have a seat."

"Thank you," she said as she took him up on his offer.

William dropped onto the sofa. "What is your relationship with Matthew?"

"I'm afraid that's a need-to-know and you don't need to know." The woman rose and pulled a handgun from the inside of her coat.

His eyes widened. "What's going on?" This couldn't be happening to him, whatever *this* was. He was the mayor of Toronto, for crying out loud. Who had the gall to hold the mayor at gunpoint, in his own home?

He stood up. "Do you have any idea who I am?"

"You will be a corpse if you don't cooperate," she said. "Sit. Back. Down."

This woman was psychotic. Looks certainly were deceiving.

"Where is my son?"

"From my understanding, he'll be here soon. Until then, let's get comfortable, shall we?"

CHAPTER 90

DANIEL WAS OUTSIDE THE AIRPORT waiting in his car for Matthew's plane to touch down. Two cop cars were parked behind him, and the officers inside were ready to escort Ian Bridges to jail.

As for Matthew, he could explain everything to his father. Daniel had kept Matthew's secrets for long enough. William Connor deserved to know the truth about his son.

To witness the heartbreak in William's eyes when he had pressed him for information on his whereabouts was almost enough to break his resolve. If it hadn't been for Sophie's life being at risk, he probably would have come clean. Surely, Matthew would understand his viewpoint, but even if he didn't, too bad.

Daniel would be there when Matthew first stepped off the plane to deliver the message personally. He was no longer going to be working between father and son. He no longer wanted to be a dividing force between flesh and blood.

His cell phone rang, and he answered, expecting it to be Matthew. Instead, it was Justin, and he was out of breath.

"Slow down. Say that again," Daniel said.

"I tracked down the phone that sent the videos of Sophie. But it's the location of—"

"Okay, breathe." If the kid didn't slow down his delivery, he'd hyperventilate before he got to his news.

"He was in contact with a woman named Veronica Vincent. Her phone signal is coming from the Connor mansion. Right now."

Daniel sat up straighter, bumping his head on the car's visor. "You must be reading something wrong."

"I'm not. I've double-checked it, triple-checked it. She's there."

"Oh shit." Daniel put the car into drive and gunned it out in front of an SUV.

A blaring horn and a cursing driver greeted him in his rearview mirror, but they'd just have to deal with it. There was a killer in the house, and William and Lauren would be home.

"Justin, send the cops to the Connor residence. Now."

Daniel tossed his cell phone onto the passenger seat and floored the accelerator. He glanced to his mirror again and noticed the two cop cars were trailing him.

Apparently, this wasn't Toronto PD's finest hour.

He fished for his phone again, and as he took a corner, it fell right in his palm. He dialed 911 to have cruisers sent out to the airport. He dropped Ian Bridges's name and hoped it reached that detective from the news, the one who had freed Sophie.

As for the two cops on his six, he'd lead them straight to Veronica.

CHAPTER 91

TORONTO WAS A WELCOME SIGHT. The feel of the runway under the plane's wheels whelmed emotion up into Matthew's throat.

Sophie Jones was just fine, or at least she would be. She may need to see a therapist, and he was more than willing to pay for that as he felt somehow responsible for the entire mess, but she was safe.

Logically, he knew none of it was his fault. He hadn't abducted her. But if it hadn't been for Vincent's personal vendetta against him, it might not have gone so far. Vincent would never forgive him for leaving her in South Africa in a fight for her life, even if she had found it attractive. But it didn't matter if she forgave him. They'd never be together. There was too big a difference between the two of them: she loved to kill and he didn't. And that was just one aspect where they differed.

Matthew had picked up on the way Robyn had looked at him after Lewis had been attacked by the anaconda. It was as if she held him responsible for what had happened, but his conscience was clear. If they hadn't taken down the Bolivians when they had, the rest of them may be buried in Paititi, if they were even given the courtesy of a burial.

The plane came to a smooth stop, and the loading platform was lowered.

Cal rushed to the exit. "Let me off this thing," he said as he headed out first.

Matthew gathered up Robyn's things for her and offered to carry her bag. Matthew and Ian had returned home mostly empty-handed, their backpacks still in a cavern back in Bolivia where they had dumped them to dive into the first lagoon. Robin smiled at him, but it seemed forced.

He put his hand on her forearm. "Are you all right? Are you in pain?"

She shook her head, and tears beaded in the corners of her eyes. "When I was shot, you called me 'baby.'"

His heart palpitated. "You heard that? I thought, maybe, with just being—"

"I heard it."

"Well, you know how I feel about you, Robyn."

She angled her head farther back to gaze into his eyes. "And you know how I feel."

He detected the softness in her tone, the fact that she felt the exact same way, but there was also a sadness, a regret.

"I know it's not our time right now," he said.

She shook her head, and with it, speared his heart.

He had to turn the conversation back to what he thought she was going to bring up before he choked on the tears he was too proud to cry. "I know you're upset about Lewis." It was silly, really. He didn't need to explain himself to her. He didn't know why he felt he had to.

"A little bit, but I understand."

"Are you sure?"

She nodded. "It was us or them, right? I get it. You didn't make him go into that lagoon, anyway. It was Juan's doing."

He put a hand on her shoulder, and she felt so small beneath his touch, so vulnerable, that he wanted to pull her in and hold her. He wanted to kiss her, to take possession of her mouth, of her being. Instead, he pressed his lips together in a firm line and lowered his head. "God, it's good to be home."

She pointed her finger at him and smiled. "You can say that again."

As they deplaned, Matthew expected police to be waiting at the base of the stairs, but there were none. He had released Ian from his bonds to the table briefly, only to zip-tie his wrists together behind his back.

Matthew followed Ian down the stairs. They'd only made it a few steps when a bloom of red stole his vision.

Chapter 92

They had one man in custody, and it wasn't even the man they had expected to find. Ian Bridges was still out there, and the lug, who went by the name of Don Reed, wasn't talking. He had demanded a lawyer and clammed up.

Brody pulled the man's background, and it was extensive. Multiple charges of assault with a deadly weapon and breaking and entering when he was younger. He even did some time back in the nineties, but the judge had gone soft on him.

But whoever seemed to have had his back then had left him out to dry now. His lawyer had yet to come through for him and soon he'd be appointed one by the city, whether he liked it or not.

It wasn't easy for Brody to sit still or leave the man alone. He wanted to beat the truth out of him. The name Amber Watts didn't bring up anything in the databases, either—at least nothing in relation to the woman he had talked to. When he had mentioned that name to Don, his eyes had glazed over.

It seemed obvious that Amber Watts was Veronica Vincent.

Brody had typed that name into the system, too, and ran it through the databases. The screen returned with many results. He should have known he'd need more to narrow it down.

"Fuller." He turned toward the approaching chief.

The man's face was pale. Something had taken a horrible turn.

Brody rose from his chair and met him halfway. "What is it?"

"Nine-one-one just got a call. There's been a shooting at Pearson International. There's a confirmed casualty, but the victim's identity has yet to be confirmed. However, just before that a caller, who identified himself as Daniel Iverson, William Connor's house manager, said that Ian Bridges was coming in on a private flight along with Connor's son and some friends. You don't think they're connected, do you?"

He didn't answer his boss's question. He had already grabbed his coat from his chair and was on the move.

BRODY FLEW THROUGH THE CITY TO THE AIRPORT. The location of the plane and the shooting would be easy to find. That's the thing with tragic events like this. Not only were they messy but they drew spectators the way gladiators did in Ancient Rome.

He immediately spotted the silver jet and headed straight for it. He flashed his badge at the security gate and they let him in. As he got closer, the casualty was confirmed by the amount of blood that sprayed the side of the plane. A sniper's shot. How that had even been arranged was almost inconceivable. It meant that the shooter was in the crowd and that they had bypassed security.

A couple ambulances were already on-site, not that paramedics could help the person who was on the other end of the bullet.

Brody jumped out of his department car and looked around for a potential sniper perch. The terminal was crowded and becoming more so by the minute. He motioned for officers to approach him.

"Cordon off this area," he commanded. "Have the public taken somewhere and get all their information."

The officers nodded, and he watched them run off to follow his orders. Eventually the crowd receded. There were still enough gawkers to make his skin crawl, but he had learned to manage that aspect of the job years ago. They just had to be put out of mind and his focus allocated to the task at hand.

Brody ran up to a medical examiner, who was leaning over the remains. He held up his badge. "Do we have an ID?"

The examiner looked up slowly. "Ian Bridges."

He ran his hand through his hair. This all began with Ian Bridges abducting Sophie Jones. Now he was dead. It was the in-between details that needed to be ascertained. But now that he knew the identity of the deceased, any fear over it being Matthew Connor was eradicated.

It was then that he noticed four adults nestled together at the back of an ambulance. He was closer now and able to see. One man was sitting on the back of the ambulance wrapped in a blanket. That man was Matthew Connor.

He scanned the two next to him, recognizing them from their photographs—Cal Myers and Robyn Garcia. The other woman was easy to identify. It was Sophie Jones. He took a step toward them when his phone rang. Caller ID showed Chief Snyder.

"Just after you left another call came in asking for patrol to go out to the Connor estate."

"The estate?"

"Apparently there is a threat to the mayor's life. Veronica Vincent. Does that name ring any bells for you?"

"I've gotta go." Brody hung up and beelined it to Matthew. "Matthew Connor, I'm Detective Fuller. You have to come with me. Right now."

Matthew hopped off the back of the ambulance. His face had streaks of pink on it. He must have been right next to Ian when he was shot.

"What is it?" Robyn asked.

Matthew was looking at Brody. His eyebrows held the same contortion his father's did when standing his ground on an issue. Brody had witnessed it during various televised press conferences.

"It's your father."

MATTHEW WAS FORTUNATE NOT TO be joining Ian in the morgue. Fate had intervened, or it was a lucky stroke of coincidence, but the moment the bullet struck Ian's head, Matthew's stride had shifted to the side. Otherwise, it would have traveled through the both of them.

The shock of it all must've been making him hear things.

"What about my father?" Fear laced through him all of a

sudden. He didn't care for the flush in the detective's cheeks.

"Do you know a woman named Veronica Vincent?"

His heart nearly stopped beating. "Y-yes."

Matthew noticed that Cal squeezed Sophie tighter and rubbed her arm.

"Well, she's at your house, Matthew."

"What is she…?" Oh God. He knew exactly. Vincent wasn't the kind to give up, and she wasn't past getting her hands dirty, and she had lost her leverage when the cops freed Sophie.

This had become personal. Again.

CHAPTER 93

"I DON'T KNOW WHAT YOU think you know about my son, but—"

"Do you just love the sound of your own voice?" Veronica paced the room. She had faith that she'd be able to escape any charges that may come her way but also knew that she was being reckless coming here. Stupid even, but she had invested too much to relinquish all claim to the City of Gold.

The door to the den swung open, and she spun to see Matthew standing in the doorway. She smiled at him. "How nice of you to join us, Matthew."

"Son?"

She put the gun back on William. "You stay right where you are. Your son and I, we have some business to take care of."

"I'm not in business with you, Vincent, and I never have been."

She laughed. He was obviously putting on a show for his father. It was then that she remembered. "Ah, he doesn't know, does he?"

"Doesn't know what?" The older man didn't look too impressed, and it was more than just being held at gunpoint.

She found his ignorance amusing. No doubt he assumed that he had his household under control. Control—the illusion that so many hungered for.

"Oh, please, let me introduce you," she said, her voice full of glee.

"No, Veronica, not this way," Matthew said.

Something softened in her belly when he spoke her first name. It took her back to that night in South Africa.

His eyes met hers. "Let me tell him the truth myself."

She stepped off to the side. Who was she to come between a father and son bonding moment? It would be their last anyway. She gestured with a jab of the gun for him to go ahead.

THIS HAD TO BE ONE of the toughest moments of his life. To not only see his father held up at gunpoint, but to know he was about to bring such disappointment to him, was breaking Matthew's heart.

He glanced at Vincent. She was probably finding amusement in the entire scenario. Holding all the cards was a position she relished more than most. Seeing people humiliated and betrayed, she enjoyed even more. But, surely, she had to know time was running out for her.

He looked back to his father, studying the creases in his brow, taking note of the lines around his eyes and his mouth. For the first time, he recognized himself in his father. And in that instant, he experienced a connection most children likely had with their parents from a very young age, but it was one he was never able to let form. When his mom had died, he'd been too busy being angry and blaming his dad for what had happened, for the fact that his father was moving on so soon. But in quick reflection, he realized that was what he'd wanted to believe. He had tainted the truth to protect his heart. If he had a distant relationship with his father, it wouldn't hurt as much when it was his time to go. But right now, Matthew grasped the fallacy in those beliefs, in his prior convictions. If his father died now without their closing the distance between them, Matthew would be buried in regret without any chance to make amends. Now was the time to come clean. And he would deliver it to his father the way he'd appreciate it most—directly.

"I'm Gideon Barnes." The truth cut from his throat. Matthew didn't know exactly what he expected. Maybe for his father to yell at him, to accuse him of stealing, of violating his trust.

Instead, a tear fell down the man's cheek. Matthew didn't remember even seeing his father cry when he'd lost his wife.

Matthew glanced quickly at Vincent, who rolled her eyes and approved that he move to the couch beside his father.

"I'm sorry that I wasn't honest with you. I wanted to tell you, but I didn't know how you'd react. I thought you'd be angry."

William faced Matthew, meeting his gaze. "You didn't want to tell me."

Matthew's heart fractured at hearing his father's voice and seeing the pain in his eyes. "I—"

William held up his hands. "I'm not always the easiest to talk to. And I admit I'd prefer for you to be an archaeologist and not a treasure hunter. I mean, haven't I provided for you enough?" He waved a hand dismissing his own question. "I'm just happy to have you home safe, son."

His father surprised him then by pulling Matthew into an embrace.

"As much as I hate breaking up this little reunion, I'm going to need to know where to collect Paititi."

Matthew pulled back from the hug and stood. "I'm not telling you anything."

She smiled coyly. "You're forgetting that I have the gun."

The door to the den burst open. Detective Brody stood in front of a crew of ETF officers.

"And I have an entire army."

EPILOGUE

"I STILL CAN'T BELIEVE MY son found the lost City of Gold." William Connor posed with an arm around Matthew, as Cal snapped a picture of them.

Cal had purchased a new camera and was entertaining multiple offers to buy photographs of Paititi. He was having fun negotiating, not that he was very open to fluctuation. He had a price in mind, and he'd accept nothing less. It was the legendary City of Gold, after all. He should be able to name his price. Besides, no one else knew where it was.

Matthew, William, Daniel, Cal, Sophie, Robyn, and a team they had hired had gone to catalog and claim the find. The pieces would be distributed to museums throughout the world, although, Matthew did negotiate a substantial finder's fee for this discovery.

"Sophie!" Cal called out for her, and she came running to his side.

From the outside, their relationship seemed stronger than ever, and Matthew was happy for them. Sophie had been through a lot, and it could have ruined everything, but she'd focused on how far Cal had gone to save her. She'd recognized his bravery for what it was: the greatest love. It had to be for one to willingly risk one's life for another's.

When Sophie reached Cal's side, he looked at her with a serious expression on his face. "We need to talk," he said.

"Okay…" She bit her lip, clearly nervous about being placed

on the spot.

"You know that house you love so much?"

"Uh-huh…"

"It's ours, if you still want it. I know that you might not want to…after everything that—"

"What do you mean *ours*?" she interrupted. "You mean, as in us moving in together?"

Cal pulled the camera over his head and handed it to Matthew. He then got down on one knee and pulled out a small box from a pocket. "Sophie Jones, will you marry me?"

Sophie covered her mouth and started to cry.

Robyn tucked herself against Matthew's side and whispered, "I'm so happy for them."

He smiled at her and mouthed, since he wasn't good at whispering, *Me too.*

Seconds passed and Sophie still hadn't responded. Cal held his pose, and Matthew was impressed by his determination.

"I said, Sophie Jones, will you—"

"Yes! Of course!" She threw her arms around him and kissed him.

Cal pulled back just long enough to say, "Matt, take our picture."

Read on for an exciting preview of Carolyn
Arnold's thrilling debut novel featuring Madison
Knight

TIES THAT BIND

CHAPTER 1

SOMEONE DIED EVERY DAY. Detective Madison Knight was left to make sense of it.

She ducked under the yellow tape and surveyed the scene. The white, two-story house would be deemed average any other day, but today the dead body inside made it a place of interest to the Stiles PD and the curious onlookers who gathered in small clusters on the sidewalk.

She'd never before seen the officer who was securing the perimeter, but she knew his type. The way he stood there—his back straight, one hand resting on his holster, the other gripping a clipboard—he was an eager recruit.

He held up a hand as she approached. "This is a closed crime scene."

She unclipped her badge from the waist of her pants and held it up in front of him. He studied it as if it were counterfeit. She usually respected those who took their jobs seriously but not when she was functioning on little sleep and the humidity level topped ninety-five percent at ten thirty in the morning.

"Detective K-N-I—"

Her name died on her lips as Sergeant Winston stepped out of the house. She would have groaned audibly if he weren't closing the distance between them so quickly. She preferred her boss behind his desk.

Winston gestured toward the young officer to let him know she was permitted to be on the scene. The officer glared at her before leaving his post. She envied the fact that he could walk away while she was left to speak with the sarge.

"It's about time you got here." Winston fished a handkerchief out of a pocket and wiped at his receding hairline. The extra few inches of exposed forehead could have served as a solar panel. "I was just about to assign the lead to Grant."

Terry Grant was her on-the-job partner of five years and three years younger than her thirty-four. She'd be damned if Terry was put in charge of this case.

"Where have you been?" Winston asked.

She jacked a thumb in the rookie's direction. "Who's the new guy?"

"Don't change the subject, Knight."

She needed to offer some sort of explanation for being late. "Well, boss, you know me. Up all night slinging back shooters."

"Don't get smart with me."

She flashed him a cocky smile and pulled out a Hershey's bar from one of her front pants pocket. The chocolate had already softened from the heat. Not that it mattered. She took a bite.

Heaven.

She spoke with her mouth partially full. "What are you doing here, anyway?"

"The call came in, I was nearby, and thought someone should respond." His leg caught the tape as he tried to step over it to the sidewalk and he hopped on the other leg to adjust his balance. He continued speaking as if he hadn't noticed. "The body's upstairs, main bedroom. She was strangled." He pointed the tip of a key toward her. "Keep me updated." He pressed a button on his key fob and the department-issued SUV's lights flashed. "I'll be waiting for your call."

As if he needed to say that. Sometimes she wondered if he valued talking more than taking action.

She took a deep breath. She could feel the young officer watching her, and she flicked a glance at him, now that the sergeant was gone. What was his problem? She took another bite of her candy bar.

"Too bad you showed. I think I was about to get the lead."

Madison turned toward her partner's voice. Terry was padding across the lawn toward her.

"I'd have to be the one dead for that to happen." She smiled as she brushed past him.

"You look like crap."

Her smile faded. She stopped walking and turned around. Every one of his blond hairs were in place, making her self-conscious of her short, wake-up-and-wear-it cut. His cheeks held a healthy glow, too, no doubt from his two-mile morning run. She hated people who could do mornings.

"What did you get? Two hours of sleep?" Terry asked.

"Three, but who's counting?" She took another large bite of the chocolate. It was almost a slurp with how fast the bar was melting.

"You were up reviewing evidence from the last case again, weren't you?"

She wasn't inclined to answer.

"You can't change the past."

She wasn't hungry anymore and wrapped up what was left of the chocolate. "Let's focus on *this* case."

"Fine, if that's how it's going be. Victim's name is Laura Saunders. She's thirty-two. Single. Officer Higgins was the first on scene."

Higgins? She hadn't seen him since she arrived, but he had been her training officer. He still worked in that capacity for new recruits. Advancing in the ranks wasn't important to him. He was happy making a difference where he was stationed.

Terry continued. "Call came in from the vic's employer, Southwest Welding Products, where she worked as the receptionist."

"What would make the employer call?"

"She didn't show for her shift at eight. They tried reaching her first, but when they didn't get an answer, they sent a security officer over to her house. He found the door ajar and called downtown. Higgins was here by eight forty-five."

"Who was—"

"The security officer?"

"Yeah." Apparently they finished each other's sentences now.

"Terrence Owens. And don't worry. We took a formal statement and let him go. Background showed nothing, not even a speeding ticket. We can function when you're not here."

She cocked her head to the side.

"He also testifies to the fact that he never stepped one foot in the place." Terry laughed. "He said he's watched enough cop dramas to know that it would contaminate the crime scene. You get all these people watching those stupid TV shows, and they think they can solve a murder."

"So is Owens the one who made the formal call downtown, then?" Madison asked.

"Actually, procedure for them is to route everything through the company administration. A Sandra Butler made the call. She's the office manager."

"So an employee is even half an hour late for work and they send someone to your house?"

"She said it's part of their safety policy."

"At least they're a group of people inclined to think positively." She rolled her eyes. Sweat droplets ran down her back. Gross. She moved toward the house.

The young officer scurried over. He shoved his clipboard under his arm and tucked his pen behind his ear. He pointed toward the chocolate bar still in her hand. "You can't take that in there."

She glanced down. Chocolate oozed from a corner of the wrapper. He was right. She handed the package to him, and he took it with two pinched fingers.

She patted his shoulder. "Good job."

He walked away with the bar dangling from his hand, mumbling something indiscernible.

"You can be so wicked sometimes," Terry said.

"Why, thank you." She was tempted to take a mini bow but resisted the urge.

"It wasn't a compliment. And since when do you eat chocolate for breakfast?"

"Oh shut up." She punched him in the shoulder. He smirked and rubbed his arm. Same old sideshow. She headed into the house with him on her heels.

"The stairs are to the right," Terry said.

"Holy crap, it's freezing in here." The sweat on her skin chilled her. It was a refreshing welcome.

"Yep, a hundred and one outside, sixty inside."

When she was two steps from the top of the staircase, Terry said, "And just a heads-up—this is not your typical strangulation."

"Come on, Terry. You've seen one, you've—" She stopped abruptly when she reached the bedroom doorway. Terry was right.

Chapter 2

The hairs rose on her arms, not from the air-conditioning but from the chill of death. In her ten years on the force, Madison had never seen anything quite like this. Maybe in New York City they were accustomed to this type of murder scene but not here in Stiles where the population was just shy of half a million and the Major Crimes division boasted only six detectives.

She nodded a greeting to Cole Richards, the medical examiner. He reciprocated with a small bob of his head.

Laura Saunders lay on her back in the middle of a double bed, arms folded over her torso. But the one thing that stood out—and this would be what Terry had tried to warn her about—was that she was naked with a man's necktie bound tightly around her neck. That adornment and her shoulder-length brown hair provided the only contrasts between her pale skin and the beige sheets. Most strangulation victims were dressed, or when rape was a factor, the body was typically found in an alley or hotel room, not the vic's own bedroom. For Laura to be found here made it personal.

Jealous lover, perhaps?

"Was she raped?" Madison asked.

Terry rubbed the back of his neck the way he did when there were more questions than answers. "Not leaning that way."

"And she's in her own house," Madison added.

The entire scenario caused Madison pain and regret—pain over how this woman's life had been snuffed out so prematurely, regret that she couldn't have prevented it. For someone who faced death on a regular basis, one would think she would be callous regarding her own mortality, but the truth was, it scared her more with every passing day. Nothing was certain. And with this case, the fact that the victim was only two years younger than she was sank to the pit of her stomach.

Terry kneaded the tips of his fingers into the base of his neck. "There is no evidence of a break-in. Nothing seems to be missing. There's jewelry on her dresser and electronics were left downstairs. There is also no evidence of a struggle. Though, her clothes were strewn on the main level."

Madison moved farther into the room to study Laura and the tie more closely. It was expensive, silk, and blue striped. Her eyes then took in a shelving unit on the far wall, which housed folded clothes, an alarm clock, and a framed photograph.

She brainstormed out loud. "Maybe it was some sort of sex game that got out of hand. Erotic asphyxiation?"

"If it was something as simple as that, why not call nine-one-one? The owner of that necktie must have something to hide."

Richards's assistant excused himself as he walked through the bedroom. Madison could never remember the guy's name.

Terry continued. "Put yourself in this guy's place if things got out of hand. You would loosen the tie, shake her, but you wouldn't pose her. You would certainly call for help."

"The scene definitely speaks to it being an intentional act." She met her partner's eyes. "But I'd also guess the killer felt regret. Otherwise, why cross her arms over her torso? That could indicate a close relationship between Laura and her killer."

Their discussion paused at the sound of a zipper as Richards sealed the woman in the black bag.

His assistant worked at getting the gurney out of the room and addressed Richards. "I'll wait in the hall."

Richards nodded.

"Winston confirmed you're ruling the cause of death as strangulation," Madison said to the ME.

"Yes. COD is asphyxiation due to strangulation. Her face shows signs of petechiae. Young, fit women don't normally show that unless they put up a fight. And there were also cuts to her wrists."

"Cuts?" Terry asked.

"Yes." Richards glanced at Terry. "Crime Scene is thinking cuffs. I don't think they've found them yet."

Madison's eyes drifted to the bed's headboard and its black powder-coated vertical bars. The paint was worn off a few of them. "She's bound, and then he uncuffs and poses her." The hairs on her arms rose again. "When are you placing time of death?"

"Thirty to thirty-three hours ago based on the stage of rigor and body temperature."

"So between two and five Sunday morning?" Terry smiled and shrugged his shoulders when both pairs of eyes shot to him.

Sometimes Madison wondered how her partner could do math so quickly in his head.

"Of course, the fact that it's cold enough to hang meat in here makes it harder to pinpoint," Richards said.

Madison noticed the light in Terry's eyes brighten at the recognition of the cliché. He knew she didn't care for such idioms and he had proven himself an opportunist over the years. Whenever he could dish them out, he would. Whenever someone else said them around her, he found amusement in it. She was tempted to cross the room and beat him, but instead, she just rolled her eyes, certain the hint of a smile on her face showed. She hated that she didn't have enough restraint to ignore him altogether.

"I'll be conducting a full autopsy within the next twenty-four hours. I will keep you posted on all my findings. Tomorrow afternoon at the earliest. You know where to find me." Richards smiled at her, showcasing flawless white teeth, his midnight skin providing further contrast. And something about the way his eyes creased with the expression, Madison couldn't claim immunity to his charms. When he smiled, it actually calmed her. Too bad he was married.

"Thanks." The word came out automatically. Her eyes were on

a framed photograph of a smiling couple. She recognized the woman as Laura, but the man was unfamiliar. "Terry, who is he?"

CHAPTER 3

HE SAT IN HIS 1995 HONDA CIVIC, sweating profusely. Its air conditioner hadn't worked for years. The car was a real piece of shit, but perfect for the crappy life he had going. He combed his fingers through his hair and caught his reflection in the rearview mirror.

He lifted his sunglasses to look into his own eyes. They had changed. They were dark, even sinister. He put the shades back in place, rolled his shoulders forward to dislodge the tension in his neck, and took a cleansing breath. With the air came a waft of smoke from the cigarette burning in the car's ashtray.

He had parked close enough to observe the activity at 36 Bay Street, yet far enough away to be left alone. At least he had hoped so. Cruisers were parked in front of the house, and forty-eight minutes ago a department-issued SUV had pulled to a quick stop.

All this activity because of his work. It was something to be proud of.

He picked up the cigarette and tapped the ash in the tray.

Statistically, the murder itself was nothing special. Another young lady. People would move on. They always did.

It was the city's thirtieth murder of the year. He was up-to-date on his statistics. But he was always that way; he was a gatherer of facts, of useless information. Maybe someday his fact-finding and attention to detail would prove beneficial.

He wiped his forehead, and sweat trickled from his brow and down his nose. The salty perspiration stung. He winced. His nose was still tender to the touch. That crotchety old man at the bar had a strong right hook.

He rested his eyes for a second, and when he opened them, a Crown Vic had pulled to a stop in front of the house. He straightened up.

A woman of average height—probably about five foot five—with blond hair walked toward the yellow tape. But it wasn't her looks that captured his interest. It was her determined stride. And something was familiar about her.

He smiled when he realized why.

She was Detective Madison Knight. She had made headlines for putting away the Russian Mafia czar, Dimitre Petrov, but the glory hadn't lasted long. People like Petrov had a reach that extended from behind bars and the rumor was that Petrov had gotten the attorney who had lost his case killed.

He must have hit the bigtime to have Knight on *his* investigation. An adrenaline rush flowed over him, blanketing him in heat. Energy pulsed in his veins, his heartbeat pounding in his ears. He strained to draw in a satisfying breath.

Tap, tap.

Knuckles rapped against the driver's-side window.

His heart slowed. His breath shortened. Slowly, he lifted his eyes to look at the source of the intrusion.

A police officer!

Stay calm. Play it cool.

He drew the cigarette to his lips. Damn, his nose hurt so much when he sucked air in that he had to fight crying out in pain. He left the cig perched between his fingers, and the cop motioned for him to put the window down.

"I need you to move your vehicle."

Thank God for his dark-tinted glasses or maybe the cop would see right through him. "Sure."

The police officer bent over and peered into the car. "Are you all right, sir?"

Following the officer's gaze to his unsteady hand holding the cigarette, he forced himself to raise it for another drag. His hand shook the entire way. "Yeah, I'm—" Her lifeless eyes flashed in his mind. He cleared his throat, hoping it would somehow dislodge his recollections. "Sure… I…I'll get out of your way immediately."

The cop's gaze remained fixed on him, eye to eye.

Could he see through him, sunglasses and all? Was his guilt that obvious?

"All units confirm a secured perimeter." The monotone voice came over the officer's radio.

The cop turned the volume down without taking his eyes off him. "What happened to your nose?"

What was this uniform out to prove?

He forced another cough and then took yet another drag. He tapped the cigarette ash out the window. The office stepped to the side, but based on the look in his eyes, he wasn't going anywhere.

He needed to give the cop an answer. His words escaped through gritted teeth. "Bar fight."

The officer nodded. His eyes condemned him. "I need you to move your car—" he drummed his flattened palm on the roof "—and try to keep yourself out of trouble."

Too late, Officer. Too late.

Also available from
International Best-selling Author
Carolyn Arnold

TIES THAT BIND

Book 1 in the Detective Madison Knight series

The hunt for a serial killer begins...

Detective Madison Knight concluded the case of a strangled woman an isolated incident. But when another woman's body is found in a park killed with the same brand of neckties, she realizes they're dealing with something more serious.

Despite mounting pressure from the sergeant and the chief to close the case even if it means putting an innocent man behind bars, and a partner who is more interested in saving his marriage than stopping a potential serial killer, Madison may have to go it alone if the murderer is going to be stopped.

**Available from popular book retailers or
at carolynarnold.net**

CAROLYN ARNOLD is the international best-selling and award-winning author of the Madison Knight, Brandon Fisher, and McKinley Mystery series. She is the only author with POLICE PROCEDURALS RESPECTED BY LAW ENFORCEMENT.™

Carolyn was born in a small town, but that doesn't keep her from dreaming big. And on par with her large dreams is her overactive imagination that conjures up killers and cases to solve. She currently lives in a city near Toronto with her husband and two beagles, Max and Chelsea. She is also a member of Crime Writers of Canada.

CONNECT ONLINE
carolynarnold.net
facebook.com/authorcarolynarnold
twitter.com/carolyn_arnold

And don't forget to sign up for her newsletter for up-to-date information on release and special offers at carolynarnold.net/newsletters.